THE PL   ON:
AN AUSTRALIAN   EST

THE PLATINUM COLLECTION

January 2018

February 2018

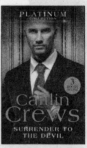

March 2018

April 2018

May 2018

June 2018

THE PLATINUM COLLECTION:
AN AUSTRALIAN CONQUEST

EMMA
DARCY

MILLS
&BOON

Published in Great Britain 2017
By Mills & Boon, an imprint of HarperCollins*Publishers*
1 London Bridge Street, London, SE1 9GF

THE PLATINUM COLLECTION: AN AUSTRALIAN CONQUEST
© 2018 Harlequin Books S.A.

The Incorrigible Playboy © 2013 Emma Darcy
His Most Exquisite Conquest © 2013 Emma Darcy
His Bought Mistress © 2004 Emma Darcy

ISBN: 978-0-263-93191-4

09-0218

MIX
Paper from
responsible sources
FSC™ C007454

This book is produced from independently certified FSC™ paper to ensure responsible forest management.

For more information visit: www.harpercollins.co.uk/green

Printed and bound in Spain
by CPI, Barcelona

THE INCORRIGIBLE
PLAYBOY

Initially a French/English teacher, **Emma Darcy** changed careers to computer programming before the happy demands of marriage and motherhood. Very much a people person, and always interested in relationships, she finds the world of romance fiction a thrilling one, and the challenge of creating her own cast of characters very addictive.

CHAPTER ONE

THIRTY.

The big three zero.

If ever there was a birthday to inspire the determination to make a change in her life, this was it.

Elizabeth Flippence assessed her reflection in the mirror with a mixture of hope and anxiety. She'd had her long brown hair cut to just below her ears and layered so that it fluffed out around her face in wild waves with bangs across her forehead. It was a much more modern look and softer, more feminine, but she wasn't sure she should have let the hairdresser talk her into the vibrant auburn colour.

It was certainly striking. Which was probably what she needed for Michael Finn to really notice her today—notice her as a woman instead of taking her for granted as his superefficient personal assistant. She desperately wanted their relationship to shift from its consistently platonic level. Two years was long enough to pine for a man who seemed fixated on not mixing business with pleasure.

Which was ridiculous. They were so well suited to each other. Surely Michael knew that in his heart. It couldn't be more obvious. Her frustration over this stand-off situation had been simmering for months, and Elizabeth had decided that today was the day she was going to try smashing down his guard. This make-over should at least capture his attention.

And the hairdresser was right about the auburn tones making her dark brown eyes look brighter. The new hairstyle also seemed to put her rather long nose in better proportion with the rest of her face. It highlighted her slanted cheekbones in a strangely exotic way and even her slightly wide full-lipped mouth looked more right somehow.

Anyway, it was done now and she fiercely hoped it would promote the desired result. When Michael commented on her changed appearance, she would tell him it was her birthday present to herself and maybe…please, please, please…he would suggest celebrating the occasion by taking her out to lunch, or better still, dinner.

She didn't want to be his Girl Friday anymore. She wanted to be his every day and every night girl. If that didn't start happening… Elizabeth took a long deep breath as she faced the unavoidable truth. Thirty really was the deadline for a woman to give serious consideration to finding a life partner if she wanted to have a family of her own. Michael Finn was her choice but if he didn't respond to her differently today, she'd probably be wasting her time to hope for any change from him in the near future. Which meant she would have to move on, try to meet someone else.

She quickly banished the downer thought. It was imperative to be positive today. Smile and the whole world smiled back at you, she told herself. It was one of Lucy's principles and it certainly worked for her sister,

who invariably carved a blithe path through life, using
her smile to get her out of trouble. A lot was forgiven
with Lucy's smile.

Elizabeth practised her own as she left the bathroom.
She was just slipping her mobile phone into her handbag, ready to leave for work when it played her signa-
ture call tune. Quickly flipping it open she lifted it to
her ear, anticipating the caller would be Lucy, who had
spent the weekend with friends at Port Douglas. Her
sister's voice instantly bubbled forth.

'Hi, Ellie! Happy birthday! I hope you're wearing
the clothes I bought for you.'

'Thanks, Lucy, and yes, I am.'

'Good! Every woman should look bold and beautiful on their thirtieth birthday.'

Elizabeth laughed. The beautiful butterfly blouse,
basically in glorious shades of blue and green but with
the wings outlined in brown and enclosing a vivid pat-
tern in red and sea-green and yellow and lime, was
definitely eye-catching, especially teamed with the
sea-green pencil skirt. The outfit was a far cry from
her usual style in clothes, but under Lucy's vehement
persuasion, she had let herself be seduced by the gorgeous colours.

'I've had my hair cut, too. And dyed auburn.'

'Wow! Can't wait to see that! I'll be back in Cairns
later this morning. I'll drop in at your office for a peek.
Got to go now.'

The connection clicked off before Elizabeth could
say, 'No, don't!'

It was probably silly but she felt uncomfortable about
Lucy visiting her at work and had always deterred her

from doing it. Because of Michael. As much as she loved her ditzy younger sister, there was no escaping the fact that men seemed irresistibly drawn to her. Her relationships never lasted long. Nothing with Lucy lasted long. There was always another man, another job, another place to go.

For several moments Elizabeth dithered over calling her sister back, not wanting this day to be spoiled by a possible distraction from herself. Yet, didn't she need to test Michael's feelings for her? He should value her worth above Lucy's honeybee attraction. Besides, he might not even see her sister drop in. The door between her office and his was usually closed.

She didn't feel right about putting Lucy off this morning. It was her birthday and her sister was happy and excited about seeing her. They only had each other. Their mother had died of cancer when they were still in their teens, and their father, who had since settled in Mt Isa with another woman, wouldn't even remember her birthday. He never had.

In any event, Michael would have to meet Lucy sooner or later if the closer involvement Elizabeth was aiming for came to pass. Accepting this inevitability, she picked up her handbag, slid the mobile phone into its compartment and headed off to work.

The month of August was a pleasant one in Far North Queensland, not too hot to walk the five blocks from the apartment she and Lucy shared to The Esplanade, where the head office of Finn's Fisheries was located. Usually she drove her little car, leaving it in the space allocated for her in the underground car park of her boss's building, but she didn't want to be tied to driving it home today. Much better to be free to do anything.

The thought brought another smile to her face as she strolled along. Michael really was the perfect man for her. Finn's Fisheries was a huge franchise with outlets all around Australia. They not only stocked every possible piece of fishing gear—a lot of it imported—but the kind of clothing that went with it: wetsuits, swimming costumes, shorts, T-shirts, hats. The range of merchandise was fantastic and Michael dealt with all of it. She loved how he never missed a beat, always on top of everything. It was how she liked to be herself. Together they made a great team. He often said so himself.

If he would just see they should take the next step, Elizabeth was sure they could team up for life and make it a very happy one, sharing everything. He was thirty-five. It was time for both of them to start building a far more personal partnership. She couldn't believe Michael wanted to remain a bachelor forever.

In the two years she'd known him his relationships with other women had never lasted long, but Elizabeth reasoned it was because he was a workaholic. It would be different with her. She understood him.

Despite all this positive thinking, her heart fluttered nervously as she entered her office. The door to Michael's was open, which meant he was already in, organising the business of the day. It was Monday, the beginning of a new week. The beginning of something new between them, too, Elizabeth fiercely hoped as she took a deep breath to calm herself and walked purposefully to the opened door.

He was seated at his desk, pen in hand, ticking off

items on a sheet of paper, his concentration so total he didn't sense her presence. For a few moments Elizabeth simply gazed at him, loving the clean-cut perfection of the man; the thick black hair kept short so it was never untidy, the straight black eyebrows that gave slashing emphasis to the keen intelligence of his silver-grey eyes. The straight nose, firm mouth and squarish jaw all combined to complete the look of the alpha male he was.

As always he wore a top quality white shirt that showed off his flawless olive skin and undoubtedly he would be wearing classy black trousers—his customary work uniform. His black shoes would be shiny and… he was just perfect.

Elizabeth swallowed hard to clear her throat and willed him to give her the kind of attention she craved.

'Good morning, Michael.'

'Good morn—' His gaze lifted, his eyes widening in shock. His mouth was left slightly agape, his voice momentarily choked by the unexpected sight of an Elizabeth who was not the same as usual.

She held her breath. This was the moment when the only-business attitude towards her had to snap. A host of butterflies invaded her stomach. *Smile*, her mind wildly dictated. *Show him the warmth in your heart, the desire heating up your blood.*

She smiled and suddenly he grinned, the silver eyes sparkling with very male appreciation.

'Wow!' he breathed, and her skin tingled with pleasure.

'Great hair! Fabulous outfit, too!' he enthused. 'You've done wonders with yourself, Elizabeth. Does this mean there's some new guy in your life?'

The high that had soared from his first words came crashing down. Associating her makeover with another man meant the distance he kept between them was not about to be crossed. Although…maybe he was tempted. Maybe he was just checking if the coast was clear for him to step in.

She rallied, quickly saying, 'No. I've been unattached for a while. I just felt like a change.'

'Super change!' he warmly approved.

That was better. Warmth was good. Elizabeth instantly delivered the planned hint for him to make his move.

'I'm glad you like it. The clothes are a gift from my sister. It's my birthday. She insisted I had to look bold and beautiful today.'

He laughed. 'Well, you certainly do. And we should celebrate your birthday, too. How about lunch at The Mariners Bar? We can make time for it if we get through this inventory this morning.'

Hope soared again. A lunch for two at one of the most expensive restaurants in Cairns, overlooking the marina full of million-dollar yachts…her heart sang with joy. 'That would be lovely. Thank you, Michael.'

'Book us a table. One o'clock should see us clear.' He picked up a sheaf of papers, holding it out to her. 'In the meantime, if you could check this lot…'

'Of course.'

Business as usual, but there was a rainbow at the end of it today. Elizabeth could barely stop her feet from dancing over to his desk to collect the work that had to be done first.

'Bold and beautiful,' Michael repeated, grinning at

her as he handed over the papers. 'Your sister must have a lot of pizzazz.'

It killed the song in her heart. He was supposed to be showing more interest in her, not wondering about Lucy. She shouldn't have mentioned her sister. But there was no taking it back, so she had to live with it.

'Yes, she has, but she's terribly ditzy with it. Nothing seems to stay in her head long enough to put any order into her life.' It was the truth and she wanted Michael to know it. The thought of Lucy being attractive to him in any way was unbearable.

'Not like you,' he said appreciatively.

She shrugged. 'Chalk and cheese. A bit like you and your brother.'

The words tripped off her tongue before Elizabeth could catch them back. The anxiety about Lucy had caused her control to slip. It wasn't appropriate for her to make any comment about her boss's brother. Normally she would keep her mouth firmly shut about him, despite the heartburn Harry Finn invariably gave her with his playboy patter. She hated it when he came into the office. Absolutely hated it.

Michael leaned back in his chair, his mouth tilted in a musing little smile. 'Working behind a desk is definitely not Harry's thing, but I think you might have the wrong impression of him, Elizabeth.'

'I'm sorry.' She grimaced an apology. 'I didn't mean to…to…'

Now she was lost for words!

'It's okay.' Michael waved off her angst. 'I know he seems very casual about everything but his mind is as sharp as a razor blade and he has his thumb on every-thing to do with his side of the business.'

Charter boats for deep-sea fishing, dive-boats for tourists wanting to explore the Great Barrier Reef, over-seeing the resort they'd built on one of the islands— it was playboy stuff compared to what Michael did. Elizabeth's opinion of Harry Finn didn't shift one iota.

'I'll try to see him in that light in the future,' she clipped out.

Michael laughed. Elizabeth's toes curled. He was so charismatically handsome when he laughed. 'I guess he's been ruffling your feathers with his flirting. Don't let it get to you. He's like that with every woman. It's just a bit of fun.'

Oh, sure! Great *fun*! For Harry Finn.

Elizabeth hated it.

However, she managed to paste a smile on her face. 'I'll keep that in mind,' she said. 'Must get to work now. And I'll book our table at The Mariners Bar.'

'Do that.' Another grin. 'We can discuss brothers and sisters over lunch.'

No way, Elizabeth thought as she walked briskly to her own office, firmly closing the door behind her to ensure that Michael didn't see Lucy when she dropped in. She didn't want her sister sparking any interest in his mind. Nor did she want Harry Finn intruding on any part of this special lunch date. This precious time together had to be about moving closer to each other on a really personal plane. All her hopes for a future with Michael Finn were pinned on it.

CHAPTER TWO

Ten thirty-seven.

Elizabeth frowned at the clock on her desk. The arrangement with the coffee shop on the ground floor was for coffee and muffins to be delivered at ten-thirty—black expresso and a chocolate muffin for Michael, cappuccino and a strawberry and white chocolate muffin for her. She skipped breakfast to have this treat and her empty stomach was rumbling for it. It was unusual for the delivery to be late. Michael hated unpunctuality and the shop tenants were well aware of his requirements.

A knock on her door had her scuttling out of her chair to open it, facilitating entry as fast as possible. 'You're late,' she said chidingly, before realising the tray of coffee and muffins was being carried by Harry Finn.

Vivid blue eyes twinkled at her. 'Short delay while they made coffee for me, too,' he said unapologetically.

'Fine! You can explain that to Michael,' she bit out, forcing her gritted teeth open to get the words out.

'Oh, I will, dear Elizabeth. Never would I leave a blemish on your sterling record of getting everything right for him,' he rolled out in the provocative tone that made her want to hit him. She was not given to violence but Harry Finn invariably stirred something explosive in her.

'And may I say you look stunning this morning. Absolutely stunning!' he rattled on as he stepped into her office, eyeing her up and down, his gaze pausing where the butterfly wings on her blouse framed her breasts, making her nipples stiffen into bullets. She wished they could be fired at him. His white T-shirt with tropical fish emblazoned on it wouldn't look so sexy on him if there were black holes through it to his all-too-manly chest.

'The hair is spectacular, not to mention—'

'I'd rather you didn't mention,' she cut him off, closing the door and waving him towards Michael's office. 'Your brother is waiting.'

He grinned his devil-may-care grin. 'Won't kill him to wait a bit longer.'

She crossed her arms in exasperated impatience with him as he strolled over to set the tray down on her desk, then hitched himself onto the edge of it, ignoring any reason for haste. The white shorts he wore emphasised his long, tanned, muscular legs. One of them he dangled at her, teasing her need for proper behaviour.

'A moth turning into a butterfly doesn't happen every day,' he happily remarked. 'I want to enjoy the glory of it.'

Elizabeth rolled her eyes. She was not going to stand for this. A moth! She had never been a moth! She had simply chosen to be on the conservative side with her appearance to exemplify a serious career person, not someone who could ever be considered flighty like her sister.

'The coffee will be getting cold,' she stated in her chilliest voice.

'Love the sea-green skirt,' he raved on. 'Matches the colour of the water near the reef. Fits you very neatly, too. Like a second skin. In fact, it's inspiring a fantasy of you as a mermaid.' He grinned. Evilly. 'I bet you'd swish your tail at me.'

'Only in dismissal,' she shot at him, pushing her feet to walk to the desk and deal with the coffee herself since Harry was not inclined to oblige. It meant she had to go close to him, which she usually avoided because the man was so overwhelmingly male, in-your-face male, that her female hormones seemed to get in a tizzy around him. It was extremely irritating.

He wasn't as classically handsome as Michael. He was more raffishly handsome—his longish black curly hair flopping around his face, crow's-feet at the corners of his eyes from being out in the weather, a slightly crooked nose from having it broken at some point in his probably misspent youth, and a mouth that was all-too-frequently quirked with amusement. At her. As it was now.

'Have you ever wondered why you're so uptight with me, Elizabeth?' he tossed out.

'No. I don't give you that much space in my mind,' she answered, deliberately ignoring him as she removed her coffee and muffin from the tray.

'Ouch!' he said as though she'd hurt him, then laughed to show she hadn't. 'If I ever get too big for my boots, I know where to come to be whipped back into shape.'

She gave him a quelling look. 'You've come to see Michael. Just follow me into his office.'

The devil danced in his eyes. 'Only if you swish your tail at me.'

She glared back. 'Stop playing with me. I'm not going there with you. Not ever,' she added emphatically.

He was totally unabashed. 'All work, no play—got to say you're safe with Mickey on that score.'

Safe? The word niggled at Elizabeth's mind as she carried the tray to Michael's door. Why was Harry so sure she was safe with his brother? She didn't want to be safe. She wanted to be desired so much, there would be no distance left between them.

Harry bounded past her, opened the door and commanded his brother's attention. 'Hi, Mickey! I held up the coffee train to have one made for myself. Have a few things to discuss with you. Here's Elizabeth with it now.'

'No problem,' Michael answered, smiling at her as she sailed in with the tray.

She hugged the smile to her heart. Michael was the man of true gold. Harry was all glitter. And she hated him calling his brother Mickey. It was rotten, schoolboy stuff—Mickey Finn—linking him to a spiked drink, and totally inappropriate for the position he now held. No dignity in it at all. No respect.

'Thanks, Elizabeth,' Michael said warmly as she unloaded the tray, setting out the two coffees and muffin on his desk. 'Table booked?'

'Yes.'

'What table?' Harry asked, instantly putting her on edge again.

'It's Elizabeth's birthday. I'm taking her out to lunch.'

'A…ha!'

Her spine crawled at the wealth of significance she heard in Harry's voice. If he was about to make fun of the situation… She picked up the emptied tray and swung around to shoot him a killing look.

He lifted his hand in a salute, pretending to plead for a truce between them but his eyes glittered with mocking amusement. 'Happy birthday, dear Elizabeth.'

'Thank you,' she grated out, and swiftly left the two men together for their discussions, closing the door to give them absolute privacy and herself protection from *that man*.

It was difficult to concentrate on work. She tried, but the clock kept ticking on—eleven o'clock, eleven-thirty, twelve. Lucy hadn't dropped in and Harry was still with Michael. Anything could have happened with Lucy. It frequently did. She might not make it into the office at all, which would be a relief, no chance of a meeting with Michael. Harry was the main problem. She wouldn't put it past him to invite himself to her birthday lunch. If he did, would Michael put him off?

He had to.

No way could a romantic mood develop between them if Harry was present. He would spoil everything.

A knock on her door cut off her inner angst. Elizabeth looked up to see the door opening and Lucy's head poking around it.

'Okay to come in?'

Her stomach cramped with nervous tension at the late visit but it was impossible to say anything but 'Yes.'

Lucy bounced in, exuding effervescence as she always did. Today she was dressed in a white broderie anglaise outfit: a little frilly skirt that barely reached midthigh, an off-the-shoulder peasant blouse, a wide tan belt slung around her hips, lots of wooden beads dangling from her neck, wooden bangles travelling up one forearm and tan sandals that were strapped up to mid-calf. Her long blond hair was piled up on top of her head with loose strands escaping everywhere. She looked like a trendy model who could put anything together and look good.

'Ooh…I *love* the hair, Ellie,' she cooed, hitching herself onto the edge of Elizabeth's desk, just as Harry had, which instantly provoked the thought they would make a good pair.

'It's very sexy,' Lucy raved on. 'Gives you that just-out-of-bed tumbled look and the colour really, really suits you. It complements the clothes I picked out for you brilliantly. I have to say you look absolutely marvellous.' Her lovely sherry-brown eyes twinkled with delight. 'Now tell me you *feel* marvellous, too.'

Lucy's smile was so infectious, she had to smile back. 'I'm glad I made the change. How was your weekend?'

'Oh, so-so.' She waved her hand airily then pulled a woeful grimace. 'But I've had the most terrible morning.'

Out of the corner of her eye Elizabeth caught the opening of the door to Michael's office. Tension whipped along her nerves. Was it Harry coming out or both men?

Lucy rattled out her list of woes, her hands making a host of dramatic gestures. 'A body was buried in the wrong plot and I had to deal with that. Then a call came in that someone was interfering with a grave. I had to go out to the cemetery and investigate, but that wasn't too bad. It was only a bereaved husband digging a hole on top of the grave to put in potting soil so he could plant his wife's favourite rose. Nice, really. The worst thing was a dog running amok in the memorial garden and knocking off some of the angels' heads. I had to collect them, load them into the van, and now I have to find someone who can stick them back on again. You wouldn't believe how heavy those angels' heads are.'

'Angels' heads…' It was Michael's voice, sounding totally stunned.

It jerked Lucy's attention to him. 'Oh, wow!' she said, looking Michael up and down, totally uninhibited about showing how impressed she was with him.

Elizabeth closed her eyes and sucked in a deep breath.

'Are you Ellie's boss?' The question popped out with barely a pause.

Elizabeth opened her eyes again to see Michael shaking his head as though bringing himself out of a daze, and Harry behind his shoulder, looking straight at her with a sharp intensity in his bedroom blue eyes she had never seen before. It gave her the weird feeling he was tunnelling into her mind. She quickly dropped her gaze.

'Yes. Yes, I am,' Michael finally answered. 'And you are?'

'Lucy Flippence. Ellie's sister. I work in cemetery administration so I often have to deal with angels.'

'I see,' he said, looking at Lucy as though she was a heavenly apparition.

She hopped off her perch on the desk and crossed the

floor to him with her hand extended. 'Pleased to meet you. Okay if I call you Michael?'

'Delighted,' he said, taking her hand and holding on to it as he slowly turned to make the last introduction. 'This is my brother, Harry.'

Elizabeth fiercely willed Lucy to find Harry more attractive. No such luck! Her hand was left in Michael's snug grasp. She raised her other in blithe greeting. 'Hi, Harry!' It was tossed at him in a kind of bubbly dismissal, which meant in Lucy's mind he didn't really count.

'Charmed,' Harry purred at her.

It floated right over her head, no impact at all.

Elizabeth's heart sank like a stone.

Lucy was intent on engaging Michael and he was obviously enthralled with her.

'I don't know if you know but it's Ellie's birthday today and I thought I'd treat her to a really nice lunch somewhere. You won't mind if I take her off and she's a bit late back, will you, Michael?' she said appealingly.

There was a terrible inevitability about what happened next.

'Actually, I'd decided to do the same myself. Lunch at The Mariners Bar.'

'Oh, wow! The Mariners Bar! What a lovely boss you are to take Ellie there!'

'Why don't you join us? It will be a better celebration of her birthday if you do.'

'I'll come, as well. Make a party of it,' Harry put in, instantly supporting the idea.

'I only booked a table for two,' Elizabeth couldn't help saying, even though knowing it was a futile attempt to change what wouldn't be changed now. Her secret dream was already down the drain.

'No problem. I'm sure the maître d' will make room for us,' Michael said, oozing confidence as he smiled at Lucy. 'We'd be delighted to have the pleasure of your company.'

'Well, a foursome should be more fun, don't you think, Ellie?'

The appealing glance over her shoulder forced Elizabeth to smile and say, 'Certainly no awkward silences with you, Lucy.'

She laughed. 'That's settled, then. Thank you for asking me, Michael. And it's good of you to join in the party, too, Harry.'

The death knell to a happy birthday, Elizabeth thought. Not only would she have to watch Michael being fascinated by her sister, she'd also have to put up with Harry getting under her skin all the time. She slid him a vexed look. His mouth quirked at her, seemingly with more irony than amusement, but that probably didn't mean anything. No doubt he was anticipating having heaps of *fun* at her expense.

This lunch was going to be the lunch from hell.

Elizabeth didn't know how she was going to get through it without throwing in the towel, having hysterics and drowning herself in the marina.

CHAPTER THREE

ELIZABETH knew she'd be paired with Harry for the stroll
along the boardwalk to the marina, and she was. There
was no point in trying to fight for Michael's company.
His preference for Lucy to be at his side had been made
so clear, pride dictated that the arrangement be accepted
with as much dignified grace as she could muster.

The two of them walked ahead and it was sickening watching the connection between them flourish-
ing. Lucy, of course, was never short of a word, and
Michael was lapping up every one of them, enjoying
her bubbly personality. It wouldn't last, Elizabeth told
herself, but that was no consolation. The damage was
done. Lucy had achieved in one minute flat what she
had been unable to draw from Michael in two years.
Even if he turned to her later on, she would never be
able to forget that.

The boardwalk ran along the water's edge of the
park adjoining The Esplanade, and she tried to distract
herself with the people they passed; couples lounging
under the shade of trees, children making use of the
play areas set up for them, boys scaling the rock-climb.
It was a relief that Harry was leaving her to her silence

for a while. It was difficult to cope with him at the best of times, and this was the worst.

She could have chosen to tell Lucy about her secret passion for her boss. That would have warned her off although she wouldn't have understood it. It simply wasn't in Lucy to pine for a man who didn't respond to her as she wanted him to respond. She probably would have looked aghast and said, 'Throw him away, Ellie. He's not that into you if you've waited this long for him to make a move.'

That truth was staring her in the face right now.

And it hurt.

It hurt so badly, she had to keep blinking back the tears that threatened to well into her eyes. Her chest was so tight she could hardly breathe. She'd been a fool to hope, a fool to think today might be the day. It was never going to happen for her.

'Ellie…'

It was a jolt to her wounded heart, hearing Harry speak her childhood name in a low, caressing tone.

'I like it,' he went on. 'Much better than Elizabeth. It conjures up a more carefree person, softer, more accessible.'

Her spine stiffened. He was doing it again, digging at her. She shot him a hard, mocking look. 'Don't get carried away by it. Lucy simply couldn't say Elizabeth when she was little. She calls me Ellie out of habit.'

'And affection, I think.' There was a look of kindness in his eyes that screwed up her stomach as he added, 'She doesn't know she's hurting you, does she?'

Her mind jammed in disbelief over Harry's insightful comment. 'What do you mean?'

He grimaced at her prevarication. 'Give it up, Ellie. You're not Mickey's type. I could have told you so but you wouldn't have believed me.'

Humiliation burned through her. Her cheeks flamed with it. She tore her gaze from the certain knowledge in Harry Finn's and stared at his brother's back—the back Michael had turned on her to be with her sister. How had Harry known what she'd yearned for? Had Michael known, too? She couldn't bear this. She would have to resign from her job, find another.

'Don't worry,' Harry said soothingly. 'You can keep on working for him if you want to. Mickey doesn't have a clue. He's always had tunnel vision—sets his mind on something and nothing else exists.'

Relief reduced some of the heat. Nevertheless, it was still intensely disturbing that Harry was somehow reading her mind. Or was he guessing, picking up clues from her reactions? She hadn't admitted anything. He couldn't really *know*, could he?

'On the other hand, it would be much better if you did resign,' he went on. 'It's never good to keep being reminded of failure. And no need to go job-hunting. You can come and work for me.'

Work for him? Never in a million years! It spurred her into tackling him head-on, her eyes blazing with the fire of battle. 'Let me tell you, Harry Finn, I have never failed at any work Michael has given me and working for you has no appeal whatsoever.'

He grinned at her. 'Think of the pleasure of saying what you think of me at every turn instead of having to keep yourself bottled up around Mickey.'

'I am not bottled up,' she declared vehemently.

He sighed. 'Why not be honest instead of playing the pretend-game? Your fantasy of having Mickey fall at your feet is never going to come true. Face it. Give it up. Look at me as the best tonic for lovesickness you could have. Balls of fire come out of you the moment I'm around.'

'That's because you're so annoying!'

Her voice had risen to a passionate outburst, loud enough to attract Michael's and Lucy's attention, breaking their absorption in each other. They paused in their walk, turning around with eyebrows raised.

'It's okay,' Elizabeth quickly assured them. 'Harry was just being Harry.'

'Be nice to Elizabeth, Harry,' Michael chided. 'It's her birthday.'

'I *am* being nice,' he protested.

'Try harder,' Michael advised, dismissing the distraction to continue his tête-à-tête with Lucy.

'Right!' Harry muttered. 'We need some control here, Ellie, if you want to pretend there's nothing wrong in your world.'

'The only thing wrong in my world is you,' she muttered back fiercely. 'And don't call me Ellie.'

'Elizabeth reigns,' he said in mock resignation.

She bit her lips, determined not to rise to any more of his baits.

They walked on for a while before he started again.

'This won't do,' he said decisively. 'We'll be at the restaurant soon. If you sit there in glum silence, I'll get the blame for it and that's not fair. It's not my fault that Mickey's attracted to your sister. Your best move is to start flirting with me. Who knows? He might suddenly get jealous.'

This suggestion stirred a flicker of hope. Maybe...

The shared laughter from the couple in front of them dashed the hope before it could take wing. Nevertheless, Harry did have a valid point. If she didn't pretend to be having a good time, even Michael and Lucy would realise this birthday treat was no treat at all for her. She had to *look* happy even though she couldn't *be* happy.

She sighed and slid him a weighing look. 'You know it won't mean anything if I flirt with you.'

'Not a thing!' he readily agreed.

'It's just for the sake of making a cheerful party.'

'Of course.'

'It's obvious that you're a dyed-in-the-wool playboy, and normally I wouldn't have anything to do with you, Harry, but since I'm stuck with you on this occasion, I'll play along for once.'

'Good thinking! Though I take exception to the playboy tag. I do know how to play, which I consider an important part of living—something I suspect you do too little of—but that's not all I am.'

'Whatever...' She shrugged off any argument about his personality. Arguing would only get her all heated again and she needed to be calm, in control of herself. Harry was right about that.

They'd walked past the yacht club and were on the path to the cocktail bar adjoining the restaurant when Harry made his next move.

'Hey, Mickey!' he called out. 'I'll buy the girls cocktails while you see the maître d' about our table.'

'Okay' was tossed back at him, his attention reverting to Lucy with barely a pause.

'No doubt about it, he's besotted,' Harry dryly commented. 'How old are you today, Elizabeth?'

'Thirty,' she answered on a defeated sigh. No point in hiding it.

'Ah! The big three zero. Time to make a change.'

Precisely what she had thought. And still had to think now that Michael had proved his disinterest in her personally.

'Go with me on this,' Harry urged.

'Go with you on what?'

'Something I was discussing with Mickey this morning. I'll bring it up again after lunch. Just don't dismiss it out of hand. It would be the perfect change for you.'

'You couldn't possibly know what's perfect for me, Harry,' she said sceptically.

He cocked a teasing eyebrow. 'I might just be a better judge on that than you think I am.'

She shook her head, her eyes mocking this particular belief in himself.

He grinned. 'Wait and see.'

She wasn't about to push him on it. Harry enjoyed being tantalising. Elizabeth had found her best course was simply to show complete disinterest. In this case, she couldn't care less what he had in mind. All she cared about was getting through lunch without showing how miserable she was.

Michael left them at the cocktail bar, striding swiftly into the restaurant to speak to the maître d', obviously in a hurry to get back to Lucy. Harry led them to a set of two-seater lounges with a low table in between and saw them settled with her and Lucy facing each other.

'Now, let me select cocktails for you both,' he said, the vivid blue eyes twinkling confidence in his choices. 'A Margarita for you, Elizabeth.'

It surprised her that he'd actually picked her favourite. 'Why that one?' she asked, curious about his correct guessing.

He grinned. 'Because you're the salt of the earth and I revere you for it.'

She rolled her eyes. The day Harry Finn showed any reverence for her was yet to dawn. He was just making a link to the salt-encrusted rim of the glass that was always used for a Margarita cocktail.

'You're right on both counts,' Lucy happily volunteered. 'Ellie loves Margaritas and she *is* the salt of the earth. I don't know what I'd do without her. She's always been my anchor.'

'An anchor,' Harry repeated musingly. 'I think that's what's been missing from my life.'

'An anchor would only weigh you down, Harry,' Elizabeth put in dryly. 'It would feel like an albatross around your neck.'

'Some chains I wouldn't mind wearing.'

'Try gold.'

He laughed.

'Do you two always spar like this?' Lucy asked, eyeing them speculatively.

'Sparks invariably fly,' Harry claimed.

It was on the tip of her tongue to say she invariably hosed them down, remembering just in time that flirting was the order of this afternoon, so she gave him an arch look and said, 'I would have to admit that being with Harry is somewhat invigorating.'

Lucy laughed and clapped her hands. 'Oh, I love it! What a great lunch we'll all have together!' Her eyes sparkled at Harry. 'What cocktail will you choose for me?'

'For the sunshine girl… A Piña Colada.'

She clapped her hands again. 'Well done, Harry. That's *my* favourite.'

'At your service.' He twirled his hand in a salute to them both and headed off to the bar.

Lucy was beside herself with delight. 'He's just what you need, Ellie. Loads of fun. You've been carrying responsibility for so long, it's well past time you let loose and had a wild flutter for once. Be a butterfly instead of a worker bee.'

At least she didn't say *moth*, Elizabeth thought wryly.

'I might just do that,' she drawled, encouraging the idea there was a connection between her and Harry.

'Go for it,' Lucy urged, bouncing forward on her seat in excitement. 'I'm going for Michael. He's an absolute dreamboat. I'm so glad I wasn't held up any longer at the cemetery. I might have missed out on meeting him. Why didn't you tell me your boss was gorgeous?'

'I've always thought him a bit cold,' she said carefully.

Lucy threw up her hands in exasperation at her sister's lack of discernment. 'Believe me. The guy is hot! He makes me sizzle.'

Elizabeth shrugged. 'I guess it's a matter of chemistry. Harry is the hot one for me.' It wasn't entirely a lie. He frequently raised her temperature…with anger or annoyance.

Lucy heaved a happy sigh. 'Brothers and sisters… wouldn't it be great if we ended up together…all happy families.'

Elizabeth's mind reeled from even considering such a prospect. 'I think that's a huge leap into the future. Let's just take one day at a time.'

'Oh, you're always so sensible, Ellie.'

'Which is something I value very highly in your sister,' Michael declared, picking up on Lucy's words and smiling warmly at Elizabeth as he returned, but he seated himself beside Lucy, who instantly switched on a brilliant smile for him, fulsomely agreeing, 'Oh, I do, too. But I also want Ellie to have fun.'

'Which is where I come in,' Harry said, also catching Lucy's words as he came back. His eyes danced wicked mischief at Elizabeth. 'Starting with cocktails. The bartender will bring them over. Here are the peanuts and pretzels.'

He placed a bowl of them on the table and settled himself beside Elizabeth, too closely for her comfort. She wanted to shift away and somehow Harry knew it, instantly throwing her a challenging look that made her sit still and suffer his male animal impact. If she was really attracted to him, she would welcome it. Playing this pretend-game was not going to be easy, but she had to now in front of Lucy.

Her sister turned her smile to Harry. 'What cocktail did you order for Michael?'

'A Manhattan. Mickey is highly civilised. He actually forgets about sunshine until it sparkles over him.'

Lucy laughed. 'And yourself?'

'Ah, the open sea is my business. I'm a salty man so I share Elizabeth's taste for Margaritas.'

'The open sea?' Lucy queried.

'Harry looks after the tourist side of Finn's Fisheries,' Michael answered. 'I take care of buying in the stock for all our franchises.'

'Ah!' Lucy nodded, understanding why Harry was dressed the way he was and how very different the brothers were.

Why she was attracted to Michael and not Harry was beyond Elizabeth's understanding. Sunshine and sea should go together. They both had frivolous natures. It wasn't fair that sexual chemistry had struck in the wrong place. Why couldn't it strike sensibly?

The bartender arrived with their cocktails.

Harry handed her the Margarita and clicked his glass against hers. 'Happy Birthday, Elizabeth,' he said warmly, making her squirm inside even as she forced a smile and thanked him.

The others followed suit with their glasses and well-wishing.

Elizabeth settled back against the cushions and sipped her cocktail, silently brooding over the totally non-sensible ironies of life. Was there any reward for being *sensible*? The old saying that *good things come to those who wait* was not proving true for her.

She wondered how long was the life of a butterfly.

Probably very short.

But it might be sweet if she could bring herself to be a butterfly—just cut loose from all her safety nets and fly wild for a while, thinking of nothing but having a good time. She should take a vacation, get right away from whatever was developing between Michael and Lucy, try drowning her misery with mindless pleasures.

The Margarita was good. And it packed quite a punch. Maybe if she stopped being sensible and had two or three of them, her mind would get fuzzy enough to put this whole situation at an emotional distance, let her float through lunch…like a butterfly.

CHAPTER FOUR

ELIZABETH stared blankly at the luncheon menu. Food. She had to choose something. Her head was swimming from two Margaritas in quick succession. Bad idea, thinking alcohol could fix anything. It didn't help at all.

'I bet I know what you're going to order, Ellie,' Lucy said with a confident grin.

'What?' Any suggestion was welcome.

'The chilli mud crab.'

Chilli. Not today. Her stomach was in too fragile a state.

'Actually, I can't see that on the menu,' Michael said, glancing quizzically at Lucy.

'Oh, I didn't really look. I just assumed,' she quickly defended. No way would she admit that her dyslexia made reading menus difficult. 'What have you decided on, Michael?'

Lucy would undoubtedly choose the same. She was so adept at hiding her disability, hardly anyone ever guessed she had a problem.

'How about sharing a seafood platter for two with me, Elizabeth?' Harry said, leaning closer to point out the platter's contents on the menu. 'You get crab on it, as well as all the other goodies and we can nibble away on everything as we please.'

'Harry will eat the lion's share,' Michael warned.

Yes, Elizabeth thought, relieved to have such ready help, making it easier for her lack of appetite to go unnoticed.

Harry instantly raised a hand for solemn vowing. 'I swear I'll give you first choice of each titbit.'

'Okay, that's a done deal,' she said, closing the menu and slanting her food-rescuer a grateful smile.

'Sealed with a kiss,' he said, bright blue eyes twinkling wickedly as he leaned closer still and pecked her on the cheek.

Her teeth grated together as heat bloomed from the intimate skin contact. The *flirting* agreement flew right out of her mind. His ability to discomfort her on any spot whatsoever had her snapping, 'You can keep that mouth of yours for eating, Harry.'

He gave her his evil grin as he retorted, 'Elizabeth, I live for the day when I'll eat you all up.'

'That'll be doomsday,' she slung back.

'With the gates of heaven opening for me,' Harry retaliated, his grin widening.

Lucy's laughter reminded her just in time that flirting shouldn't have too sharp an edge, so she swallowed her *hell* comment, heaved a long-suffering sigh and shook her head at Harry. 'You are incorrigible.'

'A man has to do what a man has to do,' he archly declared, sending Lucy off into more peals of laughter.

Elizabeth declined asking what he meant.

Nevertheless, as the birthday luncheon progressed, she schooled herself to respond lightly to Harry's banter, pretending to be amused by it, making a show of enjoying his company. At least he was very persistent in claiming her attention, forcefully distracting her from Lucy's and Michael's stomach-curdling absorption in each other, and he did eat the lion's share of the seafood platter without trying to push her into trying more than she could manage.

It was weird finding herself grateful to have Harry at her side, but just this once she actually did. Without him she would feel wretchedly alone, facing the worst scenario of lost hopes. How she was going to cope, hiding her feelings from both Lucy and Michael in the days to come, she didn't know. She hoped they would go off somewhere together after this luncheon, give her some space, release her from the tension of keeping up a happy pretence that everything was fine.

A waiter cleared the table and offered them the sweets menu. Elizabeth decided on the selection of sorbets since they should just slide down her throat without any effort. As soon as the orders were given, Harry leaned an elbow on the table and pointed a finger at his brother, claiming his attention.

'Mickey, I have the solution to my problem with the resort.'

'You have to clear that guy out, Harry,' came the quick advice. 'Once you confront him you can't leave him there. The potential for damage…'

'I know, I know. But it's best to confront him with his replacement. We walk in and turf him out. No argument. A done deal.'

'Agreed, but you don't have a ready replacement yet and the longer he stays…'

'Elizabeth. She's the perfect person for the management job—completely trustworthy, meticulous at checking everything, capable of handling everything you've thrown at her, Mickey.'

Confusion over this brother-to-brother business conversation instantly cleared. *This* was what Harry had intended to bring up after lunch—the perfect change for her. Except it wasn't perfect. Working for him would drive her bats.

'Elizabeth is my PA,' Michael protested.

'I'm in more need of her than you are right now. Lend her to me for a month. That will give me time to interview other people.'

'A month…' Michael frowned over the inconvenience to himself.

A month…

That was a tempting time frame—manageable if Harry wasn't around her all the time. The resort wasn't his only area of interest and responsibility. A month away from Michael and Lucy was a very attractive proposition.

'On the other hand, once Elizabeth gets her teeth into the job, she might want to stay on,' Harry said provocatively.

No way—not with him getting under her skin at any given moment!

Michael glowered at him. 'You're not stealing my PA.'

'Her choice, Mickey.' Harry turned to her. 'What do you say, Elizabeth? Will you help me out for a month… stay on the island and get the resort running as it should be run? My about-to-be ex-manager has been cooking the books, skimming off a lot of stuff to line his own pockets. You'll need to do a complete inventory and change the suppliers who've been doing private deals with him. It would be a whole new challenge for you, one that…'

'Now hold on a moment,' Michael growled. 'It's up to me to ask Elizabeth if she'll do it, not you, Harry.'

'Okay. Ask her.'

Yes was screaming through her mind. It offered an immediate escape from the situation with Michael and Lucy; no need to explain why she wanted to go away; a whole month of freedom from having to see or talk to either of them; a job that demanded her complete attention, keeping miserable thoughts at bay. These critical benefits made the irritation of having to deal with Harry relatively insignificant. Her heart was not engaged with him. Her head could sort out his effect on her, one way or another.

Michael heaved an exasperated sigh, realising he'd been pushed into a corner by his brother. 'It's true. You would be helping us out if you'd agree to step in and do what needs to be done at the resort,' he conceded, giving Elizabeth an earnest look. 'I have every confidence in your ability to handle the situation. Every confidence in your integrity, too. I hate losing you for a month…'

You've just lost me forever, Elizabeth thought.

'…but I guess someone from the clerical staff can fill in for a while….'

'Andrew. Andrew Cook,' she suggested.

He frowned. 'Too stodgy. No initiative.'

'Absolutely reliable in doing whatever task he's set,' she argued, rather bitchily, liking the fact that Michael found him stodgy. He'd obviously found her stodgy, too, in the female stakes.

'I take it that's a yes to coming to the island with me,' Harry slid in, grinning from ear to ear.

She shot him a quelling look. 'I'm up for the challenge of fixing the management problems, nothing else, Harry.'

'Brilliant!'

He purred the word, making her skin prickle. It instantly gave her the unsettling feeling she might have bitten off more than she could chew with Harry Finn. But he wouldn't be at her side all the time on the island. Going was still better than staying at home.

'That's it, then,' Michael said with a resigned air.

'A whole month! I'll miss you, Ellie,' Lucy said wistfully.

'The time will pass quickly enough,' Elizabeth assured her—*particularly with Michael dancing attendance.*

The waiter arrived with the sweets they'd ordered.

'We need to get moving on this,' Harry muttered as he dug into his chocolate mud cake.

'As soon as possible,' Michael agreed.

'Today,' Harry decided, checking his Rolex watch. 'It's only three o'clock now. We could be over on the island by four-thirty. Have him helicoptered out by six. We leave here when we've finished our sweets, hop on the boat...'

'It is Elizabeth's birthday, Harry,' Michael reminded him. 'She might have other plans for today.'

'No, I'm good to go,' she said, recklessly seizing the

chance to be relieved of staying in Michael's and Lucy's company any longer.

'What about clothes and toiletries and stuff?' Lucy put in. 'You're going for a month, Ellie.'

'You can pack for her, Lucy,' Harry said decisively. 'Mickey can take you home, wait while you do it, take Elizabeth's bags and arrange their shipping to the island.'

'No problem,' Michael said, smiling at Lucy like a wolf invited into her home to gobble her up.

Lucy happily agreed with the plan, her eyes sizzling with sexual promises as she smiled back at her new lover-to-be.

Elizabeth shovelled the sorbet down her throat. The faster she got out of here, the better.

'Ready?' Harry asked the moment she put her spoon down.

'Ready,' she answered emphatically, grabbing her handbag and rising to her feet, wanting to run but knowing she had to discipline herself to suffer goodbyes.

Lucy wrapped her in a big hug, mischievously saying, 'Have a lovely time with Harry, Ellie.'

'I will,' she replied through gritted teeth. Denials of that idea would not only be a total waste of time, but also prolong this whole wretched togetherness.

Michael kissed her cheek, wryly murmuring, 'I'll miss you.'

I won't miss you, Elizabeth thought fiercely, barely managing to force a smile. 'Thank you for my birthday lunch, Michael.'

'Pleasure,' he replied, his gaze sliding to Lucy.

'We're off,' Harry said, seizing Elizabeth's hand and pulling her with him.

His hand was strong and hot, wrapping firmly around her fingers, shooting warmth up her arm, but she didn't care if heat travelled to her brain and fried it right now. He was acting fast, taking her to the freedom she needed, and she was grateful for that. Once they were outside, he led her straight to the long wharf where rows of million-dollar yachts were docked on either side.

'Where's your boat?' she asked.

'Right at the end. No shuffling around. A quick, easy getaway. Full throttle to the island.'

'Good!'

He slid her one of his devilish grins. 'I must say I admire your decisiveness.'

She gave him a baleful look. 'Save your chatting up for some other woman, Harry. I played your game in front of Michael and Lucy because it suited me to do it, and I accepted your job offer because that suited me, too. As far as I'm concerned, there's work to be done and I'll do it. I don't expect to have *a lovely time* with you.'

His eyes held hers with a blast of discomforting intensity. 'No, not right now,' he drawled. 'Having had your expectations comprehensively dashed, I daresay you'll be a sourpuss for some time to come. But the island is a lovely place and I hope it will work some magic on you.'

A sourpuss...

The shock of that description halted her feet. She stared back at the blazing blue eyes, hating the knowledge she saw in them, knowledge of her hopes and the humiliation of seeing Michael respond to her sister as he had never—would never—respond to her. She couldn't wipe away Harry's perception of the situation, couldn't deny the truth, but was that any reason to be sour on him? He'd been her saviour today.

'I'm sorry,' she blurted out. 'I haven't thanked you.'

His sexy mouth moved into an ironic tilt. 'No thanks necessary, Elizabeth.'

His voice was soft, deep, and somehow it made her heart turn over.

She shook her head. 'That's not true, Harry. You were very effective in covering up my…my difficulties with how things went down today. I am grateful to you for rescuing me every time I hit a brick wall.'

'You'll bounce back, Elizabeth. Look on tomorrow as the first day of a new life—a butterfly breaking free of its confining cocoon and finding a world of sunshine. Come on—' he started walking down the wharf again, tugging her along with him '—we're on our way there now.'

The first day of a new life…

Of course, that was how it had to be.

There was no point in looking back, mourning over foolish dreams that were never going to come true. She had to put Michael behind her. Lucy would still be there along the track, her episode with Michael gone and forgotten, flitting along in her usual ditzy way. Her sister would always be her sister. It was she who had to start a different journey and being sour about it was just going to hold her back from getting somewhere good.

Harry helped her onto a large, deep-sea fishing

yacht, which undoubtedly had powerful motors to get them to their destination fast. 'Do you get seasick, Elizabeth?' he asked as he released the mooring rope. 'There are pills in the cabin you can take for it.'

'No, I'll be fine,' she assured him.

'I need you to be in top form when we arrive.'

'What do you consider top form?' She needed to know, get it right.

He jumped on board, grinning at her as he stored the rope correctly. 'Your usual self. Totally in charge of everything around you and projecting that haughty confidence you do so well.'

'Haughty?' she queried, not liking that description of herself, either.

'You're brilliant at it. Subject me to it every time.'

Only because Harry was Harry. It was her defence against him.

'I want you to give our target a dose of it when we confront him. No chatter. Just freeze him off.'

'No problem,' she stated categorically.

He straightened up and headed for the ladder to the bridge, tapping her cheek in passing, his eyes twinkling as he said, 'That's my girl!'

She barely stopped her hand from clapping her cheek to rid it of his electric touch. She clenched it into a fist and swiftly decided there would have to be some rules made about this short-term job on the island—like no touching from Harry. No kissing on the cheek, either. He was altogether too cavalier about taking liberties with her.

She was his stand-in manager, *not his girl*!

She was never going to be *his girl*.

One Finn brother had taken a bite out of her life. She was not about to give Harry the chance to take another. A month was a month. That was it with the Finns. She was thirty years old. When she'd completed this escape phase, some serious steps would have to be planned to make the best of the rest of her life.

She needed to find herself a serious man to share all that could be shared.

There was no hope of that happening with a play-boy like Harry.

'Think you can make us both a sobering coffee while I fire up the engines?' he tossed back at her from the ladder.

'Sure! Though I'm not the least bit intoxicated, Harry.' She'd sobered up over lunch.

He grinned at her. 'I am. A straight black would be good. Join me on the bridge when you've made it.'

'Okay.'

She wanted to be fully briefed on the situation she was walking into, and Harry certainly needed to be fully in command of himself before they reached the island. Not that she'd noticed any lack of command. In fact, he'd been quite masterful in manipulating Michael into complying with what he wanted. She would have to watch that particular skill of his and not fall victim to any manipulation that would end up with her in the playboy's bed!

CHAPTER FIVE

EXHILARATION bubbled through Harry's brain. Who would have thought when today had started out that he would be riding towards the end of it on this glorious high? Here he was on the open sea, carving through the waves, the problem with his thieving manager solved, and the deliciously challenging Elizabeth at his beck and call for at least a month.

Her brick wall against him was still in place, but that blind obsession of hers with Mickey was gone. Lovely, lovely Lucy had done the job, blitzing his brother right in front of her sister's eyes. And at the most opportune moment! So easy to step in and take advantage of Elizabeth's disillusioned state.

She'd found herself trapped in a situation where pride had forced her to side with him, undoubtedly kicking and screaming about it in her mind, but totally unable to disguise the fact that she reacted to him physically. Always had. She could deny it as much as she liked but sexual chemistry didn't lie, and now that Mickey was out of the picture, cultivating the instinctive attraction she couldn't quite control was going to be the most enjoyable task Harry had set himself for some time.

Ellie Flippence…

That's who she needed to be, not stiff-necked Elizabeth. Though she did have a lovely long neck. He'd often fantasised bending that swanlike column with a trail of hot kisses, melting the rest of her, too. She had beautiful lush breasts and the gorgeous butterfly wings on her blouse showed them off a treat.

This morning he'd wanted to reach out and touch them, cup them, kiss them. He'd find the right time and place for that now. The moment would come when she'd give in to good old healthy lust, and Harry intended to make it so good she'd forget all about her shattered Mickey dreams and revel in the pleasure he'd give her.

But business came first.

He definitely needed to sober up, not give away the game before Elizabeth was ready for it.

Just as well she'd worn sandals, Elizabeth thought as she moved around the galley, steadying herself to the sway of the yacht as it headed out to sea. High heels would have been disastrous in this environment. Clearly there were tricks to keeping everything safe on board. She found a drink holder attached to a sling which made transporting coffee to the bridge relatively easy, and mugs with lids like the takeaway variety used by coffee shops. There was no risk of slopping it onto her good clothes which had to last her until her luggage arrived.

A scene flashed into her mind of Lucy in their apartment, with Michael advising her on what to choose for her sister's island wear—an intimate little scene that made Elizabeth gnash her teeth. She had to stop thinking of *them* together, think about what was ahead of her instead.

Finn Island was at the high end of the tourist industry—exclusive to only twenty couples at a time, people who could pay thousands of dollars for a minimum three-day stay. She had never been there, since it was way beyond her pocket. However, the Cairns office did have a video of it, showing its attractions and facilities, so she had some idea of how it operated.

There were twenty luxury villas, a tennis court, a gym with a pampering centre offering all sorts of massages. The administration centre, boutique, restaurant and bar faced the main beach and were spread around a landscaped area with lush tropical plants and clusters of palm trees, plus a swimming pool and spa. Apart from this artfully designed section, most of the island was covered with rainforest. A creek running from the central hill provided delightful waterfalls and rock pools, and walking tracks had been made to these natural beauty spots.

Dive-boats for exploring the Great Barrier Reef were readily available, as were yachts for deep-sea fishing and small motorboats for reaching the other beaches at the various inlets around the shoreline. All in all, Finn Island provided the perfect tropical getaway…if you were rolling in money.

Guests who could afford it would obviously be demanding, expecting the best for what they were paying. Elizabeth hoped there would be no hiccups to the island's excellent reputation for providing it while she was in charge. She knew supply boats called regularly. However, how the staff operated was a mystery to her and the need for that information was foremost in her mind as she climbed the ladder to the bridge.

She sat down in the chair beside Harry's before handing him his coffee. 'Black, as requested,' she said, forcing a smile to disprove his *sourpuss* description and holding on to a fierce determination not to be prickly in his presence.

'Thanks.' He smiled back. 'We'll be there in about forty minutes.'

'I know the general layout of the resort, but I know nothing about the staff, Harry. Or how everything runs.'

'You'll learn fast enough,' he assured her. 'Basically you have three undermanagers. Sarah Pickard is the head housekeeper. She handles the cleaning staff. Her husband, Jack, is the head maintenance man, who has his own team of helpers. The head chef, Daniel Marven, runs everything to do with the restaurant. He also keeps a check on the bar and will tell you what needs to be ordered in.' He made a wry grimace. 'The guy you are going to replace was overordering and reselling elsewhere, not to mention a few other perks he was working.'

'His name?'

'Sean Cassidy. Not important for you to remember. He'll be gone within an hour of our arrival. I'll call up a helicopter to take him off.'

'Are you going to prosecute?'

He shook his head. 'Bad publicity. Besides, it wasn't major criminal stuff.'

'How did you find out he was crooked?'

'Our sommelier in Cairns remarked to me that our island guests drank an inordinate amount of wine and spirits. Surprisingly inordinate, despite the fact that we run an open bar. It rang warning bells. When Sean had his mainland leave this past weekend, I did a thorough check of all supplies and usage, and bingo! No doubt he was robbing us and has been doing it for some considerable time.'

'Will he know you were checking on him?'

'He knows I was there but I didn't tip my hand to anyone. Mickey and I still had to decide what to do about it. Any disruption is not good for business.' He flashed a grin at her. 'Which is where you come in. No disruption.'

She nodded. 'I'll do my best to make it appear a smooth transition, but I'll need some help to begin with.'

'No problem. I'll be your guide for the first few days, until you've familiarised yourself with how everything runs.'

A few days in close contact with Harry had to be tolerated. The groundwork for this management job had to be laid if she was to carry it through successfully. It was the measure of closeness she had to watch. If he started taking liberties with her person…somehow she had to deal with that if and when it happened.

'I'll get on top of it all as soon as I can,' she said with strong resolution.

Harry chuckled, his vivid blue eyes dancing with teasing knowledge as he slowly drawled, 'I'm sure you will, Elizabeth. Can't get rid of me fast enough, can you?'

She felt heat rushing up her neck and turned her face away, looking out to sea, hating how he could read her mind and provoke this reaction in her. 'I'm sure you have to keep a check on other things besides the resort,' she said flatly.

'True. Though I am aware that I'm throwing you into a position you haven't held before. I'll spend a few days with you, then drop in from time to time in case you have any problems that I can resolve.'

She wished she could say, *Don't. I'll call you if I need your help.* But he was her boss now and what he was laying out was reasonable. Problems could arise that she didn't even recognise because of her inexperience. 'Do you have accommodation kept especially for you on the island?' she asked, worrying about how *close* he was going to be to her.

'No. I'm happy sleeping aboard this yacht. The Pickards have their own private villa as they are the only ones on the staff, apart from the manager, who actually live on the island full-time. The rest work on a rotation basis—ten days here, four days on the mainland—and they're accommodated in a series of motel-like structures.'

'Is that where I'll be staying?'

He shook his head. 'You'll have your own private quarters in the administration building.'

Where Harry could make private visits.

Elizabeth grimaced at that thought. She was getting paranoid about the man. He could not get her into bed with him unless she allowed it. All she had to do was keep him at a sensible distance. It was only for a month and he wouldn't be there all the time.

'Don't be worrying about clothes for tomorrow,' he suddenly tossed at her. 'I'll get Sarah to issue you with the island uniform.'

'What's the island uniform?' she queried, not having seen that on the video.

'This...' He indicated his T-shirt and shorts and pointed to the emblem just below his left shoulder—a stitched line of waves in blue over which *Finn Island* was written in a small flowing multicoloured script to match the multicoloured fish across his chest.

She hadn't noticed the emblem before, distracted by the way the T-shirt clung to Harry's very male physique. 'I hadn't realised. Of course, you came from there this morning.'

So much had happened today, her state of hopeful eagerness this morning felt as though it had been wiped out a million years ago. Another life ago.

'Makes it easier for the guests to know who's staff and who's not,' Harry explained, adding with one of his devilish grins, 'That won't take care of your undies, though.'

He was probably having a fantasy of her naked beneath her outer clothes.

'I'll manage,' she said through gritted teeth.

He laughed. 'You can probably pick up a bikini from the boutique. Sarah can provide you with a hair-dryer and a toothbrush. Don't know about make-up.'

'I have some in my handbag.'

'No worries then.'

Only you, she thought.

Yet when they arrived on the island and confronted Sean Cassidy in his administration office, the playboy image Elizabeth had of Harry Finn in her mind was severely dented. Right in front of her eyes his easygoing attitude disappeared, replaced by a formidable air of authority. There was no semblance of light banter in his voice as he set about firing the crooked manager with ruthless efficiency.

Sean Cassidy had risen from the chair behind his office desk to greet his visitors, a smile on his face that didn't quite reach his eyes, which skated over Elizabeth and settled warily on Harry. He was a tall, lean man, dark-haired, dark-eyed, and the unheralded appearance of his boss clearly caused some tension in him.

'You're out, Sean,' Harry shot at him before the manager could say a word. 'Move away from the desk. Don't touch anything in this office. A helicopter will be arriving shortly to fly you to the mainland. Go and collect all your personal effects from your apartment. You won't be coming back.'

'What the hell...' the guy started to expostulate.

Harry cut him off. 'You know why. I have evidence of all your skimming activities. Providing you go quietly, I won't hand you over to the police at this time. If you know what's good for you, Sean, you'll stay quiet. Any bad-mouthing of the Finn family and its business operations will have consequences you won't like. Do you understand me?'

The threat had a steely edge to it that would have intimidated anyone. Sean Cassidy sucked in his breath, swallowed whatever defensive words he might have spoken and nodded. He looked shell-shocked.

'Let's go then.' Harry waved commandingly to a door in the rear wall of the office. 'I'll accompany you into the apartment to ensure you don't take anything that doesn't belong to you.'

As the man started to move as directed, Harry turned to Elizabeth, his blue eyes ice-hard, not a vestige of a twinkle in them. 'Take over the desk, Elizabeth. You're now in charge of this office.'

She nodded, her mouth too dry to speak. Her heart was beating faster than normal. The air felt charged with electricity. She was still stunned by the strike-anyone-dead energy that had emanated from Harry. In her two years of working for Michael, she had never witnessed anything like it coming from him, and she had always thought he was the stronger brother.

It wasn't until Harry had followed Sean into the apartment and closed the door that she could bring herself to actually move her feet. The desk was large and L-shaped with a computer workstation on one side. She sat in the chair that was now hers, grateful for its firm support. Witnessing the formidable side of Harry Finn had shaken her. The man was lethal, and she suddenly felt very vulnerable to whatever he might turn on her, now that she was locked into this situation with him.

That nerve-quivering blast of forcefulness... A shiver ran down her spine. Though surely he would never *force* a woman. *He wouldn't have to*, came the instant answer in her head. He was so innately sexy he could make her feel hot and bothered with just a teasing look. But he needed her here for business so maybe he would refrain from pushing anything sexual with her. Teasing was just teasing. Hopefully she could keep a level head with that.

Having cleared her mind enough to concentrate on business, Elizabeth took stock of the other office furnishings—filing cabinets, a couple of chairs for visitors, a coffee table with brochures fanned out on top of it, framed photographs of celebrities who had stayed here hanging on the walls.

On the larger section of the desk, which faced the entrance doors to administration, was a telephone attached to an intercom system with numbers for all the villas, the staff quarters and the restaurant. Beside it was a notepad and pen for writing notes or messages. On the top page were two reminders which had been ticked. *Chocs to 8. Gin to 14.* Obviously she had to deal with all requests from guests as well as handle bookings and coordinate the staff for whatever was needed.

Directly in front of her was a spreadsheet, detailing the occupancy of the villas this week—arrivals and departures. Three couples had left this morning. Their villas were vacant until another three couples arrived tomorrow. One of them was only staying three days, the other two for five. Most of the bookings were for five, only a few for a whole week. She would have to have her wits about her, coordinating the turnovers, personalising the welcomes and the farewells, memorising the names of all the guests. Wealthy people always expected that courtesy and respect.

She was matching names to the occupants of each villa when she heard the distinctive sound of a helicopter coming in. The door behind her opened and Harry led Sean, who was loaded up with luggage, out of the apartment, waving him to go ahead, pausing at the desk long enough to say, 'Hold the fort, Elizabeth. I'll be back in twenty minutes.'

He didn't wait for a reply, intent on escorting Sean to the helipad, wherever that was. The glass entrance doors to the office opened automatically for ease of access and Harry caught up with Sean as he made his exit. There was no verbal exchange between them. The ex-manager was going quietly.

Elizabeth watched Harry until he moved out of sight. Her heart was hammering again. Experiencing a completely different side of Harry Finn to the flirtatious tease she was used to was having a highly disturbing impact on her. It was impossible now to dismiss him as a lightweight playboy. The man had real substance, impressively strong substance, powerful substance, and it was playing havoc with her prejudice against him.

Michael had said this morning that Harry's mind was as sharp as a razor blade and he had his thumb on everything to do with his side of the business. That description could no longer be doubted. She'd had evidence enough today of how accurately he could read her thoughts—something she would have to guard against more carefully in the future—and she would never again underestimate how capable he was of being master of any situation.

His attraction was all the stronger for it. Dangerously so.

Nevertheless, that still didn't make him good relationship material.

He was a dyed-in-the-wool flirt with women.

And that wasn't just her judgment. Michael had said so.

Regardless of what Harry Finn made her feel, she was not going to have anything to do with him apart from the business of managing this resort for a month. He could flirt his head off with her but she would stand absolutely firm on that ground.

He was not what she wanted in her life.

She had to look for someone steady, solid, totally committed to her and the family they would have together.

Not like her father.

And not like Harry, who probably treated women as though they were a carousel of lollipops to be plucked out and tasted until another looked tastier.

CHAPTER SIX

WHEN Harry returned he was accompanied by a middle-aged woman with whom he appeared to be on very friendly terms. They were smiling at each other as they entered the office. She had short, curly dark hair, liberally streaked with grey, a very attractive face set in cheerful lines and merry hazel eyes that invited people to enjoy life with her. Of average height, her trim figure declared her fit to tackle anything, and she exuded positive vibes at Elizabeth as Harry introduced her.

'Sarah Pickard, Elizabeth.'

'Hi! Welcome to Finn Island,' the woman chimed in.

'Thank you.' Elizabeth smiled back as she rose from the desk to offer her hand at this first meeting. 'I'll have to learn a lot very fast and I'll appreciate any help and advice you can give me, Sarah.'

She laughed and gave Elizabeth's hand a quick squeeze. 'No problem. I'm only ever a call away. Harry tells me you've been Mickey's PA. I'm sure you'll fit in here very quickly.'

Mickey? The familiar use of Harry's name for his brother struck her as odd.

'Go into the apartment with Sarah, look around, see what you need,' Harry instructed. 'I'll man the desk.'

'Okay. Thank you,' Elizabeth replied, gesturing to Sarah to lead the way.

It was a basic one-bedroom apartment, spotlessly clean and pleasantly furnished with cane furniture, cushions brightly patterned in tropical designs. The floor was tiled and an airconditioner kept the rooms cool. The kitchenette was small, and its only equipment appeared to be an electric kettle, a toaster and a microwave oven.

'You won't need that for much,' Sarah explained. 'Meals will be brought to you from the restaurant. Just tick what you want on each menu. You'll find tea, coffee and sugar in the cupboard above the sink, milk and cold drinks in the bar fridge.'

Elizabeth nodded, thinking the gourmet meals provided here were a wonderful perk—no shopping for food, no cooking and no cleaning up afterwards.

'The bed linen was changed this morning so everything's fresh for you apart from these towels.' Which she'd collected from the bathroom as she'd showed Elizabeth the facilities. 'I'll send clean ones over for you. Plus a hair-dryer and toothbrush. Harry said he'd whipped you off Mickey with no time to pack anything.'

Again the familiar name usage. Elizabeth frowned quizzically. 'He's always been Michael to me. I've only heard Harry calling him Mickey. And now you.'

She laughed. 'I've known those two since they were teenagers. Jack and I looked after their parents' place in those days. I guess I was like a second mother to them. Never had kids of my own. Good boys, both of them. You couldn't be connected to better men, Elizabeth, as employers or people.'

It was a high recommendation, though probably a biased one, given Sarah's obvious fondness for them. 'They're very different,' she commented, wanting to hear more.

'Mickey's more like his dad, a seriously driven achiever. It's in his genes, I reckon. Harry's nature is more like his mum's. She had a very sunny disposition, radiating a joy in life that infected everyone around her. It was a wicked shame when...' She heaved a deep sigh. 'Well, I guess we never know the day or the hour, but I tell you, those boys are a credit to their parents. Losing them both when they did, they could have run off the rails, plenty of money to spend, but they took on the business and pushed forward. And they looked after everyone who could have been hurt by the loss. Like me and Jack.'

She paused, grimaced. 'Here I am running off at the mouth but you know Mickey. Harry said you've been working closely with him for two years.'

'Yes, I have.'

'You'll find Harry good to work for, too. Just a different nature, that's all.'

Sunny...like his mother...like Lucy. Was that why Michael was so attracted to Lucy? But why wasn't Harry? Why did he have to plague her with his endlessly provocative attention?

'I'll only be here for a month, Sarah. I'm the fill-in until Harry finds a replacement for Sean.'

'Whatever...' She waved airily. Obviously it was not something that weighed on her mind. 'I'll send over sets of the island uniform with the towels etc. Do you want short shorts, Bermuda length or three-quarters?'

'Bermuda length,' Elizabeth decided, thinking that would look more dignified for her position as manager.

'Harry thought a bikini…?'

'No. I'll wash my undies out tonight. I'll be fine, thanks, Sarah.'

She grinned. 'I love your butterfly blouse. It's just the kind of thing Harry's mum used to wear.'

Lucy's choice, Elizabeth thought. 'I'll gladly change it for tropical fish,' she said. The butterfly blouse represented failure with Michael and trouble with Harry, since he saw it as sexy. 'I'll be more comfortable here in the island uniform.'

'Well, it is easy. You don't have to think about what clothes to put on. I'll be off now. You might want to freshen up before rejoining Harry in the office.'

'Yes, I do. Thanks, Sarah.'

She was relieved to have such a good ally in the head housekeeper. It would surely make this job easier. Sarah's long association with the Finn family meant that she could be absolutely trusted, too.

What she'd said about *the two boys* lingered in Elizabeth's mind as she made use of the bathroom facilities. The plane crash that had taken the lives of Franklyn and Yvette Finn had been frontline news about ten years ago, soon after her own mother had died. She hadn't known the people so it had meant nothing personal to her at the time, yet it must have been a traumatic period for Michael and Harry, both young men, possibly still at university, having fun, believing there was plenty of time to work out what they wanted to do with their lives. It *was* admirable that they'd taken on their father's business empire instead of selling up and shedding all responsibility.

But it still didn't make Harry good relationship material. She could respect him for what he'd done. He might be very *solid* in that sense. However, that did not mean he had any staying power where women were concerned.

For the next hour she had to sit beside him at the computer workstation in the office while he went through the Finn Island website, showing her how bookings were made over the internet and their dates subsequently slotted into the island calendar. He explained how to work out all the schedules that had to be kept and Elizabeth had no trouble grasping what she had to do.

However, being so close to Harry—virtually shoulder to shoulder—did make concentration more difficult than it should have been. With their brief encounters in the Cairns office, she'd always managed to keep her distance from him, hating how he could exude a male sexiness that made her acutely conscious of being a woman whose needs weren't being answered. Now, having barely any space between them made her senses hyperalert to almost everything about him.

Her nose kept being invaded by his smell—a sharp tanginess like a sea breeze somehow mixed with an earthy animal scent. His strong, muscular forearms were a very masculine contrast to her more slender, softly rounded ones and she couldn't help noticing his long dexterous fingers as he worked the computer mouse—fingers that fascinated her into flights of erotic fantasy. He didn't touch her, not even accidentally, but she was wound up inside, expecting him to, silently schooling herself not to react as though his touch was like a hot iron scorching her skin.

She had to learn how to behave naturally around him. Whenever he glanced at her to check if she understood what he was explaining, the vivid blue eyes seemed to be tunnelling into her mind and she had to force herself to hold his gaze as she assured him everything was clear to her. Then he smiled approval which made her stupid stomach contract. He was an extremely disturbing man even when he wasn't teasing or flirting and she didn't want him to be. Hopefully his wretchedly unsettling effect on her would gradually fade away over the next few days.

People started strolling by on the path outside, heading towards the bar for predinner drinks. Harry named them as they passed. Of course he had been here over this past weekend, but it was impressive that he could identify every guest on the island and tell her where they came from, as well as how they'd come by their wealth. Elizabeth tried to commit most of what he said to memory but it was a struggle—too many of them, too quickly.

'You'll soon have them down pat,' Harry said confidently. 'I told Daniel we'd be eating in the restaurant tonight. I'll drill you on everyone at the other tables while we dine, then introduce you around before they leave.'

'That would help a lot,' she said gratefully.

'Hope you can find some more appetite than you had for lunch. Daniel will be miffed if you don't do justice to his gourmet creations.'

He knew she'd been too upset to eat much lunch but tonight she wouldn't have to watch Michael and Lucy gobbling up each other and she wanted to stop Harry from poking any further at the still-raw place in her heart. 'Actually I'm rather hungry. Must be the sea air,' she answered airily, resolving to eat everything put in front of her and show appreciation of it, regardless of how she *felt*.

His eyes glittered satisfaction. 'Remarkable what a sea change will do.'

Well, it won't extend to sharing your bed, she silently promised him as she rolled her chair back from the desk and stood up. 'Speaking of change, I'll go and swap these clothes for the island uniform before we go to the restaurant.'

Two young women on Sarah's staff—Maddie and Kate—had brought everything she needed while Harry had been teaching her the ins and outs of the website. The way they'd looked at Harry—telegraphing they thought he was *hot*—had made her wonder if he played musical beds on the island.

'Good idea!' He eyed her up and down in that lingering way that made her skin prickle. 'We wouldn't want our lady guests going pea-green with envy at how gorgeous you look in that outfit,' he drawled. 'Nor would we want their guys seeing you as more desirable than their partners.'

'Oh, really!' she huffed, crossing her arms defensively.

'Just telling you how it is, dear Elizabeth.'

'Don't *dear* me!' she snapped, still very much on edge from having to weather the sexual pitfalls of his proximity and wanting to cut off his flirting routine.

His eyebrows arched provocatively. 'What? I can't express how I feel about you?'

One of her hands sliced out in negative dismissal. 'I don't want to hear it.'

'Wrong time, wrong man, but that doesn't make it any less true.'

She rolled her eyes in disbelief. 'Let's keep to business, Harry.'

'Okay.' He gestured at the door to the apartment. 'Go and change. It will be a start to fitting in with me instead of Mickey.'

She felt purpose underlying those words, spine-crawling purpose as she turned her back on him and walked quickly from the office into the apartment, closing the door very firmly behind her.

It caused her to work up some steely purpose of her own. She would do her best to fit in on the island but fitting in with Harry on any personal basis had to stop. It had been a purely defensive move, going along with him today, using him as a shield to hide her distress. From now on she should take control of whatever happened between them. Her mind was very clear on that. She certainly didn't want to invite any sexual complications with him, which would only mess her around more than she was already messed up by the situation with Michael and Lucy.

It was a relief to shed the clothes that had fed her hopes this morning. She had a quick shower to wash away the misery of the day and give herself the sense of making a fresh start. It felt liberating donning the island uniform. This was the end of maintaining the professional image of an executive PA, at least for the next month. The casual, carefree look of shorts and T-shirt was suddenly very welcome to her.

It seemed she'd been carrying a heavy weight of responsibility for many years, ever since her mother had fallen ill with terminal cancer and her father had deserted them. The need to hold everything together for herself and Lucy had been driving her for a long time. Somehow it didn't matter so much anymore. She was on an island, away from the life she had known up until now, all by herself…except for Harry, who'd be gone as soon as she was on top of the job.

That was her main priority now—demonstrating to Harry that his guidance was no longer needed. Once she was free of his presence, this place might very well work some magic for her—time out of time to find herself again—no hanging on to what Michael thought or felt about her, no worrying about Lucy, just Elizabeth.

CHAPTER SEVEN

HARRY watched her come out of the apartment, all bright-eyed and bushy-tailed, determined to get on with the job and do it well. He admired her strength of character, her refusal to be utterly crushed by disillusionment. On the other hand, he had kept her mind very occupied these past few hours and would continue to do so until they parted for the night. That would be crunch time for her, when she was lying in bed, alone in the darkness. It would all be about Mickey and Lucy then.

He was strongly tempted to give her something else to think about—something she couldn't dismiss as easily as she had in the past, writing him off as of no account. He didn't like it. He never had liked it. Tonight might be too soon to pounce but...what the hell! She was never going to be *ready* for him. Her mind-set against getting personally involved with him was so fixed, perhaps physically shaking her out of it was the best way to go.

If he set the scene right...

An idea came to him. A private word to the chef before dinner, concentrate on business over the meal, wait until the guests had drifted off to their villas or the bar, then spring the surprise.

He grinned at her as he rose from the office chair. 'Time to see if the stars are burning bright tonight.'

She shook her head at him. 'It's not dark enough yet.' Her tone denied any interest in an activity which probably smacked of romance to her.

'Well, we can watch for them to appear from our table in the restaurant. You are allowed to enjoy the ambience of this island, Elizabeth.'

He could see her consciously relaxing, working up a smile. 'I will, Harry. I'm glad I have the opportunity to do so.'

'Good! I want you to be happy here.'

Happy...

Why not? Elizabeth thought. She should let everything else float out of her mind and embrace this experience—tropical night, stars burning bright, glorious food, lots of interesting people to meet. All she had to do was ignore Harry's insidious effect on her, and with the ready distraction of the guests around them, surely that could be kept at bay.

He led her out of the office, locked the doors and handed her the key, which made her feel secure about any unwanted attention coming from him later on in the evening. As soon as they entered the spacious, open-air restaurant, he was called over to a table where two couples were very happy with their day of diving near the reef, happy that Harry had arranged such a marvellous experience for them.

Elizabeth was introduced as the new manager. It was easy to smile at these people, easy to smile at all the other guests when other introductions were made throughout the evening. They were all having a great time and their mood was infectious, and however they'd filled in their day, the evening meal certainly topped it off.

Every course was superb. Elizabeth really enjoyed the food and complimented the chef on it, praising the attentiveness of the waiters, too. Daniel Marven definitely ran a high-class restaurant. Elizabeth couldn't see any problem arising on this front during her management month, and she was sure Sarah and Jack Pickard handled their roles just as efficiently. This could very well be a *happy* position for her.

'You have a great set-up here, Harry,' she complimented him over coffee. 'The guests are so clearly enjoying themselves.'

He leaned back in his chair, smiling at her. 'You've handled everything extremely well, Elizabeth.'

His voice was like a soft purr that somehow seemed to curl around her, adding more heat to the warmth of his smile. All evening it had been strictly business, with Harry coaching her in her managerial role, and she'd relaxed enough to actually feel comfortable with him. She was caught off guard by the switch to personal appreciation that felt as though he was physically caressing her.

Her pulse quickened. Her toes scrunched up in her sandals. He wasn't really *doing* anything, she fiercely told herself. It hadn't even been a flirtatious remark. Reacting like this was off the wall.

'Thank you,' she said quickly, fighting off the unwelcome feelings.

'No. Thank *you*,' he replied just as quickly, the smile gone, respect shining in his eyes. 'Coming in cold, taking over from Sean…you're picking up on everything much faster than I expected. This morning I had a problem. Tonight...' He spread his hands in an awed gesture. 'You're a wonder, Elizabeth.'

She floundered for a moment, his warmth and respect tearing at her heart—the heart she had given to Michael, who didn't want it. She made an ironic grimace. 'Your brother trained me to pick up on everything.'

He returned the grimace. 'Of course. Mickey would. But I'm glad you're here with me.'

And she was glad to have this getaway.

That was the bottom line.

She forced herself to relax again. Today was almost over. She'd made it through without falling apart.

As the last couple rose from their table to leave the restaurant they called out goodnights to Harry and Elizabeth, which, of course, they reciprocated. 'Colin and Jayne Melville from Goulburn,' Elizabeth murmured, shooting a triumphant grin at Harry. 'I've got them all sorted now.'

He laughed, the blue eyes twinkling pleasure in her. 'I knew you'd meet the challenge.'

Her heart did a flip-flop. The man was sinfully attractive, actually more so when he wasn't doing his playboy *flirting* stuff. Tonight he hadn't strayed into any irritating dalliance with her, focusing entirely on easing her into this new job. He'd been exceptionally good at it, too, charming the guests into talking about themselves, giving information for Elizabeth to memorise. They enjoyed chatting with him. Of course, in their eyes Harry Finn was an equal. He had the money, the looks and the self-assurance that came with both those assets.

'One more thing to do before we part for the night,' he said, standing up and moving to draw back her chair.

'What's that?' she asked, pushing herself up from the table, feeling it had been a very long day already.

'A little ceremony from the staff to welcome you,' he answered. 'It's been set up down on the deck.' He nodded towards the bar where many of the guests had gathered for a nightcap. It was directly across from the restaurant, the walkway down to the pool deck dividing the two entertainment areas. 'More private than here.'

Elizabeth had no qualms about accompanying Harry to wherever the welcome ceremony was going to be held. It was a nice gesture from the staff and gave her the opportunity to meet more of them.

There were actually two decks. The first one surrounded the swimming pool. It was strewn with sun-lounges, tables with folded-up umbrellas, and a couple of day beds flanking it. Steps led down to a lower deck, which had a large spa to one side.

A table for two was set up just in front of more steps that led straight onto the beach; white tablecloth, an ice bucket containing a bottle of champagne, two flute glasses, two bread plates with cake forks beside them. *A table for two*, in what was so obviously a romantic setting, close to the sound of waves lapping on the beach and under a sky full of stars.

Elizabeth jolted to a halt. Her pulse jumped into an erratic beat. This looked too much like a playboy setting. Was Harry about to turn into a wolf now that business was over for the day? She shot him a hard, suspicious look.

'I don't see any staff.'

'Waiting for me to get you settled,' he said, moving ahead to hold out one of the chairs for her.

Was it true? Surely he wouldn't lie when the lie could be so quickly disproved. It was okay, she told herself, taking a deep breath and letting it out slowly as she forced her feet forward and sat where Harry had directed. He lifted the bottle of champagne out of the ice bucket, popped the cork and filled the flute glasses before sitting down himself.

'A celebratory drink,' he said, smiling at her as he raised his glass, expecting her to do the same.

She did, though his smile did nothing to calm her down. Quite the opposite.

'To a new start,' he added, clicking her glass with his.

'A new start,' she echoed, hoping the staff would hurry up and appear. Her nerves were twitching. Her heart was thumping. There was too much intimacy about being alone with Harry out here, and the control she was trying to hold on to was frayed by having had to deal with too many difficult situations.

Harry's eyes caressed her with admiration as he complimented her again. 'You've been brilliant today, Elizabeth.'

For some stupid reason, tears pricked her eyes. She managed a half smile of acknowledgment and quickly sipped the champagne, needing it to loosen up the sudden lump in her throat. The day had been overloaded with tensions but it was almost over. All she had to do was hold herself together a little bit longer.

'Ah! Here it comes!' Harry said happily, looking up towards the restaurant.

Elizabeth blinked hard, set her glass down, mentally gathered herself to deal with the welcome ceremony, then turned her head to see…

Not a group of staff members.

Only one person walking down the steps.

It was Daniel Marven, carrying a cake on a platter.

She looked for others to come streaming down behind him but no one did. He proceeded to the table alone, placing the platter in front of her.

'Enjoy,' he said, smiling at her.

Happy Birthday Elizabeth was written across the chocolate icing on top of the cake. She stared at it, barely finding voice enough to say, 'Thank you.'

'Good work, Daniel,' Harry said, and the chef took off, leaving the two of them together.

A dam of tightly held emotion burst inside Elizabeth. Her birthday. Her thirtieth birthday. She'd so much wanted it to be…not how it had turned out. Tears spurted into her eyes, welling over and streaming down her cheeks. Impossible to stop them. Her heart was not strong enough to absorb any more stress. It felt as though it was breaking.

Strong hands lifted her out of her chair. Strong arms engulfed her, clamping her to a strong chest. Her head was gently pressed onto a strong shoulder. There was no resistance in her. None at all. She was as weak as a baby—a baby who had been born thirty years ago and didn't know what life had in store for her. Still didn't. And she was too much at sea to think about it…think about anything.

CHAPTER EIGHT

HARRY had not anticipated having a weeping Elizabeth in his arms. The birthday cake surprise had been planned to give her pleasure and undermine her resistance to a friendly goodnight kiss, which could have easily escalated into something more, sparking up the chemistry that she'd always been so determined to deny. He didn't feel right about taking advantage of *this* situation.

What had caused such deep distress? Was it the reminder that she had turned thirty today? Single women could be rather touchy about reaching that age goalpost, particularly if they weren't in a relationship and wanted to be. Was it the lost chance with Mickey catching up with her at the end of the day?

It was so damnably frustrating. He'd finally got her to himself. She felt good in his arms—all woman— soft, warm and curvy. Smelled good, too. He rubbed his cheek over her hair, breathing in the scent of her—a fruity shampoo and an enticing trace of exotic perfume. He patted her back, trying to impart comfort, and felt relieved when the weeping started trailing off, interrupted by deep, heaving breaths that made him very aware of the lush fullness of her breasts. He wanted to pick her up, carry her over to the nearest day bed and blow her mind with wild, passionate sex.

The emotional storm eventually came to a shuddering halt but she remained leaning on him, her head resting on his shoulder, her body still, limp, spent of all energy. His hands wanted to wander, travelling down the very female curve of her spine to her even more female bottom—the bottom that swished provocatively every time she'd turned away from him. His fingers itched to curl around it, press her body into a more intimate fit with his, stir the same desire in her that was heating up his blood, arousing the beast.

He couldn't stop himself from hardening, didn't want to anyway. Let her feel what she did to him. Let her know she was desirable even as a limp, tear-soaked rag doll. It might jolt her out of whatever sea of misery she was swimming in. Life was for living, not wallowing in a trough of depression.

Elizabeth didn't care that it was Harry holding her. It was simply nice to be held in such a secure comforting way, propping her up when she was down, not asking anything of her, just being another body emanating warmth that took the chill of loneliness from her bones.

She wished she had someone who would always be there for her like this, someone strong who would never let her down. She'd wanted to believe it would be Michael, but it wasn't. And Harry…oh hell! She could feel him getting hard! No matter that she'd been weeping all over him. He still had sex on his mind.

A flood of embarrassment poured heat into her face as she jerked her head up from his shoulder. She'd been hanging on to him like a limpet. It took a moment to unglue her hands from his back and try shoving them up his chest to make some space between them.

'Sorry...sorry,' she gabbled, frantically looking up to beg his understanding that she hadn't been passively inviting *anything*!

'Sorry for what?' he mocked, his eyes glittering a hard challenge at her.

'I didn't mean to...to use you like that.'

'You needed to...just like I need to do this.'

He whipped up a hand to hold her chin. Elizabeth didn't have time to protest, nor time to take any action to stop his mouth from swooping on hers. The impact shocked her. It was not a gentle seductive kiss. It was a full-on sensual assault, his lips working over hers, forcing them open with the strong thrust of his tongue that instantly swept over her palate, causing her whole mouth to tingle as though it had been charged with electricity.

Instinctively she used her own tongue to fight the invasion of his, angry at his bold aggression. Whether he took this as encouragement or not, she didn't know, but his hand moved to the back of her head, fingers thrusting into her hair, holding her so there was no escape from his marauding mouth. His tongue was teasing, goading, enticing hers to tangle erotically with it, resulting in an explosion of sensation that tore any sensible thoughts out of her mind.

The whole physicality of the moment was totally overwhelming. She didn't care that he pressed her lower body so closely to his that his erection furrowed her stomach. Some primitive part of her revelled in it, revelled in the hot hard wall of his chest squashing her breasts. She was swamped by a tidal wave of chaotic need to feel everything more and more intensely. Her own hands raked down his beautifully muscled back and curled around his taut male butt, exulting in the sense of taking this incredibly sexy man as hers.

It was wildly exciting, intoxicating—one avid kiss merging into another and another, inciting a fever of passion that possessed her with such power she completely lost herself in it, craving the fierce climactic union they were driving towards, the desire for it sweeping through her like a firestorm, all-consuming.

The mouth engaging hers suddenly broke the primal connection. 'Yes...' hissed into her ear—a sound of exultant triumph. Then the intimate body contact was shifted. Her legs were hoisted up and she was being carried with heart-pounding speed, cool air wafting over her hot face, reducing the fever of urgently demanding desire.

She was tumbled onto a bed and Harry—Harry!— was leaping onto it to join her there. Her eyes were wide-open now. Her mind crashed into working gear. This was one of the day beds on the deck. She'd wanted the sex that Harry was intent on having with her. Her body was still quivering at a peak of need for it. But it was madness to go on with it—madness to muddy up what should be a clean break away from everything, starting what would inevitably be a messy affair going nowhere and interfering with carrying through this management job.

He flung one strongly muscled thigh over hers and started lifting her T-shirt as he lowered his head to start kissing her again. She'd lain inert with shock at finding herself so complicit in stirring this situation. It had to be stopped. Now! Already his hand was on her breast, fingers moving under the cup of her bra, tweaking her nipple, and for a moment she was paralysed by a rebellious wish to feel more of his touch. She stared at his mouth coming closer and closer, her mind screaming that another kiss would tip her over into Harry's world.

Did she want that?

Did she?

Losing control of everything?

A flash of fear whipped her hand up to Harry's mouth, covering it just before it made contact with hers. His eyebrows beetled down in a puzzled frown.

'Stop!' she croaked.

He jerked his head back from her halting hand, his frown deepening as he shot a disbelieving 'What?' at her.

She swallowed hard to give her voice more strength. 'I don't want you to take this any further, Harry.'

'Why not?' he demanded. 'You want it as much as I do.'

She wrenched his hand away from her breast and pulled the T-shirt down. 'A momentary madness,' she excused.

'Rubbish! It's been simmering between us for years,' he insisted vehemently. 'It just came to a head and it's damned dishonest of you to back off now.'

Anger stirred. She hadn't really consented to this. He'd started it when she was at her weakest, taking advantage of her vulnerable state. 'I don't care what you call it, I don't choose to go on with it,' she said fiercely and attempted to roll away from him.

He scooped her back to face him, his eyes blazing furious frustration. 'What is the matter with you? We want each other. It's only natural to...'

'Let me go, Harry. This isn't right for me.'

'Not right?' he repeated incredulously. 'It sure as hell felt right until you suddenly decided it wasn't, but I'm not into forcing any woman to have sex with me.' He threw up the arm that had halted her rejection of any more togetherness. 'If you hadn't responded as you did...'

'I didn't mean to,' she yelled at him, her face flaming at the truth he was flinging at her.

'Oh, yes you did! Just for once you let that steel-trap mind of yours open enough for your instincts to take over and it was dynamite between us. Is that what scares you, Elizabeth?'

She hated how he could always hit the nail on the head with her. Yes, it scared her but she wasn't going to admit it. She glared resentment at him. 'I figure you're dynamite to a lot of women, Harry, and I don't care to be left in little pieces when you move on to your next piece of fluff.'

His hand sliced the air in savage dismissal of her argument. 'I don't think of you as *fluff*! Do you imagine I'd give this management job to someone I thought of as *fluff*?'

'I'm not saying you didn't believe I could do the work. But having a bit of sex on the side was on the plate, too, wasn't it?' she hurled back at him. 'And now you're peeved because I've decided not to cooperate.'

He rolled his head in exasperation. 'Peeved does not describe what I feel right now, Elizabeth.'

There was a mountain of feeling brooding behind those words and Elizabeth instantly felt threatened by it. She scrambled off the day bed, swinging around on her feet to face down any follow-up from Harry. He hadn't moved. He lay sprawled across the bed with his head propped up on his hand, his eyes searing hers with blistering accusation.

'You're shutting the gate on living life to the full,' he said bitingly. 'I don't want your cooperation, Elizabeth. I want your surrender to what we could have together.'

'That's not the life I want,' she retorted decisively.

'You're chasing dreams instead of taking on what's real.'

'*My* choice.'

'One I can't respect,' he mocked.

'I won't stay here unless you do, Harry.'

'Oh, I will on the surface, Elizabeth. You need have no fear of any unwelcomed advances from me. It will be strictly business tomorrow and any other day I'm here.'

She should have felt relieved, but there was an aching heaviness in her stomach, a drag of physical disappointment that was not about to be easily shifted. 'In that case I'll stay,' she said flatly. Where else could she go and not be faced with Michael and Lucy? One thing she could certainly say for Harry—he had the knack of blotting them out for a while.

'Your call.' His mouth took on an ironic twist as he added, 'And do feel free to call on me if you decide to change your mind and explore a different kind of life to the one you've planned so rigidly.'

She took a deep breath to ease the tightness in her chest and said, 'Well, I'm glad we have that sorted.'

'Yes, you're a regular sorting machine, Elizabeth, everything slotted into its proper place,' he drawled as he rolled off the other side of the day bed and faced her across it. 'One day you might find there's pleasure in improper activities.'

'Not today,' she said through gritted teeth, determined not to be taunted into doing anything reckless and stupid.

'No, not today,' he agreed mockingly. 'I take it you're about to say goodnight?'

'Yes.'

'I'll fetch your cake. I wouldn't want you to go without comfort food in the lonely darkness of the night.'

The cake.

She had completely forgotten it.

Wanted to forget it now but she couldn't, not with the chef having made it especially for her. She would have to eat some of it, too, show appreciation.

Harry strode down the steps to the table that had been set for them. At his orders. She was sure of that. Hoping to sweeten her up to the point where he would slide into making a move on her. Her stomach curdled at how easy she had made it for him, and how quickly she had been caught up in the dynamic sexuality he could put out at will.

Her thighs were aquiver from having been in such intimate contact with him and her breasts were still in a state of arousal. He had excited her—almost to the point of no return—and he could probably do it again if she let him. Would he keep his word—strictly business from now on unless she gave him the green light?

He picked up the cake platter. Elizabeth realised she hadn't even moved from where she'd scrambled off the day bed. If Harry saw her still standing beside it he might think she regretted her decision. She jerked into walking, rounding the bed and heading up towards the administration office.

Harry had given her the door key after he had locked up before dinner. She dug it out of her shorts pocket, anxious to have the door open and be standing right there, ready to receive the cake from him so he had no reason to come in with it. Being alone with him in any enclosed space right now would severely stretch nerves that were already wildly agitated at having to be face to face with him, just for a few moments.

It surprised her to see guests laughing and chatting in the open bar lounge as she passed by. It had seemed so *private* on the lower decks. What if any of these people had strolled down to the beach while she and Harry… It didn't bear thinking about. Reckless, shameless…her face flamed at how very nearly she had succumbed to almost a *public* sex act.

Anger simmered as she unlocked the door, opened it and turned to take the cake platter from Harry, who had virtually caught up with her. 'Did you realise there were still people up and about when you swept me off to that bed?' she demanded accusingly.

'So what?' He arched his eyebrows at her as though she was mad.

'Oh, you don't care about anything, do you?' she

cried in exasperation and tried to snatch the platter from him.

He held on to it, forcing her to meet his gaze, a blast of hot resentment burning over her own. 'On the contrary, I care about a lot of things, Elizabeth. As to your quite unnecessary embarrassment at the thought of being observed in flagrante, this happens to be a tropical island where people drop their inhibitions and feel free to have sex wherever and whenever they want it. Using that bed under the stars for some natural pleasure in the privacy of the night would not offend anyone.'

'I'm not a guest. I'm staff,' she argued furiously.

His chin jutted with arrogant authority. 'This island is mine. I can make any rules I like for whomever I like.'

'I live by my own rules, Harry,' she flared at him. 'Now let me have the cake and let's say goodnight.'

He released the platter and stepped back, nodding mockingly as he said, 'Goodnight, Elizabeth.'

Then he strode away, back towards the beach, not giving her the chance to say another word.

She was so wound up it took several seconds for her to realise the threat of him was gone—not that he'd been threatening her. It was just how she felt with him, as though in constant danger of having her *rules* undermined or blown apart.

She quickly took the platter to the office desk, set it down and returned to lock the door, telling herself she was now safe for the night. Tomorrow…well, she would deal with tomorrow when it came.

She carried the untouched cake into the apartment, shutting herself into her own private domain. In a violent reaction to the whole stressful day, she found a knife and cut the *Happy Birthday* writing off the icing. It had been a rotten birthday. No happiness at all. She'd suffered a devastating let-down from Michael, as well as what felt like a betrayal from Lucy and persecution from Harry.

Tomorrow had to be better.

She only had to put up with Harry tomorrow.

And while that might not be a piece of cake, she would stomach it somehow.

No way was she going to break up again anywhere near Harry Finn!

CHAPTER NINE

HARRY clenched his hands into fists as he strode back down to the lower deck. The urge to fight was still coursing through him. He'd barely reined it in to bid Elizabeth a fairly civilised goodnight. He certainly didn't *feel* civilised.

Okay, he'd jumped the gun with her but she'd been right there with him. Not one other woman he'd been with had ever pulled back when both of them were fired up to have sex. Being rejected like that was an absolute first, though he probably should have been prepared for it. Elizabeth Flippence had made an art form of rejecting him over the past two years.

What were her damned rules? No mixing business with pleasure? She would have mixed it with Mickey so that didn't wash. Did she have to have a wedding ring on her finger before she'd have sex? Where was she coming from to have that kind of attitude in this day and age? A thirty-year-old virgin? Harry didn't believe it. Not with her looks.

Clearly he needed to know more about her, form another plan of attack because she was *not* going to get away from him. He didn't understand why she dug so deeply under his skin, what made her so compellingly desirable, but the buzz was there and he couldn't get rid of it. What caused him even more frustration was *knowing* she felt the same buzz around him.

It was a maddening situation.

He lifted the bottle of champagne out of the ice bucket, stepped over to the edge of the deck and poured the remaining contents onto the sand. The only thing worse than flat champagne was the flat aftermath of flattened desire. He popped the emptied bottle back in the bucket and started the long walk down the beach to the wharf where his yacht was docked.

He thought of his own birthday—thirty-three last month. Mickey had thrown him a party. They always did that for each other because their parents had and neither of them could quite let go of that golden past, though they had sold the marvellous family property on the hill overlooking Cairns because it wasn't the same—couldn't be—without their mother and father there.

He remembered the great tennis parties and pool parties his mother had organised. His and Mickey's school friends had loved coming to their place—always so much fun to be had. The fishing trips with his father had been great, too. He'd had the best childhood, best teen years, a really happy life until that black day when his father's plane went down.

This resort had still been on the drawing board then. His father had been excited about building it, showing him and Mickey the plans, talking about how he would market it. After the funeral Harry had wanted this project, wanted to be physically busy, creating something, bringing his father's vision to reality. He'd lived here, worked here until it was done, organising everything for it to be a successful enterprise.

Mickey had thrown himself into managing the franchises, needing to be busy, too, both of them wanting to feel their parents would be proud of them. It had seemed the best way to handle their grief, filling the huge hole of loss with hard absorbing work. Neither of them had been interested in managing girlfriends during that dark period, not wanting any emotional demands on them from people who had no understanding of what was driving them. The occasional night out, some casual sex...that had been enough.

Over the years neither he nor Mickey had fallen into any deep and meaningful relationships. Somehow there was always something missing, something that didn't gel, something that put them off. Occasionally they chatted about their various failures to really connect with one woman or another. It always came back to how happy their parents had been together, complementing each other, and ultimately that was what they wanted in a life partner. In the meantime they floated, docking for a while with whatever woman they felt attracted to.

Harry wondered if Lucy would last with Mickey, then chewed over his own problem of even getting a start with Elizabeth.

Why was giving in to a perfectly natural attraction such a problem to her? Why not pursue it, find out if it could lead to a really satisfying relationship? Was she so hung up on her unrequited love for Mickey that she didn't want to admit that something else could be better?

Whatever…he'd get to the bottom of her resistance and smash it, one way or another.

By the next morning Harry had cooled down enough to realise he should give Elizabeth more time to come to terms with the changes in her life. He had rushed her last night. Today he would be very *civilised*. Though not necessarily according to *her* rules.

He had breakfast on the yacht, suspecting that Elizabeth would avoid having breakfast with him in the restaurant. Undoubtedly Miss Efficiency had set her bedside alarm clock for an early hour to be up and about before any of the guests, opening the office and at her desk, ready to deal with anything that came her way. She would certainly have used the convenience of a call to the restaurant to have her breakfast delivered.

As expected, she was at her desk when Harry strolled into the administration office. He beamed a warmly approving smile at her and put a bright lilt in his voice. 'Good morning, Elizabeth.'

It forced her attention away from the computer. She pasted a tight smile on her face and returned his greeting. Her big brown eyes had no shine. They were guarded, watchful. Harry knew her brick wall was up and there would be no easy door through it. The urge to at least put a chink in her defensive armour was irresistible.

He hitched himself onto the corner of the desk, viewing her with curious interest. 'Are you a virgin, Elizabeth?'

That livened up her face, her eyes widening in incredulity and shooting sparks of outrage as she completely lost control of her voice, shrilling, 'What?' at him.

'It's a simple question,' Harry said reasonably. 'Are you a virgin, yes or no?'

'You have no right to ask me that!' she spluttered.

He shrugged. 'Why is it a problem?'

Anger shot to the surface. 'It's none of your business!'

'I guess the answer is yes since you're so sensitive about it,' he tossed at her affably.

'I am *not* sensitive about it!'

'Looks that way to me.'

She glared at him, and if her eyes had been knives they would have stabbed him in a million painful places. Harry found it wonderfully exhilarating. He'd definitely got under her skin again, regardless of how firmly she had decided to keep him out.

Her jaw tightened and he knew she was gritting her teeth as she struggled to bring herself under control. Finally she gnashed out the words 'It's just none of your business, Harry. It is totally irrelevant to this job and I'll thank you to remember that.'

'Bravo!' he said admiringly.

It confused her. 'Bravo what?'

He grinned at her. 'The rule book rules. Almost forgot it there for a moment, didn't you?'

She huffed to release some of the tension he'd raised, viewing him balefully. 'I'd appreciate it if *you* didn't forget it.'

'I do apologise for the transgression.' He made a wry grimace. 'Curiosity slipped through my usual sense of discretion. However, it does give me a better understanding of you now that I know you're a virgin. Head stuffed with romantic dreams…'

'I am *not* a virgin!' tripped out of her mouth before she could stop the wave of exasperation he'd whipped up.

He arched his eyebrows in surprise. 'You're not?'

She closed her eyes. Her mouth shut into a tight thin line. Quite clearly she hated herself for biting at his bait. Harry revelled in her discomfort. Serve her right for the discomfort she'd given him last night. And it was great to have that problem box ticked off. No virginity barrier.

Another big huff. Her eyes opened into hard, piercing slits. Shards of ice came off her tongue. 'Can we please get down to work now?'

'Jumping to it,' he said obligingly, hitching himself off the desk and rounding it to view the computer screen. 'Any bookings come in this morning?'

'Yes.' She swung her chair around to face the computer and started working the mouse. 'I think I've dealt with them correctly. If you'll check what I've done…?'

For the next half hour Harry kept strictly to business, giving Elizabeth no reason to complain about his behaviour. She had a good understanding of what was required of administration. Supply issues still had to be addressed but that could wait until later. She was so uptight he decided to give her a break, let her relax for a while.

'Before the heat of the day sets in, I'm going to call Jack Pickard to take you around the resort, show you the practical aspects of how it runs. You need to be familiar with all of it,' he said, reaching for the telephone. 'I'll stand in for you here.'

'Okay,' she answered levelly, but the relief he sensed coming from her told him exactly what she was thinking.

Escape.

Escape from the pressure of having to keep denying what was undeniable…the constant sizzle of sexual chemistry between them.

Harry told himself he could wait.

Sooner or later it would come to a head and boil over.

Then he would have her.

Elizabeth took an instant liking to Jack Pickard. She probably would have liked anyone who took her away from Harry this morning but Sarah's husband was a chirpy kind of guy, nattering cheerfully about the island and his maintenance job—easy, relaxing company. He was short and wiry and his weather-beaten face had deep crow's-feet at the corners of his eyes from smiling a lot. His hair looked wiry, too, a mass of unruly curls going an iron-grey.

'Show you one of the vacant villas first.' He grinned at her. 'Before the new guests fly in this morning.'

'Do they all come by helicopter?' Elizabeth asked.

'Uh-uh. Most come by motor launch. We meet them at the jetty and drive them around to administration. Those that fly in land on the back beach and take the wooden walkway that leads here.'

Wooden walkways led everywhere, with flights of steps wherever they were needed. The one they took to the vacant villa ran through rainforest, the lovely green canopy of foliage above it shading them from the direct heat of the sun. On either side of them were masses of tropical vegetation—palms, vines, bamboo, hibiscus, native flowers.

The villa was situated on a hillside overlooking the

bay leading into the main beach. Its front porch had a lovely view and the breeze wafting in from the sea made it a very inviting place to sit in the deckchairs provided. Jack opened a sliding glass door and gestured for her to step inside.

The structure was split-level. Elizabeth entered a spacious living room—a comfortable lounge setting with coffee table facing a television set and CD player, a writing desk and chair, a counter along one wall containing a sink and a bar fridge. Above the counter were cupboards containing a selection of glasses for every kind of drink, bottles of spirits, plus tea and coffee-making facilities, a jar of home-made cookies and a selection of crackers to go with the cheese platter in the fridge, which also held a box of Belgian chocolates, fruit juice, beer, champagne, wine and plenty of drink mixers.

Up a few steps from the living area was a mezzanine bedroom containing a huge king-size bed, lots of pillows, plenty of cupboard space, bedside tables with lamps in the shape of dolphins. All the decor had a sea-and-beach theme, most of the furnishings in white and turquoise, knick-knacky things constructed from driftwood and coral and shells. White walls and polished floorboards completed the clean, airy look.

'There's an extensive library of books, CDs and games in the bar-lounge adjacent to the restaurant,' Jack told her. 'Guests can help themselves to whatever they like. You, too, Elizabeth.'

She smiled at him. 'That's good to know.'

Should fill in some lonely hours, she thought, once Harry was gone and she could get him out of her mind.

That *virgin* question still had her seething, as though *that* was the only possible reason for not getting her pants off for him. In hindsight, she probably should have said she was, put him right off his game. On the other hand, he might have fancied himself as teacher, giving her a first experience in sex. It was impossible to pin down anything with Harry. He could slide this way or that way at the blink of an eye. Which made him so infuriating and frustrating and…

Elizabeth clamped down on those feelings, forcing herself to focus on what she was seeing here. The bathroom was positively decadent, a shower for two, a spa bath, the walls tiled in a wavy white with turquoise feature tiles and turquoise towels. The long vanity bench held two wash basins and a pretty collection of shells. Everything in the villa was clearly designed to give guests pleasure.

'This is all fantastic,' she commented to Jack.

He nodded agreement. 'Sarah and I reckon Harry did a great job of it.'

'Harry? Surely he had an interior decorator fitting out the villas.'

'Oh, he had a professional finding the stuff he wanted, but how the villas are all decked out was his idea. His dad had an architect design how they're built. It was his vision in the first place, but after he died, Harry took on the whole project and saw it through to completion. Did a great job of marketing it, too.'

This information did not fit her view of Harry Finn as a playboy. It was disconcerting until she remembered that admirable work and talent had no relevance to how he dealt with women.

She and Jack moved on. He showed her the gym, which contained most of the popular work-out equipment, introducing her to staff she hadn't met yet. A large shed near the beach where the helicopter landed contained a desalination plant that ultimately provided fresh water for the resort. The power generator was also housed there.

'This beach faces west,' Jack said, pointing to the hill above it. 'Up there are the two pavilion villas, both of them occupied today so I can't show them to you. Their porches lead out to infinity pools that catch the sunset. Feels like there's just you and the water and the sky. They weren't on the original plan. Harry's idea to build them, make them really special.'

Elizabeth nodded. 'I noticed it cost more to stay in them.'

Jack grinned. 'Honeymoon paradise.'

As they continued the tour, chatting as they went along, Elizabeth realised her escort was extremely well skilled—electrician, plumber, carpenter, gardener— capable of turning his hand to any maintenance work.

She couldn't help remarking, 'How come you never started a business of your own, Jack? You're so well qualified.'

He grinned. 'Hated all the paperwork the government expects you to do. Reckon I got a plum job with Harry's dad, maintaining the property he had overlooking Cairns. Free cottage, good pay, all the fun of creating and being in a beautiful environment. Got the same deal here on the island with Harry. We've got a good life, Sarah and me. Can't think of anything better.'

'Then you're very lucky,' she said warmly.

'That we are.'

A contented man, Elizabeth thought, wondering if she would ever reach the same state of contentment. Not today. And not here with Harry waiting for her back at the office. It was awful to think of how tempted she had been last night to just let herself be swept up in physical sensation. It had been a long time—almost three years since her last semiserious relationship ended—but that was no reason to engage in casual sex.

She'd never been into bed-hopping. Trying guys out on a purely physical basis did not appeal to her. She needed to feel really connected to the person before taking the next step to absolute intimacy. If Harry considered that attitude a headful of romantic dreams it was because it didn't suit his playboy mentality. Bending her principles for him was not on, though she had to admit he was the sexiest man she had ever met, which made everything wretchedly difficult when she was alone with him.

Just one hour in the office this morning had been exhausting, having to use so much energy blocking out his physical impact on her. Of course, last night's wild interlude had made her even more sexually aware of him. She'd been out of her mind to let him go so far with her. Now she had to cope with that memory in his eyes as well as the memories he'd stamped on her consciousness.

On the walk back to administration, Jack started talking about Harry again, how good he had been at all sports in his teens—that was easy to imagine—and what a pity it was that the untimely death of his parents had caused him to drop them. 'Could have been a champion on any playing field,' was Jack's opinion.

Elizabeth could think of one sport Harry hadn't given up.

He was a champion flirt.

She hoped he wouldn't exercise that particular skill while she had to be with him for the rest of the day. So long as he kept to business, she should be reasonably okay. Nevertheless, it was impossible to stop her nerves twitching in agitation when Jack left her at the office door and Harry swung his chair around from the computer and smiled at her.

'Enjoy the tour?'

She smiled back, deciding to show appreciation of all he'd done here. 'You have created quite an extraordinary resort, Harry. I can't think of anything that could make it better.'

'If you do, let me know. I aim for perfection.'

Would he be the perfect lover?

Elizabeth was shocked at how that thought had slid right past her guard against *the playboy*. She hurled it out of her mind as she hitched herself onto the corner of the desk just as he had this morning, casually asking, 'Anything come in that I should know about?'

'Mickey called. He's putting the suitcase your sister packed for you on the helicopter bringing the guests today.' He gave her a quirky smile. 'Should save you from having to wash out your undies tonight.'

'That's good,' she said equably, determined not to be baited into being prickly.

'Lucy says if she's missed anything you need, send

her an email,' Harry went on. 'She'll bring it with her when she comes here with Mickey this weekend.'

Elizabeth sat in frozen suspension.

Her heart stopped.

Her lungs seized up.

Her mind stayed plugged on one horribly chilling thought.

Lucy…coming with Michael…to her island escape from them.

No escape at all!

CHAPTER TEN

HARRY saw her eyes glaze. She sat completely still. He knew this was a crunch moment. He waited, silently speculating on how she would react to the bombshell when she snapped out of the shock wave.

Would pride dictate that she welcome Mickey and her sister onto the island, keeping up the pretence that seeing them together did not hurt her?

Mickey was totally unaware that Elizabeth was hung up on him. So was Lucy. Neither of them would be looking for signs of hurt. It was quite possible to get through this visit, leaving them none the wiser, especially if Elizabeth was willing to let him be the man *she* was interested in. Which had to bring them several steps closer, Harry thought, willing her to choose that path.

Alternatively, since her escape from Mickey and Lucy had just been scuttled, the island no longer represented a safe refuge for her. And Harry knew he'd gone too far too fast last night, which was certainly ruffling her feathers. She might throw in this job, walk down to the back beach, wait for the helicopter to come in and fly out on it, take a trip somewhere else, not caring what anyone thought—wipe her hands of all of them.

Except she couldn't quite.

Lucy was her sister.

Lucy depended on her to be her anchor and Elizabeth took responsibility seriously. She wasn't the type to cut free. Not completely. But she might want to for a while.

Harry needed to stop her from walking out on him. Having her here on the island was his best chance with her. It gave him time to keep challenging her, wear down her resistance, make her realise they could have something good together.

Elizabeth felt totally numb. It had been such a struggle, holding herself together in front of Michael and Lucy yesterday, a struggle coping with what Harry made her feel, a struggle learning how to manage this resort as fast as she could. Now the whole reason for so much effort, the whole reason for being here was slipping away from her.

She couldn't bear to play out yesterday's scenario with Michael and Lucy again this weekend. It was too much pretence, too much pressure, too much everything with Harry hanging around, ready to take advantage of any weak moment, and she'd be tempted to use him again as a buffer. It was all horribly wrong and the worst part was she was trapped here—trapped by her own deceit.

If she walked out on the job after pretending to like being with Harry, how could she ever explain that to Lucy? It wouldn't make sense. Telling her the truth wasn't fair. It would cut into whatever happiness she was finding with Michael, tarnish it because it was causing her sister unhappiness, which Elizabeth knew

Lucy would never knowingly do. Underneath all her ditziness was a very caring heart.

Having taken a deep breath and slowly released it to get her lungs working again and feed some much-needed oxygen into the hopeless morass in her brain, she squared her shoulders and looked directly at Harry Finn—her rescuer and tormentor. There was no devilish twinkle in the blue eyes. They were observing her with sharp attention, alert to any give-away signs of what she was thinking and feeling.

He had demonstrated yesterday how perceptive he was, and remembering how accurately he had read the situation, Elizabeth felt a strong stab of resentment that he hadn't acted to protect her this time.

'You could have dissuaded your brother from coming, Harry,' she said accusingly.

'How?' he challenged. 'By saying you don't want him here? Mickey wants to see if you're managing okay. Both of them do.' His mouth lifted in an ironic tilt. 'I did spring the job on you, Elizabeth.'

'You could have said all the villas were taken—no ready accommodation for them,' she argued.

He shrugged. 'I'm not in the habit of telling lies. Besides, Mickey has a motor-cruiser. They'll be arriving in it and could just as easily sleep in it. A head count of guests at dinner would have told him we have two villas vacant this weekend and he might have confronted me about it, raising questions. Would you have liked to answer them?'

She grimaced, accepting there was no way out of this and there was no point in protesting the arrangements already made. 'Which villa did you put them in?' she asked flatly.

'Mickey requested a pavilion villa if available. Since one of them is vacant from Friday afternoon to Sunday afternoon, I've obliged him.'

A pavilion villa…honeymoon paradise!

She turned her head away, evading Harry's watchful gaze. Flashing through her mind were images of Michael and Lucy enjoying an intimate weekend—making love on the king-size bed, cooling off in the infinity pool, drinking champagne as they watched the sunset. It was sickening. She couldn't help thinking, *It should have been me with Michael. Me, not Lucy.*

For two years she had been dreaming of having just such a romantic weekend with him. Why couldn't he have found her as wildly attractive as he obviously found Lucy? Harry had no problem in seeing her as sexy. He would have whizzed her off to bed in no time flat. Almost had last night.

'They're not coming in until Saturday morning,' Harry said quietly. 'It will only be for one night, Elizabeth.'

As though that made it better, she thought savagely. Lucy would be parading her happiness with Michael from the moment she landed to the moment she waved goodbye, and during that two-day span it was going to be one hell of an uphill battle to keep pretending happiness with Harry.

Unless…

A wicked idea slid into her mind.

It grew, sprouting a whole range of seductive thoughts,

becoming a plan that promised a way to get through this weekend reasonably intact.

Harry would view it as a night of fun and games, the playboy triumphant. He wouldn't care about what she was using him for since he'd get what he wanted. And *she* wouldn't be hurt by it because she was the one directing the play, the one in control of what was to happen.

She could set aside her principles, be a butterfly flying free for one night. Maybe it was what she needed to do, use it as a catharsis, releasing all the emotional mess in her mind and heart and wallowing in purely physical sensation. Harry had proved last night he could drive up her excitement meter. Why not experience how far he could take it?

If it was good…if it was great…she could face Lucy and Michael without the horribly hollow sense of missing out on everything, especially since she would have already had what they were going to have and where they were going to have it. That part of it should kill off any sense of jealousy and envy, which were horribly negative feelings that she didn't want to have towards her sister. Lucy was Lucy. It wasn't her fault that Michael was totally smitten by her, and Elizabeth was not going to let *their* connection affect the close relationship she'd always had with her sister.

But she needed help from Harry to make all this stick.

His expert playboy help, smashing her mind with so much pleasure it took away the pain.

If he didn't cooperate with her plan… But he would,

wouldn't he? He wanted her to *surrender* herself to him and that was what she'd be doing.

She threw a quick glance at him. He was leaning back in the chair, apparently relaxed as he waited for her to respond to the situation. However, his gaze instantly caught hers, sharply searching for what was in her mind. There was no point in taking any evasive action. She had decided on what she wanted from him. Her own eyes watched his very keenly as she put the question which would start a new situation rolling.

'Do you still want to have sex with me, Harry?'

His eyebrows shot up in surprise. There was no instant *yes*. Elizabeth's heart pounded nervously as she waited for his reply, watching his eyes narrow speculatively. He was obviously digesting what this change from her meant.

'That's been a constant for me over quite a long time, Elizabeth,' he said slowly. 'I think the more pertinent question is do you finally realise that you want to have sex with me?'

'Yes, I do,' she answered unequivocally. 'But only if certain conditions are met.'

It had to be her plan or nothing.

His head tilted to one side. He was not rushing to accommodate her. His eyes watched her with an even higher level of intensity. Elizabeth held his gaze defiantly, determined not to budge from this stance. After a long nerve-racking silence, he casually waved a hand in an invitational gesture.

'Spell out the conditions.'

Elizabeth took a deep breath, fiercely willing him to fall in with what she wanted. 'The pavilion villa is empty on Friday night. I want it to be there. And then. The rest of this week we just keep to business.'

It took every ounce of Harry's control not to react violently, to absorb this slug to his guts and remain seated, appearing to be considering what all his instincts were savagely railing against. This wasn't about him and the chemistry between them. It was about Mickey and Lucy. In some dark twisted place in her mind, she probably wanted to pretend he was his brother, having it off in the same romantic setting where Mickey was about to take her sister.

No way would he be used as a freaking substitute!

It was a bitter blow to his ego that she should ask it of him. It showed how little she cared about what he thought, what he felt. He had encouraged her to use him as a blind to hide her angst over Mickey yesterday but to use him this far…it was brutal and he hated her for corrupting what they could have had together.

Hate…

He'd never felt that towards anyone. Why did she get to him so strongly? It was crazy. He should wipe her off his slate right now, find some other woman who thought he was worth having, who'd be sweetly giving, at least for a while.

Except…damn it! He still wanted the ungettable Elizabeth Flippence!

Have her and be done with it, he thought savagely.

He could use her scenario his way, add his own conditions, make her so hyped up with sexual awareness, Mickey would be blotted right out of her mind and he'd be *the man*—the only man she'd be conscious of all through the night.

She was patiently waiting for his agreement, her eyes boring into his, boldly challenging his desire for her. He sensed that some essential part of her had clicked off. She'd moved beyond caring what he said or did. The equation was simple. He either went with her plan or that was the end of anything personal ever happening between them.

'Okay,' he said calmly. 'I'll make arrangements for us to occupy the pavilion villa on Friday night.'

She nodded, the expression in her eyes changing to a knowing mockery. She had labelled him a playboy on quite a few occasions so he knew what she was thinking—a night of sex would always be amenable to him, regardless of why it was offered.

He decided to live up to her idea of him.

'As long as you'll fit in with some conditions I have in mind,' he said with a quirky little smile.

That shot some tension through her. 'Like what?' she asked sharply.

'Like not saying no to anything I want to do.'

She frowned. 'I won't do kinky stuff, Harry.'

'I'm not into sado-masochism, domination or bondage,' he assured her. 'But I don't particularly care for clinical intimacy, either. A bit of sexy fun is more to my liking.'

'What do you consider sexy fun?' she asked suspiciously.

He grinned. 'How about you wear that butterfly blouse again, without a bra underneath? Be *wicked* for me.'

Hot colour raced up her neck and scorched her

cheeks. Harry didn't care if she connected the butterfly blouse to her Mickey fantasy. He'd had a few fantasies about it himself.

'And team it with a bikini bottom with side strings that I can undo with a flick of the fingers,' he added. 'Some bright colour that goes with your butterfly. I'm sure you'll be able to find one in the boutique.'

She rolled her eyes. 'I didn't realise you needed provocative clothes to turn you on, Harry.'

He shrugged. 'I don't. I'd simply like you to look and be accessible for once. I've been hitting a brick wall with you for two years. *Accessible* has a lot of appeal to me.'

Her cheeks heated up again, making her eyes look glittery. 'Do you have anything else in mind?' she clipped out.

He waved an airy hand. 'Let me think about it. You have rather sprung this on me. If I'm only to ever get one night with Elizabeth Flippence...' He cocked an eyebrow at her. 'That is the plan, isn't it?'

'Yes' hissed out between her teeth.

'Then I want it to be a night to remember. Something extra special. The most sensual trip of a lifetime. I need to let my imagination work on it for a while.'

'Fine!' she snapped, and hopped off the desk, adopting a brisk and businesslike air. 'You have three and a half days for your imagination to flourish. Since we have the essentials settled, let's get on with resort management.'

He could almost hear the steel click in her mind. In his experience of women, Elizabeth Flippence was definitely something else. But she would soften for him on Friday night. He'd make damned sure she did!

He rose from the chair. 'I've brought up the file on all our suppliers on the computer. Go through it. Write down any questions you have and I'll be back later to answer them. Okay?'

'Okay.'

Her relief that he was leaving her to work alone was palpable.

He strode quickly out of the office, needing time apart from her, too. He was still churned up inside. A work-out in the gym should rid him of the violent energy that was currently coursing through him.

Three and a half days...

He wondered if he'd feel free of this mad obsession with Elizabeth Flippence after Friday night. He really was beginning to hate how much she got to him. Probably she hated how he got to her, too.

Was having sex the answer to settling everything?

Impossible to know beforehand.

Afterwards...

That should tell him whether to persist with trying to form a relationship with this infuriating woman or let her go. It all hung on one night and—by God!—he was going to make the most of it!

CHAPTER ELEVEN

ELIZABETH found herself rebelling against any regret over her decision to take Harry Finn as her lover for one night. It might be stupidly reckless of her to have sex with him. There would probably be consequences she wouldn't like but she refused to care about what could happen next. Just for once she would be totally irresponsible, except for the important issue of birth control, which was impossible to ignore.

She tackled Harry on that point as soon as he returned to the office. 'I'm not on the pill,' she stated bluntly. 'Will you take care of contraception on Friday night?'

'No problem,' he blithely replied. 'And incidentally, I've thought of another condition.'

Elizabeth tensed. If it was too outlandish...

'When we're in the villa, I want to call you Ellie.'

She was startled into asking, 'Why?'

He shrugged. 'A childhood name, conjuring up the age of innocence. I like that idea.'

'I'm not innocent, Harry.' Surely he couldn't still be thinking she was a virgin.

'Nevertheless, it's what I want. Okay?'

She shook her head over his whimsy but…what did it matter? 'If it pleases you,' she said carelessly.

'It *will* please me,' he asserted, then smiled at her. 'I also want to please you. If you think of anything you'd particularly enjoy on the night, let me know. Your wish is my command.'

'I prefer to leave everything in your very capable hands, Harry,' she said dryly, not wanting to think too much about it.

But she did over the next couple of days. And nights. It was weird how completely distracted she was from thinking about Michael and Lucy. The now-certain prospect of having sex with Harry made her more physically aware of him than ever, and the anticipation of it was zinging through her almost continually.

He didn't come up with any more conditions, didn't raise the subject at all, keeping their time together on a strictly business basis, as she had requested. Somehow that contributed to a sense of secretive intimacy, knowing what they were going to do when Friday night came but not mentioning it.

She found a red string bikini in the boutique and bought it, deciding it suited the occasion since she was acting like a scarlet woman, taking a lover she didn't love. Oddly enough she felt no guilt about doing it. Somehow it represented the kind of freedom she probably wouldn't feel with someone she did love. There were no dreams to be smashed, no expectations of sharing a life together. It was just a night of sexy fun with Harry Finn.

On Friday morning, Harry announced he had business in Port Douglas and would be gone for most of the day. He printed a notice that the office would be closed at 6:00 p.m. today and stuck it on the door. 'Go on up to the villa then,' he instructed. 'I'll be there. Don't want to miss the sunset,' he added with a smile that sparkled with anticipation.

'I'll bring a bottle of champagne from the bar,' she said, remembering how she had envisaged the scene with Michael and Lucy.

'No need. I'll have one ready to open.'

'What about food? Shall I order…?'

He shook his head. 'I have that organised, as well. You only have to bring yourself, Elizabeth.' He raised his hand in a farewell salute. 'Bye for now. Have a nice day.'

'You, too,' she replied, smiling back at him.

It was a genuine smile, not the slightest bit forced. Not having to keep her guard up against him all the time had made her more relaxed in his company. She had nothing to guard against since she was giving in to what he wanted from her. And if she was completely honest with herself, she wanted it, too.

He was a sexy man.

He made her feel sexy.

She was looking forward to having this experience with Harry tonight. She probably would have hated herself if she'd been seduced into it, but the sense of empowerment that came with having decided on it herself made all the difference.

Nevertheless, when six o'clock came and she was on her way to the pavilion villa, her nerves started getting very jumpy. She had never had an assignation like this before. It was totally out of character for her. But there was no turning back from it, she told herself fiercely. Everything was in place to take this step, and take it she would.

Harry was standing by the infinity pool, looking out to sea. He wore only a pair of board shorts, printed with white sailing ships on a blue background. She paused on the last step leading to the open deck, her heart skittering at the sight of so much naked masculinity—broad shoulders tapering to lean hips, bronze skin gleaming over taut, well-defined muscles. He had the perfect male physique and it tugged on some deeply primitive female chord in Elizabeth.

It was okay to feel attracted to him, she told herself.

It was natural.

On the physical level.

As though sensing her presence he swung around, his gaze instantly targeting her, piercing blue eyes raking her from head to toe, making her hotly conscious that she was still in the island uniform. She quickly held up the carry bag holding the clothes he'd requested and gabbled an explanation.

'I've just finished at the office, Harry. I thought I'd take a shower here.'

He nodded. 'Make it fast. The sun is already low in the sky.'

The glass doors to the villa were open. The layout inside was similar to the one Jack had shown her. She headed straight for the bathroom, anxious not to be found wanting in keeping to her side of their deal. One minute to turn on the shower taps and strip off her clothes, two minutes under the refreshing beat of the water, one minute to towel herself dry, one minute to pull on the red bikini bottom and put on the butterfly blouse, fastening only one button to keep it more or less together.

Accessible was what he'd asked for. He couldn't say she wasn't delivering it. The shape of her braless breasts and the darker colour of her areolae were certainly visible through the sheer fabric, and her nipples were already stiffening, poking at the butterfly wings. She hoped he had the champagne ready. Carrying this much accessibility off with any air of confidence required some alcoholic fortification.

It was only on her exit from the bathroom that Elizabeth caught a waft of nose-teasing scent coming from the mezzanine level. She looked up to where the king-size bed was waiting for intimate activity. Candles—from small to large—lit a path to it. A long sniff identified their fragrance as frangipani, the flower most reminiscent of tropical nights.

Harry must have set them up. Had he bought them in Port Douglas today? Why go to the trouble? This was not a night of romance. Did he want her to imagine it was? And why should he want that? She didn't understand. But it was…nice of him to do it.

She was smiling over what she had decided was playboy fun as she walked out onto the deck. 'Do you treat all your women to scented candles?' she asked.

He was about to pop the cork of a bottle of champagne. He paused to give her a very long, all-encompassing look that made her extremely conscious of every female part of her body. 'No. I simply associate the scent of flowers with butterflies, Ellie. An innocent pleasure,' he said softly.

His use of her childhood name instantly reminded her of how he'd linked it to an age of innocence. She wished she knew what was going on in his mind. It seemed to be off on some quirky journey tonight.

He popped the cork and reached for one of the flute glasses sitting on the low table that served the sun-lounges. A plate of lush fresh strawberries was placed beside the ice bucket that awaited the opened bottle. As he poured the champagne, Elizabeth saw that a couple of crushed strawberries lay in the bottom of the glass, making it a very sensual drink.

'Enjoy,' he said as he passed it to her, his smile inviting her to share all sorts of pleasure with him.

'Thank you, Harry,' she said appreciatively, grateful that he wasn't grabbing at her *accessibility* or doing anything off-putting.

He waved her to one of the sun-lounges. 'Relax. Looks like being a spectacular sunset.'

She sat on the lounge, not quite ready to put herself on display by stretching out on it. Harry poured champagne for himself, then clicked her glass with his. 'To our first night together,' he said, smiling as he dropped onto the adjacent lounge, propped himself against the backrest, lifted his long legs onto the cushioned base and gazed out to a sea that was shimmering like polished crystal.

It released Elizabeth's inhibitions about doing the same. This villa certainly had a prime position for viewing the sunset. The subtle colour changes in the sky would challenge any artist—impossible to capture on canvas, she thought. It truly was lovely, just watching it and sipping strawberry-flavoured champagne.

'Have you ever been to Broome?' Harry asked.

'No.' Broome was right across the country on the coast of Western Australia. She knew it was world famous for its pearls but she'd never had any reason to go there. 'Why do you ask?'

'Sunset there is amazing. People drive down on the beach, set up their barbecues, bring eskies loaded with cold drinks, play music, sit back and enjoy Mother Nature's display for them. They completely tune out from news of the world and just live in the moment.'

He rolled the words out in a low, almost spellbinding tone that was soothing, like a physical caress that eased the last threads of tension in Elizabeth's body.

'We don't do enough of it...living in the moment,' he went on in the same seductive murmur. 'Let's try to do that tonight, Ellie. No yesterdays...no tomorrows... just each moment as it comes.'

'Yes,' she agreed, happy with the idea.

They sipped their champagne in silence for a while, watching the sun slowly disappear below the horizon.

'My parents used to do this...have a sundowner together at the end of the day,' Harry said, slanting her a reminiscent little smile. 'What about yours, Ellie? Do they have a special time to themselves?'

She shook her head. 'My mother died of cancer when I was nineteen. I haven't seen my father since the funeral. He's a miner and living with some other woman in Mt Isa. It was never much of a marriage. Mum more or less brought Lucy and me up by herself.'

Harry frowned at her. 'Your father doesn't care about you?'

She grimaced. 'I think we were responsibilities he

didn't really want. Mostly when he came home on leave from the mine, he'd get drunk and we'd stay out of his way.'

'What about when your mother became ill?'

'He came home less. Didn't want to be faced with what was happening to Mum. He said it was up to me and Lucy to take care of her.'

'That must have been hard,' Harry said sympathetically.

'Yes. Though it was a special time, too. Like you said…living in the moment…because the last moment could come at any time so every good moment was precious.'

'At least you knew that,' he murmured, nodding understandingly before throwing her a wry little smile. 'Mickey and I…we didn't realise how precious those good moments were until after our parents were gone.'

'I guess that kind of sudden death is harder to come to terms with,' she said thoughtfully.

'I don't know. We didn't have to see them suffer.' He shook his head. 'You were only nineteen. How did you manage?'

'I was at business college so I could be home quite a lot. Lucy dropped out of school to look after Mum when I couldn't be there.'

'Did she pick up her education again at a later date?'

'No.' Impossible to explain that school had never been easy for Lucy. She didn't like people knowing about her dyslexia. 'She didn't want to, didn't need it to get work.'

'But without qualifications…'

'Lucy is adept at winning her way into jobs.'

'While you're the one with the steady career. That's why she calls you her anchor.'

Elizabeth heaved a sigh. 'This is a weird conversation to be having when we're supposed to be enjoying a night of sexy fun, Harry.'

'Oh, I don't know. I'd call this an intimate conversation. We have all night to get to physical intimacy. We've been on the fringes of each other's worlds for two years. I think I know Elizabeth fairly well—' he rolled his head towards her, giving her his quirky smile '—but I want to get to know Ellie tonight.'

'That's yesterday, Harry. My childhood,' she pointed out. 'It's not living in the moment.'

The blue eyes gathered the piercing intensity that always gave her discomfort. 'Ellie is inside you right now,' he said softly. 'She's the foundation of the woman you are. She directs your life.'

'That's ridiculous!' she protested.

'Is it? You're the older child, the one who helped your mother, the one who protected your sister, the one who carried the responsibility of arranging everything when your mother was ill, when she died, the one who wants a man in her life who will never do to her what her father did to her mother, to his children.'

He was digging at her again—digging, digging, digging! In a burst of frustration, Elizabeth swung her legs off the lounge, sat up straight and glared at him. 'I did not come up here to be psychoanalysed, Harry.'

He swung his legs down to the deck in a more leisurely fashion, his eyes holding hers in glittering challenge. 'No, you didn't. Ellie wanted to break out of the Elizabeth cocoon and fly free for once, didn't she?'

She hated how he could connect everything up and be so damned right about everything! It made her feel naked in far more than the physical sense. In a purely defensive action, she snatched the bottle of champagne from the ice bucket, intending to refill her glass.

Harry took it from her. 'Allow me.'

She did, letting him pour the champagne, though it made her feel he was taking control away from her, which wasn't how she'd planned to have this encounter with Harry. 'Do you probe into the lives of all your one-night stands?' she asked waspishly.

He cocked an eyebrow at her. 'What makes you think my life consists of a series of one-night stands?'

'The way you flirt. Michael said you flirt with every woman. It isn't just me.'

'Flirting can be fun. It can be enjoyable to both parties. In a way it's a search for that magic click which will lead to bed, but that doesn't happen very often. When it has, I can't recall one instance when it only lasted for one night. You've assumed something about me that isn't true, Ellie.'

'Well, this is only going to be for one night,' she insisted, needing to regain the control that seemed to be sliding out of her grip.

'Why?'

'Because…' She floundered, not wanting to say the whole idea had erupted from the fact his brother was going to be here with her sister and she hadn't really looked beyond that painful circumstance. 'I just don't want to get heavily involved with you, Harry,' she said evasively, wishing he would simply accept what she'd offered him.

'Why not? You think I'll let you down?'

Yes was on the tip of her tongue but he didn't give her time to say it.

'Did I let you down when you needed to cover up your distress over Mickey attaching himself to your sister? Did I let you down when you needed an escape from them? Have I let you down in fulfilling your requests this week, meeting what you wanted? Haven't I shown I care about how you feel, Ellie?'

She couldn't deny any of that, yet… 'It…it fitted into your own agenda,' she blurted out.

'Which is?' He bored in.

Her head was spinning from the pressure he was subjecting her to with all his questions. She had to seize on the one point she was certain of, drive it home. She set her glass on the table, stood up, challenging him to get on with what he'd been aiming for all along.

'Having me like this! *Accessible!*' She threw the words at him. 'So why don't you stop talking and take what you want with me?'

Anger burned through Harry. He'd tried to reach out to her, tried to find a special meeting ground with her. She just kept closing her mind, shutting the door on him, keeping him out. He set his glass down, rose to his feet and hurled her confrontation right back in her face.

'You want to be treated like a piece of meat instead of a woman I care about? Fine! Just stand there and let me oblige!'

CHAPTER TWELVE

HARRY saw her eyes dilate with shock.

He didn't care.

She'd invited him to take her without caring and his level of frustration with her was so high, turning away from following through on her invitation was beyond him. His hands lifted and cupped the breasts they'd wanted to cup in Mickey's office days ago. He fanned her rock-hard nipples with his thumbs. The soft sheer fabric of the butterfly blouse gave a sensual sexiness to feeling her like this, causing a rush of hot blood to his loins.

He wanted her.

He'd been burning up for her all week.

Her eyes refocused on his, still slightly glazed but clearing as she sucked in a deep breath.

Yes, look at me! he thought savagely. *Know it's me and not Mickey!*

He undid the button holding her blouse together and spread the edges apart, wanting to feel the naked lushness of her breasts against his chest. His arms slid around her waist, scooping her into firm contact with him. It felt good. It felt great.

'Harry…' It was a husky gasp.

He didn't want to hear anything she had to say. His name on her lips shot a soaring wave of triumph through him—*his* name, not Mickey's—and he was hell-bent on keeping it stamped on her consciousness. His mouth crashed onto hers, intent on a blitzkrieg invasion that would blast any possible thought of his brother from entering her head.

To his surprise her tongue started duelling with his and a wild elation burst through his brain when her hands clutched his head, not to tear them apart but to hold them together, her fingers kneading his scalp, her mouth working to meet and escalate the passion surging through him.

He pressed one hand into the sexy pit of her back, forcing her body into contact with his erection as he pulled the bikini string at her hip apart, changed hands to do the same with the other, whipped the scrap of fabric from between her legs. The lovely female curves of her naked bottom were sensual dynamite, igniting his need for her to the brink of explosion.

He tore his hands off them to sweep the blouse from her shoulders and pull it off her arms. It broke her hold on his head, broke the marauding madness of their kissing, but it had to be done. She was fully naked now, totally *accessible* to anything he wanted with her.

He bent and scooped her off her feet, holding her crushed to his chest as he strode from the deck, into the villa, up the steps to the mezzanine level. He tumbled her onto the king-size bed, snatched up the contraceptive sheath he'd laid ready on the bedside table, discarded his board shorts in double-quick time, pulled on the sheath and leapt onto the bed, rolling her straight into his embrace, not allowing any sense of separation to strike any doubts about what they were doing in her mind.

Their mouths locked again, driving passion to fever pitch. Her body was arching into his, explicitly needful. He barely controlled the urge to zero in to the ultimate intimacy with her. Only the bitter recollection of her *one night* insistence forced him to a different course of action. If this was all there was to be between them he'd satisfy every desire she'd ever stirred in him—eat her all up so he could spit her out afterwards, not be left fantasising over what he could have done.

He wrenched his mouth from hers, trailed hotly possessive kisses down her lovely long neck, tasted the tantalising hollow at the base of her throat, slid lower to feast on her sensational breasts, swirling his tongue around her provocative nipples, sucking on them, devouring them, taking his fill of her luscious femininity, revelling in the little moans vibrating from her throat, the twist of her fingers tangling with his hair.

He reached down to part the soft folds of her sex, his own fingers sliding, searching, finding the excited wetness that gave him easy entry to stroke the excitement to a much-higher level. She cried out, her body arching again, her need growing in intensity. He moved lower, determined on driving her crazy for him.

He spread the folds apart to expose the tight bud of her clitoris and licked it, slowly teasing at first, then faster, faster until she was writhing, screaming for him, begging, her legs encircling him, feet beating a drum of wild wanting. He surged up to take the ultimate plunge, but the savage need inside him demanded a last absolute surrender from her.

Her head was thrashing from side to side. He held it still. 'Look at me!' he commanded.

She blinked and looked but there was no real focus in her eyes.

'Say my name!'

'What?' It was a gasp of confusion.

'Say my name!'

'Har...ry...' It was a weak waver of sound.

'Say it again!'

'Harry, Harry, Harry...' she cried hysterically. 'Please...'

'You want me?'

'Ye-s-s-s.' She beat at his shoulders with tightly clenched fists. 'I'll kill you if you don't...'

He silenced her with a deep, thrusting kiss as he propelled his flesh into hers. When he lifted his head, the animal groan of satisfaction from her throat rang jubilant bells in his ears. She clutched his buttocks, trying to goad him into a fast rhythm, but he wanted the excitement to build and build, not explode all at once. He started slowly, revelling in her eagerness for him, the convulsive little spasms that told him she was totally engaged in feeling him—*him*, not Mickey.

He felt her creaming around him and couldn't keep controlling the rampantly growing need of his own body. It overtook his mind, oblivious to everything but the physical scream to reach climax, releasing the fierce tension raging through every muscle of his body. It pumped from him in a glorious burst of ecstatic satisfaction, and with all tension draining away, he rolled onto his side, pulling her with him, wanting to hang on to the sense of intimate togetherness as long as he could.

She didn't attempt any move away from him. Maybe she was drained of all energy, too. Whatever…she left her legs entwined with his, their bodies pressed close, her head tucked under his chin. He stroked her hair, enjoying the soft silky texture of it, thinking he still had the freedom to touch. He wondered how she was going to act for the rest of the night. Would Ellie emerge and see him for the man he was, or would Elizabeth stick to her guns?

He couldn't call it.

He told himself he didn't care.

At least he had the satisfaction of making her want him with every fibre of her being, if only for one night.

Elizabeth didn't want to move. It felt unbelievably good, cuddled up with Harry, having her hair stroked. Her mind drifted to her childhood, sitting on her mother's lap, head resting just like this while her hair was stroked lovingly. No one else had ever done it. She'd always been the one to comfort Lucy, not the other way around. It was weird, feeling comforted by Harry but…she didn't want to move.

She liked being naked with him, too, the warm flesh contact, the sense of his male strength holding her safe. It was so nice and peaceful after the storm of incredible sensation. Having sex with Harry…her mind was still blown by it…just totally unimaginable before experiencing it. She'd never tipped so utterly out of control, never been taken to such peaks of exquisite pleasure-pain, and the sheer ecstasy of floating in the aftermath of one climax after another...well, that had certainly set the bar for how fantastic sex with the right man could be.

Though she hadn't thought Harry was the right man in any other respect...or...might he be?

Maybe she had been a bit too quick to judge, misreading his character. Or maybe she was just being influenced by how *right* he was in bed for her. Most probably he was the best action man on that front for every woman he took to bed. Just because this had been special to her didn't make it special to him. But she was still glad she'd had this with Harry.

'Are you okay?' he murmured caringly.

She sighed contentedly. 'Very okay, thank you.'

'Then let's go take a shower. Once we're done there we can get in the pool and cool off.'

She *was* hot and sticky. 'Good idea,' she said.

The shower was more than big enough for two and Elizabeth was in no hurry using it this time. She enjoyed soaping Harry's great body, touching him intimately, letting him do the same to her.

'Having fun?'

The wry note in his voice made her look up. There was no amusement twinkling in the vivid blue eyes. The mocking glint in them dried up the pleasure she had been feeling, sending a chill through her as she remembered her taunt about having a night of sexy fun, rejecting having any deeper involvement with him, virtually dismissing him as a person of no account in her life. He'd been so angry—*shockingly* angry. She'd forgotten that, her mind swamped by so much else.

Instinctively she reached up to touch his cheek in an

apologetic appeal. 'I was taking pleasure in you, Harry. I thought you were taking pleasure in me.'

For a moment his mouth took on an ironic twist. Then he bent his head and kissed her, a long sensual kiss that swallowed up any worry about him still being angry with her.

Finishing off in the infinity pool was another sensual pleasure, the water like cool silk caressing her skin. 'Just stay there,' Harry instructed as he heaved himself out. 'I'll light the torches to keep the insects away and bring out the oysters with some chilled wine.'

'Oysters!' She laughed. 'I don't think I need an aphrodisiac, Harry.'

He stopped. His shoulders squared and she saw his back muscles tense. He half turned to face her, a cutting look in his eyes that ripped through the amusement in hers. 'I'm not into playboy tricks, Elizabeth. I simply remembered you liked them at your birthday lunch.'

That coldly spoken *Elizabeth* slapped her with the realisation that she was offending him every time she painted him as a playboy. Perhaps even insulting him. He'd told her straight out that the label was wrong in his eyes. Had she been doing him an injustice all this time? What hard evidence did she actually have that he used women lightly? None!

There was a sitting shelf at one end of the pool, and she settled on it, still enjoying the soft ripple of the water around her dangling legs as she thought back over the two years Harry had been dipping into her life while she'd been working for his brother. When he'd first walked into her office he'd emanated a megawatt attraction that had put her in such a tizzy physically she had instantly mistrusted and disliked his power to do that to her.

She'd reasoned that a man with so much personal magnetism was very likely to stray from any relationship since other women would always be eyeing him over, wanting a chance with him, especially when he was both wealthy and sexy. Determined not to go anywhere near that playing field, she had kept a rigid guard against his insidious assaults on her armour.

Now it felt as though she had prejudiced herself against a man who might well be worth knowing in a deeper sense than she had ever believed possible. Could he actually fulfil everything she had been looking for? His brother had definitely been more the type of character that appealed to her—solid, responsible—not dangerous like Harry. Yet Michael had not seen what he wanted in her. And was Harry really dangerous, or was that a false perception on her part?

She watched him emerge from the villa and stroll across the deck towards her, carrying a platter of oysters, a bottle of wine and two fresh glasses. He'd tucked a white towel around his waist. The sky had darkened and the flickering light of the torches he'd lit at the corners of the deck was not bright enough for her to see the expression in his eyes. Was he still angry with her?

'Shall I get out?' she asked.

'Not if you don't want to,' he answered with a careless shrug. 'I can serve you just as easily there.'

'The water's lovely.'

'Then stay.'

He set the platter on the deck, sat on the edge of the

pool and proceeded to open the bottle of wine and fill the glasses.

'I do like oysters, Harry. Thank you for remembering,' she said, hoping to erase the *aphrodisiac* remark.

He handed her the glass of white wine with a droll little smile. 'I remembered your sister saying you loved chilli mud crab, too. I know a restaurant in Port Douglas that specialises in that dish so I had it cooked for you and it's waiting in the microwave to be heated up when you want it.'

She stared at him, horribly shamed by his caring and generosity when she had treated him so meanly, using him as a distraction, even to going to bed with him in this villa because of Michael bringing Lucy here.

'I'm sorry,' she blurted out.

He frowned. 'Sorry about what?'

'My whole attitude towards you. It's been uncaring and bitchy and…and soured by things that you weren't even a part of. I haven't been fair to you, Harry. I've never been fair to you and I don't know why you're being so nice to me because I don't deserve it.' Tears suddenly welled into her eyes and she quickly tried to smear them away with the back of her hand. 'I'm sorry. I'm all messed up and I can't help myself.'

'It's okay,' he said soothingly. 'Just take a few deep breaths and let it all go. Life is a bitch sometimes. The trick is to get past the bad bits. I've been trying to help you do that, Ellie.'

Ellie… The soft caring way her childhood name rolled off his tongue brought another spurt of tears to her eyes and screwed her up inside, stirring up the craven wish for someone to take care of her. She'd been taking care of herself and Lucy for so long, she needed someone to simply be there for her. But she couldn't expect Harry to keep doing that. She didn't know how far his kindness would stretch. What she could do was bask in it for a little while.

It took quite a few deep breaths to bring herself under control enough to manage a smile at him. 'Thank you for helping me.'

'You do deserve to have nice things done for you,' he said seriously. 'Everyone does. It makes the world a happier place. My mother taught me that. She was brilliant at it.'

She sipped the wine he had poured for her, remembering Sarah Pickard's description of Yvette Finn—*a sunny nature, radiating a joy in life that infected everyone around her.* 'Sarah said you're like your mother,' she remarked, starting to reappraise the man in a completely different light to how she had previously perceived him.

He gave a wry shake of his head. 'A hard act to follow, but I try.'

'Tell me about her,' she said impulsively, wanting to understand where Harry was coming from.

He made an indecisive gesture. 'Where to start?'

'Start with how your father met her,' she encouraged.

He laughed. 'In hospital. He'd broken his leg and Mum was the only nurse who wouldn't let him be grumpy.'

'She was an ordinary common nurse?' It surprised her, having imagined that Franklyn Finn would have married some beautiful accomplished socialite.

Harry shook his head. 'I don't think anyone would

have said she was ordinary. All the patients loved her, my father included. He always considered himself extremely privileged that she learned to love him back. It took him quite some time to win her.'

'She didn't like him at first?'

'It wasn't that. She wasn't sure about how she would fit into his life. Dad was a seriously driven guy. In the end, she made up a set of rules for how their marriage could work and he had to promise to keep to them.'

'Did he?'

'Never wavered from them. She was the light of his life and he was never going to let that light go out.' He grimaced. 'In a way, I guess it was a kind fate that they died together. They were so tied to each other.'

It must have been a wonderful marriage, Elizabeth thought, wishing she could have one like it. Her own mother hadn't known much happiness in hers and the end of her life had certainly not been kind, though she and Lucy had done their best to ease the pain of it. 'I always thought Lucy could have made a great nurse,' she murmured, remembering how good she had been at cheering up their mother.

'She could have become one if she'd wanted to,' Harry remarked.

'No' slipped out before she could stop it.

'Why not? She could have gone back to school....'

'Lucy was never good at exams,' she prevaricated. Her dyslexia made it impossible for her to pass them. She was smart enough to pick up anything as an apprentice and she had a great memory, but examinations that required reading and writing within a set time simply couldn't be done. 'I don't think she had the head for study after Mum died,' she added to put him off pursuing the point. 'She was only seventeen and she took it hard, Harry.'

'Understandable,' he said sympathetically.

She sipped some more of the wine and eyed the platter of oysters. 'I think I'm ready to eat now.'

He laughed. 'Help yourself.'

'I'll get out first.'

Harry quickly rose to his feet, grabbing a towel to dry her off and wrap around her. She didn't try to take it from him and didn't protest his action when he finished up tucking it around her waist, leaving her breasts bare. 'They're too beautiful to cover up,' he said with a smile.

'I'm glad you think so,' she said a little shyly.

Exhilaration zinged through Harry. She'd dropped all the barriers. There was no rejection in her eyes, no guard up against him. And it remained like that for the rest of the evening, no bitchy barbs slung at him, no hiding what she thought or felt about anything, no shutting him out.

She might not have forgotten all about Mickey but she had definitely put his brother aside and was actively taking pleasure in finding connections with him—connections beyond the purely physical. The sexual chemistry was still there, of course, simmering between them, heightened by their newly intimate knowledge of each other, but Harry was encouraged to believe this could actually be the beginning of a relationship that might become very special.

He wasn't driven to carry her off to bed in a fury of frustration a second time. She happily walked with him and they both indulged in slow, sensual lovemaking—a sweet pleasuring of each other that was intensely satisfying to Harry. No way was this going to be a one-night stand. He wouldn't accept that. Elizabeth Flippence had opened up to him and he liked it too much to let her slip away from him.

Tomorrow he would see if her attachment to Mickey had been broken.

He wanted it broken.

It had to be broken.

CHAPTER THIRTEEN

A WOMAN I care about...

Those words spoken last night kept running through Elizabeth's mind all morning, keeping any anxiety over coming face to face with Michael and Lucy again at bay. She added up all the caring from Harry and realised no other man in her life had done as much for her—helping, comforting, pleasuring, answering her needs.

It couldn't be just about having sex with her.

There had been genuine concern in his eyes when he'd asked, 'Are you going to be okay today?' before leaving her at the office door after their night at the pavilion villa.

She'd assured him that she would be and he'd added, 'I'll be on hand.'

Ready to run interference if she needed it, as he had last Monday.

It felt really good to have him caring about her—someone she could depend on to get her through this weekend without too much heartache. Oddly enough, she wasn't feeling any heartache at all over Michael wanting Lucy, although seeing them together again might strain her current sense of being able to set them at an emotional distance.

Harry was to meet them at the jetty and transport them to the administration centre. Elizabeth felt reasonably confident about handling their queries about how well she was coping with management responsibilities. Lucy, of course, would angle for a private conversation with her, but she didn't think that would trouble her too much. She no longer felt so shattered over her lost dreams.

A few guests dropped into the office to check on arrangements they'd made for diving expeditions. There were inquiries about bookings to be answered. A couple of beach picnics had to be sorted out with the chef. Sarah Pickard came by, ostensibly to put in an order for new towels, but her eyes shone with lively curiosity about this new development between Harry and his stand-in manager.

Probably all the staff on the island knew about it by now since the villa had to be cleaned this morning, ready for Michael and Lucy. Elizabeth had decided it didn't matter but she certainly wasn't going to talk about her private life to anyone.

'Harry said it's your sister coming with Mickey today,' Sarah remarked.

'Yes,' Elizabeth answered briefly.

'That's nice.'

Elizabeth smiled. 'Yes, it is.'

'When did they meet?'

'Lucy came into the Cairns office to see me and they clicked. Simple as that,' she said airily.

'And Harry, of course, met you when he went to see Mickey.'

'Yes.'

Realising that Elizabeth was not about to be chatty, Sarah backed off, only tossing out the comment, 'Well, it's all very interesting,' as she left the office.

It wasn't interesting so much as complicated, Elizabeth thought. She didn't know if these connections were likely to lead anywhere good for either Lucy or herself. Two brothers who were close, two sisters who were close, the work situation—if things started going wrong, there could be a nasty ripple effect.

She remembered Lucy's blithe comment when Harry had been ordering their cocktails last Monday— *wouldn't it be great if we ended up together...all happy families!* Possibly it could be great if it worked out like that but Elizabeth wasn't counting on it. It was far too early to think the possibility was high.

Lucy slid out of relationships almost as fast as she started them.

As for herself and Harry, she couldn't even call it a relationship yet. All she could really say for certain was that her stance against him had been substantially shifted. And he was fantastic in bed!

It was almost midday when he called from the jetty to say Mickey's motor-launch was about to dock. Her nerves instantly started jangling, mocking any idea that she could breeze through this meeting with no angst at all. She fiercely told herself the important thing was to keep her composure, regardless of what she was feeling.

Lucy was hugging Michael's arm when Harry led them into the office—the woman in possession and obviously loving having this man in tow. Her skin was glowing, her eyes were shining and the smile on her face beamed brilliant happiness. Elizabeth's heart contracted at this evidence that her sister was over-the-moon in love.

'This island is fabulous, Ellie,' she cried. 'What a great place to work!'

'Tropical paradise,' Elizabeth responded, pasting a smile on her face and moving from behind the desk to greet them appropriately.

Lucy released Michael's arm to rush forward and give her a hug. 'Are you loving it?' she asked, her eyes bright with curiosity about the situation, which, of course, included Harry.

'Not too much, I hope,' Michael semigrowled in the background.

'It's been quite a change,' she said dryly, flicking him a sharply assessing look.

Somehow he was more handsome than ever, his face relaxed in a friendly way, his very male physique shown off in casual clothes—smartly tailored shorts in a blue-and-grey check teamed with a royal blue sports shirt. He still had the impact of an alpha man scoring ten out of ten, but she wasn't feeling it so personally anymore. He belonged to her sister now.

'A good one, I hope,' Harry slid in, drawing her attention to him.

Another alpha man—no doubt about it now—and the memory of last night's intimacy caused a wave of warm pleasure to roll through her. The piercing blue eyes were digging at her again, but she didn't resent it this time. He *cared* about what she was feeling.

'Yes,' she answered with a smile, wanting to allay his concern for her.

'Now, Harry, poaching my PA is not on,' Michael shot at him.

'Like I said before, Mickey—*her choice*,' he replied with an affable shrug.

'Okay, while you two guys argue over my brilliant sister, I want her to show me her living quarters,' Lucy put in quickly. 'You can mind the office, can't you, Harry?'

'Go right ahead,' he said agreeably.

'Come on, Ellie,' she urged, nodding to the door at the back of the office. 'Michael said your apartment was right here. I want to see everything. And while I'm at it, may I say you look great in the island uniform?'

Elizabeth laughed. 'Not as spectacular as you this morning.'

Lucy wore cheeky little navy denim shorts with a red-and-purple halter top, big red hoop earrings, red trainers on her feet and a purple scrunchie holding up her long blond hair in a ponytail.

'Am I over-the-top?' she asked.

Elizabeth shook her head. 'You can carry off anything, Lucy.'

'I wish…' she replied with a wry grimace as Elizabeth ushered her into the apartment and closed the door on the two men in the office.

Elizabeth eyed her quizzically, sensing something was weighing on her sister's mind. 'Is that a general wish or…?'

'Oh, nothing really,' came the airy reply, her hands gesturing dismissively as her gaze swung around the living room. 'This is lovely, Ellie. Show me the bedroom and bathroom.'

She stopped at the queen-size bed, her sherry-brown eyes twinkling mischief at Elizabeth. 'Have you shared this with Harry yet?'

'Actually, no.' Wanting to divert any further personal probing, she retaliated with, 'Do you want to tell me what's going on with Michael?'

She threw up her hands. 'Everything is happening! I swear to you, Ellie, I've never been this mad about a guy. I'm in love like you wouldn't believe, and while it's incredibly wonderful, it's also scary, you know?'

'In what way scary?'

She flopped onto the bed, put her hands behind her head and stared at the ceiling. 'Michael is smart. I mean *really* smart, isn't he?'

'Yes.'

'So what happens when he finds out that my brain wasn't wired right and I'm a dummy when it comes to reading and writing? So far I've been winging it as I usually do, but this is far more intense than it's been with other guys, and he's bound to start noticing I'm a bit weird about some things.' She rolled her head to look straight at Elizabeth, a yearning appeal in her eyes. 'You've worked for him for two years. Will it put him off me if I tell him I'm dyslexic?'

Having experienced how exacting he was about everything to do with work, Elizabeth could only answer, 'I honestly don't know, Lucy. Does it feel as though he's in love with you?'

'Well, definitely in lust.' Her forehead puckered. 'I can't be sure that's love, but I really want it to be, Ellie. More than I've wanted anything. I want him to care so much about having me, it won't matter that I'm flawed.'

Elizabeth sat on the bed beside her and smoothed the worried furrows from her brow. 'It shouldn't matter if he loves you. And stop thinking of yourself as a dummy, Lucy. You're very smart, and you have so many talents…any man would be lucky to have you in his life.'

She heaved a rueful sigh. 'Well, I don't want him to know yet. I couldn't bear it if…' Her eyes shot a pleading look at Elizabeth. 'You haven't told Harry, have you?'

'No. And I won't.'

'I need more time. To give it a chance, you know?'

'Yes, I know.'

'I've been running off at the mouth about me. What about you and Harry?'

Elizabeth shrugged. 'Same thing. More time needed.'

'But you do like him.'

'Yes.' The hostility towards him had completely dissipated last night, as had the steaming vexation and resentment he had so frequently stirred. As it was now, there was nothing not to like.

Lucy propped herself on her elbow, an earnest expression on her face. 'Promise me you won't go off him if things don't work out between me and Michael.'

She hadn't expected Lucy, who had always seemed to be a live-in-the-moment person, to look ahead and see complications arising from the situation. It took her by surprise. Before she could consider the promise, Lucy rattled on.

'Harry could be the right guy for you. Let's face it… he's gorgeous and sexy and wealthy and obviously keen to have you in his corner. You could be great together and I don't want *me* to be the reason for you not having a future with him. I'd be happy to see you happy with him, Ellie, regardless of what happens between me and Michael.'

Deeply touched by her sister's caring, she couldn't help replying, 'But being so madly in love with Michael, you'll hurt if he walks away from you.' Just as *she* had been on Monday—totally shattered and never wanting to see him again.

'Oh, I'll muddle along like I always do,' Lucy retorted with a wry grimace. 'I'm good at putting things behind me. I've had a lot of practice at it.' She reached out, took Elizabeth's hand and squeezed it reassuringly. 'You mustn't worry about me. Go for what you want. You deserve a good life, Ellie.'

'So do you.'

'Well, maybe we'll both achieve it. Who knows? I just want to clear the deck for you and Harry. Now tell me you're okay with that.'

Elizabeth heaved a sigh to relieve the heavy emotional fullness in her chest and finally said, 'I'm okay if you're okay.' She squeezed her sister's hand back. 'Whatever happens with either of us, we'll always have each other, Lucy.'

'Absolutely!' she agreed, the earnestness breaking into a wide grin. 'Now let's go get our men!' She bounced off the bed and twirled around in a happy dance. 'Let's have a fabulous weekend, following our hearts' desire and not thinking about tomorrow.' She paused in the doorway to the living room to give Elizabeth a wise look. 'You never know when something might strike us dead so we do what we want to do. Right?'

'Right!' Elizabeth echoed, suddenly wondering how much of Lucy's attitudes and behaviour stemmed from their mother's early death and the suffering that had preceded it. She'd only been seventeen. Would Michael wrap her in the loving security blanket she needed? It was simply impossible to know at this point.

When she and Lucy emerged from the apartment, the two men were still standing where they'd left them in the office. Michael's attention instantly swivelled away from Harry, his face lighting up with pleasure at seeing her sister again. He held out his arms in a welcome-back gesture and Lucy waltzed straight into them, laughing up at him as she curled her arms around his neck.

'All done here?' he asked indulgently.

'Yes. But I want all four of us to lunch together in the restaurant.'

He threw a quick appeal to his brother. 'That can be arranged?'

'Leave it with me,' Harry said, not exactly committing to the idea. 'Why don't you take Lucy across to the restaurant, order a bottle of wine, and we'll join you when we've cleared the way?'

'See you soon,' Lucy tossed at Elizabeth as Michael scooped her away with him.

Which left her alone with Harry.

She'd been watching Michael very intently, wishing she could see into his mind and heart, knowing now that he could hurt Lucy very badly if lust didn't turn into love. This wasn't another flash-in-the-pan attraction for her—easy come, easy go.

Was he *the right man* for her sister?

A little while ago she had believed he was the perfect

match for herself. It was hard to get her head around transferring that sense of *rightness* to the connection between Michael and Lucy, but at least it didn't hurt anymore. She felt no jealousy. No envy. Just a rather horrid sense that fate was playing a capricious trick in seeding attractions with the potential to mess up their lives.

Harry clenched his hands in instinctive fighting mode. Throughout the whole encounter with Mickey and Lucy, Elizabeth's attention had been trained on them. She hadn't looked to him for any help. Even now with them gone, her focus was inward, probably measuring her feelings and unwilling to reveal them.

Was she still obsessed with Mickey?

He needed to know.

'Elizabeth…' he said more tersely than he'd meant to.

Her gaze flicked up to his. He saw no pain in her eyes. It was more a look of curious assessment. *Of him.* Was she comparing what she'd felt for Mickey with how she now felt about him? Last night's intimacy had to have had some impact on her. She'd responded to him very positively.

'If you'd rather not have lunch with them…' he started, willing to make up some excuse for her to avoid spending more time in their company if she found it intolerable.

'No, it's fine,' she cut in. 'If it's okay with you for me to vacate the office for the lunch hour.'

'You're sure?' he asked, wanting absolute confirmation that she was free of any angst over her sister's connection with his brother.

A whimsical smile softened her expression as she

walked towards him. To his surprise and delight, when she reached him she slid her hands up his chest and linked them around the back of his neck. 'Lucy said to go get our men and right now you're my man, Harry. I hope you're happy about that,' she said in a soft seductive lilt.

Was it true?

He fiercely didn't want it to be on the rebound.

He wrapped his arms around her and pulled her into full body contact with him. No resistance. In fact, she rubbed herself teasingly against him, stirring an instant erection. Her eyes blazed with a boldness he'd never seen in them and he sensed a determination in her to take life by the scruff of the neck and give it a good shake.

Whatever… Her dream about Mickey was gone and she was choosing to have him. He kissed her and she kissed him right back, no hesitation, no inhibitions—a full-blooded response that made it extremely difficult to rein in the desire she'd fired up. It was the wrong time to race her off to bed. Mickey and Lucy were waiting for them in the restaurant and he wouldn't put it past Lucy to come looking for them if they didn't appear within a reasonable time.

Besides, the promise was certainly there that last night was not going to be the one-night stand Elizabeth had dictated.

He could wait.

He was satisfied that he'd won.

Elizabeth Flippence was now *his* woman.

CHAPTER FOURTEEN

ELIZABETH woke up on Sunday morning and was instantly aware of the man lying in the bed he hadn't shared with her before last night—the sound of his breathing, the warmth emanating from his naked body, the memories of intense pleasure in their lovemaking. Harry Finn...

She rolled onto her back to look at him, a smile twitching at her lips. He was still asleep. Her gaze wandered over every part of him that was not covered by the bed sheet—the strongly muscled shoulders and arms, the ruggedly masculine face with its slightly crooked nose, the black curls flopping over his forehead, the five o'clock shadow on his jaw. *Her man*, she thought, at least for the time being.

It felt slightly weird but definitely liberating to have thrown out her rule book on how life should be led, diving straight into the deep end with Harry and not caring if it was a big mistake. Lucy's comment yesterday—*you never know when something might strike us dead so we do what we want to do*—had made it seem stupid to deny herself what Harry could give her out of fear that she'd made a rash choice and this lovely time with him probably wouldn't last.

So what if it didn't!

She was thirty years old. Why not experience all the pleasure she could with this man? When—*if*—it ended, at least she would have had the most marvellous sex any woman could have.

She wondered if Lucy was feeling the same about Michael. Was he as good a lover as his brother? Did being *in love* make it better? It was far too soon to say she was in love with Harry but he was much—*nicer*—than she had ever thought he could be, not like a superficial playboy at all. He really did care about her feelings.

His eyes suddenly flicked open, instantly catching her looking at him. 'Hi!' he said, his mouth curving into a happy smile.

She smiled back. 'Hi to you, too!'

'How long have you been awake?'

She reached out and ran a finger down his nose. 'Long enough to wonder how this got broken.'

He laughed and rolled onto his side, propping himself up on his elbow, answering her good-humouredly. 'Rugby tackle. It made a bloody mess of my nose but I stopped the other guy from scoring a try and we won the game.'

'Sport,' she said, mentally correcting her former prejudice that had decided the injury had come out of a misspent youth. 'Jack Pickard told me you'd been good at all sports in your teens. He reckoned you could have been a champion on any playing field.'

He cocked an eyebrow at her. 'You were asking him about me?'

'No. I was being told about you. But I am asking

now. Tell me about those years, Harry. What were your proudest moments in sport?'

He was happy to talk about them, basking in her interest. For two years she had rejected knowing more about him, always projecting the attitude that he wasn't worth knowing. That glacier of disinterest had definitely thawed over the past two days.

'Did you ever dream of competing in the Olympic Games? Or representing Australia in rugby or cricket?' she asked.

He shook his head. 'I simply enjoyed sport. I never aimed to make a career out of it. Mickey and I wanted to join Dad in the business. He used to talk to us about what he was doing, what he was planning. It was creative, challenging, exciting....' He grinned. 'And you made your own rules, no toeing a line drawn for you by sport officialdom.'

'You were lucky to have a father like that, Harry.'

Not like hers.

He saw it in her eyes, heard it in the tinge of sad envy in her voice. He remembered what she had told him about her own father and realised how cautious she would be about her relationships with men, judging them on character before allowing them into her life. Playboy—womaniser—that would be a firm no-no regardless of physical attraction. No doubt she would instantly back off from anyone showing a bent towards drinking too much alcohol, as well.

A very strong-minded woman.

Her sister's anchor.

She'd been a challenge to him and he hadn't looked

any further than winning her over, having her like this, but he found himself wanting to prove she was safe with him. He was not one of the bad guys.

'I'm going to be the same kind of father to my children,' he said firmly.

It raised her eyebrows. 'You see a future with a family in it?'

'Yes, I do. Don't you?'

She looked uncertain. 'I don't know anymore. I feel a bit adrift at the moment, Harry.'

She had probably dreamed of it with Mickey and that dream was gone. He understood her sense of being adrift. He didn't know how deep it went until much later in the day.

Lunch with Lucy and Michael again before they headed back to the mainland. Elizabeth felt no stress about joining them. She wanted to observe how well they were responding to each other, watch for any pricks in their bubble of happiness. It troubled her that Lucy saw her dyslexia as a possible breaking point. She wished she could have given her sister an assurance that it wouldn't be.

It was a problem, no denying it. She suspected it played a big part in Lucy's flightiness, why relationships and jobs never lasted long. It wasn't a happy position—being thought defective. If Michael ever did think it and rejected her sister on that basis, Elizabeth knew she would hate him for it.

As soon as they were all seated in the restaurant and handed menus with the limited list of four starters, four mains and four sweets, Elizabeth mused over all of them out loud so Lucy could make her choice without having to say she'd have the same as someone else. Often in restaurants a waiter listed Specials which made a selection easy, but that wasn't the case here.

Lucy grinned at her, eyes sparkling gratitude, and it was obvious that nothing had changed between her and Michael. They still looked besotted with each other, and the meal progressed in a very congenial atmosphere.

Until they were sitting over coffee at the end of it.

'Any prospects for the position of manager here, Harry?' Michael asked.

He shrugged. 'A few résumés have come in. I haven't called for any interviews yet. Elizabeth may want to stay on now that she's on top of the job.'

'Elizabeth is mine!' Michael shot at him with a vexed look.

'No!' tripped straight out of her mouth.

The vexed look was instantly transferred to her. 'Don't tell me Harry has seduced you into staying here.'

'No, I won't be staying here beyond the month he needs to find someone suitable.'

As beautiful as the island was, it was a getaway, too isolated from a normal social life for her to stay on indefinitely, too far away from Lucy, too. Besides, if the affair with Harry ran cold, she'd feel trapped here.

'So you come back to me,' Michael insisted.

She shook her head. 'I'm sorry, Michael, but I don't want to do that, either.'

Being his PA wasn't a straightforward work situation anymore. The personal connections that had started this week—him and Lucy, herself and Harry—made it too emotionally complicated for her to feel comfortable about working closely with him.

'Why not?' he persisted.

She was acutely aware of Lucy listening and needed to dissuade her sister from thinking it was because of her. 'Being here this week made me realise I want a change. Try something different. I'd appreciate it if you'd take this as my notice, Michael.'

He wasn't happy. He glared at his brother. 'God-dammit, Harry! If it wasn't for you...'

'Hey!' Harry held up his hands defensively. 'I'm not getting her, either.'

'Please...' Elizabeth quickly broke in, feeling the rise of tension around the table. 'I don't want to cause trouble. I just want to take a different direction with my life.'

'But you're brilliant as my PA,' Michael argued, still annoyed at being put out.

'I'm sorry. You'll just have to find someone else.'

She wasn't about to budge from this stance. It felt right to divorce herself from both the Finn men as far as work was concerned. Whatever developed in a personal sense had to be something apart from professional ties, not tangled up with how she earned her income.

'Why not try out Lucy as your PA?' Harry suggested to Michael with an airy wave of his hand. 'She's probably as brilliant as her sister.'

Lucy looked aghast, panic in her eyes.

'It's not her kind of thing,' Elizabeth said firmly.

Michael frowned and turned to her sister. 'You do work in administration, Lucy,' he remarked quizzically.

'I'm the front person who deals with people, Michael,' she rushed out. 'I don't do the desk work. I'm good at helping people, understanding what they want, helping them to decide…there's quite a bit of that in cemetery administration. And I like it,' she added for good measure, pleading for him to drop the issue.

He grimaced, accepting that Lucy was no easy solution to his problem.

She reached out and touched his hand, desperate to restore his good humour with her. 'I'm sorry I can't fill Ellie's place.'

The grimace tilted up into a soothing smile. 'I shouldn't have expected it. You are a people person and I like that, Lucy. I wouldn't want to change it.'

Elizabeth saw relief pouring through the smile beamed back at him. Another hurdle safely jumped, she thought. Yet hiding the dyslexia from Michael couldn't go on forever and there was one thing she needed from him before the situation could get horribly messed up.

'I hope you'll give me a good reference, Michael.'

He sighed and turned a rueful smile to her. 'It will be in the mail tomorrow. I hate losing you but I wish you well, Elizabeth.'

'Thank you.'

Harry didn't like Elizabeth's decision any more than Mickey did. She was cutting ties with them, closing doors, and he didn't know her reasons for it. This morning he could have sworn she was over her emotional fixation on his brother but if that was true, why give up her job with him? It was a top-line position and on the salary front Harry doubted she could better it.

He had offered her an alternative but she wasn't taking up that option. It was understandable that staying on the island long-term would not suit her. She and her sister lived together and were obviously close—family who really counted as family, like him and Mickey. Apart from that, if she wanted to rejoin the social swing, Cairns was the place to do it.

He didn't like this thought, either. It meant she didn't see much of a future with him, which raised the question in his mind—how much of a future did he want with her?

She touched places in him that no other woman had, but did he do the same to her? More time together should sort that out, but there was one thing he needed to know right now because it was twisting up his gut.

Was she still using him to fight off her feelings for Mickey?

Elizabeth silently fretted over whether she had spoken her mind too soon, aware that her announcements had upset the happy mood around the table. Although Michael had accepted her decision on the surface, it was obvious from the stony glances he threw at Harry that he blamed his brother for it and was barely holding in his frustration over the situation. Her nerves picked up tension emanating from Harry. Lucy kept looking anxiously at her. No one chose to eat any of the petit fours that accompanied coffee.

As soon as Elizabeth had finished her cappuccino, Lucy pushed back her chair and rose to her feet. 'I'm off to the ladies' room. Will you come with me, Ellie?' Her eyes begged agreement.

'Of course,' she said, immediately rising to join her sister.

The barrage started the moment they were closeted in the ladies' room. 'Why are you leaving your great job with Michael? He's not happy about it.'

Elizabeth shook her head. 'It's not my mission in life to keep Michael happy,' she said dryly.

'But you always said you loved that job.'

'I did, but it's high pressure, Lucy. I didn't realise how much it demanded of me until I came out here. I don't want to be constantly on my toes anymore. I want to look for something else—more relaxed, less stressful.'

'Then it's not because of me and him?' she said worriedly.

'No,' Elizabeth lied. 'I'm sorry Michael is unhappy about it but I don't think he'll take it out on you, Lucy. If he does, he's not the man for you.'

She heaved a sigh. 'You're right. Okay. It's completely fair for you to look for something else. He's just got to lump being put out by it.'

'You can play nurse and soothe his frustration,' Elizabeth said with a smile.

Lucy laughed.

It eased the tension on that front.

However, Michael's displeasure with her decision made the farewells after lunch somewhat strained. Elizabeth hoped that Lucy's company would be bright enough to move his annoyance aside. She hadn't meant to spoil their day.

Harry followed her into the administration office, obviously intent on pursuing the issue of her leaving his

employ, as well, although he shouldn't have any griev-
ance with her. She had only ever agreed to the month
needed for him to find another manager.

Wanting to clear that deck, she swung around to face
him, quickly saying, 'I won't stay on, Harry. I didn't
promise to.'

His grim expression surprised her. The laser-blue
eyes were so hard and piercing, her heart jumped into
a gallop. The air between them seemed to gather an intensity that played havoc with her nerves.

'Why did you throw in your job with Mickey?' he
shot at her.

'I explained why,' she said defensively.

'You waffled to whitewash the true reason,' he ac-
cused. 'Tell me, Elizabeth.'

He had no right to delve into her private reading of
a highly personal situation for herself and her sister. It
was not his business. It was the involvement with his
brother that was the problem and she was not about to
spell that out.

'I'm sorry you thought it was waffle.' She shrugged.
'I don't know what else to say.'

His mouth thinned in frustration. He shook his head
at her refusal to open up to him. 'I knew you were using
me on Friday night,' he stated bitingly. 'That whole
scenario at the pavilion villa was more about Michael
and Lucy than being with me. I want to know if what
you've done with me since then and what you decided
today was also driven by your feelings for my brother.'

Her face flamed with shame at how she had used him
and her mind jammed with shock that he could believe
she was still doing it. 'No!' she cried, forcing her feet

forward to go to him, her eyes pleading forgiveness for her brutal lack of caring for *his* feelings. 'I don't even think of Michael anymore, not with any wanting in my mind or heart,' she said vehemently. 'I haven't been using you, Harry. Even on Friday night I was confused about why I was doing what I did with you.'

She reached him and laid her hands on his chest, meeting his scouring gaze with open honesty. 'Since then, I swear I've enjoyed every minute with you, wanting to know the person you are, liking what I'm learning about you. Please don't think any of it was related to your brother.'

He frowned, not yet appeased by her outcry. 'Then why not work for Mickey?'

She grimaced at his persistence. 'Maybe I just don't want to be reminded of how silly I was. A break is better, Harry.' She slid her hands up around his neck and pressed her body to his, craving the wild warmth and excitement of his desire again. 'Can we forget about Michael now? Please?'

His eyes still scoured hers for the truth. His hands gripped her waist hard as though he was in two minds whether to pull her closer or push her away. 'He's my brother,' he said gruffly.

And Lucy was her sister, whom Michael could hurt very badly.

'Does that mean I *have* to work for him or I'll lose any interest you have in me, Harry?'

Again his brow beetled down. 'That's not the point.'

'Good! Because as much as I want what you and I are having together, I won't let any man dictate how I lead my life.'

That was a core truth.

She wanted a partner in life, not a lord and master.

Harry believed her. There was a strength in this woman that had always challenged him. As much as it had frustrated him in the past, he admired the way she made a decision and stuck to it. A warrior woman, he thought wryly, one who would fight tooth and nail for what she believed was right.

Yet she was vulnerable to the womanly needs that he'd tapped into. The wanting for him was in the soft giving of her body appealing to his, the hand-lock at the back of his neck, the slight pouting of her mouth waiting for a kiss that would blow everything else away. The challenge in her eyes burned into his brain. She was his for the taking, not Mickey's, and the compulsion to take her forced him to set all reservations aside.

He kissed her.

She kissed him back.

And Harry revelled in the sense that this was a true beginning of a relationship that promised to be more *right* than any he had known.

CHAPTER FIFTEEN

ELIZABETH managed the administration office on her own throughout her second week on Finn Island. She didn't feel lonely. There were daily meetings with Sarah and Jack Pickard and Daniel Marven. Apart from them, many of the guests dropped by to chat about what they'd done or what they planned to do while they were here. Quite a few were much-travelled tourists from other countries, who couldn't resist comparing this place to other getaways they had enjoyed, always favourably, which Elizabeth thought was a feather in Harry's cap.

He'd carried through his vision for this resort with an attention to detail that was every bit as meticulous as Michael's in his side of the business. In that respect he was just as solid as his brother. In fact, he really had none of the characteristics of a playboy who cared little for anything except indulging himself with passing pleasures.

He called her each day to check on how she was doing and they had quite long conversations that always left her smiling. Contact with him didn't make her tense anymore. They discussed many things with an ease that she thoroughly enjoyed. Even the flirtatious remarks that she'd once hated, once left her steaming with anger, now made her laugh and spread a delicious warmth through her body.

It continually amazed her how much her life had changed in such a short amount of time. Giving up the Michael dream that had been gnawing at her for so long and giving in to the attraction Harry had always exerted on her…it was as though a whole lot of inner conflict had been lifted from her. She had set aside worries about the future, letting herself be a happy butterfly. When serious issues had to be faced, she would face them. But that wasn't yet.

Emails from Lucy were full of dizzy pleasure with her love affair with Michael. According to her sister, he was everything wonderful. Still early days, Elizabeth thought, but hoped the relationship would become what both of them were looking for to complement their lives. And who knew…maybe Harry might turn out to be the right partner for her?

He returned to the island on Saturday morning, strolling into the office, a wide grin on his face, eyes sparkling with pleasure at seeing her again. Her heart jumped. Her feet jumped. She was out of her chair, wanting to skip around the desk and hurl herself at him, driven by a wild eagerness to revel in all the sexual excitement his physical presence instantly aroused in her. Only a sense of decorum held her back. Or rather a very basic female instinct to have him demonstrate his desire for her first.

Her smile, however, was an open invitation to take up where he'd left off last weekend. 'Hi!' she said in a breathy rush.

He strode forward, dumped the attaché case he was

carrying on the desk and swept her into his embrace. 'Can't wait another minute,' he said and kissed her with a hunger that ignited the same hunger in her.

It was great to feel so wanted.

What made the physical sizzle between them even better was the respect he subsequently showed for her opinion. He'd brought the résumés of the most likely prospects for the position of manager with him and wanted her input on them before deciding on interviews. This sharing on a business level made Elizabeth feel like a real partner, not just for sharing a bed.

They talked about the possibilities for most of the day, weighing up the pros and cons, deciding on who would best deal with the situation. There seemed to be a wonderful, vibrant harmony flowing between them, making their lovemaking that night extra special. It wasn't until Harry chose to query her choices that the pleasurable flow was broken.

They were lying face to face, their legs still intimately locked together. Harry softly stroked the feathery bangs off her forehead, looking deeply into her eyes. 'I'd really like you to stay on here, Ellie,' he said. 'It's not too late to change your mind.'

Her chest instantly grew tight. It was difficult to resist the seductive pressure of his words when she wanted to cling onto the sweet sense of everything being perfect. 'I can't, Harry,' she blurted out.

He frowned at her quick reply. 'You've been happy here this past week. I've heard it in your voice every time I've called. And today you've been so relaxed, confident. Why not reconsider?'

'It's better that you get someone else,' she argued.

'But I like feeling you're part of my world, Ellie. It's been great this week, sharing it with you.'

She sucked in a deep breath, needing to hold firm against the persuasive pull of a future that might mean sharing his world forever. It was too soon to know, her mind screamed, too soon to commit to the possibility. She reached up and stroked his cheek, her eyes pleading for understanding.

'I'm not rejecting you, Harry. I just need to be where Lucy is. Being on this island in a permanent position is too far away.'

He heaved a sigh, his mouth turning into a wry grimace. 'You have to be there for her.'

'Yes.'

'Well, I guess I'll just have to invade your world in Cairns.'

She relaxed at his acceptance of her decision, smiling as she said, 'I hope you do.'

Harry told himself to be content with her apparent willingness to continue their relationship once she was back in Cairns. Separating herself from both Mickey and himself professionally had niggled at him. She'd been so elusive in the past, he wasn't absolutely confident that he'd won her over into moving forward with him.

They'd certainly gone beyond a one-night stand and he no longer thought this was a rebound situation. The connection between them was too good to doubt it. Still, the fact that she was severing the work connection… Harry shook it out of his mind. There was no point in letting it throw a cold shadow over the warmth of their intimacy tonight.

He had her where he wanted her.

It was enough for now.

The call-tune on his mobile phone woke him to the dim light of dawn.

Elizabeth stirred, as well, asking, 'Who'd be wanting to contact you at this hour?'

'Don't know,' he muttered, hoping it wasn't bad trouble of some sort as he rolled out of bed and retrieved the mobile from his shorts pocket. He quickly flipped it open, held it up to his ear and spoke a terse, 'Yes?'

'Harry Finn?' asked a male voice he didn't recognise.

'Yes. Who's speaking?'

'This is Constable Colin Parker. I'm calling from the Cairns Base Hospital. I'm sorry to say your brother, Michael Finn, was involved in a serious car accident earlier this morning....'

Harry's heart stopped. Shock and fear jammed his mind for a moment, fear spearing through to force out the words, 'How serious?'

'Your brother and two teenagers are in intensive care. I can't say exactly what injuries were sustained but I'm told they are extensive. Two other teenagers...'

'He's not dead.' Relief poured through Harry. Although there was no guarantee Mickey would pull through, at least he had a chance, not like their parents.

'Who?' Elizabeth cried, alarmed by what she'd heard.

It instantly recalled the high probability that Lucy had been with Mickey—a Saturday night—out on the town. 'Was my brother alone in his car?'

Elizabeth clapped her hands to her face, her eyes wide with horror, a gasp of shock leaving her mouth open.

'Yes, he was. No passengers.'

'Lucy wasn't with him,' he swiftly assured her. 'Thank you for letting me know, Constable. I'll get to the hospital as soon as I can.'

He grabbed his clothes and headed straight for the bathroom, his mind racing over which would be the fastest way to the mainland. Calling for a helicopter, getting the pilot out of bed and to the airfield—no, he couldn't bear waiting around. Best to take the yacht back to Cairns at full throttle, be on the move. He could easily summon a car to meet him at the marina, drive him straight to the hospital, no time wasted.

You hang on, Mickey, he fiercely willed his brother.

Elizabeth had wrapped a robe around her and was pacing the bedroom floor when he emerged from the bathroom. 'How bad is it?' she shot at him, anguish in her eyes.

It made Harry think she still cared a hell of a lot for his brother, which put another savage twist in his heart.

Her hands lifted in urgent plea. 'Lucy will want to know.'

Anguish for her sister or herself? He shook his head. He didn't have time to sort this out. 'He's in intensive care. That's all the cop could tell me,' he answered. 'I have to go now, Elizabeth. Will you hold on here until… until…' He couldn't bring himself to voice whatever was going to happen.

'Of course I will,' she cried. 'I'll do anything you want me to do. Just call me. I'll stand by as long as you need me.'

Yes, Harry thought. *The one who had always carried the load. Always would. The anchor.*

He walked over to her, scooped her into a tight embrace, needing a brief blast of warmth to take some of the chill out of his bones. He rubbed his cheek over her silky hair and kissed the top of her head. 'Thank you. I'll be in touch,' he murmured, then set her aside to go to his brother.

Elizabeth was not going to leave him any day soon.

Mickey might.

Elizabeth's heart bled for him as she watched him make a fast exit from her apartment. To have his parents killed in an accident and now to have his brother on the danger list from another accident…it was a wickedly unkind twist of fate.

When she had thought Lucy could be involved, too… The huge relief at hearing she wasn't made her feel guilty for being spared what Harry was going through—totally gutted with fear and anxiety. It was no empty promise that she would do anything to help. If she had the power to make everything better for him, she would. He was a good man.

So was Michael.

And Lucy would want to know that the man she loved was in hospital, possibly fighting for his life.

Where was her sister? Why hadn't she been with Michael? Had there been a bust-up between them? Questions fired through Elizabeth's mind as she used her mobile phone to make contact with her. The call tone went on for a long nerve-tearing time before it was finally cut off by Lucy's voice, sounding groggy with sleep.

Of course, it was still very early in the morning—

Sunday morning—but time didn't matter. 'Wake up, Lucy!' she said sharply. 'There's been an accident.'

'What? Is that you, Ellie?'

'Yes. Michael was injured in a car accident early this morning. He was badly hurt.'

'Michael…oh, no…no…' It was a wail of anguished protest. 'Oh, God! It's my fault!'

'How is it your fault?'

'I ate something at dinner last night that upset me. He brought me home. I was vomiting and had dreadful diarrhoea. He left me to find an all-night pharmacy, get me some medicine. I was so drained I must have drifted off to sleep. He should have come back but he's not here and… Oh, God! He went out for me, Ellie!'

'Stop that, Lucy! You didn't cause the accident and getting hysterical won't help Michael,' she said vehemently, needing to cut off the futile guilt trip. 'I take it everything was still good between you last night?'

'Yes…yes…he was so caring when I was sick. Oh, Ellie! I'll die if I lose him.'

'Then you'd better do whatever you can to make him want to live. Are you still sick? Can you get to the hospital? He's in an intensive care unit.'

'I'll get there.' Gritty determination was in her voice, hysteria gone.

'Harry was with me on the island. He's on his way. Be kind to him, Lucy. Remember he and Michael lost their parents in an accident. I have to stay here. Harry's counting on me to take care of business but I think he'll need someone there, too.'

'I understand. You love him but you can't be with him.'

Love? That was typical Lucy. Elizabeth cared about

the man and she certainly loved aspects of him, but she mentally shied from putting a boots-and-all love tag on her feelings for Harry. However, right at this moment it was easier to just let her sister think what she wanted to think.

'I need to know what's happening, Lucy. Please... will you keep me informed?'

'Sure! I'll call you with news as soon as I have it. Moving now. Over and out. Okay?'

'Okay.'

Elizabeth took a long deep breath, trying to settle some of her inner agitation. There was no more she could do about the situation, yet the need for some kind of action was twitching through her nerves. The office didn't have to be opened for hours yet. It was too early for anyone on the island to require her for anything.

She showered and dressed, then walked down to the beach, dropping onto a deckchair to simply sit and watch the sunrise, wanting to feel some peace with a world that had just changed again. Nature kept rolling on, regardless of what happened to human beings. While it could be ugly, too—cyclones, floods, droughts—this morning it had a beautiful tranquillity that soothed the turmoil in her soul.

The sea was a glittering expanse of shimmering wavelets. The sky slowly turned into a pastel panorama of pinks and lemons. The sun crept up over the horizon, shooting beams of light into the tinted clouds. It was a lovely dawning of a new day—another day that she was *alive*.

Life was precious.

More than ever Elizabeth felt a pressing need to make the most of it.

This past week with Harry had been good.

She'd felt happy with him.

Love was a big step from there but her mind and heart were opening up to the chance that Harry Finn might be the man who could and would share her life in all the ways she'd dreamed of.

CHAPTER SIXTEEN

ELIZABETH was on tenterhooks all morning waiting for news of Michael. She thought it would be Lucy who called, but it was Harry, instantly assuring her that his brother's injuries were not life-threatening as they had feared.

'He was hit on the driver's side, right arm and hip fractured, broken ribs, lacerations to the face, a lot of bruising, concussion. The doctors were worried that a broken rib had punctured his liver but that's been cleared and bones will mend.' His sigh transmitted a mountain of relief. 'He's going to be incapacitated for quite a while, but there should be no lasting damage.'

'That's good news, Harry,' Elizabeth said, her own relief pouring into her voice.

'Lucy's here. I've left her sitting beside Mickey, holding his left hand. She's certainly a surprise, your sister.'

'What do you mean?'

'He's not a pretty picture—face cut, bruised and swollen. I didn't think it was a good idea, her going in to see him. Thought she'd have hysterics or faint at the sight of him. She gave me an earbashing on how much she cared about Mickey and she was no wimp when it came to facing anyone who was suffering anything.'

Elizabeth smiled, imagining the scene. 'I told you she was good with Mum.'

'Looks like she'll be good with Mickey, too. Like Mum was with Dad. He'll need cheering up in the days to come, that's for sure. He's sedated right now. Haven't spoken to him, only to the doctors, who assure me he's out of the woods.'

'That's the important thing, Harry. Whatever the future brings, he does have a future.'

'Thank God!'

'How did the accident happen? Lucy said he'd left her to find an all-night pharmacy...'

'Drunken teenagers in a stolen car running a red light. They just slammed into him. All four of them are here in the hospital, undoubtedly ruing their stupid joy ride. I can't say I'm feeling any sympathy for them.'

Harsh words, but justified, Elizabeth thought. Nevertheless, concern for him made her ask, 'Are you okay, Harry? I know shock can hit hard and have lingering after-effects.'

He heaved another big sigh, releasing tension this time. 'I'll be fine. Got to step in for Mickey. I'll have to run the Cairns office until he can pick up the reins again. I can delegate the running of the tourist side for a while, but Mickey has always kept a very personal control of the franchises. There's no one I can hand it to.'

'I know,' she murmured understandingly, realising that his mind was racing, trying to foresee problems he had to deal with.

'I'll set up interviews with the two people we selected for the management position on the island, hopefully this week, then send the one I think is most appropriate out to you. If you'll train whomever I choose...'

'No problem,' she assured him. 'I'll get Sarah and Jack and Daniel to come on board for that, as well. We'll handle it for you, Harry. Don't worry about it. You'll have enough on your plate taking over from Michael. Just keep me informed on what's happening.'

'Will do. And thanks for...' He paused a moment, his voice gathering a husky note as he added, 'for being you, Elizabeth.'

The emotional comment brought a lump to her throat. It had been a stressful morning and she teetered on the edge of weeping now that the practicalities of the situation had been sorted out. She knew intuitively that Harry was close to breaking up, too, having held himself together to face the worst.

Having swallowed hard to clear her throat, she softly said, 'Don't be too alone in this, Harry. Anything you need to share...you can talk to me any time. Okay?'

Another pause, longer this time, making her wonder if she had stepped too far, assuming an intimacy he didn't feel with her when they weren't in bed together.

'Though I'm not into phone sex,' she blurted out.

He cracked up. Peal after peal of laughter sent her brain into a tizzy. She had no idea what it meant—a release from tension, amusement at her prudish restriction?

'Oh, Ellie! I love you,' he bubbled forth. 'I really, truly do.'

She was stunned into silence. Was this a genuine declaration or was he funning her?

'And it will kill me if you don't love me back,' he went on, slightly more soberly.

How was she to reply to that? 'Umm... Well, don't die any time soon, Harry.'

'I won't. I have too much to live for. And so do you, Ellie,' he said with conviction. 'Bye for now.'

Elizabeth didn't know what to think. In the end she decided Harry's *loving* her was simply an impulsive re-action to her helping him at a time of crisis. It was more comfortable putting it in that box than believing he was serious, because she didn't want to feel pressured about loving him back. As much as she liked him—maybe loved him—she wasn't ready to lay her heart completely on the line. It was too...*hasty*.

Harry knew he'd jumped the gun with the *love* words. They'd spilled out of him before he realised what he was saying, no consideration given to how they'd be received or interpreted and, worst of all, he couldn't *see* Elizabeth's reaction to them.

He'd spoken the truth. He knew that without any doubt now. The instinctive attraction had always been there and he'd never been able to give up on it, despite her constantly blocking it, preferring to see his brother as the more desirable man. But they were *right* together, *right* for each other. He felt it in his bones. Though he suspected she wasn't quite ready to hear or accept it.

Having given her word, she would still stand by him during this crisis. But until he was actually with her again, he'd steer clear of pouring out personal feelings. He wasn't absolutely sure that her emotions had been detached from his brother. Having sex with him—liking it, wanting it—that was certainly answering a need in her, but whether he'd won through to her heart was not certain at this point.

Patience, Harry, he cautioned himself.

Elizabeth Flippence was the woman worth keeping.

He had to convince her he was the man worth keeping.

Every day following Michael's accident, Elizabeth found herself literally hanging on calls from Cairns. She cared about Michael's progress—of course, she did—yet she grew impatient when Lucy went on endlessly about every little detail and her sympathy was sorely stretched at times. She really wanted to hear from Harry, not her sister.

Her heart always jumped when his voice came over the line and her body flooded with warm pleasure. Not once did he mention *loving* her, and despite thinking she didn't want to hear it, weirdly enough she actually did, although she was happy to simply chat with him and it felt really good to help him with problems he was encountering in Michael's office.

His confidence in her, his respect for her opinion, his desire for her input on everything, did touch her heart. Very deeply. None of her previous relationships with men had reached this level of sharing. She loved it. When he told her he was bringing his chosen candidate for manager over to the island himself at the weekend, she was thrilled at the prospect of being with him again, if only for a few hours.

He instructed her to hold a villa aside for herself from Saturday to the following Friday as the new manager would be taking over the apartment and she would probably need a week to ensure he was on top of the job. His name was David Markey and he was only twenty-eight, but he'd had experience as assistant manager at a resort on Kangaroo Island, which was down below Adelaide off the coast of South Australia. According to his résumé, he was keen to take up a position in a more tropical climate. Elizabeth had thought him a good possibility and she was glad he had interviewed well, leading Harry to choose him.

They were to arrive by helicopter on Saturday morning and the moment Elizabeth heard the distinctive noise of the rotors, her pulse started racing. She'd barely slept the night before, thinking of Harry and how it might be with him this time. It was difficult to contain the nervous excitement buzzing through her but somehow she had to keep it in check while she handled the business side of this visit.

Professionalism insisted that she couldn't run down to the back beach, waving madly like a child as the helicopter landed and flinging herself at Harry the moment he stepped out of it. Waiting in the office for the men to enter it was the right and sensible thing to do—the Elizabeth thing, she thought wryly, not the Lucy thing. But Harry was counting on her to be sensible and helpful. This was not *butterfly* time.

She'd asked Jack to meet the helicopter, introducing himself to David Markey as well as giving any help needed with luggage. While she waited, she forced herself to check through items laid out on her desk in preparation for making the job transition as easy as possible for David—a list of the current guests and the villas they occupied with a notation of activities some of them had booked today, contact numbers for the chef and the Pickards, a list of staff names under headings of housekeeping, maintenance and restaurant. It was all there waiting…waiting….

Harry led the others into the office. His vivid blue eyes connected with hers with such riveting intensity, Elizabeth was pinned to her chair while her heart rocketed around her chest. She stared back, feeling as though he was wrapping a magnetic field around her entire being, claiming her as his, tugging her towards him.

She stood. Her thighs were quivering, but her legs moved as though drawn by strings, drawn by the power of an attraction that had become totally irresistible. His smile bathed her in tingling pleasure. She was so consumed by sheer awe at the strength of feelings shooting through her, the man moving in beside Harry didn't register on her radar until her attention was directed to him.

Harry lifted his hand in an introductory wave, inclining his head towards the slightly shorter man. 'David Markey, Elizabeth.'

'Good to meet you,' the newcomer promptly said, stepping forward and extending his hand.

Elizabeth met it with her own hand, belatedly smiling a welcome. 'Likewise, David. I hope you'll be very happy working here on Finn Island.'

He was a clean-cut, good-looking young man—short brown hair, bright brown eyes with a ready smile to charm, a typical front man in the hospitality industry. 'I'm very glad to have the chance,' he said enthusiastically.

Jack had manoeuvred around the two men, wheeling two suitcases towards the door into the manager's apartment. Harry gestured towards him as he spoke to David. 'If you'll just follow Jack, he'll show you your living quarters and answer any questions you might have about them. I want a private word with Elizabeth.'

'Of course. Thank you,' was the ready reply, and taking the privacy hint, he closed the apartment door after himself.

The brief business with David had given Elizabeth enough distraction to recover from the initial impact of Harry's presence. Having regained some control of herself, she turned to him with a sympathetic smile. 'Tough week?'

'Mmm...' His eyes twinkled teasingly as he spread his arms in appeal. 'I think I need a hug.'

Her heart started racing again as she laughed and moved straight into his embrace, eager for the physical contact she had craved all week.

He hugged her tightly to him, rubbing his cheek against her hair, breathing in deeply and releasing a long, shuddering sigh before murmuring, 'There is nothing like a warm living body to make you feel better. I have so much wanted you with me this week, Ellie.'

'I wished I could have been there for you, too, Harry.'

'Can't be in two places at once,' he said wryly, tugging her head back so they were face to face. 'I'll stay here overnight if that's okay with you.'

'I was hoping you would,' she answered, openly showing that she welcomed every intimacy with him.

Desire blazed into his eyes. He lifted a hand and ran a feather-light finger over her lips. 'If I start kissing you I won't want to stop and there's no time for it now.

When Jack comes out I'll leave you with David. Sarah wants me to lunch with them, hear all the news about Mickey firsthand. You should lunch with David in the restaurant, introduce him to the guests. I'll catch up with the two of you afterwards, find out how he's doing and hopefully get you to myself for a while.'

Assured they would be together later in the afternoon, Elizabeth didn't mind seeing Harry go off with Jack, happy with the plan of action he'd laid out. She knew how fond Sarah was of both the Finn brothers, and it was nice of Harry to answer the housekeeper's concern about Michael. It was also appropriate for her to introduce David to the guests since she was known to them, having been the resident manager all week.

Over lunch, David proved to have a very pleasant manner with the guests and the restaurant staff. Elizabeth quite enjoyed his company herself. He readily answered her questions about his experience on Kangaroo Island and was keen to question her experience at this resort, garnering as much knowledge as he could as quickly as he could.

It occurred to her that it might not take a week to fill him in on everything and make sure he understood the whole working process of the island. He wasn't coming in cold to the job as she had. He was already a professional in this field. It might only take a few days and then she could get back to Cairns.

To Lucy…

To Harry…

To real life again…

Although the island *getaway* hadn't really been a getaway for her. She'd been well and truly faced with real life here—forced to accept the reality of Michael's connection with Lucy, having her misconceptions about Harry ripped apart, learning that an attraction based on sexual chemistry could gather many more levels, given the chance.

Her time here had been one of intense emotional turmoil, yet coming now to the end of it, she was ready to move forward, wanting to move forward, hopefully with Harry, who had become a very vital part of her world. No denying that. Though she was not going to spin rosy dreams about him, as she had with Michael. She would do the realistic thing and live in the moment with Harry.

The moment could not come fast enough today.

She accompanied David back to the office after lunch and they settled in front of the computer workstation to go through the booking system. It took an act of will for Elizabeth to concentrate on it. Anticipation was like a fever in her blood. She kept glancing at the wall clock, wondering how long Harry would stay with Jack and Sarah, aching for him to leave them and come for her.

It had just turned two o'clock when he entered the office, filling it with an electric energy that zapped through every nerve in Elizabeth's body.

'How's it going?' he asked.

'Fine!' Elizabeth managed to clip out.

'Fine!' echoed David.

'Well, I need to have a meeting with Elizabeth now,' Harry said, exuding the alpha male authority that had so surprised her when he'd sacked Sean Cassidy. 'After we leave, you can close the office, David. It doesn't need to be reopened until five o'clock. Take the time to settle in or stroll around, familiarising yourself with the island's attractions. We'll have dinner together this evening.' His arm beckoned commandingly. 'Elizabeth…'

'See you later, David,' she threw at him as she rose from her chair, her heart pounding with excitement at the prospect of spending at least three hours with Harry.

That gave her a lot of moments to live in…to the full.

CHAPTER SEVENTEEN

As soon as they left the office, Harry caught her hand, his long fingers intertwining with hers, gripping possessively, shooting an instant wave of tingling heat up her arm. 'Which villa is yours?' he asked.

'Number one. It's the closest to the office in case I'm needed.'

He smiled at her, his eyes twinkling admiration and approval. 'Standing by,' he said warmly.

'I don't think I'll have to stand by for long, Harry. David's very quick on the uptake.'

He nodded. 'A case of been there, done that. Do you like him?'

'Yes. I think he'll manage very well. He's at ease with the guests, too, eager to please.'

'Good!'

'I doubt he'll need me for more than a few days. When I'm satisfied he's on top of everything I'll come back to Cairns and help you in the office.' She threw him an anxious look, suddenly thinking she might have assumed too much. 'If you want me to.'

He grinned happily. 'I was going to ask if you would. Just to tide us over until Mickey can take control again. Andrew—the guy you suggested could fill in for you—

is floundering like a fish out of water under the pressure of too much responsibility. Not his bag at all. Mickey had already directed an agency to find a better replacement for you, but had yet to set up interviews.'

'I'll stay until that can be sorted out,' she promised.

'You wouldn't walk out on anyone at a bad time, would you, Ellie?'

His eyes caressed her as though she was someone very special and her heart fluttered with happiness. 'Not if I could help,' she answered, knowing intuitively that Harry wouldn't, either. He was a caring man who had looked after the people who could have been hurt by Franklyn Finn's sudden death. He hadn't walked away. Not like her father, she thought.

She didn't mind him calling her Ellie anymore. Every time he used that name she heard affection in it, and Harry's affection had become very addictive.

They mounted the steps to the villa's deck. He paused by the railing, his gaze sweeping around the bay below. 'I don't know how Mickey can stand being closed up in an office day after day.'

'He likes running the franchises,' Elizabeth pointed out. 'And since you say he has tunnel vision, I guess that's all he sees when he's there.'

'Mmm…lucky for me! I don't think I could have handled it. I'll be glad when he's back in the driving seat.' His gaze swung to target hers, the blue eyes gathering the intensity that always made her feel he was digging into her mind. 'What about you, Ellie? Have you thought of what you want to do when everything's on course again?'

She shook her head. 'I'm just taking one day at a time.'

'May I make a suggestion?'

'I'm not going to work full-time for you, Harry,' she said quickly, hoping he wouldn't try to persuade her to take up that option again. She had fallen in love with him, and while working together might be great for a while, if he lost his desire for her...

'I wasn't about to ask you to,' he said, drawing her into his embrace.

'What then?' she asked, relieved by this assurance and sliding her hands up his chest, over his shoulders and around his neck, inviting a kiss, wanting him to make love to her, craving intimate contact.

His mouth quirked teasingly. He lifted a hand and gently stroked her cheek, looking deeply into her eyes. 'I don't want you working for me, Ellie. I want you living with me. I'm suggesting that you think about marrying me. We could start a family, make a home together and hopefully live happily ever after. How does that sound?'

She was totally stunned. No way had she anticipated a marriage proposal! Her heart slammed around her chest. She stared at Harry, utterly speechless, barely able to believe what he'd just said.

The shock dilating her eyes told Harry he'd jumped the gun again. This time he didn't care. He wanted her thinking about it, wanted her knowing that he was serious about sharing his future with her. She was *the one* he'd been looking for, *the one* who would complement his life in all the ways that mattered to him. He couldn't bear her having any doubts about where she stood with him.

He had no doubts. This past week had clinched it for him. His brother was no longer a gut-tearing factor in their relationship. That had become clear in all the conversations they'd had. Caring for Mickey had not been at the heart of them. Her focus had been on him—his thoughts, his concerns, his feelings.

He wanted to banish her sense of being adrift, wanted to become *her* anchor, just as she had become his. She might not yet be ready to commit herself to marriage but he saw no harm in laying it on the line. Her mind was clearly rocked at the moment but he didn't sense any negative vibrations coming from her.

'Think about it, Ellie,' he softly commanded, then kissed her.

Elizabeth didn't want to think. She wanted to feel all that Harry made her feel. She threw herself into the kiss, hungry for the wild rush of passion between them—the passion that swept away everything else but the fierce need for each other. It surged through her bloodstream. Her body ached for him, yearned for him, silently but intensely communicating more than she could say.

Harry didn't push for any verbal answer from her. He swept her into the villa and they tore off their clothes, reaching for each other, desire at fever pitch, falling onto the bed, moving urgently to come together. She grasped him with her hands, her legs. He kissed her as the strong shaft of his flesh slid into the pulsating passage that exultantly welcomed their joining. The sheer bliss of it spread through her entire body.

Her mind sang his name…Harry, Harry, Harry….

They rode the waves of pleasure together, driving up the intensity of feeling, instinctively intent on making it more sensational than it had ever been because it was more than physical this time. Much more. Her heart was beating with love for this man, bursting with it as they both climaxed, tipping them over into a world that was uniquely theirs, an intimate sharing that Elizabeth now knew with absolute certainty she would never find with any other man.

It was only a few weeks since she had dreamed of having this with Michael. It seemed weird that in such a short time Harry had so completely supplanted his brother in every sense, but he had. And this was *real*, not a fantasy. She hugged him to her, wanting this *reality* to go on forever.

She thought of Lucy.

Did her sister feel as deeply as this with Michael?

She heaved a sigh, knowing that whatever happened in that relationship was beyond her control.

Harry planted a warm kiss on her forehead. 'Is that a sigh of satisfaction?' he murmured.

'I do love you, Harry,' she said, opening up to him. 'It may seem like an incredible turnaround, but it's true.'

He eased away enough to prop himself up on his elbow and look into her eyes. A smile slowly curved his mouth. 'I love you, too. We're right for each other, Ellie. I know you'll stand by me in all the years to come and I hope you know I'll stand by you.'

'Yes…yes, I do,' she said with certainty.

'So…will you marry me?'

She wanted to.

Lucy would want her to, regardless of what happened with her and Michael. She'd told her so, saying quite vehemently that she didn't want to be the reason for Elizabeth not to have a future with Harry.

Her long hesitation prompted him to ask, 'What reservation do you have in your mind?'

'Will you be kind to Lucy if she and Michael break up?'

It was important to her. She couldn't brush that possibility aside as though it wouldn't count in the future.

He frowned, obviously puzzled that she should be concerned about this. 'Of course I will, Ellie. She's your sister.'

'And Michael's your brother,' she reminded him. 'We could have divided loyalties, Harry.'

'We'll work it out,' he said without hesitation. 'I know Mickey would never interfere with what makes me happy and I bet Lucy would hate feeling she was any kind of block to your having a happy life with me. Am I right about that?'

'Yes,' she conceded, remembering how accurately Harry could read people.

'Then we don't have a problem,' he argued. 'They might not end up together but that won't break our family ties, Ellie. They will both wish us well.'

Yes, she could believe that. It shouldn't be too much of a problem.

'Ellie, we only have one life to live,' Harry pressed on, the intensity back in his eyes. 'We've found each other. Let's not waste time we could have together. You never know when it will be taken away from us.'

Like it had been with his parents.

Like what had almost happened to Michael.

'You're right,' she said, all doubts blown away. 'We should get married. Start having a family. I'm thirty, you know.'

His face broke into a wide grin. 'Yes, I know. And it was the best birthday of all because it brought you to me.'

She laughed, her eyes happily teasing. 'Not very willingly.'

'It was only a matter of time,' he said with arrogant smugness.

She heaved a contented sigh before challenging him one last time, her eyes dancing flirtatiously. 'Well, you're not going to waste any of it, are you? I have to be back at the office...'

His mouth silenced hers.

Her body revelled in having this man.

Her mind was at peace.

She loved Harry Finn and he loved her.

Whatever future they had together they would make the most of it, always being there for each other. That was how it should be and it was going to happen. She and Harry would make it happen because they both wanted it. Everything felt right.

It *was* right.

* * * * *

POSTSCRIPT

Dear Reader,

You have just read Harry's and Elizabeth's story. Michael and Lucy are two entirely different people. While part of their story intersects with this one—their first meeting, the romantic weekend on Finn Island, Michael's car accident—these situations will be related from their points of view in my next book, along with the highs and lows experienced by both of them in their journey towards finding out if they are right for each other. Lust is not love, and passion can turn cold when expectations are not met, when deeply set needs are not answered. The added complications of brothers and sisters can throw shadows, as well, as you've seen in this book. I hope you'll look forward to following the lives of these people. I hope you'll feel for them and want them to end up happily together.

With love always,
Emma Darcy

HIS MOST
EXQUISITE
CONQUEST

CHAPTER ONE

A DEARLY BELOVED daughter buried in the wrong plot.

A man digging up a grave.

A dog running amok in the memorial garden, knocking off angels' heads.

What a Monday morning, Lucy Flippence thought as she drove to Greenlands Cemetery, having been given the job of dealing with these situations. Just when some slack time would have been very handy, too, it being her sister's birthday. It would be really nice to take Ellie out to lunch, especially since Lucy was dying to see her in the wildly colourful new clothes with the new hairdo.

It would be like a complete makeover and highly due, given it was Ellie's thirtieth birthday. For the past two years her sister had been drowning in blacks and greys and taupes, and so caught up in being Michael Finn's personal assistant, she didn't have any other life—not one man sparking her interest.

Right now Lucy had quite a fresh understanding of this disinterest in men. The nasty incident in the Irish pub at Port Douglas had spoiled her weekend away with friends. The guy had started out a promising prince and turned into a horrid frog. It seemed to her they all did, sooner or later. At twenty-eight she had yet to meet one whose shining armour remained shiny, regardless of circumstances.

Even so, she wasn't about to give up on men. She enjoyed the exciting high of a new attraction, loved the sense of being loved, if only for a little while. It was worth the hurt of being disillusioned. As long as she lived, she was going to be out there, experiencing everything that looked and felt good. It was what her mother had told her to do—her mother who'd married her horrible frog father because she was pregnant with Ellie.

'Don't ever make that mistake, Lucy. Be careful.'

She was.

Always careful.

Especially since she didn't want to have children, didn't want to pass on her dyslexia, blighting another life with it. Putting a child through what she'd been through at school was not an act of love, and the problems didn't stop there, either. The incurable disability blocked a heap of avenues that normal people simply took in their stride.

The thought of an innocent baby being born with a wrongly wired brain like hers triggered a strongly negative recoil inside Lucy. She would not risk that happening. Which meant, of course, she would probably never marry—no real point to it if having a family was out of the question.

There was, however, always the hope of meeting a prince who didn't care about having children, or perhaps one who had a genetic fault of his own and would be happy to simply settle with having each other to love. She hadn't ruled out these possibilities. They bolstered her resolve to keep moving on, making the most of her journey through life.

The cemetery on the outskirts of Cairns came into view. It was aptly named Greenlands—everything being so very green as it usually was up here in far north tropical Queensland, especially after the big wet and before the oppressive heat of summer. August was always a pleasant month and Lucy was glad she wasn't stuck in the office, closed off from the lovely sunshine.

As she drove the van into the parking lot, she spotted a man wielding a shovel beside one of the graves. He looked elderly and Lucy instantly decided he wouldn't be dangerous to approach, not that she was frightened of doing so anyway. Her appearance invariably disarmed people.

She loved putting herself together in a fun outfit. The Sunday Markets at Port Douglas were always great for crafty stuff. The wooden bead necklaces and bangles she'd bought yesterday, along with the tan leather belt, and sandals that strapped in criss-crosses up her lower legs, looked fabulous with the white broderie anglaise miniskirt and peasant blouse she was wearing today. Her long blond hair was piled up on top of her head to show off the cute dangly wooden earrings, as well. She didn't look like officialdom and that was half the battle in getting people to confide in her.

The elderly man caught sight of her walking towards him, and stopped digging, leaning on the long handle of his shovel as he watched her approach, looking her up and down as most men did, regardless of age. She could now see two large plastic bags of potting soil lying on the ground beside him, and behind them was the top of a rose bush.

'Well, you're a pretty sight for sore eyes, girlie,' he greeted her, his mouth slowly curving into a wistful little smile. 'Visiting a loved one?'

'Yes, I always visit my mother when I come out here,' Lucy said with her own wistful smile. The man's face was so lined and dotted with age spots she guessed he was about eighty, but his body had a spry wiriness that undoubtedly came from keeping himself active.

'Your mother, eh? Must have died young,' he remarked.

Lucy nodded. 'She was only thirty-eight.' Ten years older than Lucy was now—a fact that lay constantly in the back of her mind, urging her to pack as much into her life as she could.

'What took her?' the man asked sympathetically.

'Cancer.'

'Ah, that's a hard death.' He shook his head sadly. 'Guess I should be grateful my wife went quickly. Heart gave out. Coming up seventy-five she was. Almost made it to our diamond wedding anniversary.'

'You must have had a happy marriage,' Lucy commented, wondering if it was really true. She had observed that some couples stayed together because they didn't want to face the turmoil of breaking up.

'My Gracie was a wonderful woman.' There was love and longing in his voice. 'Wouldn't have swapped her for anyone. She was the best, the only one for me. I miss her so much....' Tears welled into his eyes.

'I'm sorry,' Lucy said softly, waiting until he'd re-

covered his composure before asking, 'Are you planting that rose for her?'

'Yes,' he answered huskily. 'Gracie loved roses.
Especially this one—Pal Joey—because it has such
a beautiful scent. Not like those hothouse roses they
sell in shops. Here...' he bent down and picked up the
bagged rose bush, pointing out the one yellow rose in
full bloom '...come and smell it.'

She did. The scent was stunningly strong and beautiful. 'Oh, that's lovely!'

'I brought it from our garden. I couldn't let my Gracie lie here without some part of our garden, and this
was her favourite rose.'

'Well, Mr...?' Lucy raised her eyebrows quizzically,
needing his name.

'Robson. Ian Robson.'

'Lucy Flippence,' she responded. 'I have to tell you
I'm from cemetery administration, Mr Robson. Someone reported you digging at a grave and I was sent out
to investigate, but I can see there's no harm being done.'

He frowned over any possible interference to his
plan. 'Only want to plant the rose.'

'I know,' Lucy soothed. 'What you're doing is fine
with me. You'll tidy up afterwards, won't you? Leave
your wife's grave looking much nicer than it was before, take the empty bags away?'

'Don't you worry, Miss Flippence. I'll not only do
that, but you can count on me tending to this rose bush,
feeding it and pruning it so it will bloom beautifully
for my Gracie.'

Lucy gave him a warm smile. 'I'm sure you will, Mr

Robson. It's been a pleasure meeting you. I'll go visit my mother now.'

'God bless,' he said in parting.

'You, too.'

As she walked on Lucy had no doubt that Ian Robson had been a prince to his Gracie. That kind of devotion could only come out of a true love which lasted a lifetime. However rare that was, it was comforting to know it did happen—could happen for her if she was super, super lucky.

She stopped at her mother's grave, sighing heavily at what Ellie had insisted be printed on the headstone:

Veronica Anne Flippence
Beloved Mother of Elizabeth and Lucy

No 'Beloved Wife of George,' because that would have been a huge lie. As soon as their mother had been diagnosed with terminal cancer their father had deserted them. Not that he would have been any help during those long months of suffering. Every time he'd come home on leave from his mining job in Mount Isa he'd ended up getting drunk and abusive. Better that he had left his daughters to look after their mother, but the desertion certainly demonstrated there was not even common decency in his character—a frog of the worst order.

Ellie had found out he'd had another woman in Mount Isa and was leading a double life—a cheat on top of everything else. Lucy was glad he had dropped out of their lives. She still hated him for not giving her mother the love she had deserved. There'd been no roses in their marriage—none that Lucy could remember.

'It's Ellie's birthday today, Mum,' she said out loud. 'I'm sure you know that. I bought her a gorgeous butterfly blouse and a lovely green skirt to go with it. She's fallen into a dowdy rut and I want to break her out of it. You said for us to always look out for each other, and Ellie does more than her fair share of that, helping me over hurdles I can't leap like everyone else because of my dyslexia. I'm trying to help her to meet a prince. Guys notice colourful people. She has to give herself a chance, don't you think?'

Lucy smiled at what Ellie had told her over the phone this morning—that her long brown hair was cut and dyed auburn. That was a step in the right direction. If her sister would just lighten up a bit, have some fun, show she was enjoying herself... Guys liked that. In fact, they gravitated towards women who emitted a joy in life.

'If you can perform a miracle, Mum, it would be fantastic if two princes showed up for Ellie and me today. Okay? That would be a birthday to remember.' Lucy heaved another big sigh at the improbability of this happening. 'In the meantime, I've got to go and collect some angels' heads so they don't get damaged any more than they are already. Bye now.'

When she reached the memorial garden, she stood aghast at the number of headless angels. The dog must have been a huge German shepherd or Great Dane. It sure had run amok here. She picked up one head, realised how heavy it was, lay it back down and went to bring the van closer to the garden. It took her an hour to load them all up for transport to the stonemason.

Checking the time, she decided that job could wait until after lunch. If she didn't get to Ellie's office before twelve o'clock, her sister might go off somewhere by herself. Lucy could call her, but surprising her was better. What was a birthday without a nice surprise?

Finding a parking space close to the Finn Franchises building was impossible. Lucy ended up two blocks away from the Esplanade, where it was located. She half ran the distance and managed to arrive at Ellie's office just a few minutes after noon. Having paused long enough to catch her breath, she knocked on the door and opened it enough to poke her head around it to check if the room was occupied. Ellie—a brand-new Ellie—sat at a desk.

It put a wide grin on Lucy's face as she asked, 'Okay to come in?'

'Yes.'

Given the affirmative, she literally bounced in, twirling to shut the door behind her, then dancing over to the desk in an ecstasy of delight over the dramatic change in her sister's appearance. 'Ooh...I *love* the hair, Ellie,' she happily enthused, hitching herself onto the edge of the desk for a close look at the new style. 'It's very sexy. Gives you that just-out-of-bed tumbled look and the colour really, really suits you. It complements the clothes I picked out for you brilliantly. I have to say you look absolutely marvellous. Now tell me you *feel* marvellous, too.'

The slightly uncertain expression on her sister's face cracked into a smile. 'I'm glad I made the change.'

Then, typically Ellie, she turned attention away from herself. 'How was your weekend?'

'Oh, so-so.' Lucy waved her hand airily, then pulled a woeful grimace. 'But I've had the most terrible morning.'

She didn't want to relate the frog in the Irish pub episode. No negatives about men today, with Ellie looking so beautiful. Lucy rattled on about the rose planting at the grave and the dog damage in the memorial garden, describing the scene and what she had to do about it, how heavy the angels' heads were....

It was a really good story, yet Ellie was clearly distracted from it, her gaze sliding away, fixing on some point at the other end of the room.

'Angels' heads...' a male voice said in a rich tone of incredulous wonder.

It sent a weird quiver down Lucy's spine. She didn't know if sound vibrations could squeeze her heart, but something did. She whipped her head around, feeling an instant urge to check out the owner of *that voice*.

And there he was—tall, dark and handsome, the perfect image of a storybook prince!

CHAPTER TWO

EVERYTHING IN MICHAEL Finn's mind was blown away
by the vision of stunning femininity perched on the
edge of Elizabeth's desk. The legs hit him first—long,
beautiful legs, glowing with a golden tan, their shapely
calves accentuated by straps running up from her sandals. A white frilly skirt ended at midthigh. A white
peasant blouse hung off one perfectly rounded shoulder.
A mass of shiny blond hair was piled loosely on top of
her head, some curly strands of it escaping whatever
pins she'd used.

Her face was turned towards Elizabeth, but there
was certainly nothing jarring about its profile, and a
fascinating dimple kept flashing in her cheek as she
talked, her voice lilting with animation. Arty earrings
swayed against her lovely long neck, bangles jingled on
her arms as her hands waved around in graceful gestures, and the story she was telling was as mesmerising as the rest of her.

'Angels' heads…?'

The words spilled from his mouth, escaping from
the bubble of incredulity bouncing around his brain.
He could hardly believe the heart-grabbing impact she

was having on him, and her mention of angels added to the sense of an out-of-this-world encounter.

He was used to sizing women up before deciding if he was willing to put the time into having an ongoing relationship with them. He never rushed into a decision because it was so tedious breaking off the connection when he found it didn't suit him. But the *rush* he was feeling with this woman in his sights triggered a wildly rampant compulsion to forge a connection with her right now before she could disappear on him.

Her head turned towards him. Surprise lit her lovely face, her eyes widening as she stared at him—big brown eyes with amber sparkles in them. Shiny coral lipstick highlighted her lush, sexy mouth as it dropped open to emit a breathy, 'Wow!'

It echoed the *wow* zinging around Michael's mind, and he felt himself stirring as her gaze flicked over him, uninhibitedly checking out his physique. Her open interest in him was like an electric charge. He had an erection in no time flat—which had never happened to him at a first meeting with any woman, not even when he was a randy teenager. At thirty-five, this was a totally new experience and a slightly discomforting one. He prided himself on always being in control.

'Are you Ellie's boss?' she asked, her head tilting as though her mind was racing through possibilities between them.

Ellie...? It took him several moments to wrench his thoughts away from the rage of desire burning through his bloodstream, and connect the name to Elizabeth. 'Yes. Yes, I am,' he finally managed to answer. 'And you are?'

'Lucy Flippence. Ellie's sister. I work in cemetery administration, so I often have to deal with angels,' she said, as though needing to explain to him that she wasn't off the planet, but an ordinary human being with a proper job to do.

'I see,' he said, thinking she wasn't the least bit ordinary.

She hopped off her perch on the desk and crossed the floor to him with her hand extended. Curvy hips swayed. Perky breasts poked out at him. She was tall, slim and so exquisitely female that all his male hormones were buzzing.

'Pleased to meet you.' Her smile was entrancing. 'Okay if I call you Michael?'

'Delighted.' He took her hand and held on to it, the soft warmth of it making his skin tingle with excitement at this first physical contact.

He suddenly registered movement at his side, reminding him he'd just come out of a serious business meeting with his brother. Harry was stepping up, expecting an introduction. Was he feeling the same impact, wanting Lucy's attention turned to him, centred on him? Michael fiercely hoped not. He didn't want to fight his brother over a woman, but he would with this one. A highly primitive sense of possession was swirling through his gut.

His eyes telegraphed hard warning-off signals at Harry as he turned to make the introduction. This was no-go territory. Don't make a contest of it. They had always respected each other's interest in their targeted women, but Lucy had to be a magnet for any man. Even as he said, 'This is my brother, Harry,' Michael willed him to accept he had first claim.

His heart swelled with satisfaction when Lucy left her hand in his grasp and simply raised her other hand in a blithe greeting, tossing a 'Hi, Harry!' at his brother in a kind of bubbly dismissal.

'Charmed,' Harry purred at her.

The flirtatious tone didn't raise so much as a flicker of response. Her gaze instantly connected to Michael's again, the warm brown eyes appealing for understanding and, to his mind, much more than that to come from him. He felt her reaching out, wondering, wanting....

'I don't know if you know, but it's Ellie's birthday today,' she said, 'and I thought I'd treat her to a really nice lunch somewhere. You won't mind if I take her off and she's a bit late back, will you, Michael?'

Lunch...*yes,* he thought exultantly. He couldn't wait to have more of this enchanting woman.

'Actually, I'd decided to do the same myself,' he quickly informed her. 'Lunch at the Mariners Bar.'

'Oh, wow! The Mariners Bar!' Her eyes sparkled with golden lights. 'What a lovely boss you are to take Ellie there!'

'Why don't you join us? It will be a better celebration of her birthday if you do.'

'I'll come, as well. Make a party of it,' Harry put in, instantly supporting the idea.

Four was better than three, Michael decided. Harry had to know now that Lucy wasn't interested in him, and he could entertain Elizabeth, which took the onus of doing that off him.

'I only booked a table for two,' his PA inserted, pulling them back to arrangements already made.

'No problem. I'm sure the maître d' will make room for us,' he stated, oozing confidence as he smiled at Lucy. 'We'd be delighted to have the pleasure of your company.'

Her smile of delight was turned to her sister. 'Well, a foursome should be more fun, don't you think, Ellie?'

There was a touch of irony in Elizabeth's reply. 'Certainly no awkward silences with you, Lucy.'

She laughed, seeming to sprinkle sunshine at everyone as she happily declared, 'That's settled then. Thank you for asking me, Michael. And it's good of you to join in the party, too, Harry.'

Michael wasn't interested in having a party.

What Harry called his tunnel vision—usually applied only to his work on the franchises—had kicked in with a vengeance on Lucy Flippence. He saw no one but her. His entire focus, physical and mental, was on her. He wanted her completely to himself.

It didn't occur to him that it might not be a good idea to bed his PA's sister.

All he could think of was how to get her there as fast as he could.

CHAPTER THREE

LUCY COULDN'T BELIEVE her luck. The prince liked her, wanted to be with her. And what a prince he was, not only drop-dead gorgeous, but a billionaire to boot! Ellie had said enough about the Finn Franchises for her to know this guy was seriously wealthy, but had never mentioned he was also seriously sexy.

Which gave Lucy pause for thought as they made their way out of the building and across the Esplanade to the boardwalk that ran along the water's edge of the park leading to the marina. Was there something *wrong* with Michael Finn, something that had put Ellie off being attracted to him? Was he a terribly demanding boss? Lucy wasn't keen on *demanding* men. If he had struck himself off Ellie's possibility list, Lucy needed to know why before jumping in the deep end with Michael Finn.

Though it was a beautiful day and her heart was singing. There was no reason not to enjoy this exciting attraction while it was still lovely and shiny. As soon as they paired off on the boardwalk, the two of them in front, Ellie and Harry behind, Michael gave Lucy a smile that tingled right down to her toes.

'Tell me about yourself, Lucy,' he invited. 'How did you come to be in cemetery administration? You look as though you should be a model.'

He had silver-grey eyes—very distinctive, like the rest of him—and she was thrilled that he was interested in her, if only for a little while. Words bubbled out in an effervescent stream. She told him about her experience of modelling—its advantages and disadvantages—then tour guide jobs she'd had, and he laughed at the amusing stories about people who'd made guiding both difficult and hilarious at times. Moving on to her stint in the dance studio, she was prompted to ask, 'Do you dance, Michael? I mean, do you like dancing?'

It was a strike against him if he didn't.

He grinned at her, half singing, 'I've got rhythm... you've got rhythm....'

She laughed in delight.

'Our mother insisted that Harry and I have dancing lessons when we were kids,' he went on. 'Said it was a mandatory social skill and we would enjoy it in the end. We grumbled and groaned at having to miss sport for girlie dancing, but she was right. You could get the same adrenaline rush out of dancing as you can out of sport.'

'A case of mother knows best,' Lucy remarked.

He winced ruefully. 'She always did.'

Seeing the change of expression, Lucy softly asked, 'Does that mean your mother is not still with you?'

It drew a quizzical look. 'Don't you recall the plane crash that took both my parents?'

'No. I'm sorry, but...'

'It was all over the newspapers, the media....'

She wasn't about to admit that her dyslexia made

reading newspapers too difficult. 'How long ago was this?'

'Close to ten years.' His frown lifted. 'Maybe you were too young to take much notice. How old are you, Lucy?'

'Twenty-eight. And just over ten years ago my mother died of cancer. I didn't take much notice of anything for a while, Michael.'

'Ah…understandable.'

His face relaxed into a smile again and Lucy was highly relieved that a sympathetic bond had been established. She pushed it further, saying, 'I don't have a father, either. He deserted us before Mum died. It's just me and Ellie now.'

'Do you live together?'

'Yes. We share an apartment. Ellie is a wonderful sister.'

The voice of her wonderful sister shattered the lovely build-up of understanding. It was raised in extreme vexation, crying out, 'That's because you're so annoying!'

Startled, Lucy instantly swung around, anxious that nothing go wrong today. Michael turned, too. Seeing that she'd drawn their attention, Ellie rolled her eyes at her companion and huffed in obvious exasperation before saying, 'It's okay. Harry was just being Harry.'

Guilt swirled around Lucy's mind. Had she inadvertently lumped Ellie on her birthday with a man she didn't like, spoiling the nice lunch her sister had been anticipating with Michael? Being completely star-struck by the storybook prince, Lucy might have been blindly selfish in so quickly agreeing to a foursome, not really consulting Ellie about whether it was okay with her.

'Be nice to Elizabeth, Harry,' Michael chided, 'It's her birthday.'

'I *am* being nice,' he protested.

Ellie didn't lose her temper over nothing, Lucy thought, taking proper stock of Michael's brother. He was a very manly man, his white T-shirt and shorts displaying a lot of firm muscle and smoothly tanned skin. The slightly bent nose stopped him from being classically handsome, but the riot of black curls and the bedroom blue eyes gave him a strong, rather raffish attraction. He exuded a confidence that probably meant he was used to being popular with the opposite sex, but he'd be dead in the water with Ellie if she perceived him as a playboy.

'Try harder,' Michael advised, dismissing the distraction by lightly grasping Lucy's elbow and turning her away with him to continue their stroll together.

She couldn't dismiss it so easily. 'Does Ellie dislike your brother, Michael?' she asked, hating the feeling that this foursome had been a very bad idea.

If it was, she had to break it up, regardless of the miracle meeting with this man. A real prince who was truly, deeply attracted to her would pursue a relationship, anyway. It wasn't fair to Ellie, messing up her birthday with a man she found hard to tolerate. Better for them to dump the men and go off together, though that was tricky with Michael being Ellie's boss.

'I don't think it's a case of *dislike*,' he answered with a slightly wry grimace. 'I've never known anyone to dislike Harry. He's a natural charmer, but he does tend to ruffle Elizabeth's feathers with his flirting.'

There was flirting and *flirting,* Lucy thought, and some of it could get a bit icky.

'Don't worry,' Michael went on. 'He'll behave himself now. I've warned him.'

That made no difference if, deep down, Ellie couldn't abide the man. Lucy needed to have a private word with her, suss out the situation to her satisfaction. Impossible right here. They had walked past the park with the children's playgrounds, and were level with the swimming lagoon. Another ten minutes' stroll would bring them to the Mariners Bar, Hopefully, she would get the chance to be alone with Ellie in the cocktail lounge before they went into the dining-room.

In the meantime there was no point in not making the most of Michael's company.

'We'd got up to dancing,' he reminded her with a grin, the grey eyes lit with amused curiosity. 'Modelling, tour guiding, dancing—how did this lead to cemetery administration?'

'Oh, there's a lot of stuff in between,' she said airily. 'I was doing a beautician course while the dancing was paying off. That led to jobs in a department store and two of the holiday resorts up here.' She slanted him a twinkling look. 'I do a great foot massage and pedicure if you ever need one.'

He laughed. 'A woman of many talents.'

She loved the sound of his laugh. It echoed in her ears and seemed to ripple down to her heart, where it tripped her pulse into racing overtime.

What was she going to do if his brother was a frog? *Please don't let him be,* she silently begged. It would ruin this highly promising lunch.

Michael kept asking her questions, seemingly intrigued by her, which was a lovely feeling. Most guys wanted to talk about themselves. He gave her the sense that he'd never met anyone like her before and he couldn't get enough of her, not right now, anyway. Whether that would last... Well, nothing usually did, not on this kind of high, but Lucy couldn't help revelling in it.

Of course, he wouldn't be intrigued by her at all if he knew the truth—that she didn't just flit from one job to another because she was attracted to something new and different. More times than not she ran into an unavoidable snag because of her dyslexia, and she was either let go or moved on before she had to suffer the humiliation of being found wanting again. Her disability was a curse she had to live with, but she was determined to enjoy the good times in between being stumped by it and having to pick herself up and try something else.

Right now the promise of having a very good time with Michael Finn was thrilling her to bits, though she still had to check with Ellie that what was happening was okay with her. She wanted her sister to have a happy birthday. Men came and went in Lucy's life. Ellie was the only person she could count on to always be there for her.

They'd passed the yacht club and were on the path to the cocktail bar adjoining the restaurant when Harry called out to them. 'Hey, Mickey! I'll buy the girls cocktails while you see the maître d' about our table.'

Mickey? Mickey Finn. Lucy rolled her eyes. That was such *boy stuff!* Maybe Harry was simply an overgrown boy, irritating Ellie with his silly immaturity.

'Okay.' Michael tossed back the response, apparently accustomed to being called Mickey by his brother, and not minding it.

Whatever… The arrangement between them would give her some time alone with Ellie in the cocktail bar—time enough to check if the current scenario sucked for her sister.

Michael left them at the bar, striding swiftly into the restaurant to speak to the maître d'. Harry led them to a set of two-seater lounges with a low table in between, and saw them settled facing each other.

'Now let me select cocktails for you both,' he said, the vivid blue eyes twinkling confidence in his choices. 'A margarita for you, Elizabeth.'

It surprised her. 'Why that one?'

He grinned. 'Because you're the salt of the earth and I revere you for it.'

She rolled her eyes at his linking her character to the salt-encrusted rim of the glass that was always used for a margarita cocktail.

Though it was clever, Lucy thought, openly conceding, 'You're right on both counts. Ellie loves margaritas and she *is* the salt of the earth. I don't know what I'd do without her. She's always been my anchor.'

'An anchor,' Harry repeated musingly. 'I think that's what's been missing from my life.'

'An anchor would only weigh you down, Harry,' Ellie put in drily. 'It would feel like an albatross around your neck.'

'Some chains I wouldn't mind wearing.'

'Try gold.'

He laughed.

This quick banter between them gave Lucy pause for speculation. 'Do you two always spar like this?' she asked.

'Sparks invariably fly,' Harry claimed.

Ellie gave him an arch look. 'I would have to admit that being with Harry is somewhat invigorating.'

Lucy laughed and clapped her hands. They were playing a game, scoring points off each other. It wasn't bad at all. 'Oh, I love it! What a great lunch we'll all have together!' She cocked her head at the man who was certainly ruffling Ellie's feathers, but quite possibly in a way her sister found exciting under her surface pretence of indifference. 'What cocktail will you choose for me?'

'For the sunshine girl…a pina colada.'

She clapped her hands again. 'Well done, Harry. That's *my* favourite.'

'At your service.' He twirled his hand in a salute to them both and headed off to the bar.

A charmer, Michael had said, and Lucy could now see how it was. Ellie was attracted to Harry but she didn't trust his charm, maybe thinking he was a bit too slick with it. She should just ride with it, enjoy it, let her hair down and not care where it led.

Lucy leaned forward to press this advice on her sister. 'He's just what you need, Ellie. Loads of fun. You've been carrying responsibility for so long, it's well past time you let loose and had a wild flutter for once. Be a butterfly instead of a worker bee.'

An ironic little smile tilted Ellie's mouth as she drawled, 'I might just do that.'

'Go for it,' Lucy urged, excited by the possibility that

both the brothers could be princes. 'I'm going for Michael. He's an absolute dreamboat. I'm so glad I wasn't held up any longer at the cemetery. I might have missed out on meeting him. Why didn't you tell me your boss was gorgeous?'

'I've always thought him a bit cold.'

Lucy threw up her hands at her sister's lack of discernment. 'Believe me. The guy is hot! He makes me sizzle.'

Ellie shrugged. 'I guess it's a matter of chemistry. Harry is the hot one for me.'

Chemistry…yes! That explained everything. There was nothing *wrong* with Michael. Quite simply, there was no chemistry between him and Ellie, and no one could make that happen. It either did or it didn't. Lucy had met some really nice guys in her time, but there'd been no point in dating them. They just didn't do it for her.

She sat back contentedly, the narky questions that had been niggling at her making a complete exit, leaving her free to fall in love again.

She grinned at Ellie. 'Brothers and sisters…wouldn't it be great if we ended up together, all happy families?'

It was a lovely fantasy! Totally off the wall, because Lucy knew she wasn't good enough to hold on to a man of Michael Finn's calibre. Today was hers. Probably tonight. Maybe she would have him for a week or two if she could manage not to be found wanting by him.

'I think that's a huge leap into the future,' her sister commented, rolling her eyes at Lucy. 'Let's just take one day at a time.'

Sensible, as always.

And completely right, as always.

But Lucy was flying high and didn't want to be brought down to earth.

That could happen tomorrow or the next day or the next....

Today she was over the moon and wanted to stay there.

CHAPTER FOUR

WHILE LUCY DIDN'T believe in big dreams for herself, she saw no reason for Ellie not to have them. Her sister was brilliant at everything. No one could find fault with her. However, her personal life certainly needed brightening, and Harry Finn looked like the right man to do it if she'd simply fling the door open and let him in.

'You're always so sensible, Ellie,' Lucy chided, wanting her to lighten up and take a few risks for once.

'Which is something I value very highly in your sister,' Michael said warmly, picking up on her words as he appeared beside them and seated himself next to her on the lounge.

'Oh, I do, too,' she quickly agreed, liking him all the more for appreciating this quality in his PA. She bestowed a brilliant smile of approval on him as she added, 'But I also want Ellie to have fun.'

'Which is where I come in,' Harry said, also catching her words as he came back. His eyes danced with wicked mischief as he gazed at Ellie. 'Starting with cocktails. The bartender will bring them over. Here are the peanuts and pretzels.'

He placed a bowl of them on the table and settled

himself beside her, throwing her a challenging look that mocked any resistance to having fun with him. She flicked him a sizzling glance in return.

Definitely something hot going on between them, Lucy thought, and gave Harry an approving smile as she asked, 'What cocktail did you order for Michael?'

'A Manhattan. Mickey is highly civilised. He actually forgets about sunshine until it sparkles over him.'

Lucy laughed at the teasing reference to herself as the sunshine girl. 'And for yourself?'

'Ah, the open sea is my business. I'm a salty man, so I share Elizabeth's taste for margaritas.'

'The open sea?' Lucy queried.

'Harry looks after the tourist side of Finn's Fisheries,' Michael answered. 'I take care of buying in the stock for all our franchises.'

'Ah!' She nodded, understanding why Harry was dressed the way he was.

She knew Finn's Fisheries was a huge franchise with outlets all around Australia. They not only stocked every possible piece of fishing gear, a lot of it imported, but the kind of clothing that went with it: wetsuits, swimming costumes, shorts, T-shirts, hats. The range of merchandise was fantastic and Ellie had told her Michael dealt with all that.

She knew about the tourist side, too, having been a tour guide herself. There were Finn dive boats offering adventures around the Great Barrier Reef, Finn deep sea fishing yachts for hire, and for the really rich, the exclusive getaway resort of Finn Island, where she'd never been but would love to go.

Harry couldn't be too much of a playboy if he was

responsible for keeping these enterprises running successfully. She noticed that his white T-shirt with the tropical fish had the emblem of Finn Island printed below his left shoulder, and wondered if he'd come from there this morning. Maybe if she and Michael hit it off really well, he would take her to the glamorous getaway.

Lucy decided she could not have wished for a more exciting situation—Ellie and Harry, she and Michael. The conversation over cocktails zipped with good humour. Ellie drank a second margarita, definitely loosening up, hopefully throwing caution to the winds. A thirtieth birthday was not a time to be overly sensible.

Lucy wanted her sister to have the best possible day.

Which led to making *the mistake!*

They were handed menus as soon as they were seated in the dining-room, and instead of waiting for the others to start talking about the dishes listed, as she usually did, the fact that they were at a top-line restaurant gave her the confidence to say, 'I bet I know what you're going to order, Ellie.'

Her sister raised her eyebrows. 'What?'

Lucy grinned at her. 'The chilli mud crab.' It was her absolute favourite dish.

'Actually, I can't see that on the menu,' Michael said, glancing quizzically at her.

'Oh, I didn't really look. I just assumed,' she replied quickly, silently cursing herself for being an impulsive idiot.

Revealing her disability to a man she wanted to impress—a man as smart as Michael Finn—would make him lose interest in no time flat, and she would shrivel up inside if he got that look on his face—the look that saw her as defective. Hiding her dyslexia was always the best course. Now she had to cover up the stupid mistake.

Pretending to study the menu properly, she asked, 'What have you decided on, Michael?'

'The steak.'

'How about sharing a seafood platter for two with me, Elizabeth?' Harry said, leaning closer to point out the platter's contents on the menu. 'You get crab on it, as well as all the other goodies, and we can nibble away on everything as we please.'

Lucy instantly warmed to him even more—a sweet man, not only caring about her sister's pleasure, but also taking the meal selection heat off herself.

'Harry will eat the lion's share,' Michael warned.

Harry instantly raised a hand for solemn vowing. 'I swear I'll give you first choice of each titbit.'

'Okay, that's a done deal,' she said, closing the menu and slanting him a smile.

'Sealed with a kiss,' he said, bright blue eyes twinkling wickedly as he leaned closer still and pecked her on the cheek.

'You can keep that mouth of yours for eating, Harry,' she snapped, probably on the principle of give him an inch and he'd take a mile.

He grinned. 'Elizabeth, I live for the day when I'll eat you all up.'

'That'll be doomsday.'

'With the gates of heaven opening for me,' Harry retorted, his grin widening.

Lucy couldn't help laughing.

Ellie heaved a long-suffering sigh and shook her head at him. 'You are incorrigible.'

'A man has to do what a man has to do,' he archly declared, sending Lucy off into more peals of laughter.

He *was* fun. And totally irrepressible. She suspected that Ellie was holding out against him because she got a kick out of the sparring, as well as not wanting him to think she was an easy catch.

However, their selection of a seafood platter for two didn't help Lucy with choices. She would have to order the same as Michael, which was okay. The steak should be very good here.

Michael was amused by Harry's determined assault on Elizabeth's defences, amused by her determined resistance to his charm, too. Most women would be lapping it up. His brother was going to have to work hard to win this one over, but the battle served to keep them occupied with each other, leaving him free to pursue the connection with Lucy.

He'd been quite stunned when Elizabeth had turned up at work this morning wearing the gorgeous butterfly blouse—totally atypical of her usual style in clothes. A birthday gift from her sister, she'd said—a sister who was as different from her as chalk and cheese. She was so right about that. He could see Elizabeth as a schoolma'm. Lucy promised to be a delicious array of exotic cheeses, and tasting all of it had already become a must-do in his life.

And despite her choice of *white* clothes today—very sexy white clothes—she was definitely the butterfly, flitting from job to job as though they all had some sweet nectar for her, tasting and moving on, clearly enjoying everything that life could offer her, wanting a whole range of experiences.

Including him.

Saw him, liked him, wanted him.

His head was still spinning with the excitement of her uninhibited response to their meeting. No games, no pretence, no guard up—just lovely open Lucy letting him know she found him as sexy as he found her. It was a struggle not to be in a constant state of arousal.

He thought of Fiona Redman, his most recent ex, who'd definitely been into female power games. The convenience of having her as a sexual partner did not stack up against the annoyance of being expected to toe her lines. No woman was ever going to decide for him when he should work and when he shouldn't. The success of Finn Franchises had been top priority in his life ever since his father's untimely death, and that was not about to change any time soon.

However, he would certainly make time to satisfy this sizzling lust for Lucy. It probably wouldn't last long. The sheer novelty of her would wear off and the usual boredom or irritation would set in. He had never come across the magic glue that could make a relationship stick. He always found fault somewhere and that was the end of it. Quite possibly the fault was in him. Whatever... he was going to enjoy this woman as long as she stayed enjoyable.

The waiter returned and took their orders. Lucy chose the steak, too. Wanting to share everything with him? It was absolutely exhilarating being with her, especially when she turned those big brown eyes on him, the golden specks in them glowing with warmth.

'You said dancing lessons interfered with sport, Michael. What did you like playing?' Dimples flashed in her cheeks as she spoke.

He smiled reminiscently. 'Everything in those days—cricket, baseball, tennis, soccer, rugby.'

'Not now?'

'They were mostly schoolboy passions. I still play tennis, but only socially. I have a couple of games of squash during the week to loosen up from too much desk work, and usually a round of golf at the weekend.' She looked sublimely fit, probably from dancing, but out of interest he asked, 'What about you? Any sporting passions?'

'I can play tennis, but like you, only socially. At school I mostly concentrated on athletics.'

He grinned. 'High-jump champion?'

His instant assumption surprised her. 'How did you guess?'

'Long legs. Great shape, too.'

And he couldn't wait to have them wound around him in an intimate lock.

'You're obviously in great shape yourself,' she retorted, her eyes simmering with the same kind of thoughts, driving his excitement metre higher. Then, as though taking a mental back step, she added, 'I also play netball with a group of friends once a week. I always keep up with my girlfriends. Men can come and go, but real friends stay in your life.'

'You don't count any men as real friends?'

'A few gay guys. They're lovely people. Lots of empathy and caring.'

'No straight ones?'

Her dimples deepened as her luscious lips twitched into a provocative little smile. 'Well, sooner or later most straight men turn into frogs.'

'Frogs?' he repeated, needing enlightenment. He'd heard 'empathy and caring' loud and clear but 'frogs'?

Her eyes danced teasingly at him. 'You suddenly turn up in my life and everything about you shouts that you're a prince amongst men.'

A prince. That was a surprisingly sweet stroke to his ego.

Her hands lifted in a helpless gesture. 'But how do I know you won't turn into a frog tomorrow?'

'Ah!' he said, understanding. 'You've been with guys who haven't lived up to their promise.'

She shrugged prettily, the off-the-shoulder sleeve of her peasant blouse sliding lower on her upper arm. 'It happens,' she said in airy dismissal. 'I'm hoping not to be disappointed with you, Michael.'

The seductive challenge sizzled straight to his groin. He was up for it, all right. He wished he could whizz her straight off to bed. How long would this birthday luncheon go on—main course, sweets, coffee? At least another hour and a half. He'd give Elizabeth the rest of the afternoon off, take Lucy to his penthouse apartment. Although...

'Do you have to get back to work this afternoon?' he asked.

'Yes, I do,' she answered ruefully. 'I have to deliver the angels' heads to the stonemason, take the van back to the office, then visit the people who own the burial plot that's been mistakenly used, and hopefully persuade them that one burial plot is as good as another.'

'Tricky job,' he said with a sympathetic wince.

'Not really. It's a matter of getting them to em-pathise with the bereaved parents who have just laid their daughter to rest—how terrible it would be for them to have her dug up again,' Lucy explained. The caring in her voice moved something in his heart, reminding him of laying his parents to rest, the final closure.

Caring, empathy…he sensed something quite special in this woman. She wasn't just fantastically sexy. There was much more to her. So far it was all good.

'Are you free tonight?' he asked, not wanting to wait any longer to have her to himself.

'Yes.'

Her smile promised an eagerness that matched his for a more intimate encounter. Which made his hard-on even harder.

Fortunately, the waiter showed good timing in arriv-ing with their main course. Their conversation moved to food as they ate their steaks, which were perfectly cooked, asparagus on the side with a touch of Béarnaise sauce, and crunchy roasted potatoes.

Lucy was into cooking, loved experimenting with different combinations of ingredients. Better and bet-ter, Michael thought, looking forward to enjoying many meals with her. She had an infectious enthusiasm for life that made her company an absolute delight. He was wondering if she'd ever cooked frogs legs after bidding a frog goodbye when Harry claimed his attention, lean-ing an elbow on the table and pointing a finger at him.

'Mickey, I have the solution to my problem with the resort.'

The problem that had brought him to the office

this morning—the discovery that the resort manager was feathering his own nest at their expense. Michael frowned over the interruption. He didn't want to talk family business with his brother when he had plans to make with Lucy.

'You have to clear that guy out, Harry,' he said tersely—the same advice he'd given earlier. 'Once you confront him you can't leave him there. The potential for damage…'

'I know, I know. But it's best to confront him with his replacement. We walk in and turf him out. No argument. A done deal.'

Why was he persisting with this discussion here? 'Agreed,' he said impatiently. 'But you don't have a ready replacement yet and the longer he stays—'

'Elizabeth. She's the perfect person for the management job, completely trustworthy, meticulous at checking everything, capable of handling everything you've thrown at her, Mickey.'

That rocked him. Was Harry off his brain, wanting to mix pleasure with business? The way he'd been madly flirting…was he seriously attracted? This didn't feel right.

'Elizabeth is my PA,' Michael stated firmly, giving his brother a steely look.

Harry dug in regardless. 'I'm more in need of her than you are right now. Lend her to me for a month. That will give me time to interview other people.'

'A month…' Michael frowned over the inconvenience to himself. Harry did have a point. He needed a replacement for Sean Cassidy pronto.

'On the other hand, once Elizabeth gets her teeth

into the job, she might want to stay on,' Harry said provocatively.

Michael glowered at him. 'You're not stealing my PA.'

'Her choice, Mickey.' Harry turned to her. 'What do you say, Elizabeth? Will you help me out for a month… stay on the island and get the resort running as it should be run? My about-to-be ex-manager has been cooking the books, skimming off a lot of stuff to line his own pockets. You'll need to do a complete inventory and change the suppliers who've been doing private deals with him. It would be a whole new challenge for you, one that—'

'Now hold on a moment,' Michael growled. 'It's up to me to ask Elizabeth if she'll do it, not you, Harry.' This on-the-spot decision didn't sit well with him, particularly with his brother virtually railroading him into it, yet it was a credible solution to the problem.

'Okay. Ask her.'

Michael heaved an exasperated sigh, disliking the sense of having been pushed into a corner. 'It's true,' he reluctantly conceded. 'You would be helping us out if you'd agree to step in and do what needs to be done at the resort. I have every confidence in your ability to handle the situation. Every confidence in your integrity, too. I hate losing you for a month….'

He grimaced at the prospect. She was his right hand in the office, always understanding and delivering whatever was needed. Gritting his teeth, he muttered, 'I guess someone from the clerical staff can fill in for a while….'

'Andrew. Andrew Cook,' she suggested, which meant she had already decided to go with Harry.

'Too stodgy. No initiative,' Michael said, hating the idea of having to do without her.

'Absolutely reliable in doing whatever task he's set,' she argued.

'I take it that's a yes to coming to the island with me,' Harry noted, grinning from ear to ear.

She shot him a quelling look. 'I'm up for the challenge of fixing the management problems, nothing else, Harry.'

Good! Michael thought. Elizabeth wasn't about to mix business with pleasure. If that was on Harry's mind, as well as solving his predicament, she'd spike his guns and serve him right, given that he'd have to put up with Andrew Cook while she was away.

'That's it then,' he said, resigned to a month of having to spell out everything to his *pro tem* PA.

'A whole month! I'll miss you, Ellie,' Lucy said wistfully.

Ah, yes! A month of Lucy without her sister possibly butting into their relationship, Michael thought, realising and appreciating the one upside of this situation. It could have been tricky having his PA an ever-present watchdog while he bedded her sister. Absolute freedom from that felt good. A month might very well be the limit of this currently hot connection, anyway—everything done and dusted before Elizabeth returned to take up her position with him again.

'The time will pass quickly enough,' she assured Lucy.

The waiter arrived with the sweets they'd ordered when he'd cleared away their main course.

'We need to get moving on this,' Harry muttered as he dug into his chocolate mud cake.

'As soon as possible,' Michael agreed, looking forward to having intimate time with Lucy.

'Today,' Harry decided, checking his watch. 'It's only three o'clock now. We could be over on the island by four-thirty. Have him helicoptered out by six. We leave here when we've finished our sweets, hop on the boat....'

'It is Elizabeth's birthday, Harry,' Michael reminded him. 'She might have other plans for today.'

'No, I'm good to go,' she said.

Great! he thought. No delay to what he wanted.

'What about clothes and toiletries and stuff?' Lucy put in. 'You're going for a month, Ellie.'

'You can pack for her, Lucy,' Harry said decisively. 'Mickey can take you home, wait while you do it, take Elizabeth's bags and arrange their shipping to the island.'

'No problem,' Michael said, smiling at Lucy. 'I'll give you my phone number. Give me a call when you've finished work and I can come by your apartment this evening.'

She'd be there all by herself. Perfect!

Her eyes danced with pleasure as she agreed to the plan, and her smile was full of sensual promise.

Michael decided he didn't care what Harry did with Elizabeth.

Let them sail off into the sunset!

He was going to make hay with the sunshine girl!

CHAPTER FIVE

LUCY WAS NERVOUS. Excited, too. Much more excited than she usually was about having a first date with a new man, which was probably what was making her so nervous. Plus the fact that Michael Finn was a high-flyer and she had never connected with anyone from his level of society. She was definitely out of his league in any social sense, and more than likely he only wanted a sexual fling with her, which she might as well accept right now and not get herself in a twist about it.

Regardless of his intentions, she wanted to be with him, wanted to experience him, so no way was she going to back off at this point. Besides, a Cinderella could win a prince. Miracles could happen. Failing that, if the worst came to the worst, she could write off her time with him as a case of real lust being satisfied. Because while she had certainly fancied other guys in the past—not like this, not nearly as strongly as this—Michael Finn had her in an absolute tizzy of lust.

Just thinking of him, she was squeezing her thighs together, and when she'd been in the shower earlier, running her hands over herself, dying to know how it would feel with his hands caressing her naked body.

Even now as she prepared the Thai salad to go with the prawns she'd bought on the way home, her stomach muscles kept contracting.

He'd be here soon—another ten minutes or so. The apartment was tidy. The table was set. She'd changed into a yellow wraparound dress with a tie belt that could be easily undone, and underneath it she wore her sexiest white lace bra and panties, wickedly intent on knocking his socks off, though he probably wouldn't wear socks. Or shoes. Easily slipped off scuffs, she decided, like hers. She'd deliberately left off jewellery, not wanting it to get in the way. Her only adornment was a frangipani flower she'd picked off the tree in the front yard and stuck in her hair.

She imagined him wearing shorts and an open-necked sports shirt that could be pulled off in a second. Would he have a hairy chest? Not too hairy, she hoped, but having such thick black hair, and obviously loaded with testosterone, he was bound to have some. She couldn't wait to see, to touch. Her fingers were tingling with anticipation.

The doorbell rang.

Her heart started pounding.

Please let him be a prince tonight, she wildly prayed. *Please let him not do or say anything to put me off him. I want this night to be perfect.*

The rush of desire steaming through her made her legs feel weak as she walked to the door and opened it. Her breath caught in her throat at seeing him again— so stunningly handsome, and the silver-grey eyes shining with pleasure at seeing her. She barely managed a husky 'Hi!'

His smile was dazzling. 'I've been looking forward to this moment ever since we parted this afternoon,' he said, the lovely deep tone of his voice sending a thrill through her.

'Me, too,' she said, smiling back. 'Come on in, Michael.'

He was wearing shorts and a sports shirt—navy and red and white, a strong combination that emphasised his alpha maleness. He handed her a bottle of wine as he stepped into the living-room. 'To go with whatever you've planned to feed me.'

She laughed. 'It's only a light meal. It was a very substantial lunch.'

'Perfect!' He matched the word to the glance encompassing her appearance before adding, 'It's a light wine, too.'

A very good one, she thought as she glanced at the label—Oyster Bay Sauvignon Blanc. Almost giddy with excitement, she certainly didn't need alcohol to feel intoxicated, but she asked, 'Do you want to open it now?'

'When we eat,' he said dismissively, taking in her living space. 'This is a wonderfully welcoming room, Lucy. Did you do the decorating?'

It was a fairly standard two-bedroom apartment, one bathroom and an open kitchen combined with the living area, but she was proud of how they had turned it into their home, and Michael's approval of it was especially pleasing. She set the bottle of wine on the kitchen counter so she could use her hands to gesture at various items as she answered him.

'Ellie bought the basic furniture. I added the cushions and the wall posters and the rug in front of the lounge. We wanted it to be a cheerful place to come home to, and with the walls and floor tiles being white, the whole place virtually begged for bright splashes of colour.'

'You've done a brilliant job.' He gave her another dazzling smile, setting off a fountain of joy inside her. 'My mother was great at using colour to please the eye, too.'

Being compared to his mother felt like a huge compliment. Lucy beamed at him. 'I'm glad you like it.'

He shook his head slightly as he moved towards where she stood in front of the kitchen counter, 'There's nothing not to like about you, Lucy.'

The lovely low throb in his voice set her stomach aflutter and her heart leapt into a wild gallop when his hands started sliding around her waist. Her own hands automatically lifted to his shoulders as he drew her closer, gently pressing her lower body to his. The silvery-grey eyes darkened with a storm of feeling, searching hers for a reflection of the same storm.

'I don't want to wait any longer,' he said, the plea edged with urgent demand.

'I don't, either,' she admitted without hesitation, every atom of her body yearning to know all of him.

Her lips were already eagerly parted as he bent his head to kiss her. When his mouth made contact with hers—an incredibly sensual first taste—her head whirled with the sudden roaring of her blood. She moaned softly, deep in her throat, as his tongue slid over hers, sweeping her mouth with acute sensation. The kiss fast became more fiercely demanding, driving her into a wild response. The lust that had been simmering since the first moment of meeting flared into passionate need.

Her hands buried themselves in his hair, fingers raking through the thickness of it, grasping his head possessively. His hands clutched the cheeks of her bottom, scooping her hard against him, pressing her so close his erection furrowed her stomach, exciting her further with his strong arousal. Her whole body started aching for him. Her thighs quivered with the fierce desire to feel him inside her, and the rush of hot wetness between them begged for instant satisfaction.

The gloriously devouring mouth suddenly abandoned hers, breaking away to snatch air in ragged gasps. 'Lucy…' It was a groan of wanting.

'Yes… Yes…let's do it.' The response spilled straight off her tongue.

In a spurt of frenetic energy she pushed herself out of his embrace to lead him into her bedroom. 'Come on,' she urged, untying the belt of her dress, taking off the light garment and tossing it onto the lounge as she passed, turning as she reached the bedroom door, looking back to see how he was responding to her wanton invitation.

He'd spun around and was facing her, but seemed stunned into immobility, an incredulous look in the eyes that were raking her from head to toe. His glittery silver gaze lingered on the white lace panties and bra long enough to make the wetness hotter and turn her nipples into bullets.

'You do want me?' she asked provocatively, wondering if he was more used to leading the action than having a woman doing it.

'Oh, yes! Madly!'

The vehement reply shot a bolt of elation into a gurgle of laughter.

He tore off his shirt and hurled it on top of her discarded dress. He did have hair on his chest—a nest of black curls across the centre of it, arrowing down to where his hands were unfastening his shorts. Fascinated, she watched as he pulled them down and stepped out of his remaining clothes. More black curls framed his manhood, which was magnificently primed for action.

Her insides quaked with anticipation. Nevertheless, she never forgot caution, and didn't this time, either. The urge to step back and touch him was irresistible. She took him in her hand, fingers gently stroking the silky skin of his strong shaft as she lifted her gaze to his, appealing for understanding. 'I need you to wear a condom, Michael.'

'Right!' he said, sucking in air and shaking his head as though trying to clear it, while reaching for his shorts again and extracting a packet, holding it up for her to see. 'I did come prepared.' He raised a quizzical eyebrow. 'You're not on the Pill?'

She slid her other hand up his chest, spreading her fingers into the black curls. 'Yes, I am, but that's not protection from everything.' Her eyes flashed him a look of troubled uncertainty. 'I don't know who you've been with before me, Michael.'

He frowned. 'I assure you I'm clean.'

'I want you to be, but I won't risk my health,' she pleaded.

His mouth twisted into a rueful grimace. 'Fair

enough!' He lifted a hand to her cheek, a sympathetic look in his eyes as he stroked where she usually dimpled. 'You've been with a frog who lied to you?'

She grinned at his pick-up on frogs. 'No. I just believe in being careful.'

He grinned back. 'Okay. I'll see a doctor tomorrow. Get a clearance. Can we do without condoms then?'

She flung her arms around his neck, her eyes dancing with relief and pleasure as she rubbed her body invitingly against his. 'You're looking ahead to more of me?'

'Much more,' he assured her in his deep-throated voice.

She lifted herself up on tiptoes and kissed him, deliriously happy that he had so readily accepted her conditions, and he didn't see her as a one-night stand.

He instantly took the initiative from her, claiming her mouth with wildly erotic passion, clamping her body to his, driving up the urgency of the desire churning through both of them. He broke the raging intimacy of their kissing long enough to command action. 'Put your feet on top of mine, Lucy.'

She did and he walked her backwards, keeping her locked to him, the movement making her acutely aware of the hard muscular tension in his thighs, in his entire body. Her breasts were brushing the broad hot wall of his chest, tingling with excitement. Her skin felt electric, buzzing with sensory overload. She couldn't wait to be completely naked, too, feeling all of his maleness everywhere.

As soon as he'd turned into her bedroom, one of his hands slid to her bra clip and unfastened it. Impatient for all barriers to be gone, she unwound her arms from his neck and stepped off his feet, quickly pushing the straps from her shoulders, flinging the bra away, grabbing the top of her lace panties and pulling them down enough to lift her legs out of them.

Michael was wasting no time, either, tearing open the packet of condoms, sheathing himself. She straightened up and for one sizzling moment they looked at each other, revelling in the sight of their sexuality completely open to view. He was perfect, Lucy thought, absolutely perfect, and the glittering desire in his eyes told her she was just as excitingly perfect to him.

He startled her by suddenly swooping and lifting her off her feet, crushing her to his chest. It was a small-ish room. The bed was close by, a couple steps away.

'You bring out the caveman in me,' he said gruffly.

She laughed, bubbling over with elation at the possessiveness of his action. When he carried her onto the bed, the same streak of possessiveness swept through her as she wound her legs around his hips in aggressive ownership.

Take me, take me. The words were pounding through her mind, the fierce need to take *him* thrumming through her whole body. She was open to him, dying for him, and he didn't keep her waiting, plunging inside her so fast she gasped at the glorious sensation of the aching emptiness being totally filled, powerfully filled.

She clutched him to her, wanting to hold him there, wanting to hold on to this awesome moment, live her awareness of it to the full. 'Michael...' She breathed his name—the man who lived this moment with her.

'Open your eyes, Lucy,' he commanded.

She hadn't realised she'd closed them, keeping the

high mountain of feeling to herself. But yes, she wanted
to share it with him, have him share what he was feeling with her. She opened her eyes wide and caught the
fierce intensity in his—the need to know, the desire to
take all that she was.

'Keep them open.'

She did, watching him watch her as he began a
rhythm of retreat and thrust that slowly escalated to
a faster and faster beat, on and on until she was arching, bucking, writhing with the pleasure of it, the excitement, the exquisite tension, building, building to
a crescendo of almost agony, teetering on the unbearable. She cried out, her eyes wildly demanding release,
her hands clawing his back, her feet goading him on
in desperate need, her heart seemingly on the point of
bursting.

'Yes…' The word hissed from between his teeth and
his eyes blazed with sheer animal triumph as he drove
himself into her as deeply as he could, and the agony
shattered, melting away on wave after wave of ecstasy
emanating from the spasms that convulsed around him.

'Yes…' she echoed, with a moan of sweet pleasure,
feeling him pulsating, too, his body shuddering in his
own explosive release, his chest heaving for breath, and
when he collapsed on top of her, it seemed his heart
was drumming in sync with hers, a testament to their
utter togetherness.

Long may it last, Lucy fiercely willed.

She'd never had a man like Michael Finn in her life.

She wanted what they had right now to go on and
on forever.

Of course it wouldn't…couldn't.

Loopy Lucy—which was what the kids at school had called her—was not good enough to hold on to this top-of-the-scale man for long. *Just cherish the moment,* she told herself. *Hug it tight.* Make it a memory she could hold on to. Unless she suffered amnesia or Alzheimer's disease, nothing could take great memories away from her.

They were hers forever.

CHAPTER SIX

Wow!

For a while it was the only word in Michael's mind. He had been conscious enough of his heaviness on top of Lucy to roll onto his side, but he took her with him, ensuring their togetherness continued. She hooked her leg around him, as intent as he was on maintaining their intimate connection. Her incredibly sexy breasts were softly heaving against his chest. Her warm breath was wafting over his throat. Her arms embraced him as though she wanted to stay clamped to him forever.

She was…amazing!

So uninhibited about showing her desire for him, voicing it, moving on it… no woman in his memory had ever been so actively inviting, making him feel he was amazing to her. His heart started thumping again as he recalled her peeling off her yellow dress, revealing the lovely curve of her back, the long glorious legs and her cheeky bottom fringed in white lace. Then stepping back to stroke him…

His mind had been so blown by her he might well have forgotten the condoms if she hadn't brought up the safe sex issue. He was glad that she had. It was best to be careful. They had no history between them. Only today. But there were going to be a lot of tomorrows. He'd get a health clearance as soon as he could, do away with the condoms so there'd be nothing between him and the whole sensual experience of Lucy Flippence.

His PA's sister…

Amazing!

She was certainly the best possible consolation prize for losing Elizabeth to Harry for a month.

When Michael grew too soft for her to hold him in, she sighed and moved her head to look at him, her big brown eyes shiny with pleasure, a smile of contentment curving her mouth. 'That was fantastic, Michael,' she said happily.

'Fantastic!' he agreed, grinning in turn.

'Shall we go and have a shower together?'

'Nothing I'd like better.'

She laughed, disentangling herself from him and rolling off the bed. 'I'll go and turn the taps on. We don't have a mixer in the shower and you have to be almost a rocket scientist to get the temperature right using both taps. I don't want you to get scalded and—' her eyes danced teasingly '—I don't want you to have a cold shower, either.'

She made him laugh. She made him feel happy. He suddenly realised he hadn't felt this happy for a long time. The sunshine girl… He smiled over the aptness of the name as he followed her to the bathroom.

Showering together was another sensual delight, caressing each other with soap, doing what should have been foreplay, except they'd been in too much of a hurry. He loved her breasts, large enough to fill his hands and firm enough to hold their beautiful shape. The areolae were brown, a very distinctive frame for her enticing nipples, which he'd definitely pay more attention to later this evening…though possibly not much later. He was hardening again under Lucy's erotic ministrations.

'Mmm…' she murmured, looking down at him and cocking her head with a considering air. 'Maybe we should do what we have to do first, or we might never get it done.'

'What do we have to do?' he asked, dropping a kiss on her forehead.

'Pack a bag for Ellie. And we could open your bottle of wine and eat what I've prepared.' Lucy met his gaze, eyes twinkling with mischief. 'Not that you look as if you need to build up your strength, Michael, but it might be even better if we wait a bit.'

'Okay.' He didn't mind waiting, knowing what was coming. 'Elizabeth won't need much,' he informed her. 'She'll be wearing the island uniform while she's on duty, the same as Harry had on today—white shorts and T-shirt with the Finn Island emblem. She'll be supplied with those clothes.'

'So, it's toiletries, make-up, underclothes….' Lucy turned off the taps, stepped out of the shower, grabbed a towel for herself and handed him one as she listed the items to be packed. 'Pyjamas, dressing-gown, the gorgeous caftan I bought her for swanning around in.' She grinned at him. 'It will certainly catch Harry's eye.'

'I'm not sure that would be doing your sister a favour.'

The remark earned him a sharp look. 'You think he wouldn't be good for her?'

Michael shook his head. 'I didn't mean that.'

'What then? Ellie is very dear to me. I don't want her hurt.'

He shrugged. 'I simply have the impression she doesn't approve of my brother. The way he flirts…'

'Mmm…probably doesn't trust him yet. I think she was badly let down by a guy about two years ago. Put her right off men. Harry will have his work cut out winning her over, but she is attracted to him. No question.' Lucy wrapped her towel around her, tucking it in above her breasts.

'What about you?' he asked, wrapping his own towel around his waist.

'What about me?'

'How long have you been unattached?'

'Oh, a couple of weeks,' she answered, waving an airy hand as she headed out of the bathroom.

'You weren't devastated by the break up?'

'Not at all. I'd been going off him for some time and I finally called it a day.'

She entered a second bedroom. He followed, watching as she opened a built-in wardrobe and lifted down a medium-size travel bag from the top shelf. 'This should do,' she said, smiling at him as she turned to lay it on the bed, waving at a chair in front of a computer desk. 'Take a seat while I pack.'

He sat, noting that Elizabeth's room was very different from Lucy's—no vivid colours, less random clutter, more orderly, somehow not as endearing in personality. 'Why did you go off him?' he asked, curious about Lucy's dislikes in a man.

She rolled her eyes. 'He was getting to be a control

freak, wanting everything his way. In my book, relationships should be a two-way street. I am not going to be told what to do, what to wear or what to say, and he actually started answering for me when people asked me questions….' She threw up her hands.

'No respect for the person you are,' Michael deduced, liking her stance for individuality.

'How come you're unattached?' She tossed the question at him, returning to the wardrobe to fetch clothes.

'I wasn't available enough for the last woman I was involved with. She thought I should take off from work any time at all, specifically when she wanted me to.'

'Ah!' Lucy grinned at him as she brought an armload of garments to the bag. 'No respect for your position.'

He nodded. 'Altogether too self-centred.'

She shook her head, wryly remarking, 'It starts off good. You think it's going to be great. Then it all goes downhill.' Her eyes sparkled brightly at him. 'Let's make a deal, Michael. I won't try to change you and you won't try to change me. If we don't gel as we are, then we accept that and part with no hard feelings.'

'Sounds good to me.'

He didn't want to change one thing about Lucy Flippence. Her directness and spontaneity were a delight. He imagined her last guy had been the type to want to catch a butterfly, put it in a bottle, poison it and pin it to a board so it could never fly away and attract anyone else's eye. She was well rid of him.

'I'll just grab Ellie's toiletries and make-up from the bathroom and pack them before I add the good stuff. Don't move. I'll be right back,' she instructed.

It was strange being in his PA's bedroom. It actually felt like an intrusion of her private life, which he'd known nothing about until Lucy had enlightened him. He hoped Harry would be careful with Elizabeth, not treat her feelings lightly if he pursued the attraction that Lucy was so sure of.

Maybe a trip over to the island might be a wise move, to check out what was happening between them. In a month's time Michael wanted a fully functional Elizabeth back in the office with him, and that might not be how it would end up if his brother messed with her emotions.

Lucy waltzed back in with her plunder from the bathroom.

'Are you free this coming weekend?' he asked her.

'Free as a bird,' she answered blithely, placing Elizabeth's essentials in the bag.

Or a butterfly, Michael thought, smiling over his image of her. 'We could go over to Finn Island, see how your sister's doing, stay Saturday night and enjoy the facilities ourselves.'

Her face lit with delight and she clapped her hands in excitement at the prospect. 'I'd love that, Michael.'

'I'll call Harry tomorrow, set it up.'

'Wonderful! I know about Finn Island, of course— exclusive getaway, open bar, gourmet food—but I've never been there. Do you go often yourself?' she asked as she returned to the wardrobe to select more clothes.

'No. Harry oversees everything to do with the island.'

'I didn't mean for business.'

'For pleasure?'

'Yes. I imagine it's very romantic.'

Michael laughed. 'With the right companion, yes. It's not such a paradise with the wrong one.'

'Well, I hope it will be paradise for us,' she said, grinning at him while proceeding to load up the bag. 'This should see Ellie through. She can tell me on the weekend if she needs more.' Having zipped it shut, Lucy grinned at him again. 'Now food and wine and fun in the kitchen.'

Michael was happy with that program.

She led him back to the living room, where she whipped away her towel, picked up the yellow dress, put it on—without underclothes—and turned to him as she did up the tie belt, her eyes dancing teasingly. 'This is safer for me while cooking, but you can keep your towel, Michael.'

He did, enjoying the idea that he was as accessible to her touch as she was to his in the wraparound dress. She quickly provided glasses and he opened the bottle of wine, while she removed a prepared salad and a plate of prawns from the refrigerator.

It was fun in the kitchen. Lucy was playful, provocative and positively entrancing. She had a wonderfully expressive face and he loved watching it as she talked and laughed, loved how her dress swished with the sway of her hips and the bodice gaped with each movement of her breasts. She was so delectably female, absolutely adorable and incredibly sexy.

The meal they sat down to was perfect: prawns cooked in a Thai dressing with a touch of ginger and chilli, accompanied by a very tasty salad. Lucy ate with uninhibited relish. Just watching her enjoy the food was erotic. She emitted a joy in life that Michael realised he'd been missing ever since his parents had died.

There'd been pleasures—many of them, from many sources—but this unadulterated sense of joy bubbling over... His mother had been like that, as though every day the sun shone just for her, and life was always beautiful. The gift of happiness, he thought. Lucy had it, too. Maybe he had found the woman he could spend the rest of his life with.

The fanciful thought surprised him. What had it been—about nine hours since he'd met Lucy? She made an incredible impact, but it was far too early to be entertaining any thoughts about a future with her beyond the month he'd given himself. As she'd said herself, it starts off good then it all goes downhill. Right now it was great, but 'downhill' was probably on its way, sooner or later.

After they had cleaned up after their meal they returned to the bedroom, both of them intent on a slower build-up to ultimate intimacy. Michael loved Lucy's total lack of inhibitions, her innate sensuality, the exquisite delicacy of her tantalising caresses. She inspired him to stroke, kiss and taste her all over, revelling in her responses. It was an act of extreme control to hold off taking her until she begged him to do so, intense need making her voice shrill. His own excitement was at fever pitch and their coming together was even more incredibly satisfying than before.

He was conscious of a wildly primitive elation, almost a sense of triumph in bringing her to such a powerful peak of wanting him. She climaxed almost immediately and he exulted in the hot creaminess of her as he drove towards his own climax—a fiercely ecstatic release that left him floating in a sea of joy.

When he finally kissed Lucy goodbye that night, he carried the joy with him. How this relationship would turn out—whether they'd be compatible as a couple or not—he didn't know and didn't care. He was going to take whatever he could of Lucy Flippence until the joy of her ran out.

CHAPTER SEVEN

LUCY WAS ON cloud nine. Michael had wanted to be with her every night this week. Even on Wednesday evening, when she played netball with her friends, he'd come to the gym to watch her in action, and quite happily suffered being introduced to a group of hot, sweaty women. So far he'd been an absolutely perfect lover, showing no froglike tendencies at all. He was charming, considerate, always ready to laugh with her, have fun, and tomorrow he was taking her to Finn Island, which would surely be paradise.

Her heart was pounding with excitement as she walked along the Esplanade, anticipating their date this evening. Michael had to work late and he'd asked her to meet him at Danini's, a very chic Italian restaurant, at eight o'clock for dinner. He'd booked a table, which was just as well, because there was a crowd of people out and about—lots of tourists enjoying the warm weather, visiting the night markets and filling up most of the tables in the pavement section of the many restaurants catering to them.

'Do you want to sit inside or out?' Michael had asked her before making the booking.

'Out,' she'd answered, preferring the evening breeze off the ocean to air-conditioning, and the hustle and bustle of the street to the relative seclusion of an inside dining-room. She enjoyed watching people, and if she had to wait for Michael to arrive, it would pass the time pleasantly.

As it turned out, she didn't have to wait. Although it was five minutes short of eight o'clock when she arrived at Danini's, Michael was already seated at a table.

'You're early,' Lucy declared, greeting him with a happy smile.

'So are you,' he said, returning her smile as he stood to hold out her chair.

She laughed, instantly feeling giddy in his presence. 'I didn't want to miss out on any time together.'

'Nor did I.'

His eyes sparkled with silvery glints, and Lucy's heart was skipping with happiness as she sat down. A pina colada was on the table in front of her. 'Oh, you've bought me my favourite cocktail, too. Thank you, Michael.'

'Your pleasure is my pleasure,' he said in his deep, warm voice, resuming his seat opposite her.

He was a beautiful, beautiful man. A true prince, Lucy thought, thanking her lucky stars that she had met him. This was an experience she could treasure for the rest of her life.

He handed her a menu, which was always a tricky business for her. 'Have you decided already on what you want to order?' she asked.

He nodded. 'The veal scallopini.'

'I'll have the same.'

'What about sweets?'

She grinned at him as she closed the menu. 'I'll watch what's being served at other tables and see what appeals most.'

He laughed and set his menu aside, content to wait for her decision. A waiter arrived very promptly and took their order, leaving them both to settle back comfortably and enjoy each other's company.

'There's a charity ball at the casino next Saturday night,' Michael told her. 'I bought tickets months ago, more to contribute to the charity than with any intent of attending, but we can join a group of my friends if you'd like to come and dance with me.'

'I'd love to dance with you,' she said truthfully, though meeting his high society friends was a bit of a worry. Regardless of that problem, however, the invitation to the ball was proof he was anticipating a second week with her, which was marvellous.

'Then I'll look forward to it,' he said, looking pleased.

Lucy firmly told herself the invitation also proved Michael wasn't worried about how she'd mix with his peers. On the other hand, he was a man, and on the whole, men didn't look for shortcomings in her. It was the women who could get narky if they thought she didn't fit in with them.

Her friends had all raved over Michael. What woman wouldn't? He had everything!

His friends would undoubtedly be running a more critical eye over her.

The ball at the casino would be a test of whether their relationship could stand up in his world.

Lucy hoped she would pass it with flying colours.

Though Michael had to, as well. For him it would be a test of how well he tried to integrate her with his group of friends, whether he would stand by her side as a true prince would if she ran into difficulties, protect her if she needed protecting. It would be lovely to feel secure with him.

There had been no security in her mother's marriage—not emotional or financial or even physical security—and Lucy knew she would never commit herself to any man long-term unless she was confident she would be safe with him in every sense. Not that she was expecting long-term with Michael, just hoping for longer than her relationships with guys usually ran.

Determined to being prepared when meeting his friends, she gave him an inviting smile and said, 'Tell me about the people we'll be with at the ball.'

Happy to oblige, he described one married couple who ran a wedding bureau specialising in the Japanese market, since it was much cheaper to have a wedding in Cairns than in Japan, with the plus factor of a tropical location. Another couple owned a coffee plantation up near Mareeba on the tablelands. A third couple was making big business out of macadamia nuts, mangoes and other exotic fruits. The rest were singles, but all of them successfully established in various fields—smart, wealthy achievers.

Lucy couldn't help thinking none of them would understand her haphazard way of moving from one job to another. She wasn't *driven* to achieve anything because she had always known her dyslexia would get in the way. Enjoying herself with whatever appealed and was available was the best she could do.

'I won't fit in with them, you know,' she warned Michael. 'I'm from a different kind of zoo.'

He looked totally unconcerned, grinning at her as he lifted his cocktail glass in a toast. *'Vive la différence!'*

The tension that had been building up in Lucy eased. Michael was the only one who really counted, and he liked her the way she was.

Their meal arrived, along with a bottle of red wine to go with the veal. The meat was melt-in-your-mouth tender, the mushroom sauce was delicious and the wine, a full-bodied cabernet sauvignon, complemented both perfectly. Lucy's palate was immensely pleasured by it all and she sat back with a contented sigh when she'd finished eating.

As Michael put down his knife and fork, looking equally replete, she felt a strong sense of being watched. Her skin prickling at being the target of some intense focus, she threw a sharp glance around. Passers-by were streaming past the restaurant, none of them paying any attention to her, but the feeling persisted and her gaze was eventually drawn to a table at the adjoining restaurant.

Recognition of the guy from the Irish pub in Port Douglas came as a nasty jolt. He was staring straight at her, and when he caught her eye he lifted a schooner of beer in a half-drunk, mocking manner, a look of leering triumph on his face. He was with a group of men, probably the same ones who had been at the pub.

They'd been fun at first, flirting with her and her girlfriends, inviting them to dance—fun until they'd drunk too much. They were a bunch of good-looking men who were obviously used to getting their own way with women regardless of their behaviour. They'd yelled abuse after Lucy and her friends when they'd walked out on them.

She'd actually felt attracted to the guy staring at her now—Jason…Jason Lester. He had a gym-toned body, wicked blue eyes and a sexy bristle along his jaw, but by the end of the evening the attraction was stone-dead. And he hadn't liked being rejected by her—not one bit.

Her stomach cramped when he pushed his chair back and stood up, his gaze still trained on her. Alarm crawled down her spine. If he was intent on confrontation… She quickly reached out and grabbed Michael's hand, needing his full attention as her eyes transmitted an urgent warning.

'There's trouble coming our way,' she said quickly.

'What?' He frowned, looking past her to spot what she found disturbing. 'You mean Jason Lester?'

'You know him?'

'Played football against him in my teens.'

She hadn't imagined any connection between them and didn't have time to ask Michael whether he'd liked Jason or not, which drove up her tension considerably when the guy arrived at their table.

'Well, well, here's the honey bee again,' he drawled sneeringly, his gaze shifting to Michael, who was rising to his feet, half a head taller than Jason and more broad-shouldered, but apparently not intimidating enough to stop a jeer at him. 'Pulling in bigger bucks with you, Mickey Finn.'

'You're being rude, Jason,' Michael said tersely, his face set in stony challenge as he added, 'inexcusably.'

'Just thought I'd give you a friendly warning, Mickey.

What looks like all sweetness has quite a sting in her tail.'

'I'd prefer to discover that for myself,' he replied coldly. 'Now if you don't mind...'

'But I do mind. I want the honey bee to spell out why she turned her back on me when she's slept with half the men in Cairns.' The blue eyes lasered hers with vicious spite. 'Well, sweetheart?'

Her face flamed at the slur on her character. That he had made such a nasty crack about her in front of Michael goaded her into a wild reply. 'Even a town slut can have standards, Jason Lester, and you don't meet them.'

'After richer pickings, aren't you?' he retorted, and threw a last mocking look at Michael. 'Just so you know what you're playing with, old friend.'

He left.

Lucy sat frozen, watching him saunter off. It totally appalled her that she'd used the term 'town slut' on top of Jason Lester's numbering her ex-lovers as half the men in Cairns, making it sound as if she was actually acknowledging herself as a slut, which she wasn't. Far from it. But Michael could be starting to see her that way—as a gold-digging slut who had drawn him straight into her bedroom on their first night together.

If Jason Lester and Michael had been friends... If Michael believed him, one man to another... She couldn't think past that, couldn't bring herself to look at the prince who might at this very moment be turning into a frog.

Michael slowly unclenched his hands as he watched Jason Lester make a quick retreat back to the safety of a gang of mates seated at a table in the next restaurant. Typical of him to dive in, hit where it hurt, then run for cover. He'd always been a dirty player on the football field, grabbing guys' crotches and squeezing whenever he could. Harry had got him back in one game, delivering a bit of justice.

Certainly there was no friendship fostered between Lester and the Finn family. He hadn't come to this table to do any favours. His only purpose had been to poison the happy flow of a relationship he wanted to destroy out of some malicious sense of envy. Michael *knew* this, but he couldn't stop himself from wondering how much truth there was in the poison.

The honey bee...

It was an apt name for Lucy, flitting along in her free-spirited way and so sweet to be with in every sense.

The burning question was how many men had dipped into her honey? He might have dismissed Lester's snide crack about half the men in Cairns but for Lucy's retort that even a town slut had some standards. It had been an angry retort, hitting back, yet his own experience with Lucy—her easy, uninhibited approach to having sex—suddenly didn't feel so great to him.

This past week he had been obsessed by the pleasure of her, at the cost of his usual complete concentration on work. Even tonight he'd cut short what he should have done in the office, impatient to be with her again. Had she deliberately gone after his balls because of his 'big bucks'? He'd thought that her joy in sex was part and parcel of her nature, but maybe it was all designed to play him, to take him where she wanted him to go, en-

snare him into not looking beyond what she gave him.
Was he being fooled by this woman?

He glanced sharply at Lucy as he resumed his seat.
Her chin was up at a defiant angle. Her face was taut.
No smile. Her whole body looked tense. Her gaze was
lowered, seemingly fixed on the table next to theirs,
where the waiter was serving sweets. Michael didn't
think she was considering what to order for herself, but
he decided to pretend that she was. A bone-deep pride
insisted that Lester not see he had disturbed either of
them in the slightest.

Michael reached over and touched her hand to draw
her attention back to him. Her head turned slowly, reluctantly, and when she lifted her gaze to his he saw
her eyes were anguished.

Because what she was had been revealed…or because it deeply distressed her to have him think anything nasty of her? There was no certain way of telling
at this moment, and he wasn't about to sit in judgement
with Lester watching.

Michael quickly composed an indulgent smile and
nodded to the next table. 'Do you fancy any of the
sweets being served over there?'

'What?' she asked in a dazed fashion.

'You said you wanted to see what sweets other people
ordered before you decide,' he reminded her.

'Oh!' There was a second of utter disbelief, almost
instantly chased away by immense relief. The frozen
look on her face cracked into a smile that showered him
with a gush of warmth. 'I wasn't really looking at them.'

He squeezed her hand. 'Don't let Lester spoil your
appetite. I love the way you appreciate good food.'

The smile wobbled. 'He was so nasty. I thought...' Her eyes searched Michael's anxiously.

Again he squeezed her hand. 'He's gone, Lucy. We were enjoying ourselves. Let's wipe him out of our minds and keep on enjoying ourselves.'

She looked at him wonderingly. 'You can do that?'

'Yes.' It wasn't the absolute truth, but he grinned at her to lighten the moment and said, 'Though I'm glad you didn't sleep with him. I have standards, too, and Lester doesn't meet them.'

'I hate abusive men,' she said fiercely. 'My father was abusive when he got drunk. It was a huge relief when he dropped out of our lives.'

Michael frowned, wondering what exactly 'abusive' entailed, if there was any bad sexual history that might have led to sluttish behaviour on Lucy's part. 'Do you mean violent?' he asked cautiously.

Lucy grimaced. 'He did hit Mum occasionally. Most of the time, though, he'd just get mean and nasty.'

'What about you and your sister?'

She shook her head. 'We learnt early on to stay out of his way when he got drinking.'

Michael sensed nothing hidden behind her answer and felt relieved that there'd been no sexual abuse. He wished Lucy hadn't made that 'slut' remark. It sat uneasily in his mind, along with Lester's 'bigger bucks' remark.

'Not a happy household,' he murmured, thinking how lucky he had been with his parents.

'It was happy when my father was away in Mount Isa,' she said quickly. 'He lives there full-time now. He's a miner.'

'I see. He came home to Cairns in between shifts.'

'Yes. And it was always a relief when he left.' She shook her head again. 'Mum should never have married him. She was pregnant with Ellie at the time and more or less got trapped into it. She was on her own up here, having come from a broken home herself—no one to turn to—and she tried so hard to hold it all together. I couldn't have had a better mother, Michael.'

'Well, I'm glad of that,' he said sincerely. 'And I'm sorry your father wasn't what he should have been.'

She eyed him curiously. 'What was your father like?'

'He was great. Both my parents were. Harry and I were brought up in a very happy home.'

She sighed. 'Then you must have only good memories of them.'

'Yes.'

'I guess you'll want to give your children the same kind of happy home.'

There was a faraway look in her eyes, as though she was imagining how it might be in the future. *Whoa!* The warning shot straight into Michael's mind. He might have gone there with her before Lester had fired his bolt of poison, but he didn't want a wife or the mother of his children to have earned the reputation of being a slut.

On the other hand, his gut rebelled against giving Lucy up at this point. He'd never had sex this good, and until Lester's intrusion she had been a delight to be with. Michael still wanted to enjoy this relationship. He wasn't looking for any long-term future with her. He just wanted a continuation of what they'd been sharing all week.

The waiter arrived to clear away their dinner plates,

and diverted Lucy's attention to ordering sweets. The rest of the evening was fun and they finished it off with fantastic sex. Michael was content with that, deciding he would simply enjoy one day at a time with Lucy, take the experience for what it was—complete and utter pleasure. If it was his wealth that made her sparkle for him, he didn't care, as long as she kept sparkling. He liked the sunshine. It relaxed him. It made him feel happy.

CHAPTER EIGHT

FINN ISLAND...

Lucy drank in all she could see of it as Michael
steered his motor launch closer to the wharf where
Harry was waiting for them. They had entered a large
bay edged with a beach of very white sand, partially
shaded by masses of palm trees. It was a beautiful sunny
day and the water was a glorious glittering turquoise.
At the centre of the crescent of sand wide wooden decks
led up to the main buildings of the resort. On either
side, villas were stepped up on hills that were covered
with rainforest.

Paradise, indeed, she thought, except for the snake
in it. Last night Michael had urged her to wipe the encounter with Jason Lester out of her mind, and she had
tried to do that, relieved that Michael's interest in her
had not wavered. But somehow it didn't feel right that
he hadn't cared about what had been said. Although
she had dreaded a negative reaction from him, it didn't
seem natural for there to be no reaction at all. Unless
he just wanted the sex to continue, regardless of how
many men she had slept with.

She'd told herself not to get in a twist about it if

Michael just wanted a sexual fling with her. But if he now saw her as no better than a slut to be used...or even worse, a slut with an eye on taking a slice of his wealth... Lucy hated that thought.

It had wormed its way into her mind this morning and she couldn't get it out. She *had* slept with most of the men she'd dated for any length of time, though not on the first night. It had been different with Michael. The excitement of connecting with him had been so intense that the idea of holding him off until they knew each other better hadn't even entered her head. She'd done what she'd wanted to do, elated that the desire was so mutual.

And he'd made her feel...*amazing.*

Still did.

As though she was the best thing that had ever happened to him.

He was certainly the best thing that had ever happened to her.

Maybe she was worrying needlessly.

He'd been happy in bed with her last night, happy with her company on the boat this morning, touching her with pleasure in his eyes, holding her, kissing her. She'd revelled in the warmth of his manner towards her. If she could just get rid of this uneasy feeling that underneath it all he might have no respect for her, she would be totally happy with what they were sharing.

Harry helped Michael fasten the motor launch to the wharf and led them to a golf buggy for a quick ride to the administration centre, where Ellie was waiting for them. A track wound through the rainforest and underneath the awesome canopy of foliage formed by the incredibly tall trees were masses of tropical vegetation: giant tree ferns, palms, bamboo, hibiscus, native flowers. Lucy wondered if her sister loved working in this environment, so different to city living. Had she found it more relaxing, or was working with Harry a tense situation, given the very personal element of being attracted to him?

Ellie was not one to let down her hair in a hurry, but Lucy hoped she was letting Harry into her life. Two years of strict spinsterhood needed to be broken. Ellie was too young to give up on men. There was pleasure to be had in relationships, even though the guys might turn into frogs after a while. Lucy decided to insist they all have lunch together. It would give her the opportunity to observe what was happening between Harry and her sister.

They alighted from the buggy at a wide wooden walkway dividing the two main buildings. Michael took her arm, tucking it around his, smiling in pleasure at having her with him. Lucy's heart lurched. He was such a beautiful prince. She desperately wanted to be his princess, though she already knew this relationship would not have that happy ending.

Michael would want a family in his future. He hadn't actually said so last night, but she'd felt it in his head and in his heart, and she wasn't the one who'd be sharing that with him. Nevertheless, she still wanted to feel he loved and respected her.

Harry led them into the manager's office. Lucy beamed at her very clever sister, who rose from behind an imposing desk, looking very much in charge of everything. 'This island is fabulous, Ellie,' she immediately enthused. 'What a great place to work!'

'Tropical paradise,' Ellie replied, smiling as she moved out from behind the desk to greet them.

Lucy slipped her arm free of Michael's to rush forward and give her a hug. 'Are you loving it?' she asked, curious to know everything, especially the situation with Harry.

'Not too much, I hope,' Michael semi-growled in the background.

'It's been quite a change,' Ellie said drily, flicking him a sharply assessing look, probably checking if he was badly put out by her decision to leave him for a month. He hadn't grumbled about it to Lucy, but he probably wouldn't anyway, since their relationship had nothing to do with his work, and he'd be conscious of the fact she and Ellie were sisters.

'A good one, I hope,' Harry interjected, drawing Ellie's attention to him.

'Yes,' she answered with a warm smile, which Lucy took as a very good sign.

'Now, Harry, poaching my PA is not on,' Michael declared.

'Like I said before, Mickey—*her choice*,' he replied with an affable shrug.

'Okay, while you two guys argue over my brilliant sister, I want her to show me her living quarters,' Lucy put in quickly, wanting to get Ellie on her own. 'You can mind the office, can't you, Harry?'

'Go right ahead,' he said agreeably.

'Come on, Ellie,' she urged, nodding to the door at the back of the office. 'Michael said your apartment was right here. I want to see everything. And while I'm at it, may I say you look great in the island uniform?'

Ellie laughed. 'Not as spectacular as you this morning.'

Lucy was wearing cheeky little navy denim shorts with a red-and-purple halter top, big red hoop earrings, red trainers on her feet, and a purple scrunchie holding up her long blond hair in a ponytail. 'Am I over the top?' she asked.

Ellie shook her head. 'You can carry off anything, Lucy.'

'I wish….' she replied with a wry grimace, as Elizabeth ushered her into the apartment and closed the door on the two men in the office.

She hadn't carried off the encounter with Jason Lester with any classy panache, quite possibly adding to his nasty slur on her character with her own wild retort, and she wasn't very confident of carrying off being an appropriate companion for Michael at the ball next Saturday night. Jason's accusation that she had come on to one of the Finn brothers because of his wealth might be suspected by Michael's friends. It could also have tainted *his* opinion of her.

Ellie eyed her quizzically, sensing something was weighing on her sister's mind. 'Is that a general wish or…?'

'Oh, nothing really,' she replied airily, not wanting to unload these highly personal problems on her sister. She focused on examining the living-room of the apartment. It looked bright and cheerful, with colourful tropical prints on the cushions softening all the cane furniture. An adequate kitchenette ran along one wall.

A television and sound system were arranged against another. She gestured around, saying, 'This is lovely, Ellie. Show me the bedroom and bath.'

The very modern bathroom had everything any woman could want, and there was no stinginess in the bedroom, either. The queen-size bed had much more space than the king-size singles they had at home. She couldn't help grinning mischievously at Ellie. 'Have you shared this with Harry yet?'

'Actually, no.' She retaliated with, 'Do you want to tell me what's going on with Michael?'

Lucy threw up her hands. 'Everything is happening! I swear to you, Ellie, I've never been this mad about a guy. I'm in love like you wouldn't believe, and while it's incredibly wonderful, it's also scary, you know?'

'In what way scary?'

Because it meant too much that everything feel right between them—so much it made her terribly conscious of shadows lurking in the wings. She flopped onto the bed, put her hands behind her head and stared at the ceiling, knowing Ellie expected an answer, and finally picking a problem her sister would readily understand.

'Michael is smart. I mean *really* smart, isn't he?'

'Yes.'

'So what happens when he finds out that my brain wasn't wired right and I'm a dummy when it comes to reading and writing? So far I've been winging it, as I usually do, but this is far more intense than it's been with other guys, and he's bound to start noticing I'm a bit weird about some things.' She rolled her head to look directly at Ellie, needing a straight opinion from her. 'You've worked for him for two years. Will it put him off me if I tell him I'm dyslexic?'

Her sister frowned in thought, then slowly shook her head. 'I honestly don't know, Lucy. Does it feel as though he's in love with you?'

'Well, definitely in lust. I can't be sure that's love, but I really want it to be. More than I've wanted anything. I want him to care so much about having me, it won't matter that I'm flawed.'

Ellie sat on the bed beside her and smoothed the worried furrows from her brow. 'It shouldn't matter, if he loves you. And stop thinking of yourself as a dummy, Lucy. You're very smart, and you have so many talents.... Any man would be lucky to have you in his life.'

She heaved a rueful sigh. 'Well, I don't want him to know yet. I couldn't bear it if...' She shot a pleading look at Ellie. 'You haven't told Harry, have you?'

'No. And I won't.'

'I need more time. To give it a chance, you know?' A chance to keep this man as long as she could—to have all the pleasure of him—because it was really going to hurt when she did lose him.

'Yes, I know.'

'I've been running off at the mouth about me. What about you and Harry?'

Ellie shrugged. 'Same thing. More time needed.'

'But you do like him.'

'Yes.'

There was obviously a chance for something really good here for Ellie. Harry couldn't possibly see any bad in her. She was clever and classy and sensible, perfectly suitable to be a wife who could manage anything in the Finn world. Definitely not riff-raff—a tag Lucy suspected might be attached to herself, since she drifted aimlessly from job to job, living in the moment rather than planning ahead, because there was really nothing to plan for, not with her dyslexia blocking any way upward.

In contrast, Ellie's path forward had always been clear. The teachers at school had loved her for being so bright and studious, and she had certainly been driven by their family situation to make the most of her capabilities, building a career ever since she'd been at business college. To be so good at everything automatically commanded respect.

Lucy propped herself on her elbow, looking earnestly at her far more worthy sister. 'Promise me you won't go off him if things don't work out between me and Michael.'

Ellie looked surprised at the request, but it was important to clear away any complications in the current mix. When the relationship with Michael lost its magic, it shouldn't take the shine off Ellie's connection to Harry. Lucy didn't want sister loyalty to muddy the waters. That wasn't fair. The idea of the four of them—brothers and sisters—ending up together was a wonderful fantasy, but Lucy felt compelled to do a reality check here and now.

'Harry could be the right guy for you,' she argued. 'Let's face it…he's gorgeous and sexy and wealthy, and obviously keen to have you in his corner. You could be great together and I don't want *me* to be the reason for you not having a future with him. I'd be happy to see you happy with him, Ellie, regardless of what happens between me and Michael.'

Concern and confusion chased across her sister's face. 'But being so madly in love with Michael, you'll be hurt if he walks away from you.'

And who always stood by and tried to make things better any way she could?

Ellie did.

Being the older sister, she had an overdeveloped sense of responsibility, looking after Lucy when they were kids, stepping in when she was bullied at school for her scatty mind, taking charge of everything when their mother became too ill to manage, getting them through all the traumatic turmoil of her death and setting them up as their own little family unit. Ellie was the rock, the anchor around which Lucy had drifted, the one who made a mission of *being there,* no matter what.

No way was Lucy going to cost her sister a chance with Harry Finn.

'I'll muddle along like I always do,' she insisted. 'I'm good at putting things behind me. I've had a lot of practice at it.' She reached out, took Ellie's hand and squeezed it reassuringly. 'You mustn't worry about me. Go for what you want. You deserve a good life, Ellie.'

'So do you.'

'Well, maybe we'll both achieve it. Who knows? I just want to clear the deck for you and Harry. Now tell me you're okay with that.'

Ellie heaved a deep sigh, obviously wishing the situation wasn't complicated. But it was and there was no point in not facing it. 'I'm okay if you're okay,' she finally said, her hand squeezing back, her eyes holding the steady determination that had seen them through many troubles. 'Whatever happens with either of us, we'll always have each other, Lucy.'

'Absolutely!' she agreed, relieved to have this serious stuff settled between them.

It was time now to set about banishing shadows from both their lives. They were here on this beautiful island and two princes were waiting for them. She grinned at Ellie. 'Now let's go get our men!' She bounced off the bed and twirled around in a happy dance. 'Let's have a fabulous weekend, following our hearts' desire and not thinking about tomorrow.'

She paused in the doorway to the living room to give her often too sensible sister a wise look. 'You never know when something might strike us dead, so we do what we want to do. Right?'

'Right!' Ellie echoed.

Life could be very short.

Since their mother had died, that proven truth had never left Lucy's mind. She had to stop thinking of any kind of future with Michael and just take each day as it came.

Forget the shadows.

Live in the sun.

CHAPTER NINE

MICHAEL KEENLY OBSERVED the to and fro between Harry and Elizabeth over lunch. She definitely wasn't resisting him anymore. There was no mocking, no sparring, no challenge being thrown out. Harry didn't tease or flirt. Her smiles held genuine liking. His smiles seemed to trumpet happiness.

The writing was on the wall.

Harry was winning.

Though not necessarily to the point of seducing Elizabeth into taking on the manager's job. She and Lucy had a home together in Cairns and the sisters were close, having only each other as family. He was fairly sure she would return to her PA job when the month was up. As for having an affair with Harry, he thought Elizabeth would be very level-headed about not expecting too much from him, since she had always perceived him as a playboy. It was unlikely that she would end up in an emotional mess over him. She would be guarded against that.

He wondered now about his initial impression that Lucy had no guard up against anything. Accustomed to being with more sophisticated women, who knew how to play it cool, he had been bowled over by her apparent openness, her spontaneity, the way she seemed to freely give everything up to him—with no guile at all. It had been so different to all his previous experience of the opposite sex, but was it real or was it the cleverest artifice that could be used on a man?

Michael felt uncomfortably conflicted by this question. He wanted Lucy to be what she seemed to be. Wanted it too much. He wasn't used to feeling this emotionally involved, and he didn't like it, not when she could be playing him. He needed to settle this doubt. Hopefully, Sarah and Jack Pickard might help do that when he took Lucy to their villa for afternoon tea.

The Pickards had been a fixture in his and Harry's lives all through their teens and early manhood, with Sarah being their parents' housekeeper and Jack being the maintenance man on their property. Harry had transferred them to the island to carry out the same roles here when that suddenly empty homestead with too many memories had been sold.

They were good people. Michael was very fond of both of them. Even more importantly, he trusted their instincts. How they reacted—responded—to Lucy would tell him how they viewed her as a person, a view uncoloured by the lust she continually stirred in him.

Lucy loved the restaurant, a huge open room overlooking the swimming pool and spa decks, the beach and the bay, with lush tropical gardens on either side. The tables were well spaced, making everything feel designed for relaxation, with no crush, no hurry, just divine surroundings and divine food and wine.

Best of all, the mood around the table was relaxed, too. Ellie recommended some of the dishes on the menu, making Lucy's choices easy and natural. There was no sign of any tension between the brothers, so Michael couldn't be worrying too much about losing his PA, and there was nothing but positive vibes flowing between Harry and Ellie.

It was a great lunch.

Followed by an even better afternoon.

Michael took her up to what he called a pavilion villa. This was perched on a hillside overlooking another beach, facing west to catch the sunset. It actually had a private infinity pool at the end of its open deck. Inside was just as marvellous—a white cane lounge suite in the sitting area with plump blue-and-white striped cushions, a kitchenette running along one wall leading to a totally luxurious bathroom, also in blue and white and containing a spa bath as well as a shower definitely built for two, plus a range of bath salts and body oils and lotions in exotic containers standing ready for use.

The bedroom was on a mezzanine level—not missing out on the beautiful view— and featured a king-size bed, lots of cupboards along one wall, a luggage stool where their overnight bags had already been placed and bedside tables with lamps held up by seahorses. There were artistic arrangements of shells and pieces of coral from the reef, a wall-hanging of white net holding fish made of mother-of-pearl, and large candles giving out a faint scent of frangipani.

'This is heaven, Michael!' she declared, swinging around with her arms out in an all-encompassing gesture. *And he is what makes it heaven,* she thought. *This man who is so impossibly perfect.*

Maybe it was all too good to be true, but Lucy wasn't about to let that thought spoil this time with him. He laughed at her exuberance, moving up the steps to the mezzanine level, where she already stood in her rush to see everything.

Her eyes gloated over him, the classically handsome face, the glowing olive skin, white, white teeth, the so masculine body shown off by smartly tailored shorts in a blue-and-grey check teamed with a royal blue sports shirt. Just the sight of his strong, muscular calves made her feel weak with desire. And the great big king-size bed was waiting right behind her.

'Can we have a siesta?' she asked huskily.

He grinned, his silvery-grey eyes twinkling wickedly. 'As long as you don't expect to sleep too much.'

Oh, she loved him, loved him, loved him, locking her arms around his neck in ecstatic possession of him as he drew her into his embrace. An idea sprang into her mind—one that would give her wonderfully free access to all of him. 'Maybe I'll make you go to sleep,' she said teasingly. 'Let me give you a massage, Michael. It would be criminal not to use one of those body oils in the bathroom, and afterwards I could wash it all off you in the spa bath.'

'Well, I can't say no to that.'

'You strip off and I'll fetch a bath sheet and the oils.'

She planted a quick kiss on his mouth, then danced away from him, down the steps to the bathroom, eager to get moving on showing him how good a masseuse she was. He was already naked and throwing off the bedcover and decorator cushions when she returned, pausing a moment to ogle his taut, cheeky butt. In the flesh, Michael Finn had to be the sexiest man alive, and excitement zinged through her at the thought of having all his flesh under her hands.

He turned and caught her eyeing him. 'I think I see lecherous intent,' he said laughingly.

'I was simply measuring your muscles,' she retorted with a grin.

'Fair's fair! You strip off while I spread out the bath sheet.'

She handed it to him, put the oil bottles on the bedside table and whipped off her clothes. 'Okay, I'm naked, but no looking. This is about feeling,' she insisted. 'I want you to lie facedown, close your eyes and let me have my way with you.'

'As you wish,' he answered agreeably, doing as he was told.

Lucy tried the oils on her skin first, choosing the one with the more exotic scent. She straddled Michael, taking wicked pleasure in sitting on his sexy butt, and dribbled the oil around his shoulders and down his spine, grinning as he shuddered at the sudden coolness on his skin. 'The heat comes next,' she promised, taking sensual delight in swishing her breasts over his back as she leaned across him to put the bottle back on the table.

'I'm getting a breast massage?' he queried, amusement rumbling through his voice.

'No. I was just indulging myself.'

'Indulge as much as you like.'

She laughed and went to work on his shoulders with her hands, gently kneading his muscles. 'You're a bit tight up here. I guess that comes from working at a desk all day.'

'Mmm…that feels very good,' he murmured appreciatively. 'Where did you learn to do this?'

'Part of the beautician course. It's more for relaxing, though, not remedial stuff.'

'I'm all for relaxing. I can take a lot of it.'

'I'm going to give you the whole works.'

He sighed contentedly. 'I love your work, Lucy.'

Love me.

She willed that to happen as her hands revelled in stroking his firm male flesh, feeling the strength of his muscles, loving every part of his physique as she moved over him in a kind of sensual thrall, rubbing his arms, legs, hands, feet. The oil glistening on his skin made him look like an Olympian athlete. The scent of it grew more and more erotic to her. When she told him to roll over so she could continue the process on his front, her pulse leapt into a gallop at the sight of his fully taut erection.

She couldn't tear her gaze off it as she knelt between his legs and ran her hands over his calves and up his thighs. The urge to bend her head and run her tongue around the tip of the shaft was irresistible. He gasped. His eyes opened into glittering slits. She took him in her mouth and he groaned her name repeatedly.

Yes! she thought in wild elation as she lashed him with her tongue and pumped him with her mouth, excited beyond belief by this rabid possession of his manhood. *He's mine…. He's mine!* she thought as her own body creamed in climax.

He jackknifed up, grabbed her, lifted her, pulling

her forward to fit her over him. She took him inside her, riding him, fiercely wanting to drive him over the brink, exploding everything else he cared about into meaningless atoms so that only she existed for him. He cried out as release spurted from him in uncontrollable bursts, and she writhed over him in an ecstacy of triumph. *Mine...!*

He was moaning, tossing his head from side to side. She leaned forward, held it still and covered his face with kisses. His arms encircled her, pulling her down on top of him. She could feel his heart thumping. He rolled with her locked in his embrace, taking the more dominant position so he could kiss her as he willed, his mouth devouring hers in a frenzy of passion, as though he had to make her *his* now. His and his alone.

Lucy exulted in the sense of feeling secure with him. She needed this. It might not be absolutely real for always, but it was real enough for now. His desire for her, this marvellous intimacy, the heart-warming magic of being together...sheer bliss.

Michael didn't want to think. He just wanted to wallow in the exquisite pleasure of Lucy Flippence—what she did to him, what she gave him. Yet it was so much—so much more than he'd ever expected or received from any other woman, and it had happened so quickly. Only a week. He couldn't stop his mind from circling around the situation, trying to weigh what it meant.

Jason Lester's jibe that she was after bigger bucks with Michael could be true. She'd said herself that she belonged in a different zoo to his social circle. Had she sized him up as a mark worth pulling out all the stops for? It actually felt like a stab to his heart to even consider it, which was a warning of how deeply she was getting to him.

He hadn't really had any serious relationships—more a series of attractions that wore off for one reason or another. No woman had driven him to the point of obsession as Lucy did. He couldn't get enough of her, despite the doubts that were now jangling through his mind. Even his concentration on work had been affected this past week, and he never allowed anything to interfere with his control of the franchises.

Had something changed in him?

Did Lucy touch some chord of need that had been kept locked up inside him?

Keeping faith with his father's vision had been more important to him than anything else since his parents had died. Harry felt the same way. It was a strong bond between them. They'd poured all their energy into building on the strong business platform their father had established, possibly at the cost of a more natural lifestyle, though surely it had been in their nature to do what they'd done.

Maybe it was all about timing.

They'd succeeded in achieving what they'd set out to achieve.

Now, with Lucy suddenly bursting into his life, making him acutely aware he wanted more on a personal level…it made him feel vulnerable in a way he'd never felt before. Not in control. Knocked askew.

Again he told himself to just ride with what was happening.

It was too good not to.

Eventually the situation would sort itself out. Maybe with Jack and Sarah this afternoon.

Lucy stirred, lifting her head to smile at him, her dimples flashing endearingly. 'I'd better run the spa bath if we're to wash the oil scent off us before our visit to the Pickards.'

Weird that she'd thought of them at the same time as he had. He'd told her about the invitation on the trip out, explaining their connection to the family, and she'd seemed eager to meet them, interested in their life on the island.

'Good thinking,' he approved.

Her eyes sparkled. 'I'll use the watermelon bath crystals. That will clean us up.'

He laughed. She rolled away from him, off the bed, and headed for the bathroom in a provocative prance, swinging her delectable bottom, leaving a broad smile on Michael's face and the thought in his mind that she made him laugh a lot, putting a happy zing in his life in more ways than one.

The sunshine girl...

He enjoyed the challenge of his work, keeping on top of everything, but when he walked out of his office, Lucy's kind of sunshine was precisely what he wanted, what he needed to put his world in balance. Did he really care if it was his wealth that brought him this?

He'd prefer it not to be, but it was an integral part of who he was, which probably made it a factor in all his relationships. Except with his brother. Telling himself not to let it cloud this time with Lucy, he swung himself off the bed, rolled up the bath sheet and went to join her in the bathroom.

The spa bath was another sensual delight. She insisted on soaping him all over, her body sliding around his, then directed him to sit between her legs, his back turned to her while she shampooed his hair and gave him a scalp massage. He ended up horny and they had sex again—fun sex this time, with the bubbles from the bath crystals swirling around them.

Michael could not remember feeling more relaxed when they finally strolled down the hill to visit Jack and Sarah. He wanted them to find no fault in Lucy. He wanted today to stay as perfect as it was with this woman at his side.

Paradise...

CHAPTER TEN

LUCY WAS NERVOUS about meeting the Pickards. Normally she didn't care if people approved of her or not, but from what Michael had told her, Jack and Sarah were almost like a second set of parents to him and Harry. They *counted* in his life, so it really mattered to her that they like her.

It helped that he was holding her hand, giving her a sense of security with him, and surely they would see he was happy with her. That should help, too. And Ellie would have made a good impression on them. Her sister had real class in every way. Not that Lucy was like her. She wasn't. But they were *family*.

The Pickards' villa was positioned on flat land between the gym and the huge maintenance shed that housed the power generator and the desalination plant providing fresh water for the resort. Within easy walking distance of the administration centre, and bigger than the guest villas, it was a permanent home for them.

They were both on the veranda that ran across the front of the villa, probably eager to greet Michael and his companion when they arrived. Eager to look her over, too. Jack appeared to be spraying plants in tubs placed around the edge of the veranda. Sarah was in a rocking chair, flipping through a magazine.

As she caught sight of them, she put the magazine aside and stood up, calling out to Jack that they were coming. He set the spray-can on the veranda railing, took off his gloves and joined her at the top of the steps. They were both short, lean and wiry in physique, with iron-grey curly hair framing fairly weather-beaten faces—obviously active outdoors people. And they were wearing cheerful, welcoming expressions that eased some of Lucy's inner tension.

'It's lovely to see you, Mickey!' Sarah warmly declared.

'Likewise,' he said just as warmly. 'And this is Lucy Flippence, Elizabeth's sister.'

'My, my...you're not at all alike.' The predictable comment came as she grasped the hand Lucy offered.

'No. Ellie is as sharp as a tack and I guess most people would consider me fairy floss.' Lucy tossed off the remark with a self-deprecating smile.

'I always thought there was some magic in fairy floss,' Jack said, grinning at her as he took her hand and shook it.

She laughed, relieved that he accepted her so readily. 'I think this island is magic, and Michael tells me you've both helped to make it so.'

'Oh, we do our bit. We love it here, don't we, Sarah?'

'Yes, we're very lucky,' she agreed.

'I see you've got your roses growing well, Jack,' Michael remarked.

Lucy was surprised. 'Roses? Here?'

Jack's eyes twinkled with pleasure. 'It was a challenge, but…' he stepped back, his arm swinging out to gesture to the tubs '…coming into bloom now.'

Lucy spotted a yellow bud just opening up. 'Is that a Pal Joey?'

'Yes, it's one of my favourites,' Sarah answered. 'It has such a lovely scent.'

'I know. It's beautiful. I was at Greenlands Cemetery last Monday and an elderly man was planting a Pal Joey rose bush on his wife's grave. He said he couldn't have his Gracie lie there without her favourite rose.'

Sarah's face softened. 'Oh, how very loving of him!'

'They'd been married almost sixty years. I thought it was wonderful. Do you grow them for Sarah, Jack?'

'For both of us.' He smiled ruefully at his wife. 'But should I have the misfortune of Sarah passing first, I shall certainly plant one on her grave.'

She smiled back. 'You do that, Jack.'

Lucy sighed. 'It's so nice to meet married people who are devoted to one another. There's not enough of it.'

'You can make your own world, Lucy,' Sarah said philosophically. 'And how is it that the cemetery features in yours?'

'It's her job,' Michael put in. 'Lucy is in cemetery administration.'

That startled Sarah. 'Good heavens! Do you like it?'

'So far I do. I haven't been in it for long,' she admitted. 'It gives me plenty of opportunities to visit my mother's grave. She died when I was seventeen, and I like to chat to her, tell her what I'm thinking and feeling. It sort of settles me down when I feel a bit adrift, you know?'

She was running off at the mouth as she always did

when she felt nervous. But Sarah didn't seem to think she was weird or anything, taking her hand again and patting it in a comforting way.

'It's very sad, losing your mother so young,' she said sympathetically.

'Yes, though Ellie is great. She takes charge of everything.'

Sarah nodded. 'I can see how she'd do that. She's handling everything very well here.'

'Don't you weigh in with Harry, Sarah,' Michael quickly interjected. 'Elizabeth is my PA. This situation is only temporary.'

'Not my business,' she assured him, stepping back to wave them forward. 'Come on through. I've set up afternoon tea on the back veranda. It has a view of the beach and sea.'

'Can I help you with anything?' Lucy asked as they were led into a large living area encompassing kitchen, dining room and lounge, all furnished in a very homely way.

'I just have to boil the kettle, dear, but stay with me and chat. You can help take the cake and cookies out when the tea is ready.'

'Please tell me they're your peanut butter cookies,' Michael said with relish.

Sarah laughed. 'Would I bake you any other? Go along with Jack now. We'll be out in a few minutes.'

The two men made their exit via a back door. Sarah switched the kettle on, then turned to Lucy, her hazel eyes bright with interest. 'Your sister told me you met Mickey at the office.'

'Yes, it was Ellie's birthday last Monday and I

dropped in to see her. Harry was there, too, and we all ended up having lunch together.'

'You must have seen more of Mickey this week for him to bring you here.'

Sarah was fishing, but Lucy didn't mind answering. 'Every night! It's been amazing! I feel like I'm in the middle of a fairy tale with him. He's such a prince!'

'He is, isn't he?' she said fondly. 'So is Harry. They're both very special men. Like their parents. They were special, too.'

'Michael said he lost them about the same time I lost my mother.'

Sarah sighed. 'A terrible tragedy. But they'd be very proud of their sons. Very proud.'

Realising that this woman had to know Michael's character through and through, Lucy decided to take the risk of confiding how she felt—the doubts she had about how Michael viewed this relationship, whether it could become really meaningful to him in his mind and heart.

She made an ironic grimace and gestured helplessly. 'The trouble is I'm not sure I can live up to him, Sarah. I mean…I'm more or less a Cinderella in his world. He's asked me to attend a ball with him next Saturday night, and I'm scared stiff that I won't fit in with his friends.'

'Don't be scared, Lucy,' the older woman advised. 'If Mickey wants you with him, he'll look after you. He's very like his father. Intense about anything he sets himself to do, and extremely protective of anyone he cares for.'

But did he really *care* for her? That was the big question.

'Then I should be okay,' Lucy said with a smile, thinking she'd probably dug as far as she could dig.

Sarah smiled back. 'I'm sure you will be, dear.'

The kettle boiled and she filled a large teapot that was patterned with roses. Lucy imagined the cups and saucers set outside would match.

'You *are* lucky, Sarah. There were no roses in my mother's marriage,' she wryly remarked. 'If I ever marry, it will only be to a man who loves me enough to give me roses.'

'Can't wait!' Michael announced from behind them. 'I'm going to snaffle a cookie.'

'We're coming!' Sarah chided.

'Fine! You bring the tea. I'll take the plate of cookies and Lucy can carry the banana cake.'

'How do you know it's a banana cake? It's covered in icing,' Lucy pointed out.

Michael grinned at Sarah, his eyes twinkling with certain knowledge.

'It's banana cake,' she conceded.

'You're a treasure, Sarah.'

'Oh, you and Harry always butter me up to get what you want.' She waved to the plate of cookies. 'Take them. We'll follow you out.'

They settled around a large wooden table on the back veranda, which faced a different bay than the administration centre. 'This beach catches the afternoon sun,' Jack pointed out. 'And, of course, we get the sunset view from here.'

As would the pavilion villa up on the hill, Lucy thought happily.

'You have a gorgeous lot of bougainvillea out here, Jack,' she remarked, gesturing to the brightly coloured profusion of them surrounding the veranda.

'They don't mind the sandy soil and sea air. Easy to grow here,' he explained.

'Did you do that wonderful tropical garden around the restaurant?'

Her curiosity about the development of the resort made for an easy, relaxed conversation over afternoon tea. Jack was proud of his work and Sarah was proud of her husband's ability to turn his hand to anything. Lucy coaxed smiles and laughter out of both of them, which always promoted a happy time and reduced any chance of self-conscious tension taking hold.

Michael sat back and watched her charm Jack and Sarah. She had quite extraordinary people skills, focusing on whoever was talking, picking up on their interests, making them seem just as interesting to her. Her smiles evoked smiles, and her laughter was infectious.

When she asked about how the sea water was turned into fresh, Michael quickly suggested to Jack that he take Lucy down to the maintenance shed and show her the process. It would give him some time alone with Sarah, who was a shrewd judge of character. Her opinion of other women he'd brought here had always been spot on.

Jack was only too pleased to show Lucy anything. He was clearly very taken by her. Most men would be, Michael thought, no matter how old. *The honey bee*... Lester's name for her slid into his mind again and he frowned as Lucy and Jack left the veranda together. Lester had given it a sexual connotation, but Lucy had not been consciously sexy over afternoon tea. She was simply...very appealingly female.

'What's wrong, Mickey?' Sarah asked quietly.

He shook his head. 'Just a problem I have.'

'To do with Lucy?'

'What do you think of her, Sarah?'

'A joy to be with,' she answered with a smile.

'Yes,' he agreed. 'Anything else?'

Sarah mused for a few moments before remarking, 'She's quite different from the other women you've brought over here. More spontaneous, artless…'

'Not a scheming gold-digger?' he pressed.

Sarah looked shocked. 'Not at all! Has she done anything to make you think it?'

'I am a very wealthy man,' he said drily.

'That can be intimidating to a girl like Lucy, Mickey,' she quickly argued. 'It can make her think she's not good enough for you.'

'She's beautiful. She's sexy. She's fun. That's a fairly good trade-off, Sarah.'

'If you have a lot of self-esteem, and I don't think she has,' Sarah replied thoughtfully. 'There's not much ego running around in that girl. She focuses on other people, doesn't want the spotlight turned on herself.'

'Because she's hiding something?' Michael queried, wondering if that was the case.

'I don't know. Her comment about being fairy floss compared to her sister made me think she knew she could never compete with Elizabeth, possibly from an early age. So she conceded all that ground and chose a different path for herself—one that didn't demand more than she felt capable of doing.'

'She is the younger sister. Elizabeth called her ditzy,' Michael recalled.

Sarah shot him an ironic smile. 'That's probably a good cover for feeling inadequate.'

He frowned over that possibility. 'I doubt Lucy feels inadequate. She's held quite an amazing array of jobs—model, beautician, tour guide, dancing teacher, amongst other things. It's as though she's drawn to try anything and everything. She dropped out of school to nurse her mother, who died of cancer, and never went back to complete any formal education—said she had no head for study after that. But I think she manages to do quite well for herself.'

'Where was Elizabeth when her mother was dying?'

'At home. Already at business college, so I imagine Lucy did the bulk of the nursing.'

'While Elizabeth prepared to take on the future.' Sarah nodded in understanding. 'Would you say the sisters are close?'

'Yes. Very different but very close. Lucy called Elizabeth her anchor.'

'When she feels adrift…that's what she said about visiting her mother's grave.' Sarah gave Michael a very direct look. 'You don't have a scheming gold-digger on your hands, Mickey. I'd say if Lucy is hiding anything, it's something she feels very vulnerable about. Be careful how you treat her.' His friend's serious expression cracked into a smile. 'She sees you as a prince.'

Michael grinned at her. 'Until I turn into a frog. According to Lucy, most princes eventually turn into frogs.'

Sarah laughed. 'She is a delight, that girl! In some ways, she's very like your mother. A joy to be with.'

Yes.

It was exactly what had been missing from his life, ever since his mother had died.

That was the chord Lucy struck in him—a much deeper need than the lust she stirred. A need for that emptiness to be filled.

'It's been good talking to you, Sarah,' he said appreciatively.

Someone he could trust.

Someone who would never lie to him.

He needed that, too.

If Lucy was covering up something she didn't want him to know, trying to keep him blinded with her fairy floss, he couldn't really trust her.

What did she feel she had to keep hidden?

The number of men in her past?

Maybe he should have questioned her about that last night. Maybe he should do it now. But remembering the anguish in her eyes after Lester had left them with his poison, Michael didn't want to bring that back and spoil this weekend with her. *Let it ride for a while,* he told himself again. But he wouldn't forget that Lucy could be keeping something from him—something that was important for him to know before this relationship went much further.

CHAPTER ELEVEN

LUCY COULD NOT have wished for a more marvellous time with Michael. The afternoon tea with the Pickards had been relatively stress-free. She had not felt any negative vibes coming from either of them. They were really nice people. Michael had then suggested a game of tennis, which had been great fun, followed by a dip in the infinity pool, drinking champagne as they watched the sunset. A romantic dinner for two on the deck below the restaurant had been a highlight finish to their day, eating superb food to the lapping of waves on the beach, under a star-studded sky.

On Sunday morning they slept in after a long night of making love. The fruit platter in the refrigerator was breakfast enough, since they were having an early lunch with Harry and Ellie before setting off to the mainland. Lucy wanted to see them happy with each other, as happy as she felt with Michael.

It was another beautiful, sunny day and harmony flowed between the two brothers and sisters as they sat in the restaurant, enjoying the fine cuisine. Ellie had mused out loud over the choices for each course, making decisions easy. It caused Lucy to reflect how lucky she was to have a sister who cared about her problems.

All through her school years, Ellie had tried to help her with reading and writing. She'd researched dyslexia on the internet and downloaded programs that might untangle the confusion in Lucy's mind. When they hadn't produced a miracle, she'd spent hours and hours coaching her to learn things off by heart. Without Ellie she would never have passed her driving test, which had allowed her to get jobs that wouldn't have been possible otherwise. Lucy owed her sister a debt she could never repay. It was good to see her eyes twinkling happily at Harry. Ellie deserved a prince.

Again Lucy couldn't help thinking how wonderful it would be if all four of them could end up together. That was a *big* dream—an impossible dream—but she was sailing along in a bubble of bliss, until Ellie dropped her bombshell.

They were sitting over coffee when Michael asked, 'Any prospects for the position of manager here, Harry?'

He shrugged. 'A few résumés have come in. I haven't called for any interviews yet. Elizabeth may want to stay on now that she's on top of the job.'

'Elizabeth is mine!' Michael shot him a vexed look.

'No!' The denial tripped straight out of Ellie's mouth.

Lucy was shocked into staring at her sister, who suddenly looked very serious and determined.

Michael, too, was taken aback. 'Don't tell me Harry has seduced you into staying here.'

'No, I won't be staying here beyond the month he needs to find someone suitable,' she replied quietly and calmly.

'So you'll come back to me,' Michael insisted.

She shook her head. 'I'm sorry, Michael, but I don't want to do that, either.'

'Why not?' he persisted.

'Being here this week has made me realise I want a change. To try something different. I'd appreciate it if you'd take this as my notice.'

He wasn't happy. He glared at his brother. 'Goddammit, Harry! If it wasn't for you—'

'Hey!' Harry held up his hands defensively. 'I'm not getting her, either.'

'Please…' Elizabeth quickly broke in. 'I don't want to cause trouble. I just want to take a different direction with my life.'

'But you're brilliant as my PA,' Michael argued, still annoyed at being put out.

'I'm sorry. You'll just have to find someone else.'

The relaxed atmosphere around the table was completely shattered. Everyone was tense. Lucy could hardly believe Ellie had come to this decision. It was like a rejection of both brothers, and the reason she gave… What direction *did* she want to take from here? Shutting herself off from two great careers made no sense.

'Why not try out Lucy as your PA?' Harry suggested to Michael with an airy wave of his hand. 'She's probably as brilliant as her sister.'

Panic instantly welled up in Lucy. *No, no, no!* screamed through her mind. She wasn't Ellie. She could never be like Ellie. She begged help from her sister with her eyes.

'It's not her kind of thing,' Ellie said firmly.

Michael was not put off, turning to remark quizzically, 'You do work in administration, Lucy.'

'I'm the front person who deals with people, Michael,' she stated, her stomach in absolute turmoil. 'I don't do desk work. I'm good at helping people, understanding what they want, helping them to decide.... There's quite a bit of that in cemetery administration. And I like it,' she added for good measure, pleading for him to drop the issue.

He grimaced in frustration.

She reached out and touched his hand, desperate to restore his good humour with her. 'I'm sorry, but I can't fill Ellie's place.'

The grimace slowly tilted up into a soothing smile. 'I shouldn't have expected it. You are a people person and I like that, Lucy. I wouldn't want to change it.'

Relief poured through her at having crossed this tricky hurdle without having to spell out why she'd be such a hopeless alternative to her sister.

'I hope you'll give me a good reference, Michael,' Ellie said, drawing attention away from Lucy.

He sighed and turned to her. 'It will be in the mail tomorrow. I hate losing you, but I wish you well, Elizabeth.'

It was a fairly graceful acceptance of the situation, but Lucy was extremely sensitive to the fact that the congenial atmosphere around the table was not about to resume. Tension emanated from Harry. It was obvious he didn't like this decision, either.

'Thank you,' Ellie said, nodding to Michael.

Case closed.

Except it wasn't.

Stony glances were being exchanged between the brothers. Frustration simmered from both of them. No one chose to eat any of the petit fours that accompanied coffee. Nothing was going to feel good until Michael and Harry cleared up their differences, which could be done only by leaving them alone together. Apart from resolving that problem, Lucy was also anxious to query Ellie about her reasons for leaving the PA job with Michael.

Had turning thirty hit her hard, triggering this sudden desire for change?

Or did the decision have something to do with foreseeing a bad outcome for the relationship Lucy had entered into with Michael? Ellie might not want to be around him if he let her sister down, and maybe she believed that was going to happen, complete with some horrible emotional fallout. If she was acting on that belief...Lucy inwardly recoiled from the idea. She would hate it if anything she did mucked up her sister's career.

As soon as Ellie had finished her cappuccino, Lucy pushed back her chair and rose to her feet. 'I'm off to the ladies' room. Will you come with me, Ellie?'

'Of course,' she said, immediately rising to join her.

The moment they were closeted away, Lucy confronted her, determined to learn the truth. 'Why are you leaving your great job with Michael? He's not happy about it.'

Ellie shook her head. 'It's not my mission in life to keep Michael happy,' she said drily.

'But you always said you loved that job.'

'I did, but it's high pressure, Lucy. I didn't realise how much it demanded of me until I came out here.

I don't want to be constantly on my toes anymore. I want to look for something else—more relaxed, less stressful.'

Was this the truth? Ellie had always been ambitious, and walking away from such a top-level position seemed like a complete turnaround from achieving what she'd aimed for. On the other hand, Lucy knew nothing of high pressure jobs, never having had one, so Ellie might actually need to give it up and move on.

'Then it's not because of me and him?' Lucy asked worriedly, wanting to believe this decision was as straightforward as her sister made out.

'No,' she replied, her eye contact remaining absolutely steady as she laid out what she thought. 'I'm sorry Michael is unhappy about it, but I don't think he'll take it out on you, Lucy. If he does, he's not the man for you.'

Lucy hadn't got that far in her own thinking. Her main concern had revolved around Ellie sacrificing her job out of some sense of protective loyalty. If there were personal repercussions from Michael because of his frustration over the situation…well, that simply wasn't acceptable. He would not be the man for her. It would be frog territory. Lucy was not so blindly in love that she couldn't see that. This was a test he would have to pass or there was not even a small future for them.

She heaved a sigh to relieve the tightness in her chest, gave her sister a quick hug, then looked her directly in the eye. 'You're right. Okay. It's completely fair for you to look for something else. He's just got to lump being put out by it.'

'You can play nurse and soothe his frustration,' Ellie said with a smile.

Lucy laughed, more in the grip of hysteria than from any amusement. She desperately didn't want things to start going wrong between her and Michael, but if they did, she had to be as sensible as Ellie. However seductive a fairy tale fantasy was, in the end there was no escaping from reality.

Michael couldn't recall ever being at serious odds with his brother, but he was right now. He'd lent Elizabeth to him to facilitate the quick removal of a crooked manager. He could tolerate not having her on hand for a month, but losing her altogether had not been on the table.

Just one week over here and she was handing in her resignation as his PA. He didn't buy her reason for leaving him. Something had happened and that *something* had to do with Harry. Michael waited until the two sisters had closed themselves in the ladies' room, safely out of earshot, and unleashed his anger.

'This is bloody nonsense!' he hissed at Harry. 'Elizabeth never showed any dissatisfaction with her work situation. Whatever I threw at her, she ate up, and came back for more. And I paid her what she was worth. She's completely on top of her job. Why the hell would she want to take a different direction? The only thing that makes sense is you've thrown a spanner in the works, Harry.'

'If she wants a different direction, why isn't she staying on here?' he retaliated. 'She's on top of this job, too. It's not me pulling the strings, Mickey.'

'Then what is it?' he demanded testily.

Harry eyed him grimly. 'I'd say it's Lucy.'

'That's nonsense, too! Lucy was just as shocked as I was at Elizabeth's resignation.'

'Wake up, Mickey!' Sheer exasperation laced Harry's voice. 'You're having it off with your PA's younger sister—a sister she's more or less been a mother to after their own mother died. From the moment you took up with Lucy, Elizabeth's resignation has probably been on the drawing board. Seeing how it is for her sister this weekend undoubtedly clinched it.'

'What do you mean?'

Harry rolled his eyes. 'Even to me it's obvious that Lucy's head over heels in love with you. Elizabeth would be well aware that your relationships have never lasted long. You might end up hurting her sister very badly.'

'And I might not!' Michael retorted heatedly. 'I might want to keep this relationship.'

Harry shrugged. 'Whatever… But you introduced a personal element that wasn't there before.'

'What about you? Don't tell me you haven't got very personal with Elizabeth this week.'

'Which is probably why she won't stay on working for me, either,' Harry retorted, then threw up his hands in exasperation. 'I don't know what's going on in Elizabeth's head. I wish I did. I do know that once she makes up her mind, she follows through, so we both have to accept her decision whether we like it or not.'

Michael huffed in frustration. 'Okay,' he conceded. 'It's not your fault.'

'Definitely not,' Harry vehemently insisted.

'Dammit! Why did Lucy have to be her sister?'

'You be careful how you treat her, Mickey. I don't

want your affair with her messing up what I might have with Elizabeth.'

Michael shook his head over complexities he hadn't considered. 'We've never been mixed up like this before, Harry.'

'I'll tell you now. I'm not letting Elizabeth go if I can help it.'

He was deadly serious.

'I'm not about to let Lucy go, either.' Not in the foreseeable future. There was absolutely no point to ending it within a month, since Elizabeth wasn't coming back to work for him. He could let it go on for as long as it pleased him.

Harry nodded. 'So…are *we* sorted, Mickey?'

'Yes, sorted.'

Which didn't mean he liked the situation, but at least he agreed Harry wasn't to blame for it. Elizabeth had pulled the trigger on the professional side, quite possibly swayed by the personal elements of two brothers and two sisters becoming emotionally entangled. Lucy had called her *'the sensible one.'*

Michael castigated himself for not seeing this coming, yet he hadn't known the nature of the relationship between the two sisters when he'd been bowled over by Lucy last Monday. He'd begun to see it more clearly in his conversation with Sarah yesterday, but he still hadn't anticipated this breakaway by Elizabeth.

It seemed an extreme action.

And he resented the assumption that he might treat Lucy badly.

He had never treated a woman badly.

Yet both Sarah and now Harry were warning him to

be careful with how he treated Lucy. That didn't make a lot of sense, either. She hadn't come across to him as a fragile personality, more like a free spirit, flitting around, trying anything that appealed to her. If their relationship took a wrong turn, surely she would flit somewhere else, not fall in a heap and need massive support from her sister.

Regardless of what he thought or felt, Elizabeth's decision had been made and there was no point in sweating it. He didn't regret picking up with Lucy even if it had lost him his PA. She could become very important to his life—a joy not to be missed or set aside. And he still had three weeks of having her to himself before her sister returned to Cairns—time for the relationship to consolidate, if it was going to—without any outside influence interfering with it.

Michael didn't believe being 'head over heels in love' meant a relationship was on unbreakable ground. It was probably a fair description of how he felt about Lucy right now—infatuated to the point of obsession. But this could be a fairy floss stage, melting into nothing in the end.

He wanted to share a deep, abiding love with a woman.

As his father had with his mother.

He needed more time with Lucy to know if she was *the one* he'd been waiting for.

If she wasn't, he would let her down as lightly as he could.

She might see him as a frog, but he sure as hell wasn't a gross cane toad!

CHAPTER TWELVE

LUCY COULDN'T HELP fretting over the impact of Ellie's decision. The goodbyes after lunch had a strained edge to them, and Harry had called up Jack to drive her and Michael to the jetty in the golf buggy, not choosing to do it himself. She sensed he couldn't see the back of them fast enough, and Lucy was sure he'd be very quickly demanding more explanation from Ellie. He was no longer wearing the expression of a winner.

Michael was harder to read. He chatted to Jack on the way to the jetty in a normal manner, and he held her hand, which was comforting. Jack helped him cast off, and it wasn't until they had left the island behind that Lucy plucked up courage enough to ask, 'Do you feel Ellie has let you down, Michael?'

He made a rueful grimace. 'I can't say I understand her reason for resigning, but every person has the right to choose what to do with their life. I won't argue with that but…she'll be a hard act to follow. It's going to be difficult finding someone to fill her shoes.'

Lucy tried to explain how Ellie might feel. 'I think it has to do with her turning thirty. And the apartment is paid for now, so she doesn't have to feel responsible about keeping a roof over our heads. If you've got that security you can afford to cut free a bit. I guess that's where she's at, Michael.'

He shot her a quizzical look. 'I wondered if it had anything to do with us being connected.'

Lucy shook her head. 'Ellie says not.'

'You asked her?'

'Yes. It just seemed too coincidental somehow. Although I had cleared it with her yesterday morning—like, whatever happens between you and me shouldn't affect what she and Harry could have together. The same should have applied to her job. I told her I'd just pick myself up and move on if it came to us parting.'

His mouth twitched with some private amusement. 'You would, would you?'

'Not easily,' she said archly, pleased that he wasn't grumpy. 'But I would. It's not good to hang on to things that have to be put behind you.'

He laughed, took one hand off the steering wheel of the motor launch and reached out to draw her into a hug. 'That's my Lucy!' he said warmly, and dropped a kiss on her forehead. 'I love the way you look at things.'

Love... Her heart drummed with happiness.

On the work front he was definitely put out by Ellie's resignation, but there was no overflow of negative feeling onto what they had together. He was still a prince to Lucy. She laid her head contentedly on his shoulder and sighed away all her inner angst.

'Thank you for a wonderful weekend, Michael.'

He planted another kiss on her forehead and gave her a tighter hug. '*You* made it wonderful.'

Pure bliss! Michael had passed this test with flying

colours. The only nasty little niggle remaining in her mind was the possible fallout between Ellie and Harry. Lucy *wanted* him to be her sister's prince.

Later that evening, after Michael had left her apartment, she headed straight into Ellie's room to email her. The great thing about modern technology was the common practice of using shorthand texting that cut out a lot of letters in words. Lucy could manage this simplified communication fairly well, though Ellie could get the gist of any garbled stuff she typed, so it wasn't a problem, anyway.

She kept it short.

M & I R OK. R U & H OK?

As soon as she woke up the next morning she rushed to the computer hoping for an answer. A new message popped into the inbox and yes, it was from Ellie. It opened with a smile sign, which instantly put a smile on Lucy's face, then the confirmation: H & I OK.

Still two princes, Lucy thought happily, and the week passed brilliantly without anything happening to put even a slight crack in that sweet belief. It gave her more confidence about going to the ball with Michael. She was sure he would smooth over any shortcomings she might have in the company of his friends.

On Saturday he took her out to lunch, saying they probably wouldn't be fed until quite late tonight so they might as well enjoy a good meal early in the afternoon and have plenty of energy for dancing. He drove them to the Thala Beach Lodge, which was located between

Cairns and Port Douglas and perched on top of a steep hill with magnificent views of the coast and sea.

The restaurant was open-air, with high wooden ceilings and polished floorboards, and their table for two overlooked the rainforest that covered the hillside down to the beach. Lucy once again covered up her dyslexia, remarking to the waitress that everything on the menu looked marvellous, and asking what were the most popular choices. That made it easy to pounce on the coconut prawns, followed by a chocolate fudge brownie with pistachio nuts, roasted banana and butterscotch sauce. This time it was Michael who chose to have 'the same', which gave Lucy a pleasant sense of complacency about her disability.

Maybe he would never notice it, or by the time he did, hopefully he wouldn't care about it, because there was so much that was good between them.

Like enjoying this delicious lunch together.

Like making love back in her apartment until she had to chase Michael off so she could do all she had to do to look her absolute best for the ball.

Lucy didn't own a ball gown. She had thought of borrowing one of the costumes from the dance studio where she'd worked, but decided the competition creations might look out of place in a crowd that was bound to be sophisticated. In the end, her tangerine bridesmaid dress seemed the best choice. It was a simple, long, figure-hugging shift with a knee-high split at the back for ease of movement. The square neckline was low enough to show the upper swell of her breasts—definitely an evening gown look—and the straps over the shoulders were linked by three gold rings.

With the honey-tan tone of her skin, blond hair and brown eyes, the tangerine colour looked great on her, and the garment was spectacular enough in itself not to need much dressing up—just gold hoop earrings, her slimline gold watch, the gold bangle Ellie had given her on her twenty-first birthday, the gold strappy sandals that were perfect dancing shoes, and a small gold handbag for essential make-up repair items.

She washed and blow-dried her hair, twirling it up into a topknot, and using a curling wand on the loose tendrils that dangled down from it. She kept her make-up fairly subtle, carefully highlighting her eyes and cheekbones, wanting to look right for the company she was to be in tonight, but she did gloss her tangerine lipstick. The dress demanded it and she wanted to look right for herself, too.

Certainly Michael had no problem with her appearance. When he arrived to pick her up he took one look at her and shook his head in awe, murmuring, 'You take my breath away.' Then he gave her a sparkling grin, adding, 'Not for the first time!'

She laughed. 'You do the same to me.'

He was always stunningly handsome, but dressed in a formal dinner suit he was truly breathtaking. Excited simply to be with him, Lucy stopped worrying about other people. She was going to dance all night with this beautiful, fantastic man and have a wonderful time.

However, her exhilaration was inevitably overtaken by nervous tension as they entered the casino ballroom, the need for Michael's friends to find her acceptable rising with every step she took. She tried to reassure herself with the fact that Sarah and Jack Pickard had liked her, but they had been an older couple, probably not as inclined to be as critical as a peer group.

The table Michael led her to was half occupied. They obviously weren't the first of the party to arrive, nor the last. The men stood as Michael started the introductions, and Lucy did her best to fit the names she had memorised to the faces. These were the three married couples he'd told her about, and they eyed her with interest—a new woman on the scene.

'Where did you meet this gorgeous lady, Mickey?' one of the men asked.

'She burst in on me at work and I instantly decided...' his eyes twinkled at Lucy '...I needed her in my life.'

Her heart swelled with happiness at this public declaration.

'Ah! A business connection then,' his friend concluded.

'You could say that. Though my connection to Lucy now extends way beyond business.' He gave her a hug. 'I'm here to dance her off her feet tonight.'

They all laughed. One of the women archly commented, 'He is a very good dancer, Lucy. If you can't keep up with him, hand him over to me.'

'No chance!' Michael told her. 'Lucy has done the dance studio thing. I'm out to prove I can match her.'

'Well, you look like a good match,' another woman remarked, smiling at both of them.

Lucy no longer felt tense and nervous. They were all looking at her in a friendly manner, willing to accept her into their company. Michael had set them on that path with his admiring comments, and they were happy to go along with him. Like a true prince, he'd made the situation easy for her, and she had no trouble carrying on a conversation with these people, using the information he'd given about them to focus on their lives and interests.

Once the band started up, he swept her off to the dance floor. He had great rhythm and was so sexy, Lucy could barely contain the excitement he stirred in her. Dance followed dance. He challenged her with intricate moves and she challenged him right back. Other couples made more room for them on the floor, standing back to watch and applaud their display of expertise. It was wildly exhilarating and they were both breathless when the set ended and they made their way back to the table.

The rest of their party had arrived. More introductions were made. Lucy was on too much of a high to feel nervous about them. Besides, they were all grinning at them, with one commenting, 'You two are hot, hot, hot! That was a sizzling performance on the dance floor.'

Michael laughed. 'I've never had a partner like Lucy.'

'And he's so good I'm only just still on my feet,' she said, sliding her arm around his waist and leaning into him as though close to collapse.

He hugged her shoulders and glanced inquiringly at the men. 'Who's pouring the champagne? My lady needs a refreshing drink.'

Champagne, dancing, fun company, the burgeoning hope that Michael might see her as a partner in every sense... Lucy realised the concern about being a Cinderella at this ball was completely wiped out. She felt like a princess. Not even a clash with Michael's ex in the powder room could dim the stars in her eyes.

The unexpected confrontation with the beautiful brunette was not pleasant. Lucy was refreshing her lipstick at the vanity mirror when the woman beside her turned to face her with a spiteful glare.

'Just who are you?' she demanded.

Startled, Lucy retorted, 'Who are *you?*'

'Fiona Redman.'

The name meant nothing to Lucy. 'So?'

'Michael Finn was mine until a month ago,' she spat out. 'I want to know if you're the reason he dropped me.'

'No. I've only known him for two weeks.'

She gnashed her teeth over that information, her dark eyes glowering meanly at Lucy. 'Well, don't expect to keep him. He's notoriously fickle in his relationships. Business always comes first with him.'

Lucy made no reply. She was recalling Michael's description of this woman as too self-centred.

'He might be as handsome as sin and great in bed, but he'll just use you and toss you away like all the rest,' the woman jeered.

'Thank you for warning me,' Lucy said politely, and made a quick escape, smiling over her mother's old saying, 'the soft word turneth away wrath.' It had always worked for her, putting people off their rants. It was obvious that Fiona Redman was as jealous as sin, having lost 'her catch', and Lucy was not about to let her spoil this brilliant night with Michael.

He hadn't let Jason Lester spoil anything between them.

What they had together was special. It had nothing to do with anyone else. Michael's past relationships simply hadn't proved *right,* just as hers hadn't. As far as Lucy was concerned, a small future with each other remained shining brightly at this point in time.

Michael had taken the opportunity to visit the men's room while Lucy was in the ladies', not wanting to lose any time together. He was washing his hands when another guy claimed his attention, sliding a highly provocative comment at him.

'I see you've snagged the best piece of arse in Cairns.'

Michael frowned at him. 'I beg your pardon.'

'Luscious Lucy.' This was accompanied by a leer. 'Great for sex. Pity she's such an airhead. I enjoyed her for a while. I'm sure you will, too. But trying to put some order into her mess of a mind wore me out.'

The control freak, Michael thought.

The guy flicked water off his hands and made one last rotten comment. 'She should keep her mouth for what it's good at.'

He walked out, leaving Michael untroubled by the 'airhead' tag, but disturbed at having Lucy described as 'the best piece of arse in Cairns.' It made him recall Jason Lester's remark that she'd slept with half the men in the city. Michael didn't believe this was true, certain that Lucy had more discrimination than that, yet it once more raised the question of how many men she had pleasured in the past, and how she had learnt to give so much pleasure.

He told himself it didn't matter.

He revelled in her uninhibited sensuality, her utterly spontaneous response to the sexual chemistry between them. He was glad she was like that, and however it had come about should not concern him. Apart from which, the disparaging comments had come from men Lucy had rejected—men who were missing out on what they wanted from her.

Michael returned to their table, determined to banish the niggles about her past. If she was hiding things she didn't want him to know...so what? He liked what he had with her in the present, and wasn't about to mess with it.

She was already seated, her lovely face alight with interest in the conversation amongst his friends. He took the empty chair across the table from her for the sheer pleasure of watching her smiles, the dimples flashing in her cheeks, the golden twinkles in her sherry-brown eyes, the slight heave of her perfect breasts when she laughed.

Luscious Lucy...

The phrase slid into his mind and stuck there.

They were served a seafood banquet. He watched the sensual way she forked oysters into her mouth, the relish with which she ate chunks of lobster, the licking of her lips to capture any escaping dipping sauce with the prawns, the sheer love of good food that shone through her enjoyment of the sumptuous supper.

Luscious Lucy...

There couldn't be a man alive who wouldn't think of her in those terms. Everything about her was sexy. Michael was strongly aroused simply watching her. It was difficult to contain the desire she stirred in him, the need stealing his appetite, making him impatient for the stack of gourmet food to be eaten and cleared away.

Finally the band started up again. They began with a slow number—a jazz waltz. *Perfect,* Michael thought, gesturing in invitation to Lucy as he rose from his chair. While he skirted the table, she rose from hers, as eager as he was for physical connection. He took her hand. She squeezed his. A few strides and he was swinging her into his embrace, holding her close, legs brushing against each other in the sensual intimacy of the dance.

He was acutely conscious of his erection furrowing her stomach, her breasts pressing into his chest, the warmth of her breath feathering the skin of his neck. He wanted her so badly it was almost a sickness inside him. He wanted her to himself, completely to himself.

The control mechanism in his mind snapped.

The question that should have stayed unasked came out of his mouth in a harsh rasp.

'How many men have you slept with, Lucy?'

She stopped dancing with him.

Her hands slid down to his chest, pushing to create distance between them. She looked up, stared at his face, her eyes blank of all expression, as though she was staring through him at something else.

And Michael knew instantly what it was.

The frog inside him.

He could almost feel himself turning green, and though he wanted to push back that fatal tide of colour, it was impossible to erase the words he had spoken. They hung between them, waiting to be answered—words that might well cost him a woman he wanted to keep in his life.

He wasn't ready to lose Lucy.

He might never be ready to lose her.

She'd become an addiction he didn't want to end.

CHAPTER THIRTEEN

LUCY FELT SICK.

She couldn't understand why Michael had asked that question now, on this night of nights, when everything had seemed so good between them. She had expected it—dreaded it—a week ago when Jason Lester had made that crack about her having slept with half the men in Cairns, which she had made worse with her 'town slut' remark.

Her stomach roiled with nausea.

Had she done something *sluttish* tonight? Lucy frantically searched her mind for some word or action of hers that might have triggered bad thoughts along those lines.

Nothing.

She'd simply been herself.

And if Michael couldn't accept her for the person she was...

'It doesn't matter!' he fiercely muttered. 'Forget I asked, Lucy. It was a stupid question.'

It jerked her into refocusing, meeting his eyes, searching them for truth. 'It does matter to me, Michael,' she quietly stated, hating the fact that he might think her indiscriminately promiscuous.

He grimaced in self-disgust. 'I ran into your latest ex—the control freak—in the men's room. He made some remarks about you. I shouldn't have let what he said bother me, but coming on top of Lester's...' Michael shook his head as though trying to rid his mind of images he didn't want there.

'People who want to cast nasty aspersions on others usually make sex the centre of them. Especially men, I've found. But women, too,' Lucy said, instinctively mounting a counter-attack out of a desperate need to defend herself. 'I was confronted by *your* ex—Fiona Redman—in the ladies' room. Her words were you were great in bed, but you used women up and tossed them away.' Lucy summoned up a wry little smile. 'I didn't believe you were so callous.'

'I'm sorry,' he declared. 'It's just that you're...' He paused, struggling to explain, probably hating that he'd put himself in the position of having to explain.

'What, Michael? Does it bother you that I feel free to enjoy sex as much as you do?'

'No!' He sliced the air with his hand—a sharp, negative gesture. His eyes blazed with intensity of feeling. 'I love how you are with me, Lucy.'

Not enough, she thought. *Not enough.*

Her stomach started cramping.

She clutched it, trying to stop the rolling of pain. Something was wrong. This wasn't just emotional stress. It was too physical. Had she eaten something that was violently disagreeing with her?

Defiantly determined to finish what Michael had started, she lifted her chin and faced him with her truth. 'To answer your question—'

'Don't!' he commanded tersely.

She went on, disregarding his denial of any need for it. 'I've probably slept with as many men as you have women. I've seen no reason not to have the pleasure of sex when it promised to be pleasurable. I've found each experience quite different, because the men were different. And when it came it you, Michael, it was very special.' Tears spurted into her eyes. 'So special…'

Her throat choked up. Her stomach heaved. Bile shot into her mouth. She turned blindly, desperate to get to the ladies' room before she started vomiting.

Strong hands gripped her shoulders, halting any attempt at flight. 'Lucy…' It was a gruff plea.

'I'm sick! I'm going to be sick!' she cried, clapping her hand over her mouth as she doubled over, pain shafting her lower body.

No more talk. Nothing but action, Michael moving her, supporting her, collecting one of his friends along the way to look after her in the ladies' room. Lucy barely had time to sink down on her knees in a toilet cubicle before the contents of her stomach erupted. The convulsions kept coming, even when there was nothing left to vomit. Then she was hit by diarrhoea and that was just as bad. It felt as though her whole lovely night was going down the toilet, along with the relationship she'd hoped to have with Michael Finn.

Michael waited outside the ladies' room, anxious over Lucy's condition and cursing himself for probably contributing to her sudden bout of illness with his stupid question about other men. Everything she'd said back to him was totally reasonable. *Totally*. He should have known it without asking. He should have realised that a free spirit like Lucy would take what she wanted from life and not feel she had to account for it to anyone else. And neither should she.

He'd acted like a jealous man instead of being grateful for having her light up his life, and any sense of jealousy appalled him. It was not the attribute of a rational man, which he'd always prided himself on being. This overwhelming obsession with Lucy had to stop. It was getting out of hand. He needed to pull back from it, be less intense about the feelings she stirred in him.

Though he might very well have wrecked any choice to do anything about it.

Was he now an irredeemable frog in her eyes?

Certainly, he'd killed the light in them—the light that had told him he was special.

She was special.

And he desperately wanted another chance with her.

If she walked away from him tonight, shut the door on him…

His hands clenched. He had to fight, win her back, convince her he would never again make the mistake of holding her to account for anything she might have done before they'd met. Only what they had together was important. That was what he cared about. The future without her in it looked too empty of any joy to even contemplate such an outcome. He would not accept it.

The door to the ladies' room opened. He'd asked Dave Whitfield's wife, Jane, to do what she could for Lucy, and it was a relief to see her coming out. He needed to know what state Lucy was in, whether there was some positive action he could take. Every fibre of his being was intent on changing the situation as it stood.

Jane made a sympathetic grimace. 'Not good, I'm afraid. She's violently ill. I think it must be food poisoning, though the rest of us seem to be fine. Maybe there was a bad oyster in the seafood banquet, and Lucy lucked out, being the one to eat it.'

'What should I do?' Michael asked, feeling helplessly locked out of doing anything.

'I think you'll either have to take her to hospital emergency or...does she have someone to look after her at home?'

'I'll look after her.'

'She might need some medication, Mickey. I'll go back and stay with her until she's okay to get moving.' Jane frowned. 'Though if this keeps up we might have to call an ambulance. I'll let you know if that's the case.'

'Thanks, Jane.'

'It's such a shame!' She shook her head over the mishap as she turned back to the ladies' room.

Shame was right, Michael thought savagely. Shame on him for causing more upset to Lucy when she had started to feel unwell. He had to make up for it, be all she needed him to be. The minutes dragging by felt like hours as he waited for more news. Other women entered and left the ladies' room, glancing curiously at him as they passed. He didn't care what they thought. Only Lucy mattered. He remained on watch.

Finally the door opened and Jane shuffled out, supporting Lucy, who looked completely debilitated—with no colour in her face at all. Even the bright orange lipstick had been wiped off. Her eyes were bleary, as though they'd been washed by a river of tears. Her shoulders were slumped and it was obvious she was too physically drained to stand up straight.

Michael moved quickly to draw her to his side, taking over Jane's supporting role. There was no resistance to his action. Michael suspected she was grateful to have anyone holding on to her.

'She wants to go home, Mickey,' Jane informed him. 'I think the worst is over, but she's fairly shaky. I'll get her bag and fetch Dave. If you give him your keys and tell him where you've parked, he can drive your car to the front of the casino, ready for you to put Lucy in. Okay?'

He nodded. 'Thanks, Jane.'

There was so much he wanted to say to Lucy. but she was in no condition to listen, and he knew it would be selfish of him to push any issues in these circumstances. She needed kindness and comfort.

Jane quickly organised the easiest possible exit from the casino, accompanying them to the car, which Dave had waiting for them. She opened the passenger door and Michael lifted Lucy into the seat and secured her safety belt.

Lucy mumbled 'Thank you' to everyone. Michael quickly expressed his gratitude for his friends' help, anxious to get her home. She was so limp and listless, he worried over whether to take her to the hospital instead as he settled in the driver's seat and started the engine.

'Are you sure you don't need medical attention, Lucy?' he asked.

'Just want to lie down and sleep,' she answered, sounding exhausted.

It was probably the best option, he thought as he set off for her apartment. There wasn't much comfort in waiting for attention in a queue at the emergency room of a hospital, and maybe the worst was over. She wasn't sick during the trip home. Once there, he took her keys out of her bag and carried her into the apartment—a move she weakly protested wasn't needed, but he did it anyway, wanting to hold her in his arms.

He stood her up beside her bed, unzipped her dress, slid it off her arms so it could drop to her feet, before he sat her down and worked on removing her under-clothes and gold sandals. Her skin felt hot and she shivered several times, obviously feverish. He picked out the pins holding up her hair, running his fingers through the falling tresses to ensure they were all gone, before gently lowering her to the pillows, lifting her feet onto the bed and tucking the doona around her.

'Good of you, Michael,' she murmured with a ragged sigh. 'It's okay for you to go now. Thank you.'

She closed her eyes, and the sense of being shut out of her life twisted Michael's gut. If she'd consigned him to the frog species, according to the fairy tale, the only way to change that was for her to kiss him, willingly and caringly. Somehow he had to win his way back into her heart, persuade her to overlook his crass question as to-tally irrelevant to their relationship. Which it truly was.

'I'm not leaving you,' he muttered with fierce deter-mination, sitting on the bed beside her and gently strok-ing her hair away from her hot forehead. 'You're not okay, Lucy. You're running a fever. Do you have any medication here that might lower your temperature?'

She sighed again, whether in exasperation at his

persistence or with her illness, he couldn't tell. Her eyelashes lifted slightly as she answered, 'Bathroom cupboard.'

Her voice was flat. The slitted look she gave him revealed nothing of what she was feeling towards him. 'I'll find it,' he said, and went to the bathroom.

There was a packet of pain tablets that were supposed to lower fever. He took them and went to the kitchen to fill a glass with water before returning to Lucy. He lifted her up from the pillows, fed her the tablets and held the glass to her lips. She gulped down some water. Michael was thinking she was probably dehydrated when she suddenly hurled off the doona, erupted from the bed and staggered towards the bathroom.

Apparently her stomach couldn't tolerate anything in it. Michael had to stand by helplessly as she was convulsively sick again. 'I think I'd better take you to hospital, Lucy,' he said worriedly.

'No…no…' She shook her head vehemently. 'Just help me back to bed. I'll sleep it off.'

Did she want to sleep him off, too?

What could he say?

What could he do?

He tried to make her comfortable again. He dampened a face-cloth and laid it across her forehead, then remembered the cup of ice Harry had been given to suck when he was in hospital with a broken nose. Lucy was definitely dehydrated. He found a tray of ice cubes in the freezer, emptied most of it into a large tumbler and set it on her bedside table. Her eyes were closed again. Not wanting to leave her without any ready access for help, he took her mobile telephone out of her gold hand-bag and laid it on the bedside table, too.

'Listen to me, Lucy,' he said urgently. 'I'm going to the all-night chemist to ask the pharmacist for advice. Hopefully, he'll have something to settle your stomach. I'll be back soon. Try to suck some of the ice I've left here for you. I've put your phone within easy reach, as well, so you can call me if you need to. Okay?'

'Okay.'

It was barely a whisper of sound. Michael thought she was beyond caring. He hurried out to his car and drove towards the centre of town, where he knew the all-night chemist shop was situated. He was still in two minds about overriding her decision and taking her to hospital. The most important thing right now was to get her well again. Then he could work at making her understand how special she was to him.

He didn't see the car coming at him from the street to his right. The traffic lights at the intersection were green his way. He was focused on where he was going and what he had to do. He felt the impact, then nothing else. All consciousness ceased.

CHAPTER FOURTEEN

THERE WAS A persistent tune penetrating the fog in Lucy's sleep-laden head. On and on it went, until she was conscious enough to realise it was the call-tune of her mobile telephone. Still groggy, she flung an arm out to the bedside table, fumbled around until her hand found the source of irritation. She wanted to shut it off, but some vague memory of Michael leaving the phone beside her to call him made her lift it to her ear.

'Yes…what?' The words emerged in a slurred fashion. Her mouth was dreadfully dry. Her tongue felt furred. It was a huge effort to speak at all.

'Wake up, Lucy!' someone ordered sharply. 'There's been an accident.'

A woman's voice. It sounded like her sister. And saying something about an accident. On the island?

Lucy hauled herself into a sitting position and tried to concentrate. Having pried her eyes open, she could see there was some very early-morning light coming from her window, but it was still an ungodly hour to call anyone.

'What?' she asked again. 'Is that you, Ellie?'

'Yes. Michael was injured in a car accident early this morning. He was badly hurt.'

'Michael…oh, no… No…' Shock cleared her mind in no time flat. The memory of him bringing her home, looking after her, going out to get something for her stomach shot straight into it. 'Oh, God!' she wailed. 'It's my fault!'

'How is it your fault?' Ellie asked worriedly.

'I ate something at dinner last night that upset me. He brought me home. I was vomiting and had dreadful diarrhoea. He left me to find an all-night pharmacy to get me some medicine. I was so drained I must have drifted off to sleep. He should have come back, but he's not here and… Oh, God! He went out for me, Ellie!'

'Stop that, Lucy! You didn't cause the accident, and getting hysterical won't help Michael,' she said vehemently, cutting off the futile guilt trip. 'I take it everything was still good between you last night?'

'Yes…yes… He was so caring when I was sick. Oh, Ellie! I'll die if I lose him.'

She forgot she had probably already lost him. All she could think of was how special he was, how much she loved him.

'Then you'd better do whatever you can to make him want to live,' Ellie sharply advised. 'Are you still sick? Can you get to the hospital? He's in an intensive care unit.'

'I'll get there.' Gritty determination quelled every vestige of hysterical panic.

'Harry was with me on the island,' Ellie went on. 'He's on his way. Be kind to him, Lucy. Remember he and Michael lost their parents in an accident. I have to stay here. Harry's counting on me to take care of business, but I think he'll need someone there, too.'

'I understand. You love him but you can't be with him.'

At least that was good—Ellie and Harry teaming up together. Lucy couldn't let herself dwell on where she and Michael were in their relationship when he was fighting for his life in an intensive care unit.

'I need to know what's happening, Lucy,' Ellie said in a softer tone. 'Please…will you keep me informed?'

'Sure!' Clearly, the situation deeply concerned her sister, too, with Michael being Harry's brother, as well as a man she had worked closely with for two years. 'I'll call you with news as soon as I have it. Moving now. Over and out. Okay?'

'Okay.'

Moving was not easy. Lucy was still weak and shaky. Her head whirled as she forced her legs to take her to the bathroom. Nothing in her stomach, she thought, but was too scared of being sick again to eat or drink anything. Somehow she had to make it to the hospital and not look like the total wreck she saw in the vanity mirror.

Slowly, carefully, she cleaned herself up, brushed her hair and applied some make-up to put colour in her face. Bright clothes, she decided, wanting to make Michael smile…if he was up to smiling at all. She refused to let herself think he might die, though it was impossible to banish the anxiety spearing pain through her heart.

It took a while to put clothes on, since she needed to sit down more than once until her rockiness subsided. She selected the yellow wraparound dress to remind him of the great sex they'd shared, and the pretty shell necklace that might recall their wonderful time together on Finn Island. He would surely want to live to have those pleasures again.

Being in no condition to drive safely, she called for a taxi to pick her up and take her to the hospital. On the trip there she kept wondering where the accident had happened, and how it could have been so serious when traffic in the city had to move at a relatively slow pace. Had Michael been speeding, wanting to get back to her quickly? Had she unwittingly been the cause of it?

Her mind was awash with tormenting questions when she finally arrived at the intensive care unit. Before she could properly inquire about Michael at the nurses' station, Harry suddenly appeared at her side and swept her off to the waiting room, his grim expression filling her with fear. He sat her down and stood over her as he gave her the information she most needed to know.

'It's not too bad, Lucy. His injuries aren't life-threatening. He was hit on the driver's side, right arm and hip fractured, broken ribs, lacerations to the face, a lot of bruising, concussion. The doctors were worried that a broken rib had punctured his liver, but that's been cleared, and bones will mend.' Harry's sigh transmitted a mountain of relief. 'He's going to be incapacitated for quite a while, but there should be no lasting damage.'

'Thank God!' Her own relief was mountainous, as well. 'How did it happen, Harry?' She was still anxious to know that.

'Drunken teenagers in a stolen car ran a red light and slammed into him as he was driving across an intersection. They're all here, too. Needless to say, I don't have much sympathy for them.'

Another huge roll of relief. The accident wasn't Michael's fault. Nor hers. It was simply a case of being in the wrong place at the wrong time, although he wouldn't have been there but for her. Still, the food poisoning was an accident, too, and there was no point in fretting over it. Moving on was the only way to go.

'Can I go and see Michael now?'

Harry grimaced. 'I don't think that's a good idea.'

'Why not?'

'Well, to put it bluntly, he's barely recognisable. It will come as a shock to you. They've stitched the cuts on his face, but it's very bruised and swollen. He's also sedated to keep the pain at bay, and it's best if he stays that way. If you start screaming or carrying on—'

She cut him off very sharply. 'Harry Finn, I nursed my mother while she slowly died from cancer. Nothing is worse than seeing someone you love wasting away. I am no wimp when it comes to facing people who are suffering, and I am not stupid. I care a lot about Michael and no way would I do anything to wake him up to pain. I just want to be with him.'

Surprise at her vehemence gave way to a look of respect for her. He nodded. 'Then I'll take you to him.'

'Good!'

She pushed herself up from the chair and steadied herself for the walk to Michael's bedside. Harry took her arm, which helped her stay reasonably steady. 'Have you called Ellie to let her know Michael will come through this?' she asked, as he led her back to the intensive care unit.

'Not yet. I've just finished talking to the doctors. Since there's no critical danger, they won't operate on

Mickey until tomorrow morning. I've insisted on the top surgeon.'

'I'm glad about that, but do call my sister, Harry. She's anxiously waiting for news.'

'As soon as you're settled with Mickey,' he promised.

It was better if Ellie heard everything from Harry, Lucy thought. She would call her sister tonight, hopefully after Michael had woken up and she had more personal news.

Harry certainly hadn't exaggerated Michael's facial injuries. Seeing him did come as a shock, but she swiftly told herself all this was a temporary phase. He would heal. Harry pulled up a chair for her to sit beside the bed, and she sank gratefully onto it, reaching out to take Michael's left hand in hers, mindful that his right arm had been broken. His flesh was warm. No matter how ghastly he looked, he was alive, and she fiercely willed him to want her in his future.

Though she wasn't sure how much of a future he would want with her. His questioning last night about how many men she had slept with had not left her with a good feeling. It seemed judgemental in a nasty way. He'd told her to forget it, that it didn't matter, but he had brought it up so it obviously meant something to him. Had her answer satisfied him?

She'd become too ill to assess his reaction to it. Whatever he'd thought, he'd been good to her, sticking around, bringing her home, doing his best to look after her. Still a prince, in that sense. She could only hope there wasn't a frog lurking inside him.

Her head ached. Harry had left the room, probably

to make the call to Ellie. Lucy felt too tired to think anymore. Besides, it seemed pointless. There would be no answers until Michael woke up. She rested her head on the bed beside the hand she was holding. The effort to get here had drained her of what little energy she had after being so sick. She slid into sleep without realising it was happening.

A hand gripping hers hard jerked her awake. Michael's swollen black eyes were opened into thin slits. Having drawn her attention, he croaked out, 'Where am I?'

'In hospital, Mickey,' Harry answered, rising from a chair on the other side of the bed to put himself in his brother's line of sight. 'Don't move,' he commanded. 'You have broken bones.'

'How? Why? I can't open my eyes much.'

'You were in a car accident and your face copped a beating. So did your body,' Harry told him bluntly.

'How bad?'

'You'll mend, but it will take some time.'

'It hurts to breathe.'

'Broken ribs.'

'Car accident… I can't remember.'

'Concussion. The doctors warned me you might not regain any memory of last night.'

Lucy shot an inquiring glance at Harry. He hadn't told her that. How much memory might be blotted out? And would it stay blotted out?

He nodded to her. 'Lucy's here. I'll go and fetch the doctor on duty. I was told to do that as soon as you were conscious. He'll answer any questions you have, Mickey.'

Michael squeezed her hand as he shifted his limited vision to her. 'Lucy,' he said, as though he loved her name.

She squeezed back, smiling at him. 'You're going to be okay,' she assured him.

'I remember we had lunch at the Thala Beach Lodge. What happened last night?'

'We went to a ball at the casino. We danced for hours until they served a seafood banquet. Something I ate gave me food poisoning. You took me home, then went out to an all-night chemist to get me some medication. Harry told me a stolen car slammed into you at an intersection—a drunken driver running a red light.'

He shook his head slightly and winced. 'I don't remember any of that.'

'Don't worry about it.'

'Food poisoning…last night… You must feel wretched, Lucy.'

Her heart turned over. Here he was, caring about her when he was all broken up and obviously hurting.

'I'll live,' she said dismissively. 'I had to see you, be with you, Michael. Ellie called me with the news and I was frightened you might not make it through.' She smiled to lighten up the situation. 'I was going to hang on to you like grim death until you did.'

'That's my girl,' he said with a ghost of a smile.

It was so blissful to hear him say that, as though nothing had changed between them.

Harry returned with the doctor and Lucy moved out of the way of any medical checking that had to be done, standing at the end of the bed and holding the foot railing for support. She did feel wretched. A glance at her

watch told her she'd actually slept with her head on
Michael's bed for over three hours, which should have
helped, yet her legs were still weak and shaky.

The doctor went through a schedule of procedures,
explaining what would be done and when. He answered
questions, then administered an injection of morphine
before he left.

Michael turned his attention to her. 'You must go
home and rest, Lucy. You need recovery time from food
poisoning, and I'll probably be out of it for most of today
and tomorrow.' He shifted his gaze to his brother. 'Make
her go, Harry.'

'I will,' he promised.

She didn't want to, but saw the sense in it. 'I'll go,'
she said, moving around to his side to take his hand
again, pressing it with fervent caring. 'I'll come back
tomorrow evening. I hope the operation goes well, Michael.'

'Don't worry about it. Hip operations are run-of-the-
mill stuff these days.'

She leaned over and kissed his lips very softly. 'I'll
be thinking of you every minute,' she murmured.

Harry accompanied her out of the hospital and put
her in a taxi. 'Take care of yourself, Lucy,' he said
kindly. 'I think my brother will need you in the difficult days to come.'

It was nice that he thought she was an important part
of Michael's life. Maybe she still could be if Michael
never remembered questioning her about past sexual
partners. Initially he had dismissed the Jason Lester
encounter. It was the run-in with her most recent ex
last night that had reignited the issue in his mind. If

that was now wiped out… Lucy couldn't help hoping everything would be right between them.

She desperately wanted to hold on to her prince.

She couldn't bear it if he turned into a frog.

CHAPTER FIFTEEN

FOR MICHAEL IT was a hell of a week. The broken arm was a nuisance because he couldn't use it. The broken ribs gave him pain with every movement, and he had to move. The nurses got him out of bed every day after the hip operation, walking up and down a corridor to ensure his muscles kept working around the piece of titanium that had been inserted.

On top of that was his frustration at having to leave his business to Harry, who was making a good fist of handling the franchises under his instructions, but didn't have the sense of creativity needed to take any new initiatives. Which wasn't really a problem. That could wait for Michael's return. He simply wasn't used to not controlling everything himself. It would have been easier for Harry if Elizabeth had been on hand—the perfect PA—but she was stepping in for him on the island while he was tied up here.

The accident couldn't have come at a worse time, incapacitating Michael when he had no one in the office he trusted to take over in any capacity whatsoever. Andrew Cook was next to useless, needing someone to tell him everything, and there hadn't been time to find a competent replacement for Elizabeth.

The only bright spot in his current life was Lucy.

He was intensely grateful she had decided to over-look his frog blunder at the ball, calling into question her sexual experience. He still didn't remember the car accident, but memories of everything preceding it had come swimming back to him after the hip operation.

He'd actually been afraid she wouldn't visit him again, since he wasn't about to die, but she had turned up on Monday evening and every evening since, chatting to him in her wonderfully bubbly fashion, massaging his feet, giving him her beautiful smile, not at all concerned that he looked like Frankenstein's monster.

Michael had been moved to a private room with his own television to make time pass less tediously. He had no complaints about the care given to him from the medical staff. The physiotherapist was particularly good. His friends dropped in to see him, bringing him gifts to keep him in reasonably good cheer. Harry kept him informed of business issues and was always good company. But it was Lucy who brought sunshine into his room. She made him feel lucky to be alive and very lucky to have her in his life.

Today he was glad it was Saturday, not a workday for her, and she'd promised to visit him this morning. While he waited for her he struggled with the newspaper he'd asked to be delivered to him. It was the *Sydney Morning Herald* and its pages were large. Having the use of only one arm, handling them was awkward, and most of them slid off the bed onto the floor as he tried to separate out the financial section, which he liked to read each week.

He finally managed it, and having found an article

that interested him, he was frustrated again by his vision blurring over the little print. Probably an after-effect of the concussion, he reasoned. The swelling had gone down and his eyes were back to normal, but this was obviously yet another thing he would have to wait out.

He was darkly brooding over the frustrating aspects of his situation when Lucy walked in, all bright and beautiful, instantly lifting his spirits. She'd put up her hair in a kind of tousled topknot, and her eyes were sparkling, her dimples flashing, her smile totally enchanting. She was wearing purple jeans teamed with a purple-lime-and-white top in a wildly floral print, long dangly purple-and-lime earrings and a set of matching bangles.

He smiled. 'You look fantastic, Lucy!'

She laughed. 'I like dressing up. It's fun.'

Fun like a carnival full of happy surprises, he thought.

She'd brought him a surprise, too, holding out to him a perfect yellow rose in a long-stemmed glass vase.

'Look! Isn't it beautiful, Michael? I was out at the cemetery yesterday and the old man who planted a Pal Joey rose on his wife's grave was there. He cut this off for me, but it wasn't quite in full bloom so I waited until today to bring it to you.' She placed the vase on his bed-side table. 'Just the glorious scent of it will take away the hospital antiseptic smell and make you feel better.'

'I'm sure it will. Thank you, Lucy.'

'My pleasure.'

She leaned over and kissed him. Desire for her had already kicked in and he wished he could crush her to him, but his ribs were still a problem, so he had to suffer her moving away to pull up a chair.

'Wow! You've made a mess of this newspaper,' she said, bending over to shuffle the dropped pages into a manageable bundle.

It reminded him of the article he'd wanted to read, which was still on his bed, and he needed a distraction from the rush of hot blood Lucy stirred with her sexy derriere bobbing around. 'Just leave them in a pile and sit down, Lucy. There's something I want you to read to me. The little print has me defeated at the moment. My vision keeps blurring. It's an article in this financial section.' He picked it up and held it out to her.

She took it somewhat gingerly and sat down, frowning at the opened page. 'The financial section,' she repeated slowly, sounding troubled. She looked up with a quick, appealing smile. 'Wouldn't it be better if Harry read it to you? Then you could discuss whatever's in it together. I'm simply not into that scene, Michael.'

'Harry has gone over to the island with the guy who's to take over the job of manager as soon as Elizabeth can train him into the job. I don't expect him back until tomorrow. Besides, I don't want to discuss it,' he argued. 'I simply want to know what it says. It's been annoying me, not being able to read it. It will only take five minutes, Lucy. Please?'

The smile was gone. She gave him an anguished look. 'I'd really rather not.'

'Why not?'

Surely it was only a small favour to ask. Why put it off? Why was it a problem to her? She'd lowered her lashes to hide the strange anguish he'd seen, and her body was tensing up as though readying itself to spring from the chair. All this was incomprehensible to him.

'Lucy?' he pressed, needing to have her odd reaction cleared up.

She slowly set the section of newspaper he'd given her on the bed, drawing her hands back to pick at each other nervously in her lap. She drew in a deep breath, then met his gaze squarely as though facing a feared inquisitor.

'I can't, Michael,' she said flatly.

Still it made no sense to him. 'What do you mean... you *can't?*'

Her chin lifted slightly. 'I was born with dyslexia. I've always had difficulty with reading and writing.'

Dyslexia...

He didn't know much about it, only that letters in words got jumbled up to people who had that disability.

Lucy gave a wry little shrug. 'I can usually wing my way through most situations.' Her eyes were bleak with vulnerability as she added, 'But I've been sacked from jobs because of it and dumped from relationships because of it. I know I'm no match for you, Michael. I just wanted to have you love me for a little while.' Tears glittered. 'And you have, quite beautifully.'

It sounded perilously close to a goodbye speech to Michael. 'Now hold on a moment!' He cut in fast and hard. 'This isn't the end for us. I won't have it, Lucy. You're my girl, regardless. What I want is for you to tell me about your dyslexia. Share it with me. You don't have to hide it from me.'

She bit her lips. Her head drooped. Her eyelashes worked overtime, trying to blink away the tears. Her distress was heart-wrenching. She was such a beautiful person, and clearly this disability had been a blight on her life that she'd kept dodging and fighting, determined to make the most of who she was and what she could be. That took amazing strength of character, in Michael's opinion, and he admired her for it. To keep picking herself up and moving on from where she wasn't wanted, and find joy in something else…that was something very few people could do.

As he waited for Lucy to compose herself, his mind raced back over the past few weeks, picking up clues he'd missed. The mistake about chilli crab being on the menu that first day; her habit of choosing specials that were verbally listed by a waiter, when they were dining out, or observing what other people were eating and asking for the same; her panic at the idea of taking on Elizabeth's job as his PA, with Ellie staunchly supporting her, protecting her younger sister from being embarrassed by her disability.

He understood so much more about Lucy now: why she had been the one to drop out of school to nurse her mother, why she'd taken up hands-on jobs rather than desk ones, why few of them lasted very long, why advancement in any kind of serious career would be unlikely for her. The bookwork would be too hard to manage. She'd done what she could, probably relying a lot on Elizabeth's support.

Her anchor…

No matter what happened Lucy would always have her sister, who could be counted on to never waver in her love and support. Michael could see Elizabeth in that role.

He recalled Sarah Pickard's reading of Lucy, and realised now how accurate it was. Being ditzy was a good cover for feeling inadequate, she'd said, while he'd scoffed at the idea of Lucy feeling inadequate about anything. But the dyslexia did make her feel that way, which was why she hid it. Sarah had also been spot on about there being not much self-esteem in Lucy. How could there be if people kept putting her down because of her disability?

'Lucy, I think you're marvellous,' he said softly, wanting her to feel good about herself.

Her lashes flicked up and her tear-washed eyes searched his for truth.

'I do,' he asserted more strongly, holding her gaze with steady conviction. 'No matter how many people have cast you adrift because of your dyslexia, you haven't retreated from the world. You keep on setting out on another path and giving it your best. That drive to keep going, to keep finding joy in the world…you *are* marvellous, Lucy.'

'But…' she frowned at him, a wary uncertainty in her eyes '…you must see I'm defective, too.'

'Who isn't in one area or another?' he quickly answered, thinking *defective* was a particularly nasty word to be attached to Lucy. 'Harry says I have tunnel vision, not seeing anything except what's directly in front of me. You're in front of me, Lucy, and I like what I see.' Michael reached out to her. 'Give me your hand.'

Slowly, she lifted one hand and put it in his. He squeezed it reassuringly. 'I don't care if you can't read or write. I like having you with me. Now smile for me again.'

It was a wobbly smile, but at least there was a glimmer of hope in her eyes. 'I can read and write, Michael. It's just very slow and painstaking. I'm much better at memorising things. That's how I got my driver's licence. Ellie drilled me until I knew all the answers off by heart and could recognise the questions. She's always been great like that, giving me help when I needed it. Though I don't like asking too much of her. I try to get along by myself.'

'You do very well by yourself,' Michael said admiringly. 'I would never have guessed you had any disability.'

She made a wry grimace. 'It's not something I want people to know. I'd rather be seen as normal.'

'You're way above normal, Lucy. You're very special.'

The smile came back. 'My mother used to say that. She used to say my smile was worth a thousand words.'

'She was right,' Michael assured her.

'It doesn't always help, though. The guy I was with before you—the control freak—used to make lists of things he wanted me to do. His handwriting was too hard to work out, so I just ignored the lists and did whatever I wanted. He got really angry about it and called me an airhead.'

'So you walked out on him.'

'Yes. I guess I could have explained, told him about the dyslexia, but I don't like abusive people. My father was very abusive to my mother.' She shook her head. 'I don't want that in my life.'

Michael nodded. 'Quite right! It's not acceptable.'

She beamed a brilliant smile at him and there was sunshine back in the room.

Knowing what he now knew, he should have decked that guy in the men's room for calling Lucy an airhead, though violence wasn't acceptable, either. Instead of standing up for her, he'd been distracted by the sexual angle, which had led him into frog territory. Never again, he silently vowed. No man would like losing Lucy, and bruised egos undoubtedly prompted trying to damage her in the eyes of any other man she favoured.

Michael wondered how much abuse she had suffered because of her dyslexia. 'Your school years must have been hard, Lucy,' he said sympathetically, thinking of teachers who might not have spotted her disability for quite a while, and other kids calling her stupid.

'Yes and no. I was good at sports, which helped, winning me some approval for what I could do, and I did make friends who stuck by me. But schoolwork was a nightmare and I copped some bullying, which was fairly nasty. I was an easy target for those who liked to feel superior.'

'Tell me about it,' he urged, wanting her to unload all she had kept inside and be free of it with him.

Lucy could hardly believe that Michael was so accepting of her disability, not seeming to see any wrong in her at all. He kept encouraging her to talk about it, the problems it had caused her, how she had skirted around a lot of them. She made fun of some of the situations, and it was strangely exhilarating to laugh together about them. Other more distressing experiences drew nothing but sympathy from him, even admiration at how well she'd survived them, not letting them destroy her spirit to find pleasures to enjoy.

They talked all day, and when Lucy finally left Michael, she was almost on a giddy high from sheer happiness. The sense of freedom from having to keep her dyslexia hidden from him was so exhilarating she wanted to dance and whirl around and clap her hands.

Michael liked her as she was.

He might even love her as she was.

And he was very definitely a prince.

CHAPTER SIXTEEN

LUCY WAS IN THE habit of going straight from work to visit Michael. She did not stay long on Thursday evening because Harry was there, making arrangements about Michael's release from hospital on Friday, and Ellie had returned from the island, satisfied that the new manager could handle everything. It had been almost three weeks since she'd seen her sister and was eager to hear all her news and share her own.

Ellie was in the kitchen making a salad when she arrived home. 'Hi, Lucy!' she greeted her with a smile. 'Have you eaten?'

'No. Is there enough for two?'

'Sure! There wasn't much food here so I shopped.'

'I've been with Michael most of the time.'

'How is he today?'

'Still in considerable discomfort but he can manage with a walking stick so they're letting him out tomorrow.'

She nodded. 'Harry told me. I'll be helping in the office until Michael's ready to take over again. I'll train my replacement, too, make sure there's someone competent to assist him when I'm gone.'

'That's good of you, Ellie. Do you have some idea of what you want to do after that?'

'Oh yes!' She grinned. 'There's a bottle of Sauvignon Blanc in the fridge. How about you open it and we'll drink to the future?'

Lucy was happy to see her sister in such high spirits. The month on the island had made a big difference to her. Or Harry had. She opened the bottle of wine, filled two glasses and handed one to her sister. 'Is it a bright future with Harry?' she asked hopefully.

'He's asked me to marry him. And I'm going to, Lucy.'

'Oh, that's great news!' Lucy put down her glass to give Ellie a big hug. 'I'm so happy for you!'

'I'm happy, too. I really believe we're right together.'

Her eyes sparkled. Her skin glowed. Love was beaming out of her. Lucy's heart swelled with joy for her sister, who truly deserved a good man who would always care for her.

Ellie eased back from the hug to give her a searching look. 'How's it going with Michael?'

'Hey! You're not to worry about that. I want you and Harry to ride off into the sunset together without a care in the world. You promised not to let me get in the way, remember?'

'Yes, and I won't, but I'm not about to stop caring about you. I take it you're still in love with him.'

'Oh, I love him to bits and I think he cares about me, too. Though this accident has sort of interrupted things.'

'Lucy, it needs to be more than great sex.'

'I know.' But he hadn't yet remembered asking her

about sex with other men, and that might raise its ugly head again.

'When you phoned me last Sunday, you said he had no problem with your dyslexia. That's good, isn't it?'

'It's amazing! I hated having to reveal it but he was unbelievably nice to me about it. And it's such a relief to have it out in the open, not having to hide it.'

'Then it's made no difference to how he treats you.'

'None at all. I love being with him, Ellie.'

'Well, from what Harry tells me, he loves being with you, too.' Her face relaxed into a smile. 'Who knows? We might all end up in one happy family.'

'We might,' Lucy agreed, but she couldn't quite bring herself to believe it.

Having a lovely fantasy was one thing. Having it become reality was quite another. As much as she loved Michael, marriage was something else. Michael Finn was the kind of man who would want children, and although he admired how she had managed her life with dyslexia, she didn't think he'd want his own children to be afflicted by the disability.

There was no guarantee she wouldn't pass it on to any baby she had. She had kept pushing that unpalatable truth aside in the pleasure of having a wonderful relationship with an absolute prince but it was never going to go away. It was okay for Ellie to have a family. She didn't have the faulty gene. And Lucy was delighted that this was now a solid prospect for her sister with Harry.

As for herself, she had decided long ago that having children was not a fair option so a marriage with family was not going to happen. She thought living together was fine as long as both people were content with the situation. So far none of her relationships had proceeded to that level of acceptance of each other. She would love to be with Michael all the time but the wish for an always future with him was probably a dream that wouldn't come true.

However, she was not about to give up feeling happy with him as long as he felt happy with her. Live each day as it comes, she kept telling herself. One never knew how long a life would be. Michael's accident was a sober reminder of that truth.

As the days went by in the third week since the accident, far from feeling happy with them, Lucy began to panic about the non-arrival of her period. She was never late. The contraceptive pill she used kept her right on schedule with her monthly cycle. Except there was one night when she hadn't taken it—the night of the ball when she'd been too sick to think of it. Then with the shock of Michael's accident, she hadn't thought of taking a morning-after pill, either.

After their splendid lunch at Thala Lodge, they'd made love for hours before parting to dress up for the ball. That long and late sexy afternoon now loomed as the big danger. Yet surely, surely, fate couldn't be so unkind to punish her with an unplanned pregnancy because of one night's unlucky illness. She'd always been so obsessively careful, mindful of her disability and also of the misery an unplanned pregnancy had caused her mother, leading her into an unhappy marriage. It wasn't fair that this should happen to her.

By the fourth week, Lucy couldn't keep pushing the issue aside, couldn't keep desperately hoping this was simply some glitch in her system which would soon correct itself. She steeled herself to take a pregnancy test, needing to know if it was positive or negative. Living in this uncertainty was draining her of any joy in life. Michael had even queried if she was under stress at work. It was growing impossible to be her normal self.

She bought the test kit, rose early the next morning, shut herself in the bathroom and did what she had to do, fiercely willing the result to be negative. She held her breath as she watched the chemicals react. Her heart was a painful hammer in her chest. Her mind chanted *please, please, please…*

There was no kind fate.

As she stared at the positive result the blood drained from her face and the bottom fell out of her world. The shock of it was overwhelming. She fumbled the lid of the toilet down and sat on it, bending over to stop herself from fainting, sucking in deep breaths to clear the whirl of black dots.

Her mind kept railing against the terrible truth. It shouldn't have happened to her. It wasn't fair. The life she had managed so far was spinning completely out of control. She was adrift, more deeply than she had ever been. There was no way back, no way forward that wasn't a frightening blur.

When she felt strong enough she picked up all evidence of the pregnancy kit, took it to her bedroom and hid it in her wardrobe. Her first instinct was always to hide problems. This one was too big to be faced yet. She climbed back into bed, pulled the bedclothes over her head and curled up in the foetal position, wishing she'd never been born.

Time passed in a fog of misery.

Ellie called out to her but she couldn't bring herself to answer. She wanted everything to just go away. Her sister did not oblige, knocking on her door, coming in, asking what was wrong.

'Sick. Not going to work,' she mumbled. 'Tell Michael I can't visit him today.'

'What kind of sick?' Ellie asked worriedly. 'Can I get you anything?'

'No. Just go, Ellie. I want to sleep it off.'

'Well, call me if you need me,' Ellie pressed.

'Mmmh…'

She couldn't *need* Ellie with this. It would spoil what should be a happy time for her sister. It had to be kept hidden, at least until after Ellie's wedding to Harry. Even then, she wouldn't want to be a burden on their marriage.

This pregnancy made everything so difficult.

Especially with Michael being Harry's brother.

Her mind shied away from thinking about Michael. If she told him about the pregnancy and he felt obliged to offer marriage she would hate it, hate it, hate it. It was impossible to see anything working well in these circumstances. Besides, he might doubt it was his child, and she would hate that, too.

Tomorrow she might be able to come to some decision about him. Until she could work it out sensibly it was better not to talk to him at all, so she reached out to her bedside table and switched off her mobile phone, needing to prevent him from calling to ask how she was. She needed time to come to grips with everything.

Michael hated being incapacitated. He could move around his apartment—slowly—and do quite a bit for himself—

slowly—but until his right arm and ribs mended, he was useless in the office. He was trying to wean himself off pain-killers, too, which meant he was in fairly constant discomfort. At least he wasn't so concerned about what was happening with his business now that Elizabeth was here helping Harry. She wouldn't miss a thing, never had.

Though it did amaze him that Harry had decided to marry her. He'd had no idea that the attraction had gone so deep. On either side. He remembered Elizabeth being irritated by Harry's flirting and Harry had definitely considered her a challenge he wanted to win, but it was still a surprise that they felt so much for each other. A good surprise. He had no problem with Elizabeth being his sister-in-law. She was a very admirable woman—Lucy's anchor—responsible, trustworthy, caring, and very smart. Harry had made a fine choice for a lifelong partner.

It had actually spurred him into considering Lucy in the same light for himself. She was very different to her older sister, more endearing in lots of ways. He admired the core of strength underneath her vulnerabilities and she was certainly very caring. Smart, too. Dyslexia didn't limit her intelligence. He knew he wanted her in his life, but his life was abnormal at the moment. This was not the time to be considering a future with anyone.

He spent an hour browsing through some brochures on new fishing gear, having spread them out on the dining-table for easy access. At ten o'clock Elizabeth entered the apartment, bringing his coffee and chocolate muffin from the cafe on the ground floor, as she'd done every day when she'd been working for him.

'How are you doing this morning?' she asked brightly.

'Well enough,' he answered, smiling over their old routine. He'd resigned himself to finding a replacement for her but he doubted anyone could be as good.

'Lucy's not so well,' she remarked, setting the coffee and muffin on the table next to his left hand. 'Must have caught some bug or other. I left her in bed, too sick to go to work, so she won't be coming around to visit you today.'

He frowned over this news. 'I thought she wasn't quite herself the last couple of days. No joy bubbling over. I'll give her a call.'

'Leave it for a while, Michael. She said she wanted to sleep it off.'

'Okay. Thanks for the coffee.'

He waited until lunch time to call Lucy but couldn't get through to her. Her phone was dead. It stayed dead well into the afternoon. It concerned him that she felt too sick to want any communication with anyone. He remembered the yellow rose she had brought him in hospital to make him feel better and on impulse, made a call to Jack Pickard.

'It's Michael Finn, Jack. I have a favour to ask.'

'Ask away, Mickey,' he invited cheerily.

'You know the Pal Joey rose Lucy admired when we were over on the island. Do you happen to have one in bloom?'

'Several. Sarah was commenting on them this morning.'

'Would you cut one for Lucy? I'll send a helicopter over to have it collected. If you'd have it ready to go…?'

'I'll meet the helicopter with it myself,' he promised. 'Lovely girl, Lucy.'

'Yes, she is. Thanks, Jack. It should arrive within the hour.'

He immediately set about making the arrangements required to have the rose delivered to his office before five o'clock, then called Elizabeth to let her know to expect it.

'I want you to take it home to Lucy. Tell her it's from me to make her feel better and ask her to call me. Okay?'

'Will do,' she promised. 'Nice gesture, Michael. I'm sure Lucy will appreciate it.'

It left him smiling. Hopefully Lucy would be well enough to chat to him tonight. She made him forget about pain. He badly missed having sex with her and frequently cursed his broken bones for making him inactive on that front. Four weeks down and probably another four to go, he told himself, determined on making the fastest possible recovery. He just had to be patient. Lucy was still there for him, despite his blunder at the ball.

Lucy remained hiding in bed when her sister came home. Earlier in the day she'd cried herself to sleep and although that merciful oblivion was no longer her friend she was trying to hang onto it, dozing on and off, not ready to face what had to be faced. She heard her door open and Ellie coming into the bedroom, moving quietly so as not to disturb her. She kept her eyes closed, not wanting to be questioned.

'Are you awake?' Ellie asked softly. 'I've brought you a cup of tea and a rose from Michael.'

A rose?

Lucy's mind was in such a mess, it clutched wildly at the hope that Michael truly loved her and would love her no matter what! She hitched herself up, eyes opened wide, heart thumping, only to see Ellie setting down a yellow rose in the same glass vase she had used to take her gift to Michael in the hospital.

Yellow, not red.

Not red for love.

Tears welled into her eyes so fast they overflowed and trickled down her cheeks. Her sister saw them before she could hide the emotional eruption. There was no escape from her immediate concern. Even as she flopped back down on the pillow and closed her eyes Ellie was sitting on the bed beside her, stroking her forehead, asking, 'What's wrong, Lucy?'

'Nothing,' she muttered.

'I don't believe you. Tell me what it is.'

'Just sick.'

'Sick with what? Your forehead isn't hot so you're not running a fever. And why have you got your phone switched off? Neither I nor Michael could reach you today.'

'Didn't want to be reached. Leave me alone, Ellie,' she said plaintively. 'I'm not up to talking.'

'You're hiding, Lucy,' came the voice of certainty.

'No. Just sick.'

'You're sick because you're bottling something up. You've done this before, going into retreat and churning over stuff you don't want to tell me about.'

'Please…let me be, Ellie,' she begged, quickly hiding her face in the pillow to stop the quizzing.

Her sister huffed in frustration. 'Well, at least call

Michael and thank him for the rose. He went to a great deal of trouble and expense to get it for you.'

'It's the wrong colour,' she mumbled into the pillow, tears gushing again.

'What do you mean…the wrong colour?' Ellie continued to probe. 'Michael said it was a special rose you particularly liked. He actually called Jack Pickard for one he'd grown over on the island and had it flown to Cairns by helicopter so I could put it here for you to smell. Now that deserves a thank you call from you, Lucy,' she declared with firm authority. 'I don't care how sick you are over whatever you're sick about. I'm switching your mobile on now and…'

'Don't!' Sheer panic jerked Lucy up, her arm flying out to snatch the mobile from her sister's grasp.

'What on earth…?' Ellie cried in shock.

Lucy clutched the mobile to her chest. 'I can't talk to him! I can't!'

'Why not?'

'Just leave me alone,' she pleaded.

'No, I won't!' Ellie wore her determined look. 'This has gone far enough. Tell me what's wrong, Lucy. I'm not going away until you do.'

Lucy bit her lip. It didn't stop the tears from falling.

'Tell me!' Ellie commanded.

Lucy shook her head. 'You can't fix it, Ellie.'

Her sister took a deep breath. 'Have you found out you've got cancer, like Mum?'

It was such a shocking leap she gasped, 'No…no…'

'Well, thank God for that!' Ellie regathered herself and drove forward. 'We've faced a lot together, Lucy.

It doesn't matter if this can be fixed or not. We face it together. So tell me what the problem is right now.'

Her sister…her anchor…

It was who Ellie was—through and through—and she was not about to let that part of their lives change.

Lucy's resistance collapsed.

This problem did have to be faced, and Ellie was right.

It was better faced together.

CHAPTER SEVENTEEN

MICHAEL PROWLED AROUND the penthouse apartment, banging his walking stick on the tiled floor, too unsettled to sit down and have breakfast with Harry.

'Ask Elizabeth to come straight up here when she arrives at the office,' he commanded his brother.

'Just because neither of them wanted to take calls last night...' Harry began in an overly reasonable tone.

'I want to know why,' Michael insisted. 'And I want to know now!'

'Okay!' Harry lifted his hands in surrender. 'As long as you remember to be kind to Elizabeth. It's not her fault if Lucy's sick and doesn't feel up to chatting.'

'It's more than that,' Michael muttered. 'I can feel it in my bones.'

'Probably because they're broken,' Harry muttered back at him.

'You don't know Lucy like I do,' Michael shot at him. 'I think she might be backing off me now that I'm getting better.'

'For what reason?' Harry eyed him in an assessing fashion. 'I know you've become used to her pandering to your every need this past month. I hope you haven't just been using her for that, Mickey. She is Elizabeth's sister.'

'No. That's not what it's about.' He couldn't forget feeling himself turning into a frog at the ball. Lucy wouldn't desert someone in need and he had been needy since the accident. She was big on empathy and caring. But now that he was well on the mend, other issues could be looked at and acted upon. He didn't want to confide something he was ashamed of to Harry. 'Please…just tell Elizabeth I need to talk to her.'

'Will do,' Harry finally agreed.

He had an impatient wait until Elizabeth did enter his apartment and the wary expression on her face instantly set off alarm bells in his head.

'Good morning, Michael,' she said so formally he sensed her keeping mental or emotional distance from him, which raised his inner tension several notches.

'Elizabeth…' he acknowledged with a nod, waving to an armchair in his living room '…have a seat.'

He propped himself on the wide armrest of its companion chair, directly facing her as she gingerly settled onto the deep cushion. 'What's happening with Lucy?' he asked point-blank.

Elizabeth held his gaze with a hard searching look of her own before calmly stating, 'Lucy is pregnant.'

'Pregnant…' he repeated dazedly, the shock of it sending his mind reeling.

'Because she was so sick the night of the ball, followed up by your accident, she forgot to take her contraceptive pill. Just one night she was off track, Michael. And unfortunately, you'd had a long session in bed that afternoon just prior to the ball. So that's how it happened.'

She didn't have to plead for his understanding. The circumstances were crystal clear. Knowing how obsessively careful Lucy was about safe sex, Michael could picture her deeply distressed by the outcome of this one mishap. He realised this was at the core of her withdrawal from him this past week. It was a big reason. A huge reason. But she should have shared it with him, not kept it to herself.

'Why didn't she tell me?' he shot at her sister.

Again the hard, searching look. 'Do you accept that you're the father, Michael?'

'Of course I accept it! Why wouldn't I?'

'Lucy thinks you might not believe you are. She thinks you're hung up on how many lovers she's had in the past. She said you asked about them that night.'

Michael gritted his teeth, knowing he'd painted himself as a frog, savagely wishing he could change the green into unblemished white.

Elizabeth sucked in a quick breath and continued, 'If it's a concern that will always be on your mind...'

'No!' He sliced the air with his hand in emphatically negative dismissal. 'It was prompted by what other men had said about Lucy but virtually at the moment I was asking the question I realised it was irrelevant to me. Irrelevant to us. And I've regretted bringing it up ever since.'

Elizabeth heaved a huge sigh of relief. 'Well, I'm glad we don't have that problem. I couldn't like you if you thought badly of my sister.'

'I don't. I love your sister, Elizabeth.'

The word slid straight out of his mouth before he'd even realised how true it was.

It evoked a doubtful look. 'Lucy doesn't know that, Michael, and to us *love* is a big word. Please don't use it lightly. Not in this situation.'

'I'll tell her. We'll work it out,' he asserted strongly.

Another sigh. Another doubtful look. 'You know about Lucy's dyslexia. She never planned to marry. Never planned to have children.'

Horror speared into his mind. 'She's not thinking of having an abortion?'

'No. Lucy has too much respect for life to choose that route, but she is upset about the possibility that she'll pass the disability on to her child. And she thinks you might not welcome a…a less than perfect child.'

The mountain of Lucy's vulnerabilities was rising up in front of him. She not only feared rejection from him but rejection of their child, as well. He suddenly had a very sharp memory of Sarah Pickard remarking that Lucy might think she wasn't good enough for him. In fact, Lucy had actually said so herself—*I know I'm no match for you.* This was a mountain he had to scale…somehow.

He shook his head over ever having considered her a possible gold-digger. That was so far from the truth—a million miles from the truth. She hadn't *planned* anything, hadn't expected anything of him, except that he would sooner or later turn into a frog and the pleasure of being with him would be over.

His jaw set in fierce determination. This frog was going to leap every mountain she put in front of him.

This frog was going to be the prince Lucy had wanted him to be.

'Thank you for being open with me, Elizabeth,' he said sincerely. 'I'll take it from here.'

She rose from the armchair, hesitating before heading for the door, her eyes meeting his in eloquent appeal. 'All four of us are going to have to live with whatever you decide, Michael. You must make it an honest decision. Trying to be honourable will only bring more hurt in the end.'

Honourable…standing up when he didn't really want to.

'Lucy and I will always have each other,' she went on. 'You don't have to be a part of her life. You understand? You must be honest so we know where we're going and can work out how best to do it.'

He nodded, seeing very clearly the crossroads where they all stood—two brothers and two sisters. Elizabeth and Harry were solid. They would move forward together. He and Lucy were looking down the barrel of very divergent paths if he didn't make the right moves— moves that had to be right for both of them. At the centre of those crossroads was a child who would tug at all of them, making the paths intersect throughout the future, causing conflict or bringing joy.

Elizabeth was at the door, about to open it, when he thought to ask her, 'How did Lucy respond to the Pal Joey rose you took home with you yesterday?'

Her reply was preceded by a wry grimace. 'She burst into tears. When I asked what was wrong she said it was the wrong colour.'

It made no sense to him. 'It's always yellow.'

Elizabeth sighed, her eyes sad as she answered, 'I think Lucy wanted a red rose from you, Michael.'

'Red...' he repeated, not immediately understanding.

'For love,' she spelled out. 'But please don't give her one unless you truly, truly mean it.'

She left, having made the situation with all its complications as clear as she could.

A great PA, Michael thought.

Then he turned his mind to Lucy and the child who would be theirs.

Decisions had to be made.

He wanted his sunshine girl back. She was dwelling in shadows, some of which he'd cast, others caused by the disability that had darkened many parts of her life—a disability she feared would blight their child's life. Somehow he had to pull her out of those shadows.

He thought of what Elizabeth had said about Lucy never having planned to marry, never having planned to have children. It made perfect sense of her having sex whenever it promised to give her pleasure. There was no moral issue involved, simply a need to feel loved for at least a little while.

Which was all she'd wanted from him. She'd told him so in the hospital when he'd more or less trapped her into revealing her dyslexia. She wasn't expecting to be loved for a long while. Her acceptance of that ruled how she thought, how she lived, making the most of every good moment.

He understood her now.

He understood it all.

And he realised how very critical it was that he make the right decisions.

CHAPTER EIGHTEEN

MICHAEL WAS COMING to talk to her tonight. Harry was bringing him to the apartment. Ellie was virtually standing over her, insisting this meeting be faced. No hiding. No bolting from it. No shutting her mind to the fact that this issue would touch all of them in the future. She had to listen and think very carefully about the decisions she made.

Having been instructed of all this, Lucy felt sick again—sick with nervous tension. She'd barely been able to eat any of the pasta meal she'd made for their dinner. Nevertheless, regardless of how she *felt*, pride demanded that she not *look* sick to the two Finn brothers.

She spent the hour before the eight o'clock deadline making herself appear bright and beautiful, determined to have Michael believe that the sunshine girl would pick herself up and move on, bringing up their child in her own way. After all, she was best equipped to do it, having firsthand experience at living with dyslexia. There was no need for him to concern himself about either of them.

Ellie had assured her that he did accept the child was his—no question. If this was true, he would probably offer financial support, which she would take. It was the sensible thing to do. Her own employment prospects would take a dive, being a single mother. In fact, whatever help he offered she would accept for their child's sake.

Having thought this through, Lucy was feeling a little more settled in her mind when the doorbell announced the brothers' arrival. Her heart, however, rocketed around her chest like a wound-up toy. They were early. It was only ten minutes to eight. She wasn't quite keyed up to face them yet. As Ellie moved to open the door, some self-protective instinct made Lucy step into the kitchen, putting the counter bench between her and the men who had changed their lives.

It wasn't Michael who entered. Nor Harry. Ellie opened the door wide to a delivery guy who was carrying a stunning arrangement of red roses—dozens of them clustered tightly together in a dome shape, and rising from the centre of this was a stick which held an amazing pom-pom of roses to top it all off.

'This is for the coffee table,' the guy said, moving in to place the gift as directed.

He was followed by two more delivery people whom he quickly instructed. 'That one is to go on the kitchen bench...'

More red roses, but fewer of them in this arrangement—a very artistic Japanese style.

'...and that one on the dining table.'

This was more a posy of red roses in a small dainty vase, perfect for its placing.

Fortunately Ellie had enough composure to thank the delivery people and see them out. Lucy was blown

out of her mind. The sheer extravagance of the gift was
dazzling. What it might mean…what it was supposed
to mean…could she believe it? She kept staring at the
roses…so many of them…red for *love*.

The doorbell rang again. Her gaze jerked to Ellie
who was still standing by the door.

'Are you okay, Lucy?' she asked, her hand on the
door-knob, pausing before turning it, waiting to be assured that her sister had herself under control.

Lucy nodded, grasping the end corners of the bench-
top to hold herself steady. Her mind was a whirl. Her
heart was drumming in her ears. Her stomach was
cramping in nervous agitation. Everything she'd thought
of saying to Michael had turned into a jumbled mess.
Just listen and watch, she fiercely told herself. What he
said, how he looked when he said it…that would tell her
where she should go from here.

Ellie opened the door.

Michael entered first—still the most handsome
prince in the world, commanding her total attention
and tugging on everything female inside her. As on
her very first night with him he was casually dressed;
grey shorts, a grey and white striped sports shirt with
buttons down the front—undoubtedly easier for taking
off with his hurting ribs—scuffs on his feet. One of his
hands was gripping a walking stick. The other held a
single rose which wasn't red. It was pink and white.

Confused and hopelessly distressed, Lucy was barely
aware of Harry following his brother in, pausing beside
Ellie, speaking to her in a low voice. It was a jolt when
suddenly they were both gone, the door closed behind
them, leaving her alone with Michael and a roomful of

roses that surely represented some kind of emotional pressure she would have to fight. Panic welled up. She needed her sister standing beside her, needed an anchor to stop her from being drawn into a bad place.

'There's nothing to be frightened of with me, Lucy,' Michael said, his deep rich voice pouring out in a soothing tone.

She swallowed hard, trying to clear the constriction in her throat. 'I'm sorry,' she managed to get out, gripping the counter edge even harder. 'I'm sorry for complicating your life like this. It wasn't meant to happen.'

'I know it wasn't meant to happen but I'm glad that it has.' He smiled at her, pushing one of the kitchen stools closer to where she stood and hitching himself onto the other. 'It doesn't complicate my life, Lucy. In fact, I'm seeing everything very clearly now.'

She shook her head. 'I don't understand.'

'Sit down and relax. We'll talk about whatever you don't understand.'

She unglued her hands from the bench-top, reached out for the stool and dragged it around to the other side of the counter to where Michael was seated, feeling safer with putting solid distance between them. She couldn't allow herself to be persuaded into doing something wrong. Having sat down she gestured to the roses on the kitchen bench beside her.

'You've never said you love me, Michael,' she flatly reminded him, her eyes searching his for any sign of insincerity.

'I'm saying it now.' His gaze held hers with intense conviction. 'I love you and I want to marry you, Lucy.

When we were on the island, I heard you say to Sarah that you'd never marry a man who didn't love you enough to give you roses. What you see here now is a promise there will always be roses in our marriage.'

Pain stabbed her heart. It killed her to say it but she had to. 'I won't marry you, Michael.'

'Why not?'

'It's wrong to marry because of a child. It's what my mother did, thinking it was for the best, but it wasn't. I promised her I'd never do that. No matter how good the intentions, it's bound not to turn out well.'

He didn't look at all deterred by this argument. He rolled right on over it. 'I'd agree that good intentions don't guarantee a good marriage. I think there has to be love between the couple involved for a marriage to work well and from what you've told me, I don't believe your father loved your mother. It's different for us, Lucy. I genuinely want you in my life and I believe you want me. Can you truthfully say you don't?'

'It's not as simple as that!' she cried, agonised by the need to keep on the right track here. 'Our child might have dyslexia too, Michael, and that wouldn't have been what you've planned for yourself.'

'I didn't *plan* anything for myself,' he swiftly replied. 'Somewhere on the back-burner in my mind was the hope that one day I might meet a woman with whom I could have the kind of relationship my father had with my mother. You're that person, Lucy—the woman who lights up my life. And I'm sure our child will light up both our lives, dyslexia or not.'

She couldn't let him just gloss over a condition he'd never lived with. 'You don't know what it's like…the confusion, the frustration, the realisation that you're not normal like other kids. The light goes out sometimes, Michael, and it's hard, learning how to turn it back on.'

The silvery grey eyes glittered with determination. 'Lucy, I promise you it won't be the problem it's been for you. We'll be on the lookout for it in however many children we have, get early professional help if it's needed.'

Children? He was looking ahead to having more than one child with her?

'I've been researching dyslexia on the internet,' he went on confidently. 'There's a lot that can now be done—programs that weren't available to you. But over and above that, we will both be *there* for our children. That's what counts most, isn't it, having a mother and father who love you, who think you're very special regardless of any disability?'

He spoke so caringly, Lucy's resistance to the idea of marriage began to crack. She wanted this man so much and she wanted her child to have a loving father. Yet there was another issue that could stalk and break the happy future together he was painting.

She sucked in a deep breath, released it in a shuddering sigh and looked at him with knowing wariness. 'What if you run into other men I've slept with in the past, Michael?'

His gaze did not waver from hers. 'I haven't forgotten I turned into a frog that night of the ball. I've been intensely grateful that you seemed to let me get away with it, staying by my side these past few weeks.'

'I didn't want you to die, didn't want to lose you, but I wasn't thinking there could be long future for us as a couple,' she quickly explained. 'You made me feel bad that night.'

'I know. And it's made me feel bad ever since. Please believe me when I now say I don't care if you've slept with *every* man in Cairns. If you'll marry me, Lucy, I'll always think I'm the lucky one for getting to keep you.'

The regretful tone, the vehemence of his plea to her...listening to him was playing havoc with her emotions. She so desperately wanted to believe him, yet... 'How can I be sure of that, Michael?'

'Give me the chance to prove it. I want to be your prince, Lucy. I want to love you, protect you, fight your battles for you, be your champion always. If you'll just favour me with your smile...'

The appeal in his voice, in his eyes, was irresistible, tugging at the corners of her mouth.

'...I'll conquer the world for you,' he finished with a flamboyant grin.

A gurgle of laughter erupted from her throat. This was all so impossibly romantic...the stuff of dreams... but it was washing straight through the cracks in her protective armour, swamping her heart, tugging at the love she felt for him.

He twirled the pink and white rose around in his fingers. The beautiful scent of it tickled her sense of smell.

'This rose is called Princess of Monaco. I want to give it to you because you're my princess, Lucy. I want to buy us a home with a garden where I can grow this rose so you'll always be reminded that you're my princess and I love you.' He held it out to her. 'Will you accept it from me?'

A river of emotion in full flood drowned the doubts

she had tried to hold onto. She couldn't stop her hand from reaching out and taking the perfect princess bloom, lifting it to her nose so she could breathe in the glorious scent. She couldn't stop the smile beaming her happiness at Michael—her prince. Her *true* prince.

It spilled into words. 'I love you, too.'

Desire blazed in his eyes. 'I wish I could race you off to bed, Lucy. I'd use that rose to caress every part of you so you'd be totally immersed in its scent and feel totally immersed in my love for you.'

'Oh! I do like that idea!' She gave him a saucy smile as she slid off the stool and rounded the bench to where he sat. 'We don't need to race, Michael. We can get there at a reasonable pace together. Will Harry keep Ellie away for a while?'

'Until I call him to come and get me.'

'Then we can take our time, can't we?'

'Lucy, I won't be able to...'

'But you can turn me into a rose garden and I can take you to the moon, my love,' she said, framing his beautiful face with her hands and kissing him with all the sensual promise of pleasure she could give him without any action on his part that might give him pain.

The fire she lit in Michael's groin demanded instant compliance with whatever Lucy wanted to do. He didn't care if there was some collateral pain. He wanted this intimacy, wanted to love her, wanted to feel her love for him.

She took him further than the moon. She made him burst into heaven and float there, feeling like a king, and he knew with absolute certainty that she would always be the queen in his life. She was the right woman for him. She was the perfect woman for him—an exquisite addiction that would never end. And he silently vowed that nothing would ever mar their happiness with each other.

CHAPTER NINETEEN

IT WAS THE last day of her job with cemetery administration and she'd been asked to supervise the return
of the repaired angels' heads to the memorial garden.
Lucy was happy to be driving out to Greenlands, wanting to visit her mother's grave. Beside her on the van's
passenger seat was a florist box containing the rose she
planned to place there.

She arrived before the stonemason and was on her
way down the rows of neatly tended graves when she
spotted the elderly man who had planted the Pal Joey
rose for his wife. She raised her free arm and waved,
calling out, 'Hi, Mr Robson! It looks like your rose-
bush is thriving.'

His face lit up with pleasure. 'Miss Flippence! It is
doing well, isn't it? And what have you got there?'

He set off down a cross path to meet up with her.

'It's a thank you gift for my mother,' she explained,
pausing to wait for him so he could admire it and have
a little chat. He was lonely, having lost his beloved wife.

'Ah! A Princess of Monaco,' he said as soon as he
was close enough to recognise the bloom. 'Good choice!
Wonderful scent!'

'Yes! My husband-to-be is going to plant one for me when we build our home,' she said proudly.

'Well, congratulations!' he said warmly. 'You look so happy. I wish you both all the best.'

'Thank you. I've never been so happy. It's like a miracle, finding someone who really loves you.'

'I guess you're going to visit your mother to tell her all about it.'

'Yes.' Lucy gave him a confidential smile. 'I think she worked the miracle for me. I asked her to, you see?'

His eyes twinkled at her. 'Then I'm sure she did. God bless you, girlie! Go on now and thank your mother.'

Such a nice man, Lucy thought as she walked on. There *were* princes in this world and she and Ellie were incredibly lucky to be loved by two of them.

Having placed the box at the foot of her mother's headstone, she sat on the lawn facing it, hugging her knees and tilting her head back to look up at the clear blue sky.

'If you're looking down at me, Mum, I hope you can see how magically everything has turned out since Ellie's birthday, and thank you so much if you've been a guiding spirit in it all. This is my last day on the job here because Ellie and I have a double wedding to plan and so much else besides. The four of us are looking at properties for our future homes and trying to figure out what will suit us best. And, of course, I'm three months pregnant and Michael doesn't want me doing too much so the job has to go. I'll still come and visit you though I won't be adrift any more. Isn't that wonderful?'

She heaved a happy sigh and lowered her gaze to the gift she wanted to share with her mother. 'This is the rose Michael gave me when he promised to always be there for me, my knight in shining armour. He chose it because it's called Princess of Monaco and I'm his princess, Mum. Remember how some of the schoolkids used to call me Loopy Lucy because of my dyslexia? I never thought I'd be anyone's princess. Sometimes I can hardly believe it but Michael really does love me. He makes me feel it all the time. And I love him with all my heart.'

Aware that the stonemason may well have arrived in the memorial garden by now, Lucy pushed herself upright and blew a kiss to the headstone. 'Ellie and I will be thinking of you on our wedding day. We know you would have loved to be there, seeing us as brides, and we know you would be proud of us. We followed what you told us—*Never commit your life to a man who doesn't love you and be absolutely sure he's a man you can love for the rest of your life.* We got it right, Mum, so you really can rest in peace.'

She lifted her arms high and twirled around in a happy dance, laughing with the sheer joy of being alive and being loved. She was Michael's princess bride. Nothing could be more *right* for her. And it felt so good.

So...good.

A miracle.

God bless everyone, she thought.

To feel this blessed was wonderful beyond words!

* * * * *

HIS BOUGHT
MISTRESS

CHAPTER ONE

ANGIE BLESSING did not feel particularly blessed on this fine summer Sunday morning. In fact, the bright sunshine was giving her a headache. Or maybe it was her relationship with Paul that was giving her the headache.

Here she was, sitting in his Mercedes convertible, being driven home to the apartment she shared with her best friend and business partner, Francine Morgan—her choice because she didn't want to go yacht-racing with Paul today—and instead of thinking how lucky she was to be the love interest in the life of one of Sydney's most eligible bachelors, she was thinking of Francine's current bible: *The Marriage Market After Thirty—Finding the Right Husband For You.*

For the past three years she'd been Paul Overton's *partner.*

No proposal of marriage.

The really troubling part was, if he got down on his knees right now and asked her to marry him, Angie wasn't sure she'd say yes.

'Don't forget we've got the fund-raising dinner next Friday night,' he tossed at her as he drove down her road at Cremorne, conveniently situated on his way to the Royal North Shore Yacht Club.

More politics, Angie thought. Just like the party last night. Everything with Paul was politics, making influential connections, building a network of pow-

5

erful support that would back his ambition to go into
parliament. His current career as a barrister had little
to do with a love of the law. It was more a showcase
for his rhetorical skills, a step towards what he really
wanted.

'Angie...?' He threw a frown at her, impatient with
her silence.

'Yes, Paul. It's marked in my calendar,' she said
dutifully, hating the way she was little more than an
ornament on his arm at such functions. 'And we have
the ballet on Wednesday night,' she reminded him,
relieved at being able to look forward to that date.

'I don't think I'll be able to go. The case I'm on
this week needs a lot of preparation. Big trial, as you
know, and the media will be covering it.'

Angie gritted her teeth. Ballet was *her* thing. But,
of course, that wasn't important to his career. He
could have worked on his case preparation today instead of yacht-racing, though naturally it wouldn't occur to Paul to give up one of his pleasures.

'Take Francine with you,' he suggested brightly.

'Right!' she bit out. No point in arguing. Waste of
breath.

He pulled the Mercedes into the kerb outside her
apartment block, engine idling, which meant he
wasn't about to get out and open the passenger door
for her. Angie wondered if the romance went out of
every relationship after three years. Was being taken
for granted the norm?

Paul beamed her a rueful smile. 'Hope the queasy
stomach settles down soon.'

Her excuse for not spending today with him.

She returned the smile. 'Me, too.'

He wasn't going to kiss her. Couldn't afford to catch a tummy bug with the big trial on this week.

'You do look peaky,' he commented sympathetically. 'Look after yourself, Angie.'

He wasn't about to, she thought.

'I'll call you during the week,' he added.

Sure. To check I'm okay for Friday night when you need me again.

'Fine,' she said, struggling to rise above her jaundiced mind-set.

Paul was the most handsome man she'd ever met: tall, broad-shouldered, instantly impressive, dark wavy hair swept back from what she thought of as a noble forehead, riveting dark eyes that captivated with their sharp intelligence, a strong male face to complement his very male physique. He came from a wealthy family, was wealthy himself, and she could share a brilliant future with him if he ever got around to offering it.

'Have a nice day,' she forced out, then opened the door and swung herself out of the car.

She watched him drive off—the A-list man in his A-list car—and seriously wondered if Paul saw her as an A-list woman. She probably projected the right image: tall, long blond hair, slim enough to wear any clothes well, though her figure was too curvy for classic model proportions, good skin that didn't need make-up to cover blemishes, the kind of clear-boned face that always photographed well though she certainly didn't consider herself beautiful. Her eyes were her most attractive feature, probably because they were an unusual sage green.

When it came to self-presentation, she was good, having learnt that this art was an asset in her line of business. People who hired professional help from an interior design company had more confidence in a professional who was well groomed and colour co-ordinated herself. She definitely had the image Paul liked but did she have the right *substance* for him to consider her marriageable?

Was being a successful career woman enough?

No wealthy family in her background. No political pull there, either. Her parents were both artists with antigovernment attitudes, perfectly happy for their daughter to make her own choices in life, but staunchly into alternative society themselves. They were hardly the right people for Paul to have as in-laws, though Angie knew her parents would never thrust themselves into *his* limelight.

Besides, they lived so far away, right up the north coast at Byron Bay. They'd never actually been a fac-tor in her relationship with Paul, not like *his* parents who seemed to accept her. On the surface. But was she suitable as a lifetime partner? More importantly, did she want to be Paul Overton's lifetime partner?

It had once been a dazzling prospect.

Now, Angie wasn't so sure.

In fact, she was beginning to feel she might well have wasted three years on a rosy dream which was fast developing wilting edges. She headed into the apartment block, wondering if Francine had found her Mr. Right last night at the *Dinner for Six*—a group of thirty-something singles wanting to meet their match, this being her friend's latest dating ploy in hunting for a husband.

She found Francine sitting on their balcony over-looking the bay, Sunday newspapers spread on the table in front of her, a mug of coffee to hand, and the gloom of failure denying any interest in the lovely morning or anything else. She was still in her pyjamas. Her dark curly hair was an unbrushed tangle. Smudges of last night's mascara gave her grey eyes a bruised look. Slumped shoulders added to her air of dejection.

'Struck out again?' Angie asked sympathetically, stepping outside to join her friend.

'Too earnest. No spark,' came the listless reply.

The thirty-something men were probably as desperate to impress as Francine was, Angie thought. 'Maybe they'd be more relaxed on a second date.'

'Bor…ing.' Francine rolled her eyes at her. 'And they'd be all over me like a flash if I gave them a second chance. Hot to trot, all of them.'

'Well, you did look hot in that red dress last night.'

Positively stunning, Angie had thought, the fabric clinging to Francine's gym-toned body, plus some provocative cleavage showing due to the purchase of a new push-up bra. Her figure was petite but certainly very feminine. Pretty face. Gorgeous hair. Francine was a knockout when she set out to be aggressively attractive.

'I need to light a fire in the right guy when I meet him,' she expounded. 'That's what the book says. Stand out from the crowd. Be positive and memorable. Always look my best.'

'Not exactly practising that this morning,' Angie teased, trying to lighten her up. 'What if I'd walked in here with a friend of Paul's in tow?'

'So I would have blown it. I'm just having some down time. Besides, you're not supposed to be here. What happened to yacht-racing?'

She shrugged. 'I didn't feel like it.'

'Easy for some,' Francine muttered darkly, then slammed her hands on the table and rose to her feet. 'Okay. Clean myself up. Go to the gym. Spread myself around. I'm doing it.' Grim resolve was in her voice and on her face as she marched off towards the bathroom.

'You might need to relax more yourself.' The words tripped out before Angie could think better of them.

Francine wheeled on her, spitting mad. 'Don't give me advice! You've had your Mr. Right for so long you don't know how it is for me, Angie. Or what it's like out there on the dating scene. And I'm not settling for just anyone!'

'Neither you should,' Angie quickly agreed, not even sure that *settling* for Paul was an option. Her confidence in his rightness for her was also at an all-time low.

'All these years, building up our business, you said yourself I'm brilliant at marketing our design company,' Francine ran on heatedly.

'You are,' Angie acknowledged.

'I've even snagged the Fullbright contract for us.'

A plum contract, worth a lot of money to them.

'So I should be able to market myself and get the result I want,' Francine said decisively. 'That means I have to sell what my husband-to-be finds appealing. And let me tell you I'm not going to leave any stone unturned. I'm thirty years old and I want a husband and children in my future.'

Having delivered this firm declaration, Francine marched on to the bathroom.

They were *both* thirty years old, Angie thought, taking her friend's empty mug to the kitchen, intent on brewing some fresh coffee for herself. They'd spent their twenties establishing their business, working hard, climbing up in the world. The Fullbright contract proved they'd reached the top level in their field—being given the job of colour co-ordinating a fabulous new block of luxury apartments situated right on the harbour shoreline. That success should be very sweet. And it was. But they were women, too, and priorities definitely changed as the biological clock started ticking.

Angie told herself she probably shouldn't be feeling so discontented with Paul. So what if the excitement and passion in their first year together had waned! It probably did in every relationship, giving way to a comfortable sense of being able to count on each other. It was unrealistic to expect everything to be perfect. Hadn't she accepted that maintaining something workable demanded a fair amount of compromise?

Except Paul never compromised on anything.

She hadn't noticed this at first. Now she was probably noticing it too much. But if she broke off with him…It was scary to think of herself being suddenly single again, out there in the thirty-something dating scene. Francine's total dedication to her mission seemed far too extreme to her, yet…would she begin to feel just as desperate, given no readily available prospects?

Maybe she should count her blessings with Paul instead of being critical.

Yet he had never once brought up the subject of marriage.

Three years…

Was he ever going to?

Was she just a handy habit to him, one he'd shed when the time came to make a marriage that suited his ambitions?

The coffee percolater pinged, and she poured herself a mugful, then wandered back out to the balcony with it, her mind hopelessly riddled with doubts.

The newspapers did not provide the soothing distraction she needed. Angie tried focusing her thoughts on the Fullbright contract, planning how best to handle the scheduled meeting with Hugo Fullbright himself, scheduled for next Thursday morning. The billionaire property developer was bound to be demanding and she'd need to impress him with her answers. At least she was confident of achieving that.

Francine re-emerged, looking very bright and bouncy, dressed in spectacular lime green lycra shorts and a matching midriff top, ready for her trip to the gym. 'I've made up my mind,' she announced. 'I'm going to spread my net wider.'

'A new strategy?' Angie queried.

'I've spent eight months doing what the book recommends with only dud results. The thing to do now is grab attention big-time.'

'How?'

'I read about a really bold scheme in the newspaper. I get my photo scanned, blown up, and plastered on a billboard placed at a busy city intersection. Anyone interested can contact me on the Internet.'

Angie's jaw dropped in shock. 'A billboard!' she gasped.

'Major public exposure,' Francine rattled on, apparently uncaring about any negative outcomes. 'Should bring in a huge number of guys for me to choose from.'

'You're using your face and name on a public billboard?' Angie was appalled. 'What about crackpots and perverts and...'

'Not my *real* name. More of a teaser which will be a password to reach me through a third party on the Net. I'll be protected, Angie.'

'But people will recognise your face.'

'So? No harm in being a celebrity. Probably do me a power of good.'

'Francine, what about our business associates? What are they going to think?'

'I don't care what they think. Business is business. We deliver what our clients want. Nothing wrong with me going after what *I* want.'

'But a billboard...it's so...so public!'

'Are you going to be ashamed of me?' Francine bored in belligerently.

'No! No, of course not. I'm just worried for you. What you might end up having to handle.'

'Let me worry about that. I'm simply giving you fair warning so you don't get a shock when the billboard goes up. I'm off to the gym now.'

Cutting off any further argument.

Angie didn't like the idea one bit. It horrified her. On the other hand, she wasn't a go-getter type, not like Francine whose job it was to bring in the interior design contracts for Angie to work on. In any event, nothing she said was going to change her friend's mind, and it was probably better to stay silent on the highly sensitive issue of how to reel in Mr. Right.

Angie hoped Paul wouldn't see the billboard.

He'd be scathing about her friend's blatant self-publicity.

But it wasn't *his* life and he would never have

Francine's problems. Any amount of eager women would leap at the chance to be Paul Overton's Miss Right, no need for him to advertise what a prize he was. Angie decided she would stick loyally by Francine, regardless of the consequences of her scheme.

Three days later, the inevitable was announced. 'It will be up tomorrow,' Francine informed her as they settled in their seats at the ballet. Her eyes were dancing with excited anticipation.

'Up where?' Angie asked, trying her utmost to hold back any dampener on the happy sparkles.

'You'll see it on your way to the Fullbright meeting tomorrow.'

And see it she did the next morning.

No one crossing the Sydney Harbour Bridge by car, bus, train or foot could miss it. Angie almost drove into the back of the car in front of her. Not because she was agog at seeing Francine's face on the billboard. She'd been mentally prepared to see it somewhere.

The shock—and it was totally mind-blasting—was in seeing her own face on the billboard.

Hers!

And underneath it the caption—*Foxy Angel*!

CHAPTER TWO

HUGO FULLBRIGHT had a very good view of the billboard as the cars in front of his slowed to a crawl approaching the toll booths at the southern end of the bridge. It amused him to check out the passing parade of people brave enough to hang themselves out in public. Six new faces on it this morning. The blonde stirred his interest. *Foxy Angel*.

Few women looked that good. Probably a computer enhanced photograph. Undoubtedly she would prove a disappointment to the guys who leapt on her bandwagon. Logic insisted that something had to be wrong for *her* to need this medium to get a man. But she sure was a winner on the billboard.

Foxy Angel… Hugo grinned over the teaser. Great marketing. Intriguing suggestion of naughty but nice. Just the mix he liked himself. Except he didn't care for the *naughty* part to be inspired and driven by cocaine.

It had hit him like a brick when he'd found Chrissie snorting a line of it at the party last Saturday night. And her argument—'But, darling, sex is so much more fun when I'm on a high.'—was not what a man wanted to hear, as though the pleasure he gave didn't do enough for her.

Goodbye, Chrissie.

Hugo had no regrets over that decision. To his mind, people who depended on recreational drugs to *perform* weren't in control of themselves or anything

15

else. He didn't tolerate it in any of the top executives in his company and he wasn't about to tolerate it in the woman closest to him. Besides, illegal substances were illegal, bound to lead to messy situations.

Having passed over the bridge and beyond sight of the tantalising photo on the billboard, Hugo concentrated his mind on the fast approaching meeting with the colour co-ordinator for his new Pyrmont development. He'd purchased three old warehouses along the harbour front, then had them torn down to accommodate this project. Since he'd be putting million-dollar prices on each luxury apartment, he wanted a top class job done on their visual presentation.

It was important to impress that on the specialist he'd contracted, so best he did it personally, let the woman know he wasn't interested in any cost-cutting that might have a negative effect. A quality finish was essential. He was happy with the architectural design but *the finish* should be the icing on the cake.

Attention to detail—that was the key to success.

Nothing overlooked.

One of the ground floor apartments had been turned into a temporary business centre for on the job requirements and supervision. Hugo mentally approved the security system for the garage as he parked his car, and the exclusive access system to each apartment as he moved on to enter the company *office*. He greeted his people there, left instructions for Miss Blessing to be escorted to the meeting room, and for refreshments to be brought ten minutes after she arrived.

The meeting room had been set up at the far end of the open living area where a wall of glass allowed a spectacular view of the harbour and its ever-changing traffic. It comprised a rented lounge setting with a large square coffee table. Hugo didn't bother sitting down. He stood looking out, watching various boats going past—cruisers, yachts, ferries—glancing at his watch to check the time.

The woman was late. Five minutes. Ten minutes. Unpunctuality always niggled him. It disregarded the value of his time, invariably shortening his temper. When he finally heard the footsteps signalling her arrival, he had to school himself not to display impatience as he swung around to greet her.

In actual fact, any sense of impatience shot right out of his mind as recognition hit. The long blond hair was swinging naturally around her shoulders just as he'd imagined it could, the face was an exact replica, no computerised touch-up to make her features more attractive, no blemishes on that glowing skin, and the unusual green eyes were even more fascinating in real life…

Foxy Angel!

Not only living up to her photograph, but delivering the complete goods with stunning oomph!

Her figure was femme fatale class—lush curves where there should be lush curves, stunningly outlined by a citrine silk dress that shouted sensuality, and long shapely legs enhanced by sexy strappy highheels. High impact stuff. No doubt about it. Hugo felt a hot tingling in his groin, a charge of adrenalin shooting through his body, excitement fizzing in his brain.

It was fantastic luck that Chrissie was gone from his life, because this woman was walking into it, ringing bells that said he had to have her.

And she was available!

The trick was to win her before a horde of eager beavers jumped on the billboard bandwagon.

Angie was used to guys giving her the once-over but Hugo Fullbright's comprehensive head to foot appraisal felt more sexual than most and it bothered her. It bothered her even more that he made no attempt to switch to business meeting mode. And he looked unbelievably sexy himself, stunning blue eyes simmering with bedroom interest, a tantalising little smile that smacked of sensual satisfaction lurking on his mouth as he watched her walk towards him.

A wave of his hand dismissed her escort.

His focus did not deviate from Angie, and her heart gave an agitated skip as she realised Hugo Fullbright was probably a blitz operator in more than property development. Paul might be classical male but this guy was animal male in spades. And he radiated the kind of magnetic intensity Russell Crowe brought to his movies.

His thick black hair was cut short but it still had an untamed look about it. His skin was darkly tanned, suggesting he lived more under the sun than away from it. His body was encased in tailored sophistication—a beautiful grey suit that had a sheen of blue silk running through it—yet she had the sense of a strong, lithe physique, like that of a big jungle cat, wired to pounce.

It took all her willpower to step up to him, offer her hand, and make her vocal chords perform at a natural pitch. 'Mr. Fullbright, I'm Angie Blessing.'

'Angie…' He rolled her name off his tongue as though tasting it for honey. The vivid blue eyes twinkled with wicked teasing. 'Short for Angel?'

Her heart sank like a stone. He'd seen the billboard, connected her to it. 'No. Angela,' she answered sharply, desperate for some diversion. 'But everyone calls me Angie.'

'I think Angel suits you better,' he mused, holding on to her hand, his thumb fanning her skin, shooting heat into her bloodstream.

She felt her cheeks burning. Her mind was torn over what to do—ignore the allusion to the billboard or confront it? This was business. Business! It was wrong to get into anything personal.

'I do apologise for being late, Mr. Fullbright,' she rushed out.

'Hugo.' He smiled invitingly.

'I had an urgent call…'

'I imagine you'll be getting many urgent calls. I'm sure I'm not the only man who…*likes what he sees.*'

The direct reference to the words on the billboard—*If you like what you see, contact…*—was too pointed for Angie to dismiss. She took a deep breath and plunged straight into trying to clear the murky waters of this meeting.

'Mr. Fullbright…'

'Hugo,' he slid in, and started to lift her hand as though he intended to kiss it!

She snatched it out of his grasp, firmly claiming, 'A mistake was made!'

He moved his now empty hand into a lazily elegant gesture that requested more information. 'A mistake?'

'The person who composed that billboard used the wrong half of a photograph sent in by my friend,' she said heatedly, Francine's frantic excuse doing little to stop her blood from boiling on this issue.

'A friend,' Hugo Fullbright repeated mockingly,

not believing a word of it. Then he grinned. 'You don't have to hide behind a friend, Angie. I'm not in the least perturbed by your enterprising move. It cuts straight to the chase, doing away with any need for preliminary manoeuvres. I admire the sheer nerve of it.'

Angie realised that nothing she said was going to change his mind. The *friend* cover was too often used to insert distance from a personal interest. He'd seen her image on the billboard and any mistake seemed too improbable. Angie wondered if she could sue the billboard people for damages. Francine had promised to fix everything but Francine wasn't here right now and somehow Angie had to get this meeting on a business footing. It didn't matter what he *thought,* as long as he...

'I'm just letting you know you needn't be *foxy* about this,' he dropped into the silence, benevolently forgiving what he saw as pretence. 'In fact...'

'Mr. Fullbright,' she swiftly cut in.

'Please make it Hugo.' Charm on full blast, making her heart pitter-pat like a fluttering shuttlecock being batted around her chest.

'Hugo,' she conceded, taking another deep breath to calm herself down. 'I'm here on a professional basis.'

'So you are. Sorry for confusing the issue.' His smile was very white and patently apologetic, so why was she thinking of a wolf in sheep's clothing?

It was the animal thing again.

Male on the prowl.

All her instincts were picking it up and reacting to it, throwing her into a fluster because he was terribly attractive and the situation was making her feel more vulnerable than she should be. She'd been with Paul for three years and this man…she couldn't imagine this man without a woman in tow, married or otherwise.

'Though I can't help thinking how fortuitous this meeting is,' he ran on. 'Both of us…currently unattached…'

Had he read her mind? Those blue eyes were dynamite.

'…and I do, indeed, like what I see.'

It was a very pointed statement of personal interest and intent. He wanted her. Or, at least, wanted to try her out, see how she fitted with him.

And to Angie's intense embarrassment, she felt her body responding positively to it, telling her in no uncertain terms that she would like to have the experience of this man on a very personal level.

In spite of her attachment to Paul!

'Could we…' She swallowed hard to remove the weird constriction in her throat. 'Could we talk business now?' Her voice sounded slurred, husky, desperate, embarrassing her further.

A delaying tactic. A *foxy* tactic. His interpretation of this request danced through the amusement in his eyes. 'By all means tell me…what you want to tell me,' he invited, gesturing to the lounge setting. 'Would you like to sit down?'

'Yes. Thank you,' she jerked out, and hoped her suddenly tremulous legs would carry her to the leather sofa without any graceless teetering in her high-heeled sandals.

She made the move without mishap, deliberately choosing to seat herself in the centre of the sofa, delivering the hint for him to settle for an armchair, leaving her with enough personal space to feel comfortable. Which he did. Though it didn't lessen her physical awareness of him one bit. In fact, it was probably heightened, being able to see all of him, sitting with a relaxed waiting air, confident he would eventually get the outcome he wanted one way or another.

Angie fiercely concentrated on business, determined to stay professional. 'I don't know how hands-on you are on this project…' she started.

Disastrously.

Because he instantly inserted, 'My involvement in any project is never without a hands-on approach.' The quirky little smile had a double-edged kick as he added, 'You have my full attention, Angie.'

'Right!' She wished he wouldn't keep sucking the breath out of her. 'The concept I've decided upon for designing the colour co-ordination in these apartments…'

'I've already approved the concept.'

Oh great! Now he was pulling the mat out from under her professional feet. 'Then why am I here? What point is there to this meeting?' she demanded, losing her cool under the barrage of heat she felt coming from him.

His straight black eyebrows slanted in a kind of quizzical self-examination of his motives. 'Well, I'd have to say it's developed more points since I made the initial request.'

Since he saw her photo, advertising she was available!

Angie gritted her teeth, waiting for a *business* answer.

He grinned, aiming all his megawatt masculinity at

her. 'But the primary aim was simply to meet you and assess for myself if you will deliver what you promise.'

Her stomach curled. The only assessment going on in his eyes was centred on how much pleasure he might find in having her with him on a very personal level—whether she'd live up to whatever he thought she'd been advertising on the billboard!

'We have a contract,' she bit out. 'Ask anyone our company has dealt with. We have always honoured our contracts and delivered on schedule.'

'That has been checked, Angie,' he smoothly assured her. 'But even within the letter of the contract, some things can be fiddled and often are.'

Foxy.

Was that word going to haunt her on this job?

'What I want is a quality finish,' he continued. 'No cost cutting.'

'The prices we've quoted on materials are precise,' she shot in, emphatically adding, 'We have never compromised on quality. It wouldn't even occur to us to do so in this job. Our design company has a reputation to maintain.'

'And I willingly concede you do project a high-quality image, Angie.' Warm appreciation in his eyes. Too warm. 'It reinforces my feeling that I've made the right choice.'

His choice.

As though she had no say in it!

On the other hand, if he was talking about giving them the contract...best not to make any reply. Besides, her chest had tightened up again, rendering her breathless and speechless.

Hugo Fullbright smiled his white wolf smile. 'I just

wanted to impress on you that I don't believe in cutting costs when going after what I want.'

'Fine!' she choked out.

'So we now have an understanding of where we both stand,' he concluded.

'Yes.'

Point achieved, meeting over. Angie told herself to get up and take her leave. She uncrossed her ankles, planted her feet on the floor, ready to rise from the sofa...

'I'm flying to Tokyo tomorrow morning,' he tossed at her. 'Back Sunday night. What you might call a long weekend.'

Angie remained poised where she was, wondering what this had to do with her.

'A bit of business,' he explained offhandedly. 'I built a resort in Queensland for a Japanese consortium. They probably want to run other plans past me but primarily it's a hospitality trip—wining, dining, sightseeing.'

'Nice for you,' she commented, not knowing how else to respond.

'For you, too, Angie...' A wicked challenge sparkled in his eyes. '...if you'd like to come with me.'

Tokyo.

She'd never been to Japan.

And being whisked off there by him...

Shocked at these wayward thoughts—he was *wickedly* attractive—Angie pulled herself together and frantically tried to find an appropriate reply. Rejection in this situation was very tricky.

'Thank you. But I've never thought it a good idea to mix business with pleasure. It could develop into an awkward situation between us.'

'I would agree...if you worked directly for me. But you'll be working independently on this contract. Your own boss with absolute autonomy.' The white wolf smile flashed again. 'In fact, this trip may very well provide some beneficial business contacts for you and your design company.'

He was so smooth.

And appealing.

Even making business mixed with pleasure a plus instead of a minus.

Angie couldn't believe how tempted she was. Accepting such a proposition was tantamount to being gobbled up by this marauding man. It would be such a wild thing to do. Besides, there was Paul. The fundraiser dinner on Friday night. Why hadn't she thought of that before?

'I'm sorry. I have other plans—commitments—this weekend.'

'Fair enough,' he accepted gracefully, though his eyes were weighing how serious her commitments might be.

Angie flushed with embarrassment as she remembered the billboard—the vast flood of replies Francine was expecting through the Internet. Was Hugo thinking she wanted to check them out before picking *him?*

Useless to state again that her photo was a mistake.

No way would he buy the friend excuse.

She pushed up from the sofa, too agitated to remain seated a moment longer. 'Thank you for your time. I hope you have a great trip to Tokyo,' she rattled out, forcing the offer of her hand to make a polite, *businesslike* farewell.

He stood up in all his overpowering maleness, making Angie quake inside. Instead of taking her hand, he reached inside his suit jacket and extracted a slim, gold card-holder. 'Let me give you my card.' He opened it and pressed all his contact details into her hand, smiling a sensual promise as he said, 'Should you change your mind about Tokyo…give me a call.'

'Yes. Thank you,' she babbled, and somehow managed to stretch her mouth into a bright smile. 'Goodbye.'

'Until next time,' he purred.

Jungle cat, just biding his time for another opportunity to pounce.

Angie could feel him watching her walk away from him. Every nerve in her body was tingling as though a field of highly charged electricity was emanating from him. His card was burning in her hand. She tried to think of Paul—Paul who might or might not marry her—but Hugo Fullbright and a trip to Tokyo with him were terrible distractions.

Of course she couldn't do it.

She wouldn't.

She wasn't the type of person to throw all caution to the winds, dump a man who had every reason to expect love and loyalty from her, and leap into a relationship with someone else.

It just wasn't right.

CHAPTER THREE

THE moment Angie stepped into their official office and showroom at the trendy end of Glebe Road, Francine leapt to her feet from behind her desk and was in full spout, frantically trying to appease the wrath she felt coming her way, the forerunner of it being the urgent call that had made Angie late for her meeting with Hugo Fullbright.

'I've been onto the billboard people. Told them you were threatening to sue for damages. They apologised profusely for the mistake, but they can't get your photo off and mine on until tomorrow. They'll print a public apology if you want, Angie. I know it's partly my fault for giving them the photo of the two of us, but it was the best one ever taken of me, and I swear it was clearly specified which half to use. I don't know why the technician got it wrong. But I'm terribly, terribly sorry that he did.'

Her wildly flapping hands moved into wringing. 'Did...ummh...Hugo Fullbright recognise you like you thought he might?' Her grimace imagined the worst but anxiously hoped for a let off.

Angie heaved a long loosening-up sigh, resigning herself to the fact that what was done was done. A mistake had been made and Francine had clearly worked hard at correcting the situation, so there was no point in carrying on about it.

'Yes, he did recognise me,' she answered, rolling her eyes to lighten the fraught mood. 'He had *Foxy*

Angel on his mind from the moment I walked into the meeting.' Which reminded her to ask, 'Why on earth did you pick that name? He related it straight to Angie.'

Francine scrunched up her shoulders as though defending herself from an imminent attack. 'I thought it would appeal to men's fantasies.'

'Well, it certainly did the trick,' Angie dryly informed her, though everything Hugo Fullbright had aimed at her had not felt like a fantasy at all. It had been very direct and highly disturbing.

'Were you...horribly embarrassed?'

'Yes, I was horribly embarrassed.' *And tempted.* Though best to put that out of her mind now. 'Hugo Fullbright didn't believe the billboard photo was a mistake. He said he admired my nerve and invited me to accompany him to Tokyo for a dirty weekend.'

If she put it in those terms, the temptation would go away. It was probably true, too, if he thought the billboard photo meant she'd do anything for a man.

Francine's jaw dropped.

Angie had to smile.

Tit for tat in the shock department.

'A pity it wasn't you at the meeting,' Angie ran on, needing to lighten up about what had happened. 'Hugo Fullbright is as handsome as the devil, as wealthy as they come, plus sex appeal in spades and currently unattached. You missed out on quite a catch!'

'Damn!' Shock collapsed into disappointment at the lost opportunity. 'All my meetings leading up to signing the contract were with the architect and he was seriously married with children. I never got to meet the boss man.'

'Francine…' Angie eyed her friend with deep exasperation. 'Can't you see there's a big down side to this scheme? Guys who might not take no for an answer. I was lucky that Hugo Fullbright was gentleman enough not to really come on to me.'

'I can handle it.' Francine's grey eyes flashed reckless determination. 'And let me tell you if Hugo Fullbright is all you say he is, I would have been off to Tokyo with him like a shot. You've got to seize the main chance, Angie, make it work for you. That's how it is out there. You've been safely ensconced with Paul so long, you've got blinkered eyes.'

'Paul…' Angie's inner tension geared up several notches at the reminder of her long-term relationship which could very well be in serious jeopardy. She should have been worrying about it instead of…

'He wouldn't have seen the billboard, Angie,' Francine offered in anxious hope. 'Not travelling from his apartment at Woolloomooloo to the law court at Darlinghurst.'

Angie shook her head. 'It doesn't have to be Paul. Can you really imagine that not one of his friends or colleagues, having known us as a couple for years…not one of them would have driven across the Sydney Harbour Bridge this morning without noticing the billboard and recognising *Foxy Angel* as me?'

'It *is* possible,' Francine argued. 'I mean…they wouldn't be expecting it to be you.'

'Hugo Fullbright took one look at me—one look—and had no trouble whatsoever in making the connection.'

'But anyone who knows you—really knows you—would think they're mistaken. You're so straight, Angie. It's not your kind of thing at all.'

Why did that suddenly make her feel she'd lived her life in a straitjacket, limiting her options instead of expanding her horizons?

Francine rushed into apology again. 'I'm sorry. Truly, truly, sorry. If it causes trouble with Paul, just lay all the blame on me, where it belongs, and I'll tell him so myself. I won't mind if he considers me a hopelessly ditzy woman who doesn't know which side is which.'

That wasn't going to help. Paul would be furious. Mistake or not, he'd find the whole photo thing offensive.

'Surely he's big enough to laugh it off,' Francine suggested tentatively.

More likely he'd drag it into the law court, demanding redress. Though that could turn into a distasteful circus. Possibly he would choose to laugh it off on the principle of least said, soonest mended.

'We'll cross that bridge when we come to it,' Angie said on a helpless sigh. Her own state of confusion about how she felt towards Paul—and Hugo Fullbright—was making her stomach churn.

'Right!' Francine clearly hoped for a reprieve on the Paul front. 'So…ummh…was there any business in the meeting with Hugo Fullbright?' she asked warily. 'I mean…this didn't have some negative effect, did it? The contract is watertight.'

'We have his full approval to go ahead with our concept.'

'Great!' Huge relief.

Angie wished she could feel relief. The next best thing was distraction. 'Let's get to work, Francine.'

They worked.

Every time the telephone rang, Francine pounced

on it, anxious to divert any possible trouble from Angie. At lunchtime she offered to go to the local delicatessen to buy them both salads, thus avoiding the chance that Angie might be accosted by some guy wanting *Foxy Angel* to fulfil his fantasies.

It was a very special salad—Thai beef with mango.

Angie's favourite.

Except her stomach was in no condition to appreciate it. She wondered if sushi would be easier to swallow, then wrenched her wayward mind off Tokyo and Hugo Fullbright and determinedly shoved lettuce leaves into her mouth.

The telephone rang.

Angie's stomach knotted up even further as she listened to Francine rattling out what had happened with the billboard, pulling out all stops to explain the mistake. It had to be Paul calling. And the way Francine was wilting was warning enough that he was not amused. Having exhausted all avenues of appeasement, she limply passed the receiver over, grimacing defeat.

'Paul...demanding to speak to you.'

Angie took a deep breath. 'Paul...'

'Our relationship is over!'

Just like that!

Not even a stay of judgement.

Angie was totally poleaxed, speechless.

'I can no longer afford to have you at my side,' he ranted on. 'I have been subjected to intolerable comments and sniggers from my colleagues all morning...'

'But...it's not my fault,' she managed to get out.

'Irrelevant!' he snapped. 'I do not intend to spend my time trying to explain away a mistake that no one will believe anyway. I've told people I severed our relationship last weekend and if you have any decency at all, you will back that up. If asked. The only saving grace from this mess is that I didn't go to the ballet with you last night. Goodbye, Angie.'

The line was disconnected before she could say another word.

The shock of this—this brutal dismissal from his life—stirred a turbulent anger that broke every restraint Angie would normally keep on her temper. She rose to her feet, marched over to Francine's desk and slammed the receiver down on the phone set, startling her friend into looking agog at her.

'What…what happened?' she asked nervously.

Angie ungritted her teeth and bit out, 'He dumped me.'

'He…' Francine swallowed hard. '…dumped you?'

'Three years together and he shoves me out in the cold, just like that!' Angie snapped her fingers viciously, growing more and more inflamed by the injustice of it all.

'I'll go and grovel to him, Angie. I'll…'

'Don't you dare!'

'But…'

'If Paul Overton came crawling to me on his hands and knees I wouldn't take him back,' Angie hurled at her, wheeling away and tramping around the office, working off a surge of violent energy and venting her ever-mounting outrage. 'It shows how much he cared about me. No love. No loyalty. No taking my side. Just wiping me off as though I was too tainted for him to touch anymore.'

She scissored a furious gesture at Francine who

was all galvanised attention. 'Even a criminal gets to have extenuating circumstances taken into consideration. And I'm innocent. Completely innocent.'

'You're right,' Francine gravely agreed. 'He doesn't deserve you.'

'He even backdated our separation to last weekend so he could save his precious pride in front of his precious colleagues, distancing himself from any action I've taken since then.'

'Mmmh…I wonder if he told them this was your revenge for being…'

'Francine!' Angie yelled in sheer exasperation.

It rattled her into trying to excuse her speculative mind-frame. 'I was just working it through…'

'I didn't do it, remember?'

'Completely and utterly innocent,' came the emphatic agreement. 'Uh…there's someone at the door, Angie,' she quickly added with the harried air of one wanting to grasp any distraction.

Angie swung to confront the intruder.

It was a florist delivery boy, carrying in a spectacular arrangement of exquisite orchids. He paused, glancing inquiringly from one to the other.

'Miss Angie Blessing?'

'That's me,' Angie snapped, eyeing him balefully. At this point in time, no male could be trusted.

'These are for you.'

'Fine. Thank you.'

She waved in the direction of her desk. He set the delivery down and scooted, undoubtedly aware that he'd blundered into an area mined with highly volatile sensibilities.

Angie glared at the gift.

Who would be sending her flowers?

Extremely expensive flowers.

There hadn't been time for Paul to start regretting his decision. If he ever did.

It was a very artistic arrangement, Japanese in style. This latter thought put a tingling in Angie's spine. It drove her over to the desk to unpin the attached note and read it.

A taste of Tokyo—Hugo.

The dark place in Angie's soul unfurled to a lovely blast of light. Hugo Fullbright didn't think she was too tainted to have at his side. He wanted her there. And he really valued her company. These perfect orchids had definitely cost him a small fortune.

'Right! I'm going!'

'Going where?' Francine asked in bewilderment.

'To Tokyo. With Hugo Fullbright.' She headed around the desk to get her handbag where she'd stowed his card.

Francine rocketed to her feet. 'Angie…Angie…just hang on a minute. This isn't a decision you should rush into.'

'Why not? You said yourself you'd go with him. Seize the main chance.' She found the card and held it triumphantly aloft as she moved to the telephone, abandoning all sense of caution on this wild plunge into a different future.

'It's not your style,' Francine argued frantically.

'And where did that get me? Dumped. Cast off. Devalued to nothing. This is the new me, Francine, and nothing you say is going to stop me.'

'But…'

'Not another word. I'm going.'

She snatched up the receiver and stabbed out the numbers printed on the card for Hugo Fullbright's

personal mobile telephone. Francine sank back onto
her chair, rested her elbows on the desk and covered
her face with her hands, emitting a low groan denot-
ing inescapable disaster. The buzzing call signal in
Angie's ear drowned out the mournful noise.

'Hugo Fullbright.' The name was rolled out in a
deep sexy voice.

Angie's stomach curled. She screwed it to the sticking point. 'It's Angie Blessing. I've changed my
mind.'

'A woman's prerogative,' he said charmingly.

'The flowers are truly lovely.'

'They reminded me of you. Beautiful, appealing,
with a fascinating hint of the exotic.'

Angie's pulse rate accelerated but she determinedly
kept her voice calm. 'Thank you.'

'Our flight to Tokyo leaves at ten-thirty tomorrow
morning,' he went on matter-of-factly. 'I'll have my
chauffeur call for you at nine.'

His chauffeur. That was one up on Paul. Not that
she cared about Paul anymore. Not one bit!

'Can you be ready by then?'

A reminder that she'd been late for their meeting
this morning. 'Yes,' she said firmly. 'I'm not normally unpunctual.'

'Good! Now I do need your home address.'

She gave it.

'I'm very glad you changed your mind, Angie.' He
was back to purring.

Her heart started hammering. She told herself that
having the very personal attention of a jungle cat
would certainly broaden her horizons, not to mention
tripping off to Tokyo. It was time to live dangerously.
And best not to let Hugo Fullbright know there was

any apprehension in her mind. He was thinking *Foxy Angel*—bold and enterprising.

'I look forward to seeing you tomorrow, Hugo,' she said, deciding that was a reasonably foxy reply.

'Until tomorrow.' The purr positively throbbed with pleasurable anticipation.

Angie quickly put the receiver down. 'Done!' she said, not allowing the slightest quiver of doubt to shake her resolution.

Francine dragged her hands down enough to look at her with huge, soulful eyes. 'Please...please... don't blame me.'

'What for? I'm grateful to you, Francine. You showed Paul up for what he was.'

'A skunk,' she said with feeling.

'Absolutely. You saved me from wasting more time on him, liberating me so I can take a step in a new direction.'

'But is this direction right for you, Angie?' she worried.

'Won't know until I'm in Tokyo.' She grinned at Francine as she collected her handbag, wanting to show there would be no hard feelings between them, whatever the outcome of this adventure with Hugo Fullbright.

'Angie, you shouldn't think of it as a dirty week-end,' Francine anxiously advised.

Seeing her friend's genuine concern, Angie paused to give her the real truth. 'I don't care, Francine. Hugo really got to me this morning—made me wish I wasn't with Paul. I want to take this chance with him. Come what may.'

'You're not flying off the rails because of what Paul's done?'

Angie took a deep breath and slowly shook her head as she examined her feelings with absolute honesty. 'I'm so mad at Paul because I'm angry with myself for staying with him for so long. I knew it wasn't right. And I knocked Hugo back this morning because of him. I knocked him back and I'm not going to knock him back again. Paul never really focused on me. Hugo…' The sheer magnetism of the man tugging on her—just the thought of being with him tugging on her. '…he's something else, Francine, something I want to be part of, and now that I'm free of any sense of loyalty to Paul, I'm seizing this chance!'

Angie grabbed the arrangement of beautiful, exotic orchids and sailed out of the office, determined on pursuing this course of action wherever it led. She was thirty years old with nothing to lose. Hugo Fullbright beckoned very brightly—the man himself, the trip to Tokyo, the flowers, the chauffeur…all making her feel this might very well be the trip of a lifetime.

She wanted to go with him.

And go she would.

CHAPTER FOUR

HUGO FULLBRIGHT put away his mobile phone and relaxed back into the plush leather seat of his Bentley, grinning from ear to ear, enjoying his triumph. 'I won, James,' he said to the man driving him to his next meeting. '*Foxy Angel* is mine.'

'Congratulations, sir. Though I had no doubt you would win, once you set your mind on it.'

Hugo laughed, brimming over with good humour. He had to hand it to James. As his household executive, the man was brilliant. Only twenty-seven when Hugo had hired him four years ago—a New Age butler trained to do whatever was required of him: chauffeuring his boss, shopping, doing household chores, cooking, serving meals, co-ordinating the social calendar, making travel arrangements.

All that on top of the traditional trimmings—the art of etiquette, protocol, wine appreciation. Not to mention also being equipped with computer skills and having experience in conflict resolution.

Certainly James Carter was one of his best acquisitions, highly efficient and wonderfully discreet. He made the perfect confidant for Hugo because he was privy to all his affairs, both business and personal, and could be trusted with anything. Of course, he was paid very well, as befitting a top executive, and to Hugo's mind, he was worth every cent of his six-figure annual salary, plus perks.

Life moved very smoothly with James handling all

the details. Hugo appreciated that. So what if the guy was gay! Probably better that he was. James' mind was definitely on his job. A man's man. One hundred per cent. And like many gay guys, he had a great eye for stylish clothes, a great eye for everything.

Hugo knew that his suitcase would be perfectly packed ready for him to leave for Tokyo tomorrow morning, and best of all, Angie Blessing was going with him. 'You should see her in the flesh,' he said, the pleasure of it rolling through his voice as he remembered the amazing physical impact she'd had this morning. 'Well, you will see her.'

'Nine o'clock tomorrow morning,' James affirmed. 'I've written down the address.'

'Sex on legs...'

'You do seem to fancy legs, sir. All those models you've dated.'

Hugo frowned. The comparison was wrong. 'Angie Blessing is blessed with everything. Brains as well as beauty,' he corrected.

In fact, she put Chrissie Dorrington so far in the shade, on every count, he wished he'd met Angie long before this.

'Sounds like you might have hit the jackpot, sir.'

He might very well have. He could hardly wait to have his *Foxy Angel* to himself tomorrow. 'Thank you for finding the right florist, James,' he said appreciatively.

'Did the trick, sir?'

'A timely piece of persuasion.'

'If I may say so, sir, your timing is always impeccable. It's a pleasure to work for you.'

'Thank you.'

James was pleased everything had turned out well. He absolutely adored working for Hugo Fullbright. Not only was his employer suitably wealthy—cost no object with anything to do with his private life—but he had a flamboyant personality, never stuffy or boring. There was always something *happening*. It made life interesting, exciting, challenging.

And he was generous. Not a mean bone in his body. Generous with praise, and best of all, generous in showing his appreciation financially. James knew there wasn't a butler in Sydney with a higher wage than his.

Some of the rather peevish older butlers did not consider Hugo Fullbright *a gentleman*. He was one of the new rich, a racy bachelor, not really respectable. A bunch of bloody snobs, James thought, probably eaten up with envy. For one thing, they had to drive around in black Daimlers or silver grey Rolls-Royces, some even in an ordinary Mercedes. *He* had charge of a brilliant red Bentley. Mega-dollars with panache! No one could beat that!

All the same, James did feel it was time for his employer, who was now thirty-eight, to get married and have children. It would round off his life. James' life, as well. He'd been trained to look after kids and since it was most unlikely he'd ever have any of his own, there was no doubt in his mind that Hugo Fullbright's children would be fun. Definitely entertaining little creatures. How could they not be?

It would be very interesting to meet *Foxy Angel* tomorrow. Miss Blessing surely had a flamboyant personality, as well, or she wouldn't have put herself up on that billboard. This could be the perfect match.

James started planning what he'd pack for Tokyo.

The new Ian Thorpe brand underpants—very sexy—
the Armani suit for dinner engagements—smooth sophistication—the Calvin Klein jeans for sightseeing—
brilliant for showing off a taut, cheeky butt—the
Odini black leather battle-jacket—some women were
kinky for leather...

Ah, yes! If Miss Blessing was *the one*...still, it
wasn't up to him. He'd do his bit to aid the process,
should she be good enough for his boss. The billboard
act *was* a bit dodgy. He'd know better tomorrow.

CHAPTER FIVE

THE doorbell rang at precisely nine o'clock.

Angie was ready. At least she was ready to go. She wasn't sure she was ready for this new situation with Hugo Fullbright—there was a swarm of butterflies in her stomach—but she'd weather it somehow and hopefully come up smiling. Which reminded her to put a smile on her face as she opened the door, starting off as she meant to go on, all bright and breezy.

'Good morning,' she lilted, determined that it would be good.

A surprisingly young man in a smart grey chauffeur's uniform tipped his cap to her while his eyes made a swift appraisal of his boss's new woman. Angie tensed, wondering if she passed muster. While it was summer in Australia, it was winter in Japan, so she'd teamed fine black wool pants with a frayed edge cropped jacket in black chenille, the latter very form-fitting with a diagonal hook and eye opening down the front which left a hint of cleavage on show, but not too much. Looking *foxy* wasn't really her style.

The chauffeur apparently approved, beaming a cheery smile right back at her. 'Good morning to you, Miss Blessing. My name is James Carter, answering to James.' He gestured to her suitcase and carry-on bag over which she'd slung her faux-fur leopard print overcoat, deciding it was definitely appropriate for wearing in the company of a jungle cat. 'Ready for me to take?'

'Yes. Thank you, James.'

'If you don't mind my saying so, Miss Blessing, I do like Carla Zampatti clothes. Always that subtle touch of class,' he said as he set about collecting her luggage.

Angie was so amazed at having the designer of her outfit recognised she barely got out another, 'Thank you.'

It dawned on her that the chauffeur was gay, which amazed her even further. The very macho Hugo Fullbright with a gay chauffeur? Well, why not? If he could pick a woman from a billboard photo, the man clearly had eclectic tastes in the people he drew into his life.

She didn't have to say goodbye to Francine who had left for work half an hour ago, squeezing Angie's hands as she said, 'Please…if things go wrong…just don't blame me.'

Angie would have much preferred a cheerful 'Good luck!' She was nervous enough as it was about what she was doing.

James led her down to the street where a gleaming red Bentley stood waiting. A red Bentley with cream leather upholstery! This was travelling in a style Angie had never experienced before. It made her feel like royalty, sitting in the back seat of such a car. The smile on her face did not have to be forced one bit.

Magnificent flowers.

Magnificent car.

Would the man match up to them?

And if he did, could she keep him?

She would hate it if she discovered that dirty week-

ends were his style when it came to women, picking
them up and putting them down at his leisure, easy
come, easy go. If he gave one hint of that she would
not take the flight to Japan. She hoped it was an irresistible impulse on his part, as it was on hers.

'Will Mr. Fullbright be meeting me at the airport,
James?' she asked, once they were on their way.

'We'll be picking him up from the Regent Hotel,
Miss Blessing. He has a business breakfast there this
morning. It was scheduled a week ago,' came the
obliging information and explanation for his absence
from her side.

'Thank you.'

A very busy man. And this trip to Tokyo had a
business connection, as well. Angie wondered if he
had room in his life for a wife and children. Not so
far, and she judged him to be in his late thirties. Or
maybe he was divorced. A bad marriage record. She
needed to find out these things, though that kind of
thinking was probably leaping too far ahead.

They drove over the harbour bridge. Angie checked
the billboard, needing to know if her photo had been
removed. She breathed a huge sigh of relief when she
saw that Francine's image had replaced hers, then
barely smothered a groan as she read the new caption—*Hot Chocolate*. Francine would have men's
fantasies zooming!

Still, how could she criticise?

Foxy Angel had caught Hugo Fullbright's interest.
Though that was a double-edged sword. Angie didn't
know if he was genuinely attracted to her or caught
up in a fantasy that appealed to him.

James used the car phone to alert his boss to their
imminent arrival at the Regent Hotel. Running to

schedule was clearly an important issue to such a busy man. Every minute counted. In fact, as the Bentley pulled up at the main entrance to the hotel, Hugo Fullbright was making his exit. Perfect timing.

Angie barely had a minute to compose herself before James was holding the passenger door open, and the man she was committed to spending the next three days with swept into the car, filling it with a vibrant energy. He flashed his white wolf smile at her and her heart hopped, skipped and jumped all over the place.

'Hi!' he purred, his eyes gobbling her up.

Angie knew the Bentley was air-conditioned but it suddenly felt very hot in there. 'Hi to you, too,' she replied with as much aplomb as she could muster. He was also wearing all black, a superbly tailored suit, silk shirt, and no tie. She found her gaze glued to the bared little hollow at the base of his throat until he spoke again.

'You look ravishing.' He rolled the R and Angie couldn't help feeling it was like a drum-roll anticipating many hours of ravishment.

Her toes curled.

'I was trying for beautiful, appealing, and exotic,' she tossed back at him.

He laughed. It was a laugh of pure enjoyment and Angie thought this weekend might be a lot of fun with him, if she could just let her hair down and go with it. For a long time there hadn't been any real fun with Paul. It was well past time she enjoyed life again, though she hoped for much more than a quickly passing enjoyment with Hugo.

The Bentley was in motion again, carrying her off with this man on very possibly the adventure of a lifetime—one that might lead to a lifetime of adventure! Maybe that was a hopeless fantasy but Hugo Fullbright certainly inspired it.

'Did your business breakfast go well?' she asked, interested in how he spent his time.

'A group of investors wanting to be in on my next property development. I'll let them know.' He reached over and took her hand, his thumb lightly fanning her skin again, sending electric tingles up her arm. 'I want to forget business now and learn more about you.'

Changing rooms.

'Is that how you manage your life, Hugo?' Angie asked curiously. 'Switching from one room to another? No cross-overs?'

'I don't want to bore you,' he purred, giving her the full riveting focus of his bedroom blue eyes.

Which was very flattering, having all his attention concentrated on her. Angie didn't know why she felt it was a smoke haze designed to keep her distant from the man behind the sexy charm, but her instincts demanded she challenge him.

'You think I'm some dumb blonde to be buttered up for her bed-worthiness?'

A sound suspiciously like a snort of amusement came from the driver's seat.

'Now how could I think that, Angie, when I'm trusting you with a huge budget to deliver the perfect finish for my apartments?' Hugo smoothly challenged back. 'I merely thought we could both take time out from work for a while. Enjoy each other's company without business intruding.'

'Fine! Just so you know I want to learn more about you, too.' And she gave him a long penetrating look to emphasise her interest was not purely sexual, nor centred on her own desirability to him.

He grinned. 'Well, I'd have to say I'm already flattered by the removal of your photo from the billboard.'

Heat scorched her cheeks. She barely bit back the impulse to state the truth again, which, of course, was *the straight* thing to do. And where would that get her? The sure knowledge that he wouldn't believe her anyway held her tongue. Her mind frantically composed a *foxy* reply.

'It seemed the decent thing to do since I'm not available...until further notice.'

Which put him on trial, competing for her interest. Best for him not to think she'd wiped every other guy out because he'd stepped forward. She'd had quite enough of the male ego from Paul Overton. No way was she going to let Hugo Fullbright think he could take her for granted because he considered himself so great!

He weighed her reply, his dynamite eyes twinkling appreciation of it. 'A move I respect,' he said. 'Thank you for giving me pole position. I promise I'll do everything in my power to ensure you won't regret it.'

And the power was coming at her in huge swamping waves. Angie just managed to collect her wits enough to continue the conversation. 'Interesting that you should use a car-racing term...pole position...and here you are with a very sedate Bentley.'

His brows drew together in mock disappointment. 'You don't like this car?'

'I love it. I'm just wondering why you chose it.'

'Can't I love it, too?'

'I would have thought a red Ferrari more your style. Dashing, glamorous, powerful…'

Something dark flickered in his eyes. 'No, I'm not into sports cars.' His mouth tilted sardonically. 'I wouldn't want any woman to think I'm the kind of man who needs one to make him a desirable male.'

Intriguing that he was touchy on the point. 'So the Bentley is…a perverse choice?' Angie queried, trying to probe for more.

'No.' He shrugged. 'It's simply *my* choice. A positive liking, not a negative reaction to something else.'

'They say a car does reflect the character of the man who owns it,' she mused, thinking of Paul with his Mercedes sports convertible—an establishment car with macho appeal.

'Tell me what this car stands for to you?' Hugo inquired, amused by the idea of testing her theory.

Angie paused to think about it, intuitively knowing her answer would be important in his judgement of her. 'Firstly, it yells very solid wealth. But also seriously classy style. Not something transient. It's the kind of car you could own all your life without its ever going out of style or losing its impact. Yet the red says its owner is not conservative. It's a bold choice, probably expressing his nature. I also think it's a statement that he doesn't care what other people think. Yet the high respectability of the car reassures them he can be trusted to deliver the goods, whatever they are.'

He nodded thoughtfully. 'An interesting analysis.' His mouth quirked. 'So you think I'm bold.'

Considering his blitzkrieg approach to her— 'Very,' she said with feeling.

'And you like that?' His eyes were twinkling teasingly again.

Angie's chest tightened up. Thoughts of sharing a bed with him—being bold—whizzed around her mind. 'It's...different,' she finally choked out.

He lifted her hand to his lips and pressed a very sensual kiss on her palm, his eyes never leaving hers as he did it. *'Vive la difference,'* he murmured with that throbbing purr of anticipation in his voice humming along every nerve in Angie's body.

She didn't even notice the Bentley slowing to a halt.

'Airport, sir,' James announced from the front seat.

'So...we begin our journey together,' Hugo said, still with the eye-lock that pinned Angie to her decision, despite the reality of the situation rushing in on her.

James was out of the car, holding the door open for them to alight. Hugo did not release her hand. He swung himself out and drew Angie after him. She arrived on the pavement adjacent to the international departure entrance, completely breathless and acutely aware of the man holding her.

Was she ready to go with him...accepting everything it entailed?

Was she really?

This was the moment of truth.

She could cry off, ask James to drive her back home again or get a taxi, cut every personal connection to the man. It was a woman's prerogative to change her mind. She could still do it. How was it going to feel right if she was just giving in to...*lust?*

Hugo was having no trouble with it. But men didn't, did they? They just followed their natural an-

imal instincts. It was only women who wanted more.
And she did want more than just sex. He was an
amazingly attractive, fascinating man. But if she
turned away from him now, what were the chances
he would pursue his current interest in her? He'd admired her sheer nerve in putting her face on a billboard! Wimping out of the weekend might completely wipe out his interest in her.

Hugo Fullbright was a bold man looking for a bold
partner. She could regret being bold, but wouldn't she
always regret not being bold? A man like him might
only come her way once in a lifetime.

Seize the main chance!

She didn't realise she'd squeezed his hand until he
shot her a quizzical glance. 'Nervous?'

'A bit!' she admitted. 'It's just hit me that I'm actually going to Tokyo with you.'

He flashed her a reassuring grin. 'I'll look after
you, Angie. I've been there before. Don't worry about
it.'

It wasn't the foreign country angle that was worrying her. However, she'd fretted away enough
minutes for James to have acquired a luggage trolley
and stacked everything ready to go. There it was in
front of them, Hugo's bags and hers, about to be consigned to a Qantas jet that would fly them both to
Japan.

Francine's advice slid into her mind—*You
shouldn't think of it as a dirty weekend.*

'I won't,' she said decisively.

'Good!' Hugo approved, thinking she was answering him.

James handed Angie her coat and tipped his cap.

'I hope you have a splendid journey, Miss Blessing,' he said chirpily.

'Thank you.'

He turned to Hugo. 'And you, sir, all the best! I'll check with the airport for your landing time on Monday morning.'

'Do that, James,' he said dryly. 'You might also need to see a doctor about your nose.'

'My nose, sir?'

'I've never heard you snort before.'

'I do beg your pardon, sir.' He frowned apologetically. 'A temporary ailment. I'll see to it.'

'Try to get it fixed before Monday morning.'

'You can count on it, sir.'

'I'm sure I can. Thank you, James.'

The chauffeur actually clicked his heels before turning away to round the Bentley, heading back to his driver's seat.

Hugo was smiling in some private amusement as he took charge of the luggage trolley. 'Nice coat,' he remarked, nodding to the leopard faux-fur hanging over her arm.

'I thought you'd like it,' she said, resolutely banishing any quiver from her legs as she walked at his side into the departure hall.

'Is that another piece of character analysis?' he asked in teasing challenge.

She shot him a foxy glance. 'You remind me of a jungle cat.'

'Ah! Survival of the fittest?'

'Slightly more dangerous than that.'

He laughed, making Angie's mind fizz with what might very well be dangerous pleasure.

But she wouldn't worry about that anymore.

It was not going to be a dirty weekend.

She refused to even think it might be that for him. It was going to be a getting-to-know-you fun weekend.

Wild, probably irresponsible, but didn't every woman deserve to just let her hair down and go with the flow without worrying about consequences for just a little while? Angie reasoned she could be sane and straight again when she came home. Until then she'd ride along on Hugo Fullbright's wave and if he dumped her at the end of it…well, at least she wouldn't be wasting three years on him.

CHAPTER SIX

HUGO decided he should probably try to get some shut-eye himself. They were four hours into their nine-hour flight to Tokyo and it would inevitably be a late night with his Japanese hosts once they arrived. Angie was out like a light, stretched out comfortably on the almost horizontal bed set up by the handy controls on their first-class seats.

He smiled over her apology for her drowsiness— the champagne on boarding the plane, the wines accompanying a very fine lunch, not much rest last night. He didn't mind. Her uninhibited pleasure in travelling first-class, happily accepting everything offered, enjoying it, had made it a delight to be with her, and gave him cause to reflect that too many of his companions in recent years had been picky women, demanding special food and drinking only mineral water on flights.

Not that he'd minded that. It was sensible to drink water and faddy diets seemed to be all the rage these days, but it was infinitely more companionable to have a woman with him who shared his lust for every pleasure in life.

Maybe the difference came from Angie's background. As with himself, there'd been no family wealth behind her. She'd climbed her own ladder, just as he had. Her parents had been flower children, and even now lived in an alternative society community up near Byron Bay, selling their arts and crafts to tourists.

Career-wise she'd well and truly earned her success, having the guts to get out on her own and capitalise on her talent for design, not riding on the back of anyone else. No doubt there would have been years of tight budgeting. That had to give an extra edge to enjoying the best of everything now. It did for him.

His own parents had chosen to live up on the North Coast, too—Port Macquarie, where he'd built them a retirement home with every luxury he could provide. They were happy there, and he dropped in on them when he could. Their only current concern was he hadn't found a nice girl and settled down to produce grandchildren for them.

Could Angie be the *nice* girl?

Hugo was bemused by the thought. He really had no yen to settle down. He liked his life just the way it was. Besides, he didn't need a wife. James ran a household probably better than any woman could. And Hugo was never short of feminine company when he wanted it.

Although…there was the matter of quality versus quantity. There were certainly qualities in Angie Blessing that lifted her…but this was only the beginning of their relationship. Far too soon to make a judgement, especially when it came to marriage.

Even more especially when it came to having children, which was the biggest responsibility of all. Possibly he would want them someday, but that could wait. He had no biological clock ticking. Besides, he'd want to get married first, and basically, he didn't trust any woman enough to hand her that much power over his life.

Angie's remark about sports cars had reminded him of Paul Overton, his arch-rival at school. The guy had been born with everything—good looks, brains, strong athletic ability, *and* a silver spoon in his mouth, the son and heir of a very wealthy establishment family with connections in the top legal and political circles. But that wasn't enough for Paul. He had to be number one at everything and it had always rankled him when Hugo pipped him for some prize or other.

And there was definitely no accident about the revenge he'd taken for those slights to his overweening ego. Being given a Porsche on his eighteenth birthday had handed him the tool to snag Hugo's girlfriend, and he'd deliberately set out to do it. Right in front of him. With smug triumph.

The guy was a top barrister now, probably manoeuvring his way towards a seat in parliament. If he ever made it to Prime Minister, Hugo sure as hell wasn't going to vote for him. But Paul had inadvertently taught him a lesson about women. They were inevitably drawn to what looked like the higher prize. And these days, if the prize didn't live up to their expectations of happily married life, there was always the divorce settlement to look forward to.

No thanks.

He'd worked too hard, risked too much, won too many battles to hand over half the spoils to a woman who'd done nothing to contribute to them. He was quite happy to share them, as with Angie here and now, as long as he had the controlling hand.

Even with Angie, whom he found so very appealing on many levels...would she have come with him on this trip if he wasn't a top runner in the wealthy bachelor stakes? If he hadn't sent her flowers that few men could afford, reinforcing what was on offer? He'd certainly won her, but had he won her because the price was right?

Irrelevant really. He had her with him, which was what he'd wanted. And she hadn't done any running after him, actually backing off when he'd offered himself, certainly not leaping at the invitation. At least, she'd provided him with a challenge—quite a rare event—and while she'd opened up a lot about herself since they'd been in flight, there was still something cagey about her, keeping a reserve while testing him out, as though there were other things more important to her than his surface attributes.

Foxy Angel....

Could be a lot of fun while it lasted, Hugo thought with much pleasurable anticipation, and pressed the controls to lower his seat into the bed position. Best that he be well rested for tonight, too. He wanted to enjoy every aspect of Angie Blessing, and be in top form to do precisely that.

A feather-light touch on her cheek tingled into Angie's consciousness, followed by the purring sound of Hugo Fullbright's voice.

'Wake up, sleeping beauty.'

No dream.

Her heart kicked out of its slumberous rhythm. Her eyes flew open. He was right next to her, instantly taking her breath away with his white wolf smile.

'We're about ninety minutes from Tokyo...'

She'd slept for hours!

'...and light refreshments are being served. Probably

best you eat something before we land. It will be a late dinner tonight,' he warned.

Angie bolted upright, a flood of embarrassment heating her face. 'I'm so sorry. I thought I'd only doze for a while.'

'No problem.' His grin was positively wicked. 'Nice to know you don't snore.'

Which turned up her temperature even more. 'I'll go and tidy up. Back in a minute.' She grabbed her handbag and scooted away, needing time out to regain her composure, not to mention urgent repairs to her make-up.

The reminder that she'd be *sleeping* with him to-night had completely flustered her again. She'd put it out of her mind once they'd boarded the plane, de-termined to focus on having fun and enjoying Hugo's company. And he'd let her do that, not pushing any-thing *physical,* happy to indulge her in a getting to know you conversation. It had made her feel com-fortable with him—as comfortable as she could be, given that he was a very sexy man and she was un-deniably excited by him.

Those dynamite blue eyes twinkling at her, warmly appreciative, admiring, teasing, laughing…above all, really interested in her. It hadn't felt like just a flir-tatious game, filling in time until he could pounce. It had felt…good. Very good.

Angie tried to wash the heat from her face with a thorough dousing of cold water. She was being silly, worrying about tonight. Hugo liked her. She could tell. And the liking was definitely mutual. Besides, if she wanted to say no, she was sure he would respect that. Her instincts told her he would turn away from forcing any woman to do what she didn't want.

A matter of pride.

Though he hadn't bragged about how clever he'd been in targeting the real estate market as a money-maker, starting off with buying and selling, building up funds so he could move into property development. She had virtually dragged the details out of him. His attitude had been more dismissive than proud.

Yet he was a self-made billionaire and Angie couldn't help but admire the enterprising way he'd achieved that. Nothing handed to him on a plate...unlike Paul. Though that was probably unfair. Paul wouldn't be where he was if he hadn't applied himself to using all his attributes very effectively. They were just different men, coming from different places.

Vive la difference...

She smiled over the phrase Hugo had used as she got out her make-up bag, needing to put on her best face for whatever was waiting for her in Tokyo.

It also made her feel good that Hugo hadn't looked down his nose at her parents' lifestyle or been critical of it in any way, musing that she must have had a free and happy childhood, allowed to pursue whatever interests she liked, no pressure to meet expectations.

He was the late and only child of more elderly parents, not pushy people either, but his achievements had given them a lot of pleasure and he liked doing things for them. Angie thought it was great that he'd built them a luxurious retirement home in the location of their choice. Definitely a loving son.

It was a warming thought to take back to her seat beside him, having restored her face to presentability and brushed her hair back into shape.

The cabin steward was hovering, waiting to serve the light refreshments. Her seat was upright again, the tray lifted out ready to be lowered. Angie quickly settled, apologising for the delay.

'There's no hurry. We have plenty of time,' Hugo soothed.

She flashed him a quick smile. He really was a nice man, though he was looking at her again as though he'd prefer to taste her rather than what the cabin steward was offering. It gave Angie goose bumps.

As soon as they were served, she opened up a conversation, desperately needing the distraction of talk to lessen the physical effect he had on her. 'Tell me about the people we're meeting tonight, Hugo. I'll probably need to practice their names so I'll get them right.'

He obliged her, describing the men and what positions they held, repeating their names until she'd memorised them and was pronouncing them correctly.

'Can you speak Japanese?' she asked, wondering if she was going to be a complete fish out of water at their dinner.

'Yes. I learnt it at school and have polished up my knowledge of it since then,' he answered matter-of-factly. 'But don't worry about a language barrier, Angie,' he hastened to add. 'Since we're their guests, they'll be speaking English.'

'Oh! Well, that's a relief.'

He laughed, his eyes caressing her with a warm approval that set her heart pitter-pattering. 'I'm glad you care enough to learn their names,' he remarked.

'It's only polite.'

'And good business.'

'I believe in being prepared.'

He cocked a wickedly challenging eyebrow at her. 'For everything?'

'I wasn't prepared for you,' she shot back at him.

He grinned. 'Taken by surprise. Jungle cats do that.'

Would he pounce before she could think? A primitive little thrill shocked her into wondering if she wanted that, wanted the responsibility of making the decision shifted off her shoulders. Her gaze dropped nervously to his hands. Somehow it reassured her that his fingernails were neatly manicured. He wouldn't be rough. Sleek and powerful. Her stomach contracted as she imagined him bringing those assets into play, but she wasn't sure if it was fear or excitement causing havoc with her inner muscles.

She forced her mind back onto safe ground. 'Since you can speak the language, would you please teach me the correct greeting and how to say thank you in Japanese?'

Again he obliged her, coaching her pronunciation as she practised the phrases, letting her become comfortable with the foreign words, amused by her satisfaction in being able to remember them and say them correctly. He made a light game of it, passing the time pleasantly until they landed at Narita Airport.

The business of disembarking and collecting their luggage made Angie very aware that she was now actually in Japan, with nothing familiar around her, and the only person who knew her here was Hugo Fullbright. It made her feel dependent on him, which was rather unsettling, but he smoothly took control of everything so she had nothing to worry about. Except how he might take control of her.

They were met by a smartly dressed chauffeur and Angie wondered why he was wearing white gloves, which stood out in stark contrast to his dark uniform. They were ushered to a gleaming black limousine. Along the top of the passenger seat was a spotless, and obviously freshly laundered white lace covering, precisely where heads might rest.

Angie looked curiously at it as she settled beside Hugo, prompting him to explain, 'The Japanese are big on hygiene. You'll find Tokyo a very clean city.'

Different culture, different customs, she thought, wondering what other surprises were in store for her.

Hugo took her hand, giving it a reassuring squeeze. 'You'll love it, Angie. Although it's too dark now for you to see, the overall impression of the city as you drive in is of a huge white metropolis. There aren't the masses of red roofs you see when flying over Sydney. Tokyo is the whitest city I've seen anywhere in the world.'

Of course he would notice that, being a property developer, Angie thought, but it was a fascinating fact to hoard in her mind, which was altogether too busy registering the sensations being stirred by his closeness to her, now that they were virtually alone together and he was holding her hand again.

Hugo continued to talk about features of the city as they were driven to their hotel, pointing out Disneyland as they passed it. She hadn't known there was one here. Nor had she known about the Tokyo Tower that was constructed similarly to the Eiffel Tower, only higher.

As a tour guide, Hugo added a great deal of interest to the trip, yet Angie was far more conscious of him as a man, and while he appeared perfectly relaxed, she sensed a simmering energy waiting for the right moment to burst into action.

Occasionally his gaze would drop to her mouth when she spoke back to him, watching the movement of her lips, as though imagining how they'd respond to his. There were flashes of dark intensity behind the sparkle in his eyes. The hand holding hers did not remain still, his fingers stroking, seemingly idly, yet to Angie's mind, with sensual purpose, stirring thoughts of how his touch would feel in other places. Sometimes he leaned closer to her, pointing something out, and the tantalising scent of some expensive male cologne accentuated his strong sexiness.

When they reached the Imperial Hotel, they were driven to the VIP entrance and met by a whole entourage of hotel management, everyone bowing to them, then taking charge of their luggage and escorting them along wide corridors, up in a classy elevator, right to the door of their suite and beyond it to ensure everything was to their satisfaction.

It was mind-boggling treatment to Angie. She'd imagined this kind of thing only happened to royalty or heads of state or famous celebrities. Was Hugo considered *a star* by the Japanese? She was certainly moving into a different stratosphere with him. This suite had to be at least presidential. The floral arrangements alone were stunning.

She was still trying to take it all in as Hugo chatted to their entourage and ushered them out, dealing smoothly with the situation as though he was born to it. Angie was way out of her depth, yet she couldn't deny it was an exhilarating experience to be given so much courtesy and respect. All because she was with *this man,* she reminded herself. It was enough to turn any woman's head.

As he walked back to where she stood, still dumb-struck by the extraordinary world she'd stepped into, Hugo gestured towards the bathroom and warned, 'We don't have a great deal of time before the call will come for us to be taken to dinner. Would you like to shower first?'

Angie nodded as a swarm of butterflies attacked her stomach again. Bathroom…naked…with him prowling outside in this very private suite.

'Let me take your coat.'

His hands were on the collar, drawing the coat off her shoulders, down her arms. He was standing so close, face to face, Angie's breath was helplessly trapped in her lungs. He tossed the coat on an arm-chair. Then his hands were sliding around her waist, his mouth smiling his wolf smile, his eyes sizzling now with sexual challenge.

'It feels I've been waiting a long time for this,' he purred, and Angie had a panicky moment at the thought of being devoured by him.

Yet as soon as his mouth claimed hers, she knew she'd been waiting for this, too, wanting to know how she'd feel when he kissed her, needing to know, hop-ing it would settle the questions that had been buzzing around in her mind. She slid her arms up around his neck, closed her eyes, let it happen, all her senses on extreme alert.

It didn't start with any marauding forcefulness, more a seductive tasting that charmed her into re-sponding, sensual lips like velvet brushing hers and the electric tingling of his tongue gliding over them, inviting—inciting—her to meet it, to open up to him, to explore more.

A slow kiss, gathering an exciting momentum as Angie was drawn into a deeper, more intimate journey with him, and she felt the pressure of his hands, gathering her closer, bringing her into full body contact with him, gliding over her curves as though revelling in their soft femininity, loving it.

Somehow his touch gave her the sense of being intensely sexy, making her acutely aware that she certainly hadn't felt this desirable to Paul for a long time. Maybe it was simply the wild pleasure of finding this dangerous gamble with Hugo was stirring sensations that some primal need in her wanted in order to make the risk right. Angie's mind wasn't really clear on this as it was being bombarded by impressions of the hard, strong maleness of the man who was holding her, kissing her as though he was enthralled by what she was giving him.

Then all thought disintegrated as he kissed her a second time, her mouth totally engaged with his in an explosion of passion so invasive that her whole body yearned to be joined with his, and exulted in knowing he was similarly aroused, desire becoming a vibrant urgency that could not be ignored.

And to Angie's confusion afterwards, it was Hugo who backed away from it, not she. He moved gently, not abruptly, slowly lessening the white-hot ardour, disengaging himself, taking a deep breath. 'We don't have enough time, Angie,' he murmured, his voice uncharacteristically rough, strained. 'You'd better go and have your shower now.'

She went, though how her quivering legs carried her into the bathroom she didn't know. The image of herself in the vanity mirror seemed like that of a woman in a helpless daze. How could there be so much incredibly strong feeling coursing through her? She'd barely met Hugo Fullbright…and all her worry about saying no to him…while here she was with her whole body screaming yes.

Having managed to undress and cram her long hair into a shower cap, Angie turned on a blast of water and tried to wash herself back to normal. Conscious of time being in short supply, she didn't linger under the sobering spray, quickly drying herself and donning the bathrobe supplied by the hotel. Cap off, clothes scooped into her arms, and she was out of the bathroom, calling to Hugo, 'It's all yours.'

He'd stripped down to his underpants!

Her gaze instantly veered away from them, though she barely stopped herself from staring at the rest of his bared physique—more definitively muscular than Paul's, very powerful thighs, and smoothly tanned olive skin that gleamed as though it was polished. No hair at all on his chest. Somehow she forced herself to keep moving towards her suitcase which was set on a luggage stand, ready for her to open.

'Thanks,' he said, flashing her an approving smile for not holding them up too long as he headed for the bathroom.

Angie dressed as fast as she could, her heart pumping overtime as she castigated herself for comparing Hugo to Paul. Hugo Fullbright was his own man. Paul was gone from her life. It was just difficult to wipe three years out in what was little more than a day. Even more difficult to come to terms with the fact that she'd been intimate with one man last week and was now about to plunge into intimacy with another.

But she hadn't really been happy with Paul, she frantically reasoned.

And Hugo was…special.

Incredibly special.

It didn't matter how soon it was and how fast it was happening, not to admit she wanted him was stupid. Better to be *straight* with herself—and him—than play some *foxy* game that would leave them both frustrated. Games weren't her style. Never had been.

Though whether this relationship would have any future in it or not, she had no idea. Francine would think she was mad not to suss that out first, and she probably was mad. Maybe she'd have second thoughts about it all before they returned to the hotel after dinner.

She'd chosen her Lisa Ho outfit for tonight— crushed velvet in shades of green; a Chinese style jacket with long fitted sleeves flaring at the wrist, and a long slim-line skirt that flared gracefully below her knees. Black high heels with sexy crossover ankle straps. She'd just seated herself at the well lit dressing table to attend to her grooming when Hugo emerged from the bathroom, a towel tucked around his hips.

Angie's heart was already galloping. It positively thundered as he stripped off and set about dressing. He was not acting in any exhibitionist way, just going naturally about the business of putting his clothes on, perfectly comfortable with having a woman in the room with him, chatting to her as though everything was absolutely normal.

She couldn't help thinking he was used to these circumstances. Inviting a woman away for a weekend was probably as familiar to him as it was unfamiliar for her to accept such a proposition. Which begged the question—was she just one of a queue that suited him far more than any permanent relationship would? An endless queue of women he found desirable at the time, but who'd always have a *use by* date?

Angie wasn't happy with that thought.

Yet it seemed to fit.

He wasn't married.

He'd never been married.

The telephone rang—notification that their car had arrived.

Angie quickly grabbed her small evening bag and stood up, ready to go. Hugo put down the telephone receiver and his gaze swept her from head to foot, before lingering on the row of buttons fastening the front of her jacket. *He* was now dressed in a superb pin-striped navy suit, looking both moody and magnificent.

'Will I do in this outfit?' she asked nervously, willing her legs to get steady so she could walk safely in these precarious shoes.

His face lightened up as he smiled with a touch of irony. 'You do...extremely well...in every sense.'

Her whole body flushed.

'I'd have to say the same of you,' she tripped out, trying to keep a level head.

He laughed. 'Then we clearly make a fine couple.'

And Angie carried that wonderfully intoxicating thought with her as they started out for their first night in Tokyo.

CHAPTER SEVEN

HUGO found it difficult to keep his mind focused on appreciating the hospitality of his hosts, let alone pursuing their subtle interest in future business. Tonight he was definitely not on top of the game. In fact, he was seriously distracted by Angie Blessing.

He couldn't remember the last time he'd been so excited by a woman. His usual control had slipped alarmingly when he'd kissed her. He'd actually struggled to assert it again, having to fight his reluctance to part from her, despite the tight schedule that demanded other action. And even now the provocative row of buttons down the front of her jacket was playing havoc with his concentration.

Ironically enough, his hosts were charmed by her, as well. Maybe it was an innate business sense coming to the fore, or simply a genuine interest in them and their country, but she delighted them with the very positive energy she brought to this meeting. Hugo mentioned the work Angie was doing on his latest project and they presented her with their business cards and respectfully requested hers. She was definitely quite a hit with them, doing herself proud. And him.

He could not have chosen a better partner—he frowned over that word—*companion* for this weekend. Why had he thought *partner*? Angie Blessing had been very accurate in naming herself *Foxy Angel*. She was demonstrating that right, left and centre—

clever and beautiful. It was okay to admire her, want her in his bed, but it would be stupid of him to lose his objectivity with this woman. Bad enough that he was currently sucked in to thinking about her all the time.

No doubt that would change soon, Hugo assured himself.

Anticipation was insidious.

Satisfaction would put his mind back in order.

Angie's mind was dancing waltzes with Hugo Fullbright. A bridal waltz featured very strongly. Pure fantasy at this point, but it buoyed her spirits enormously to mentally see them as a well-matched *couple,* fitting perfectly together.

In every sense.

Not just sexual!

This dinner party was turning out to be very much a pointer in that direction, much to Angie's relief and delight.

Their Japanese hosts seemed to like her, even giving her their business cards. Not that she expected anything to come of their taking hers, but it was a mark of respect, and best of all, Hugo had talked up her talent for interior design, making the point that she was very successful in her area of expertise—an accolade that made her a focus of interest, as well as him.

His ego had not demanded she simply be an ornament on his arm, though it was his business that had brought him to Tokyo. To Angie, it was an amazing thing for him to do. She tried to return the favour by being as congenial a guest as it was possible for her to be.

Which wasn't difficult. She was truly having a marvellous time—dining in a private room in this obviously high-class Japanese restaurant. The walls were
made of the traditional paper screens, lending a
unique ambience, and while they did sit on cushions
on the floor, luckily there was a pit under the table to
accommodate legs—a concession for Westerners?

They were served by wonderfully graceful
Japanese ladies dressed in kimonos, and each course
of what seemed like a never-ending banquet was artfully presented. Much of the food Angie didn't recognise but Hugo helpfully explained what it was
whenever she looked mystified. She was happy to try
all the different tastes. The seaweed soup was the only
course she couldn't handle. Three mouthfuls and her
eyes were begging Hugo to be released from eating
more.

He grinned and lifted his little cup of sake, indi-
cating she could leave the soup and appreciate the rice
wine instead. The sake was surprisingly good and
Angie had to caution herself not to drink too much
of it. Her level of intoxication was already incredibly
high, just being with this man who made her feel
valued and appreciated and understood.

Of course, he did want her, as well.

There was no ignoring what was all too evident in
the way he looked at her whenever there was a lull
in the conversation. It was a wonder the buttons on
her jacket didn't curl right out of their eyelet fasten-
ings from the searing intent in those bedroom blue
eyes. Angie could feel her breasts tingling with a tight
swelling in response and knew she wouldn't try to
stop him from undressing her once they were alone

in their suite again. The very thought of it excited her.

His hands, his mouth, his body, the kind of person he was…everything about him excited her. She felt as though all her lucky stars were lining up to deliver the best that life had to offer tonight. No way in the world could she turn her back on it.

The time finally came for them to take leave of their hosts. Angie found herself babbling in a kind of wildly nervous exhilaration during the limousine ride back to the hotel. Hugo was not nearly so verbose, patiently listening to her gush of pleasure in the marvellous evening.

Patiently waiting.

Making no move to pounce.

Waiting…waiting…

The reality of what was about to happen didn't really hit Angie until they were on their way up to their hotel suite, the elevator doors closed, locking them into the small compartment, no one else with them, alone together. The feeling that she was now cornered rushed in on her, choking her into silence.

She needed Hugo to say something light to break her tension, to ease her into the next inevitable step, to somehow make her more comfortable with the idea of *sleeping* with him, but he didn't. The hand holding hers gripped more tightly, as though affirming she was caught—no escape. And the waiting was almost over. A matter of minutes…seconds…and he'd have her exactly where he wanted her.

The elevator doors opened onto their floor. Her feet were drawn into matching his steps while her heart thumped a rapid drum-roll and her mind whirled like a dervish, wildly trying to rationalise the choice she'd made.

Hugo hadn't forced her into anything.

She was here of her own free will.

Wanted to be with him.

All she needed was for him to kiss her again.

It would feel all right then.

He opened the door to their suite, placed a hand at the pit of her back, gently nudging her forward, a guiding hand, perfectly civilised, not the paw of a panther poised for the kill. And she was not walking into a dark, dangerous jungle. He switched the lights on for her to see she was once again in luxurious surroundings.

The curtains had been closed, blocking out the night view of the city. The door behind her was closed. Rather than look at the bed which loomed too largely in her mind, Angie fastened her gaze on the magnificent floral arrangement gracing the coffee table in the lounge area.

Her shoulders were rigid when Hugo lifted her coat from them, removing it for her. It was no more than a gentlemanly courtesy. He didn't try to make it more. She fiercely told herself to relax but her body had gone completely haywire as she felt the heat of his nearness to her, smelled the cologne he used.

'Have I assumed too much, Angie?'

The loaded question snapped her into swinging around to face him. He'd tossed her coat aside and was unbuttoning his suit coat, but his eyes stabbed straight into hers, probing like twin blue lasers.

'What…' It was barely a croak. Her mouth was so dry she had to work some moisture into it before she could get out the words. '…what do you mean?'

A mocking glint challenged her as he bluntly stated, 'You're frightened.'

'No, I'm not,' she shot back at him, instinctively denying any form of cowardice.

His coat joined hers on the dividing bench between the bedroom and living areas. His eyes derided her assertion as he began undoing his tie. 'I've been with too many women not to know how it is when they're willing...and eager...to go to bed with me.'

'Maybe that's the problem...too many women,' she defended hotly. And truthfully, as the thought of being only one in an ongoing queue burst into her mind again.

His mouth tilted ironically. 'I'm not in my teens, Angie. Neither are you,' he added, hitting the raw place Paul's dumping had left.

'So I should know the score?' she retorted with a bitter note he instantly picked up on, his eyes narrowing, weighing what was behind the response.

Her cheeks burned with guilt and shame. Hugo had every right to assume what he had and it was terribly wrong of her to give him a negative reaction because of Paul. She wasn't being fair.

'I'm not into keeping scores,' he said with a careless shrug. The tie was tossed on top of the coats. He flicked open the top buttons on his shirt, then started removing the cufflinks from his sleeves, dropping his gaze to the task in hand.

The cufflinks were black opals, rimmed with silver. Angie watched his fingers working them through the openings, savagely wishing she'd kept her mouth shut.

'Nor am I into bed-hopping,' he went on matter-of-factly. 'Every woman in my life has had my exclusive attention until such time as the relationship broke down…for whatever reason.'

'Why did your last relationship break down?' The question slipped out before she could clamp down on it, curiosity overriding discretion.

His gaze flicked up as he slid the cufflinks into his shirt pocket. His eyes mocked her need to know as though it shouldn't be important to her. But he did answer her in a sardonic fashion. 'I caught Chrissie snorting cocaine. I'm not into drugs, either. She'd lied to me about staying off them.'

Chrissie… Her mind latched onto the name, though it meant nothing to her. Just as Paul would mean nothing to Hugo. A new relationship should start with a clean slate. Why was she messing this up?

Hugo turned away from her, moving over to the bed. 'What about you, Angie?' he tossed back over his shoulder. 'Do you need an artificial high to unleash yourself sexually?'

Contempt in his voice.

For her or for Chrissie? Angie took a deep breath, needing to recapture his respect. 'No, I don't. Nor would I want to stay involved with someone who used drugs.'

'Glad to hear it. Makes people unreliable.'

He sat on the end of the bed and started removing his shoes and socks, not the least bit perturbed about her watching him undress. Weirdly enough, Angie didn't feel in any way threatened by it. His detached manner seemed to place her on some outer rim, having no influence at all on what he did. Yet she knew intuitively he was very aware of her presence and he was waiting again, waiting for her to give him something to work with.

The problem was she couldn't make herself move. Any physical approach felt like a horribly false step, like throwing herself at him, which he'd surely view cynically at this point. And she couldn't think straight enough to know what would be the right thing to say.

He tucked his socks in his shoes—a tidy man who obviously preferred a *tidy* life—and sat upright, the expression on his face suggesting he'd been struck by an idea that he found oddly titillating.

'Are you a virgin, Angie? Is that why you're so nervous?'

'No!' The denial exploded from her, throwing her into more anguished confusion over what she should do to correct the negative impressions she hadn't meant to give this man, especially when he was the most attractive man she'd ever met.

He cocked his head consideringly. 'Have you been…attacked by a man?'

She shook her head, mortified that he should judge her as sexually scarred by a bad experience.

He stood up, casually rolling his flapping sleeves up his strong muscular forearms as he strolled back towards her. 'Are you worried about protection?' he inquired, frowning over her frozen attitude. 'If that's the case…' He paused, waving to the far bedside table. '…I did bring a supply of condoms with me. You have no need to fear unwelcome consequences.'

'Thank you,' she choked out, feeling an absolute idiot for getting herself into such an emotional tangle when he was being perfectly civilised and looking after everything like the gentleman he clearly was.

A wry little smile sat provocatively on his lips as he slowly closed the distance between them and lifted his hand to stroke his knuckles gently down her burning cheek. 'I'd have to say this is not what I expected of *Foxy Angel.*'

She wanted to say—*Just kiss me*—but what came blurting out of her mouth was, 'I'm not *Foxy Angel.*'

It shocked him into a freeze on action. 'Pardon?'

'*Foxy Angel* is *Hot Chocolate.*'

He shook his head as though she wasn't making sense.

'On the billboard this morning.'

'It was a different photo. Different woman.'

'Yes. It was the photo that should have been used yesterday with the caption of *Foxy Angel.* Francine had to change the name to something else to avoid confusion.'

'Francine…' Again he shook his head, not taking it in.

'I tried to explain to you at our meeting that a mistake had been made. You didn't want to believe me. But the truth is that my friend had sent in a photo of the two of us and the technician had used the wrong half. Francine is the one who's marketing herself.'

'This is absurd,' he tersely muttered.

'Worse than absurd,' she retorted heatedly, and before Angie could think better of them, more damning words tripped out. '*You* took the wrong impression of me, and my partner of three years was so humiliated by the billboard he dumped me cold.'

The cloud of irritation and confusion instantly dissipated. The air suddenly sizzled with electric energy as dangerous bolts of lightning were hurled at her from Hugo's eyes. 'So what is this? Your revenge on men?'

Her heart contracted under the violent force of his

reaction. A convulsive shiver ran down her spine. But her mind rose to the challenge, sharp and clear.

'No. I came with you because I wanted to. Because I'm attracted to you. But I've never done anything like this before and…'

'And you got cold feet,' he finished for her, the frightening electricity instantly lessening.

'Yes,' she admitted, sighing with relief at his quick understanding. 'I'm sorry. I didn't mean to be such a fool…' She gestured her inner anguish. '…when it came to this.' Her eyes begged his forgiveness. 'I knew what you expected…'

Hugo's mind was spinning, fitting all the odd pieces into this new picture of Angie Blessing, realising everything about her made better sense now. 'It's okay,' he quickly soothed, playing for time, needing to get the action right when he moved in on her.

No question that he had to if he was to be certain of keeping her, and keeping her was now his prime objective. He wanted this woman and it was abundantly clear that he had to make his claim tonight. Letting her off the hook would only give her more time to doubt her decision to come with him, more time to think about the guy who'd dumped her, perhaps wanting him back, hoping he would reconsider and call her on Monday.

The attraction she'd admitted to was real.

There'd been ample proof of that in the way she'd responded to him before they'd gone out to dinner.

Hugo could barely quell the raging desire to blot the other guy out of her mind. Gently, gently, he told himself. He'd never seduced a woman before—never had to—but if he had to seduce Angie Blessing, he would.

This woman was going to be his.

CHAPTER EIGHT

FRANCINE was right.

Dirty weekends weren't her style.

The relief at getting everything straight with Hugo was so enormous, Angie felt totally light-headed. Even her heart was skipping happily as though a terrible pressure had been lifted. Especially since Hugo had told her it was okay with him, accepting that he had been at fault, too, disbelieving her explanation of the mistake. Though she shouldn't have played up to the false identity. Any form of deception was wrong.

'I should have told you the truth before I accepted your invitation,' she said ruefully.

He smiled. Not his wolf smile. There was a warm caress in his eyes, making her feel better. 'I'll take that omission as a measure of your wanting to be with me,' he said, a hint of appeal taking the ego edge out of his statement.

'I did. I do,' she eagerly assured him.

'Then it's all good, Angie. Because if you had laid it out to me, I would still have pressed the invitation. *Foxy Angel* had its appeal but only because it was attached to you.'

She could feel herself glowing with pleasure.

It truly was okay.

Hugo was attracted to her, not some fantasy.

He tilted her chin, locking her gaze to the powerful intensity of his as he softly said, 'Believe me, the guy was a fool for letting you go. But I almost feel kindly towards him because he opened the door for me.'

His hand slid up over her cheek with a feather-light touch, the kind of reverent touch used in feeling something precious, wanting a tactile sense of what made it so special. Angie's breath caught in her throat and she stayed absolutely still, feeling thrilling little tingles spreading over her skin.

'And I now have enough time with you to show *I* value you,' he went on. 'Far more than he did.'

The purr of his voice was thrilling, too, not threatening at all. And what he was saying hit deep chords of truth. Paul hadn't valued her. He'd thrown her away like garbage, while Hugo treated her not only as an equal partner, but as a woman whose feelings really mattered to him.

'It's easy to get blinded by familiarity, Angie,' he murmured caringly. 'Not seeing what else there can be, only feeling safe with what you've known before. But I want you to look at me, feel how it is with me, give it a chance. Will you do that?'

'Yes...' She wanted to very much, was dying for him to kiss her as he had before.

He did.

Though so gently at first, it was even more tantalisingly sensual, giving her plenty of time to relax into the kiss, and Angie revelled in his obvious sensitivity to how she was reacting, responding. She understood he was exerting maximum control for her sake, wanting her to feel right with him, and this understanding removed any inhibition she might have had about moving closer to him, lifting her arms to wind them around his neck, inviting a deepening of the kiss, wanting to give as he was giving.

It was only fair.

Yet he seemed to shy away from trying to incite the passion he'd stirred before, his mouth leaving hers to graze around her face, planting warm little kisses on her temples and eyelids as his arms enclosed her in their embrace, one hand drawing its fingers slowly through her hair as though enjoying its silky flow around them.

'Everything about you feels good to me,' he murmured. 'Your hair…' He rubbed his cheek over it. '…your skin…' His lips trailed down her cheek to her ear which he explored very erotically with his tongue, arousing sensations that zinged along every nerve in Angie's body. '…the lovely soft curves of your body. All of you…beautiful,' he whispered, his breath as tingling as his tongue as he expelled warm air on a deeply satisfied sigh.

She couldn't even begin to catalogue his appeal to her. It was fast becoming totally overwhelming. Her mind was swimming in a marvellous sea of pleasure, revelling in his appreciation of her and loving his intense masculinity.

His fingers caressed the nape of her neck, slowly traced the line of her spine to the pit of her back. Then both his hands were gliding lower, gently cupping her bottom, subtly pressing her into a closer fit with him.

He was aroused.

Oddly enough, given her *cold feet*, it was not a chilling reminder that she was playing with fire, more a comforting reassurance that he really did desire the woman she was, a very warming reassurance that everything within her welcomed—more than welcomed when he kissed her again, not holding back this time, a long driving kiss that exploded into a passionate need to draw her into wanting all he could give her.

And Angie did want it.

It didn't matter that joining with this man might be premature, ill-considered, foolishly impulsive. She forgot all about being one of a queue. He was with her, wanting her, and she was wanting him right back, exulting in the fierce excitement he stirred, anticipation at fever-pitch, her whole body yearning for the ultimate experience of his.

'Angie…' His forehead was resting on hers, both of them gasping for breath. Her name carried a strained plea.

'Yes,' she answered, tilting her head back so he could see the unclouded need for him shining straight from her eyes.

A quick smile of relief, a sparkle of wild wicked joy. 'Is that giving me permission to undo the eight buttons that have been giving me hell all night?'

The lilting tease in his voice evoked a gurgle of laughter, erupting from her own relief and pleasure in him. 'You counted them?'

'Many times.'

He kept her lower body clamped to his, blatantly reinforcing her awareness of the desire she'd stirred, making her feel elated at her own sexual power over him as he lifted a hand to the top button, his fingers deftly releasing it from its loop.

'This one should have dissolved under the heat I subjected it to.'

The laughter welled up again.

Next button. 'Then this one should have popped open of its own accord, knowing it would get obliterated if it didn't.'

'Buttons are not sentient beings,' she said, feeling quite deliriously happy.

'But they do have two functions,' he carried on, attacking the rest. 'Opening and closing. And I didn't want you closed to me, Angie.'

Having unfastened the form-fitting bodice, his hand slid underneath it, around to the back clip of her bra, working it apart without the slightest fumble, demonstrating an expertise which might have given Angie pause for thought about that queue again, except for the swiftness of his warm palm cupping her naked breast, his fingers gently kneading its soft fullness, his thumb fanning her nipple into taut excitement, and the deep satisfaction purring through the 'Ah…' that throbbed from his throat, telling her how much he loved touching her like this.

For several moments she did nothing but revel in the way he was taking this new intimacy, the wonderful sense of his pleasure in it. Her breast seemed to swell into his hand, craving his caressing possession of it, greedy for all the exciting attention he was giving.

'Take off my shirt, Angie.' A gruff command, instantly followed by the compelling plea, 'I want to feel your touch.'

Yes pounded through her mind, though it was more a response to her own rampant desire to touch him. Her gaze swam to the row of buttons he'd left in place. Her hands lifted, eager to dispose of them, dispose of the shirt, too, bare his chest, shoulders, arms, letting her see, letting her feel the raw flood of his strong masculinity, absorbing it through her palms, skin against skin.

His breathing quickened as she glided her hands

over muscles that seemed incredibly smooth yet pulsing with a maleness which totally captivated the instinctive part of her that responded to beautiful strength in a man. And he was beautifully made. Perfect physique. It was exciting to feel the rapid rise and fall of his chest under her touch, knowing his heart had to be drumming in unison with hers.

His hand moved to her other breast, electrifying it into extreme sensitivity. 'Your jacket…get rid of it.' Hoarse need in the demand. His eyes were closed, a look of totally absorbed concentration on his face.

Exhilarated by how much he was into *feeling her,* Angie didn't hesitate, freeing herself of both jacket and bra, almost throwing herself against him as she flung her bared arms around his neck. And in the same instant he released her breast to wrap her in a crushing embrace, his mouth capturing hers, invading it with mind-blowing passion, possessing it with deep rhythmic surges, inciting a chaotic need that drove her into a frenzied response.

Waves of heat were swirling through her, crashing through her. He undid the zipper of her skirt, pushed it down over her hips—hips that wriggled their mindless consent, eager to feel closer to him. With seemingly effortless strength he lifted her out of the falling garment, scooping her off her feet and whirling her over to the bed, moving so fast Angie was still giddy from their wild kiss as he laid her down and completed the final stripping—her shoes, hose and panties—no asking permission now, just doing it with an efficient speed that screamed intense urgency, echoing the torment of coiled tension in her own body.

His eyes glittered over her, taking a searing satisfaction in her nakedness, and her heart suddenly quivered uncertainly over the rightness of what was happening here. Was it too soon? Had he cornered her into surrendering to his power? Her mind felt too shattered by raging need to think coherently.

He shed the last of his clothes, and it was as though the veneer of civilised sophistication—the gentleman image—was instantly shed, as well. He emerged from it like some primitive powerful warrior, his taut skin shimmering over muscles bristling with explosive energy, his magnificent maleness emanating a challenge that telegraphed he could and would stand up to anything, confident of battling any odds, vanquishing all opposition, winning through.

And the wolf smile was back.

Yet when he moved onto the bed, it was with the lithe prowling grace of a great jungle cat, inserting a knee between her legs, hovering over her on all fours, his head bent towards hers, his eyes blazing with the avid certainty that she was his to take as he willed…a mesmerising certainty that made every nerve in Angie's body quiver, whether in trepidation or anticipation she had no idea.

She wasn't ordinarily a submissive person. She'd always prided herself on being independent, capable of holding her own when dealing with life in general, yet she felt herself melting under the sheer dominance of this man, not wanting to fight for her own entity, yearning to merge with him, lose herself in him if that was how it was going to be.

Mine, he thought, revelling in the surge of savage triumph that energised every cell in his body, priming him to burn himself into Angie Blessing's consciousness, to put his brand on every part of her delectable femininity, use whatever means would bind her to him, take her as no man had ever taken her before.

Her eyes had a drowning look.

He felt a momentary twinge of conscience.

Dismissed it.

She'd said *yes.*

He swooped on her mouth and it said *yes,* too, her tongue as fiercely probing as his, engaging in an erotic tango that goaded him to do it now, appease the ache, fulfil the need. But that would be far too fast, not serving his purpose, and he forcefully controlled the raging temptation, tearing himself out of it, trailing hot sensuous kisses down her throat, savouring the wild gallop of her pulse-beat at the base of it.

He wanted to devour her, make her feel totally consumed by him. He moved lower, engulfing her breast with his mouth, drawing the sweet flesh deep, lashing the taut nipple with his tongue, sucking it into harder prominence, and he exulted in the convulsive arch of her body, the wild scrabble of fingers in his hair, digging, tugging, blindly urging the ravishment of her other breast. Which he did with a passion, feeding off her response, loving the vibrant taste of her, the headiest aphrodisiac he'd ever experienced.

He could hear her ragged breathing, the little moans that erupted from her throat, felt the tremors of excitement under her skin as his hand circled her stomach, his fingers threading through the tight silky curls below it, delving into the softly cushioned cleft at the apex of her thighs, caressing the slickly heated flesh, finding the most hidden places of pleasure, stroking them, feeling her inner muscles pulsing to his rhythmic touch, the hot spill of her excitement, the intense peaking of her clitoris.

He levered himself down, captured it with his mouth, moved his hands to cup her bottom, rocking her, thumbs pressing into the inner walls of the passage now yearning to welcome him. Not yet. Not yet. He drove her towards the sweet chaos of a tumultuous climax, feeling her exquisite tension spiralling higher, so high it lifted her body up to bow-string tautness.

He knew when it began to shatter, heard her cry out, exulted in her frenzied desire for him. Her hands plucked frantically at his head, his shoulders, her thighs quivering out of control, her body begging for his.

A wild energy charged through him as he surged over her, positioning them both for the entry she craved. He barely had sense enough to snatch up a condom from the bedside table and sheath himself with it before thrusting deep to settle the maelstrom of need, sharing her ecstatic satisfaction in the full penetration, feeling the ripples of her climax seizing him, squeezing, releasing, squeezing, releasing.

He held her thrashing head still and silenced her cries with a kiss meant to soothe and reassure and bring her into complete tune with him, waiting for more, wanting more, slowly tasting the promise of it, realising this was only a beginning of a sensual feast that could keep rolling on and on.

Her response was white hot at first, an almost anguished entreaty to finish it now, fast and fiercely, riding the storm of sensation he'd built to its ultimate limits, and Hugo was hard-pressed to hold on to his control, to calm her, enforcing a more conscious awareness of an intimacy that could be prolonged, that he was ruthlessly determined on prolonging so it would linger in her memory, obliterating every other memory of sexual connection she'd experienced before this.

No ghosts in this bed tonight.

Only him.

Taking absolute possession.

Angie could hardly believe Hugo was not choosing to ride the crest of her own turbulent pleasure, that he'd answered her need to feel him inside her, then stopped, as though it was enough for him to give *her* satisfaction.

Which couldn't be right.

Yet he made it feel right…the way he was kissing her…so caringly. It gave her the sense that he really treasured this gift of herself, and being so intimately joined with her was very special to him, too special not to pause over this first climactic sensation, deepening the delicious merge with a kiss that added immeasurably to how good she felt with this man.

Her inner chaos seemed to coalesce into a more intense awareness that circled around the strong core of his sexuality, anchoring her as she began to float on a warm sea of ecstasy. Her arms were strangely limp, but she managed to wrap them around him, wanting to hold all of him.

'Stay with me, Angie. Come with me,' he murmured.

The sensation of him starting to move inside her was marvellous, slowly, slowly leaving her to close tremulously behind him, retreating to the outer rim, then just as slowly pushing forward again so that her muscles clutched joyously at his re-entry, eager to have him sink as deeply as possible, wanting absolute possession of all he could give her.

He burrowed an arm under her hips, changed angles, teased, tantalised, delighted…exquisite pleasure peaking over and over again. Angie had never known anything like it…intoxicating, addictive, fantastic…her whole body keyed to feeling him, loving him, voluptuously revelling in this mind-blowing fusion.

Her legs wrapped around him, instinctively urging a faster rhythm. Her hands luxuriated in moving over him, feeling the tensile strength, wickedly wanting to test his control, make it break, draw him into the compelling overdrive that would end in his surrendering all his power to her. Somehow that was becoming more important than anything else…to take his mastery from him, make him lose himself in her, bring him to an equal place where the togetherness was truly the same.

She strained every nerve into focusing on making it happen, determined on exciting him to fever-pitch, caressing, pressing, goading with her hands, legs, kissing his shoulders, his neck, tasting him with her tongue. He laboured to catch his breath and she exulted in the tightening of his muscles, his thighs becoming rock-hard as need surged from them, forcing the more sensual rocking into a glorious primitive pounding, and she heard her own voice wildly crying *Yes…Yes…Yes*…to the beat of it.

Even more exhilarating was the animal roar that came from his throat when he finally rammed impossibly deep and spilled himself in great racking spasms, making her almost scream with the pleasure of rapturous release—her own and his, pulsating through both of them. A passionate possessiveness swept through Angie as he collapsed on top of her. She cupped his face, brought his mouth to hers, and sent her tongue deep in fierce ownership.

It seemed for a moment he was completely spent—or surprised. It gave Angie a brief, heady taste of being in control, seizing an initiative, but that quickly blurred as he responded, striking sweet chords of satisfaction before ending the kiss and carrying her with him as he rolled onto his back, tucking her head under his chin and holding her enveloped in his embrace.

Putting himself in charge again, she thought, smiling contentedly over being Hugo Fullbright's captive. There was no trepidation attached to it now. Her body was still thrumming with the pleasure he'd given. Or was it taken?

Didn't matter.

She wondered if this had just been normal sex for him. It certainly hadn't been for her—unmatched by anything in her previous experience. It might have been driven by sexual attraction but it had felt as though he was making love to her—if only physical love—brilliant, all-consuming physical love. Far from regretting her capitulation to it, Angie was intensely grateful to know how it could be with the right man.

The right man...

Had she fallen in love with Hugo Fullbright?

So soon? So quickly?

Or was she simply dazed by his expertise in making her *feel* loved?

And appreciated.

And valued.

He might make all the women he chose as his companions feel like this to begin with. What happened afterwards? How would it be tomorrow, the rest of the weekend, beyond that? For all she knew he was only intent on a *dirty weekend* with her! Though he had asked her to take a chance on him, give him time.

It was silly to start fretting over not being able to keep him in her life. That was out of her control. Hugo would undoubtedly do what he wanted to do, and whether that meant with her or without her only time would tell. Though not too much time. Not even if she loved him madly, was she going to spend three more years being dangled on the bait of a possible commitment.

If she was *right* for him...

'You're not relaxed anymore, Angie,' he said, one hand sliding into her hair, fingers seeking to read her mind. 'Tell me what you're thinking.'

She sighed away the edginess that had bitten into her contentment, then thought there was no point in not being open with him. He'd said quite plainly he didn't want her closed up. 'Just wondering how temporary I am for you.'

'Would you like not to be temporary?'

'Now there's a leading question, dodging right past mine.' She raised herself up to see if there was any hint of reservation in his eyes and was surprised to find amusement dancing at her. 'What's funny?' she demanded.

'You...thinking I might have had enough.' The wolf grin flashed out at her. 'Believe me, Angie, I'm already hungry for more of you, and if you'll excuse me while I go to the bathroom, I'll be very happy to come back and convince you of it.'

She hadn't actually been referring to sex, but he was rolling her onto the pillow next to him, extracting himself, heading for the bathroom to get rid of the protection he'd donned. The back view of him as he strode away from her was just as awesome as everything else about him. *Alpha Man,* Angie thought, and wondered why every woman in his past had failed to hold on to him. They must have wanted to. Did *she* have whatever it took to hold his interest beyond the bedroom? To become a lifetime partner?

Her gaze moved to the bedside table where a heap of condoms had spilled out of the packet he'd put there, ready for action. He hadn't asked her if she was on the pill, perhaps not prepared to risk her telling a lie about that, or simply protecting himself against any health issues. Did he always use them as a matter of habit? Did it indicate a freewheeling sex life?

He'd certainly come amply prepared for this weekend.

But given the *Foxy Angel* angle, and her unquestioning acceptance of his invitation, why wouldn't he?

What would Francine have done in this situation?

Seize the chance.

Angie took a deep breath and fiercely told herself to simply go with the flow until it didn't feel right. She had two more days with Hugo Fullbright—two days constantly in his company, in bed and out of it. By the time they landed in Sydney on Monday morning, she should know if there was a real chance of forging a relationship that would take them far beyond this weekend.

CHAPTER NINE

'THE breakfast buffet in the Imperial Viking Room has to be seen to be believed,' Hugo had declared. 'And I'm *very* hungry this morning.'

So was Angie—so much energy expended last night, until sheer exhaustion had drawn them into a sleep. And again on waking up. If she wasn't in love with Hugo Fullbright, she was definitely in lust with him. He was an amazing sensualist with incredible stamina, and never in her life had Angie been made so aware of her body, which now tingled with excitement at simply a twinkling glance from this man.

Clearly he was very much into physical pleasures. Now food.

And he was right about the breakfast buffet. Hugo shepherded her around the incredible banquet laid out for people to serve themselves whatever took their fancy—every possible taste catered for: Asian, Continental, English, and all of it superbly presented to tempt appetites. Perfect fruit. Exotic pastries and croissants. Never had she seen such a wonderful selection of breakfast dishes.

'I'm going to be a pig,' Angie muttered as she kept loading a plate with irresistible goodies.

'Good! Saves me feeling guilty about indulging myself in front of you,' Hugo remarked.

She flashed him a curious look. 'Do you ever feel guilty about anything?'

He grinned. 'Rarely. Because I don't take what

isn't offered or paid for. And let me say that having you share my appetites is a joy I'd hate you to feel guilty about. Let's wallow in piggery together.'

She had to laugh.

Somehow he took any sense of sinfulness out of lusty greed, choosing to view their breakfast as an adventure into gourmet delights, encouraging her to sample far more than she would normally have done.

'Now we have to walk it off,' she told him when they finally gave up on trying anything more.

'I'll take you for a walk around the Ginza district.'

'What's there?'

'Shopping.' The blue eyes sparkled knowingly. 'The way to a woman's heart.'

It was true that most women loved shopping. And most men hated it. 'You don't have to indulge me. I'd rather we do something we'll both enjoy.'

'It's my pleasure to indulge you, Angie,' he happily assured her.

She *was* in love with him.

Absolutely drowning in beautiful feelings.

They left the Imperial Viking Room in high good humour, Angie more curious to see what the central shopping district in Tokyo offered than wanting to buy anything. She found the tour fascinating; with designer boutiques stocking clothes from all around the world, yet shops catering to distinctly Japanese culture, as well, like the one that stocked an astonishing array of umbrellas in every shade of every colour, some beautifully hand-painted or embroidered or featuring exquisite lace insertions.

'Women use them in summer to protect against the sun and heat. The streets of Tokyo are a mass of colourful umbrellas,' Hugo informed her.

'You mean like parasols?'

He nodded. 'Reduces the glare, too. Sunglasses aren't so popular here.'

'I'm not a big fan of sunglasses everywhere. Especially when people wear them indoors where there's no glare at all. It's a very irritating affectation.'

'Guarding their self-importance,' Hugo laughingly agreed.

Angie was glad he didn't seem to have any affectations, despite his VIP status. But his idea of indulging her hit a very wrong chord when he led her into a department store where the ground floor was completely taken up with displays of fabulous jewellery: gold, diamonds, pearls, every gemstone imaginable beautifully crafted into spectacular pieces.

Angie's gaze skimmed most of it in passing, recognising it was not in her affordable range, but she did stop to look at some fascinating costume jewellery, intricately worked necklaces that were exquisitely feminine and brilliantly eye-catching. They were designed like high-necked collars that sprayed out from the base of the throat, and one that was woven into a network of delicate little flowers particularly attracted Angie's eye.

It was displayed on a black plastic mould and she couldn't help touching it, thinking how wonderful it would look with her black strapless evening dress.

'Try it on,' Hugo urged, beckoning a salesgirl to help with it.

'I'm not wearing the right clothes,' Angie demurred, having donned a brown skivvy under her leopard print coat. However, she was tempted into asking how much the necklace cost in Australian currency.

The salesgirl whipped out a calculator, fingers darting over the buttons. She held it out for Angie to see the display box. Over twelve thousand dollars!

'Garnets,' the girl explained, seeing her customer's shock at the price.

'Thank you,' Angie replied, firmly shaking her head.

'Let me buy it for you,' Hugo chimed in.

Another shock which instantly gathered nasty overtones, making her query the kind of relationships he'd had throughout his long bachelorhood—mercenary women who'd jumped on him for everything? She wasn't like that and needed him to know it.

'No,' she said emphatically.

He frowned at her. 'It would be my pleasure to…'

'If you think this is the way to my heart, you couldn't be more wrong, Hugo.' A tide of scorching heat flooded into her cheeks. 'I'm not here to get what I can out of your large wallet. If that's what you're used to from other women, no wonder you don't trust what they feel for you.'

She'd gone too far.

Spoiling all the beautiful feelings between them.

Her stomach contracted in nervous apprehension as the blue eyes lost their bedroom simmer, sharpening into surgical knives that aimed at cutting through to the very heart she had steeled against *his pleasure* this time.

'What do you feel for me, Angie?' he asked very softly.

Too much. Too much, too soon, she thought, frightened to admit it when he'd just put her into the category of *bought* women. 'I was enjoying your company up until a moment ago,' she answered guardedly. 'And I'm sorry you made that offer. It puts me on a level I don't like.'

'Then please accept my apology,' he rolled straight back at her, his expression instantly changing to charming appeal. 'The offer was not meant to insult your sense of integrity. It was a selfish impulse on my part. I wanted to see you wearing the necklace. Wanted to see you taking pleasure in my gift.' His smile set her heart fluttering again. 'Will you forgive my self-indulgence?'

Confusion swirled in Angie's mind. Had she got it wrong, leaping to a false assumption about his attitude to previous relationships with women? He could certainly afford to indulge himself—the Bentley, travelling first-class everywhere, the best of everything. And she had accepted his invitation to share it all with him at no financial cost to herself.

Her pride might be leading her astray here. She wasn't used to being with a man like him. Nevertheless, she could not accept such an outrageously expensive gift on such short acquaintance, especially when that short acquaintance involved sharing his bed. It smacked of…sexual favours being paid for…and everything within her recoiled from being thought of in those terms.

'I'm sorry, too,' she said hesitantly, her hand lifting in an agitated gesture of appeasement. 'This just isn't…my scene.'

'Then let's get out of here.' He took possession of her hand and smoothly drew her into walking with him towards the exit. 'It's not far to the Sensoji

Temple—a must see in Tokyo. We could take in the east garden of the Imperial Palace, as well.'

The tension in her chest eased as he resumed his role of tour guide, coaxing her into chatting cheerfully with him, erasing the awkwardness she felt over having made such a *personal* stand about the jewellery.

Even so questions lingered in her mind.

Did he really care about the person she was...what she thought, what she felt? Or was he just a very deft womaniser, well practised at pushing the right buttons to win him the response he wanted? How much could she trust in how he seemed to be?

Hugo worked hard at recovering the ground he'd lost with Angie Blessing. Big mistake offering to buy her the necklace, putting her right offside with him. Her refusal to accept it from him had not been a ploy to make her seem different to the women he'd dated in recent years. She *was* different. No doubt about that.

And he hated the doubt he'd put in her eyes.

Hated it with a passion.

Which surprised him.

Why did he care so much about her trusting him? Certainly she'd got to him, harder and faster than he'd ever been stirred before. Last night, and again this morning, having her was more exhilarating—intoxicating—than...impossible to come up with even a near comparison. She was pure sensual magic in bed. And very, very appealing out of it.

The man who'd dumped her had to be an ego creep. Giving her up over a technician's mistake was so incredible to Hugo, it seemed only logical that the guy would be grovelling for her forgiveness come

Monday. Which meant no more false steps between now and then, opening the door for a possible reconciliation. Angie Blessing was going to be his for as long as he wanted her, and at this point in time, Hugo wasn't putting any limit on the relationship he intended to set up with her.

The temple proved a good distraction from personal issues. The huge wooden Thunder Gate and the enormous red lantern welcoming people to the temple grounds immediately caught Angie's interest. All the activity in the main hall fascinated her: people buying fortunes and good luck charms, people praying or rubbing the billowing smoke from the bronze urn on themselves for its curative powers.

They wandered down to the colourful souvenir shops and Angie happily bought three beautiful fans, hand-painted in the Japanese artistic style: a sky blue one for her mother, a dramatic black one for Francine—currently named *Hot Chocolate* on the billboard—and a very delicate pink one for herself.

'Why the pink one for you?' Hugo asked, curious about her choice.

She laughed, a self-conscious flush blooming in her cheeks, her lovely green eyes seeming to question it herself. 'I guess all girls love pink, Hugo.'

'I thought that was little girls,' he countered, thinking her answer was evasive.

'Maybe it's genetic and it never really goes away, however grown up we think we are.'

'You're not feeling grown up today?' he teased, hooking her arm around his again as they walked on, wanting her as physically aware of him as he was of her, determined on reinforcing the strong sexual connection they had.

Her lashes fluttered at him in a sidelong glance. 'You must know you make me feel very much a woman.'

He grinned at the admission. 'You make me feel very much a man.'

She sighed. 'I don't think you need any help in that department.' They were passing a shop with a display of Samurai swords and she stopped to view the display. 'In fact, that's what you should buy for yourself, Hugo.'

'What would I do with a sword?' he quizzed. 'At least you can use a fan.'

'It would be a visual symbol of what you are.'

'A Samurai warrior?'

She met his amused look with deadly serious eyes. 'I think you were born a warrior. You've learnt to put a civilised cloak over it but my instincts tell me that's your true nature.'

Her instincts were sharper than he'd realised. He'd always thought of himself as a competitor, in any arena he chose, and the will to win, or at least put in his best possible effort to win was very strong in him. 'So you see me as a fighter,' he mused, wanting to probe her thoughts further.

'A bit more than that,' she answered dryly. 'A fighter fights. A warrior sets out to conquer, determined on making his way past anything that stands between him and his goal.'

Her pinpointing of the difference lit red alert signals in Hugo's mind. How had she got this far under his skin? Most women were blinded by surface things, seeing no further than his obvious assets. Why was Angie Blessing different? What made her different? Or had he somehow revealed more of himself to her than he had to anyone else?

He swiftly decided to turn her perspective into a positive score for him. With a wry little smile, he said, 'If you think this Samurai warrior is viewing you as his Geisha girl in Japan, you're wrong, Angie.'

'I'm not here just to pleasure you?' she lightly tossed at him, but he heard the testing behind the question.

He wrinkled his brow in mock dismay. 'I thought the pleasure was mutual. Don't tell me you've felt obligated to fall in with what I want.'

'Obligated…no. Though there is a certain… expectation…attached to generosity which is all one way and I'd prefer the scales to feel more balanced.' She paused, then delivered a punch line he was not expecting at all. 'So let me buy you a sword, Hugo.'

He held up a hand of protest. 'You wouldn't let me buy you the necklace.'

'Too much on top of this trip to Japan, which I did accept.'

She was still unsettled by the idea of his *buying* her. Best to clear this issue her way right now, or it might continue to niggle, regardless of what he said. 'Hmmm…why do I sense there'll be a sword hanging over my head if I don't agree?'

'Because you're a very perceptive person?' she suggested with a grin that knew she'd won this point.

'Then let me see how perceptive you are, Angie,' he challenged, making a game of it. 'Make it your choice of sword for me.'

'Now you're putting me on my mettle,' she quipped back.

He laughed and escorted her into the souvenir shop, not really caring what she chose. If she needed some symbol of equalising the situation, let her have it. The only tension he wanted between them was that wrought by sexual desire, waiting to be satisfied.

The Samurai wore two swords—one long, the other short. Angie selected a long one which also happened to be a Japanese Navy Officer's issue sword with the Navy arsenal mark of an Anchor stamped in it. Its scabbard was black lacquered wood, very handsome. The quoted price was over two thousand dollars—more expensive than all three fans together—and it surprised Hugo that Angie didn't quibble over the price, offering her credit card without hesitation.

Was she proving she was a woman of independent means? That it was important to her to be perceived as such by him? A woman who would not be swayed even by great wealth into doing anything she didn't want to do?

He'd been presented with more expensive gifts by other women, mostly clothes they fancied seeing on him, accessories that were blatant status symbols, or *objets d'art* they thought would look good in his house. None of them had carried any real personal meaning, neither for him nor the giver.

The sword was different.

And it made him feel uncomfortable.

It was impossible to gloss over it as though it was a nothing gift, irrelevant to what was happening between them. It was a very pertinent statement, both about Angie Blessing and himself. And Hugo had the strong sense that she was pulling him into a deeper place than he'd ever been before with a woman.

As they left the shop, he couldn't stop himself from asking, 'Why a Naval Officer's sword?'

Her eyes sparkled with her own satisfaction in the choice. 'Because I can see you as a swashbuckling pirate, too, going after all the booty you can get.'

'Do I get the fair maiden, as well?' tripped straight off his tongue. She was happy with him again. It was amazing how good that felt.

She laughed, completely relaxed with him now that he'd accepted *her* gift. 'Since you've carried her off on your ship, and she's already succumbed to…' Her eyes mischievously subjected him to a once-over. '…the physical pleasures you promised…'

'And delivered?' He arched his eyebrows in a rakish query.

'Mmmh….'

The sexily satisfied hum zinged into his bloodstream, arousing strong carnal urges.

'I'd say that was a given,' she concluded, and the happy grin on her face was completely uninhibited, no shadow of any reservations about being with him.

'Let's head back to the hotel,' he said, instantly quickening their pace from a slow stroll. 'I'm feeling hungry again.'

But not for food.

CHAPTER TEN

IT HAD been an absolutely brilliant weekend, Angie thought, wishing it didn't have to end. Though, of course, time inevitably marched on and here they were in the first-class lounge at Narita Airport, waiting for their flight back to Sydney to be called. Hugo caught her smothering a yawn and shot her a rueful smile.

'Have I worn you out?'

'No. Just happy tired.' She smiled back to prove it. 'Thank you for sharing Tokyo with me, Hugo. I've loved every minute of it.'

'You made it a pleasure, Angie,' he said warmly, his bedroom blue eyes sparkling at her, making her pulse skip yet again.

But it hadn't all been about sex, she assured herself. Yesterday afternoon they had left the hotel again to take in the amazing view of the city from the Tokyo Tower's observation platform, even being able to see as far as Mount Fuji, which had been covered by snow. Then they had visited the East Garden of the Imperial Palace and drank tea in the pavilion there…until the urge for more intimacy had them hurrying back to their suite.

He was such a fantastic lover he could trigger a flood of desire just with a look. Even when they were with his Japanese hosts last night, dining at a teppan-yaki bar on the top floor of a skyscraper overlooking the city lights, eating prawns flown in from Thailand, crayfish from Sydney, and the famous Japanese Kobe steak, she was sure their appetites had been highly stimulated by the physical pleasures they had just shared, not to mention the simmering anticipation of more to come once the evening was over.

Fabulous, addictive sex.

With the deep sense of loving running all through it.

Or was she fooling herself about that? Could such feeling not be mutual? Hugo hadn't said anything. But then, neither had she. Too much, too soon?

Angie knew she wouldn't have protested if Hugo had kept her in bed all day today. Nevertheless, she was glad he'd taken her on the harbour lunch cruise, showing her more of Tokyo, spending time just talking to her, giving her the sense that he really did care about the person she was, above and beyond their wonderful compatibility in bed.

'What do you plan to do tomorrow?' he asked.

'Come back to earth with a thump, I guess. Get back to work. Face up to real life again.'

He frowned, observing her sharply from narrowed eyes. 'This weekend hasn't felt real to you?'

'It might not have been anything extraordinary to you, Hugo, but to me…' She shook her head, amazed at all they'd done together in incredible harmony. '…it's like I've been on a magic carpet ride.'

'And you expect it all to disappear in a puff of smoke?' he quizzed half-mockingly.

She hoped not. Desperately hoped not. But maybe he was referring to the *Tokyo* experience. 'I'll always have the memory,' she assured him with a grateful smile.

'No regrets?'

Her heart sank. It sounded horribly like a cut-off line. Pride forced her to say, 'None. A marvellous experience in every respect.'

'Are you saying goodbye to me, Angie?'

Shocked into realising he was misinterpreting her comments, she immediately shot out, 'Why would I want to?'

'You're not seeing me as part of your *real life,*' he whipped back, a hard, cutting edge to his voice. 'And I'm very aware I've served as a distraction from that this weekend.'

Paul…

He was referring to her acceptance of his invitation because Paul had dumped her. The weird thing was, Hugo had literally wiped her partner of three years right out of her mind and it was another shock to be reminded of him.

'Tactically, it was the best move you could have made to put yourself out of reach for a few days,' Hugo went on. 'Let him stew over his incredibly stupid and rash decision. My bet is he'll call you at work tomorrow…'

'No, he won't! Paul burnt his boats by telling—'

'Paul? Paul who?'

'Overton.' The name tripped out under Hugo's driving pressure and Angie grimaced over the absurd situation that her ex-partner should be thought of as any kind of rival by the man who had so totally superseded him.

'Paul Overton.' Hugo drawled the name as though tasting it with all the relish of a warrior given a mission that was very much to his appetite.

'He's a barrister in the public eye and the billboard blotted my copybook beyond repair as far as he is concerned,' Angie rattled out, determined on setting the record absolutely straight so Hugo understood there was no contest involved. 'I do not expect a call from him tomorrow or any time in the future. Nor do I want one. He is out of my life,' she added emphatically, her eyes flashing defiance of any disbelief on Hugo's part.

Which was ridiculous, anyway.

How could he even think she would want any other man but him after all the intimacy they had shared? Yet he was looking at her with such burning intensity, Angie felt herself flushing, as though she was somehow at fault, not giving him enough assurance that she saw a future with him. On the other hand, *he* hadn't made any firm arrangement to see her again.

Why bring up Paul now? And ask her about no regrets? It certainly hadn't *felt* like a dirty weekend, but maybe she had coloured it far too rosily with her own feelings. For all she really *knew,* Hugo might like to spend his time off work focusing on a desirable woman, enjoying saturation sex. Everything he'd said and done could have been a tactical play to win what he wanted. Was he thinking she could take up with Paul again…no harm done?

Angie's stomach started clenching.

Deciding directness was called for she asked straight out, 'Are you about to say goodbye to me?'

His face relaxed into a wolfish grin. 'No. Definitely not. I want a lot more of you, Angie Blessing. A lot more. I'm nowhere near finished with you.'

His reply should have eased her inner tension but the words he'd used and the predatory gleam in his eyes set her mind into a panicky whirl.

Finished…

It implied an end.

When he'd had enough.

As with all the other women who'd been in his life? Did he walk away and leave them behind once his appetite for them had been satisfied? She was still new to him. How long would she last?

Stop it! she fiercely berated herself.

Hugo had asked her to give a relationship with him a chance. And she would. Because it would be self-defeating not to since she felt so much *was* right with him. But she also had to learn from her mistakes, not hang on beyond what was a reasonable time for a commitment to be made. Hugo was obviously still in lust with her, but love was what she wanted, the kind of love that nothing could shake or break.

Faith in each other.

Loyalty.

Emotional security.

Her mind and heart were gripped by these needs as she heard their flight being called. Both she and Hugo rose instantly from their armchairs, action providing relief from the tension of the past few minutes. They were about to say goodbye to Tokyo but not to each other, and possibly to reinforce his intent, Hugo tucked her arm possessively around his for the walk to the boarding tunnel.

'Believe me, I'm real,' he murmured in her ear as they set off together.

She flashed him a quick smile, acutely aware of the hard muscled solidity of his claim. 'What do you plan to do tomorrow?' she asked, wanting more than his magnetic sex appeal to make her feel right with him.

'Make damned sure you don't dismiss me as a dream,' he softly growled.

Angie laughed, a wild irrepressible happiness bubbling up again, chasing away the fears of being foolishly blind to where she might be going with this man. If he was leading her down a garden path, the garden was certainly worth looking at before she closed the gate on it.

Hugo was all the more determined to keep Angie Biessing in his life now. She was a prize, definitely a top quality prize for Paul Overton to have hung on to her for three years, despite her less than sterling silver family background.

And there was such a delicious irony in the situation!

Good old Paul's overweening ego had fumbled the catch and who was there to pick up the ball? None other than the hated rival who'd pipped him at the post so many times throughout their teen years that Paul had stooped to using his parents' wealth to rip Hugo's girlfriend off him.

Not this time, Hugo vowed.

In fact, he would take great pleasure in rubbing Paul Overton's nose in the fact that Angie had moved on to him, and there'd be no buying her back. Hugo could more than match anything the Overtons had to offer by way of wealth. He had the means to shower Angie with whatever her heart desired.

Though he'd have to be careful not to overstep the mark there. She took pride in being a lady of independent means. Nevertheless, wealth was a seductive tool and Hugo intended to wield the power it gave him. He certainly wasn't about to hand any advantage to Paul Overton, who'd undoubtedly come out fighting, once he was made aware that his loss was Hugo Fullbright's gain.

But he wouldn't win, not by hook or by crook.

And how sweet it would be to see him face this defeat!

Indeed, Hugo was brimming over with exhilaration at the thought of this future confrontation as he and Angie settled themselves in the plane and they were handed glasses of champagne. He clicked Angie's in a toast, his eyes flirting outrageously with hers, promising pleasures to come.

'To Tuesday night.'

She effected an arch look, though her whole body language telegraphed yes to whatever he wanted. 'What's happening on Tuesday night?'

'I think I can manage one night without having you at my side. I'll give you tomorrow to catch up on business and sleep, but come Tuesday…dinner at my place?'

No hesitation. Big smile. 'I'd like that.'

'I'll pick you up at seven.'

'Fine.'

She happily drank to the arrangement and Hugo was satisfied nothing would change her mind. Paul Overton's pride would not allow him to call her. Not until he knew who had taken his place in her life. Which he'd discover only when Hugo chose to reveal it…with maximum impact.

A public spotlight would be perfect.

Hugo made a mental note to get James doing all the undercover work on that. With his butler network it should be no problem for him to ascertain what would be a prime meeting place and do whatever was required for Hugo and Angie to be present, parading their relationship.

Of course, by the time that was put into action, it would be too late for Paul to make a recovery.

Hugo was ruthlessly determined on ensuring it was too late.

Far too late.

He was not about to give up this woman.

Not to anyone!

CHAPTER ELEVEN

As the Bentley crossed the Harbour Bridge, taking her home from the airport, Angie swivelled around in her seat to look out the back window and check the billboard. Amazing to think only a few days had passed since it had caused such a change in her life!

The photo of Francine—*Hot Chocolate*—was still on it, as it should be since her friend had paid for a full week's advertising. It was only Monday morning. Three full days of exposure so far, four more to go. Angie wondered if it had brought in any real possibilities for the outcome Francine wanted.

Hugo's gaze followed the line of hers. 'Your business partner,' he said, recalling what she'd told him.

'Yes. Francine Morgan.'

'Does *Hot Chocolate* really describe her?'

Angie grimaced. 'Probably *Foxy Angel* is more true to Francine's character but she couldn't use that after the mistake was made of putting my face with it instead of hers. I think, in her angst over the situation, she just went for something madly provocative.'

'Stirring the pot.'

'I just hope it doesn't backfire on her, landing her in big trouble. Francine is my best friend as well as the marketing force in our design company. We share the apartment, too.' Angie checked her watch. They had landed at six-thirty, but being first-class passengers, there'd been virtually no delay in the arrival procedures at the airport. It was only seven-thirty now. 'She'll still be at home.'

'Then I'll get to meet her.' Spoken with warm anticipation.

Angie glanced sharply at him, remembering he'd admired her friend's enterprising nature, though he'd attributed it to herself at the time. 'Francine may want to steal you from me,' she said wryly.

He laughed and squeezed her hand. 'No chance.'

Her heart tap-danced in pleasure, yet to Angie's mind, in the marriage market he was a prize that any woman would covet. Even fight over. 'You must know you're a very attractive package, Hugo.'

His eyes instantly lost their twinkle of amusement and acquired the searing intensity of twin blue lasers. 'I'm very much taken by you, Angie. Don't doubt that for a minute.'

It was good to hear.

Nevertheless, the plain truth was they'd basically spent an exclusive weekend together, no intrusion from their normal social circles, and most of the time dominated by the strong sexual chemistry between them. Angie couldn't help wondering how their relationship would fare, given the various pressures of their day to day lives, not to mention the judgements of people who were close to them.

She looked at the chauffeur in the driver's seat. James had greeted them cheerfully at the airport, welcoming them home. He appeared to have his attention completely focused on the road, but he was probably listening intently to whatever was going on in the back seat. He gave no indication of it, not by so much as the tiniest snort, but he had to be fitting her into the context of Hugo's previous women, making comparisons.

Would he favour her or work against her if he saw the relationship turning serious? He might not care to have any woman interfering with his running of Hugo's household. Why hadn't Hugo married before this?

He's been waiting for me, Angie told herself in a determined burst of positive thinking. It was what she wanted to believe, and when they arrived at her apartment and Hugo escorted her inside, briefly making the acquaintance of Francine before taking his leave, his manner definitely reflected that she—Angie Blessing—held prime position in his heart.

'Wow! What a sexy hunk! Those eyes…and he's obviously smitten with you, Angie,' was Francine's comment the moment Hugo had gone. 'No need to ask how the weekend went. I bet he's dynamite in bed.'

'It wasn't just sex,' Angie protested, flushing at the inference that nothing else mattered.

'Got to have the spark to start with,' came the knowing retort. 'And Hugo Fullbright is sparking on all cylinders! It's clear to me that you two are up and running, Angie. And good for you, I say! Even better for me.' She rolled her eyes in relief. 'Takes away my guilt over Paul. Who, I might add, has made no contact though he must have seen that *my* photo has gone up on the billboard, proving what we told him was true.'

'The truth was irrelevant,' Angie said dryly, drawing up the handles of her bags, ready to roll the luggage into her bedroom. 'Come and tell me how *Hot Chocolate* fared while I unpack.'

'Brilliant! I'm snowed under with responses,' Francine declared, pirouetting with glee as she danced ahead to open Angie's bedroom door for her. 'I've got bug eyes from reading them through on the computer this weekend.'

Angie shot her a look of concern. 'I thought the name you used might draw some gross stuff.'

Francine waved an airy hand. 'I've eliminated all those.' Her eyes twinkled with happy anticipation. 'Kept only the clever ones. And don't you worry. I'm vetting them very carefully. If they don't come up to my exacting standards...no meeting.'

'What precisely are your exacting standards?'

She grinned. 'Someone who works hard at winning me.'

Angie cocked a challenging eyebrow. 'There doesn't have to be a spark?'

'Oh that, too. Naturally I'm asking for photographs. After all, they have seen mine.'

'You think you can tell from a photograph?'

As Angie heaved her larger bag onto the bed, ready to unpack, Francine bounced around to the other side, wagging a confident finger. 'The eyes have it,' she asserted. 'Your Hugo has just demonstrated that. I look for sparkly, intelligent, wicked eyes.'

'Wicked?'

'Definitely wicked.'

'That might not be husband material,' Angie warned, once again reminded that Hugo was a longtime bachelor, though he had certainly gone all-out to win her. But what if winning was an end in itself?

'Well, at least I should have a lot of fun finding out,' Francine declared, totally undeterred from her mission for marriage.

Fun…or heartbreak?

Angie shook off the doubt.

Tomorrow night she'd be with Hugo again. Nothing was going to stop her—or Francine—from pursuing what seemed right for them.

Hugo focused his mind on what had to be done as James drove him home to Beauty Point on Middle Harbour. 'I want you to acquire two tickets for all the upcoming ballet performances, James,' he said, having decided that was top priority.

'Ballet, sir?' The astounded tone was comment enough on Hugo's previous lack of interest in that artistic area.

'It's never too late to try something new.' Especially with Angie, Hugo thought.

'Of course not, sir. One's experience can always be broadened.'

'Exactly. Have you seen a ballet, James?'

'Oh yes, sir. Never miss a performance. It's always quite splendid. I'm delighted to hear Miss Blessing enjoys it, too.'

Hugo noted the warm approval in his voice—definitely a recognition of top quality. No doubt this would facilitate James' co-operation in securing what was required.

'In fact, sir, I have prime seats already booked for the ballet season. No problem to give them to you for the…uh…duration.'

'Very kind, James, but the duration could be longer than such self-sacrifice could stand. See if you can book more.'

'As you wish, sir,' came the cheerful response.

Apparently the idea of a *long* relationship met his

approval, too. Hugo wondered how Angie had scored so many positive points in his butler's book. While James had invariably acted with faultless courtesy towards the women Hugo had brought home in the past, he usually remained extremely circumspect in any remarks about the relationships. Still, there was no time to reflect on this change right now. Instructions had to be given.

'When you unpack, you'll find a Samurai sword in my bag. I'll leave it to your good taste to find the best way of displaying it in my bedroom. Some place it can't be missed, James.'

'A sword, sir?' he repeated in some bemusement.

'A gift from Miss Blessing.'

'I will see that it's *prominently* displayed, sir.'

'Before tomorrow night.'

'Do I understand Miss Blessing will be…uh… joining you tomorrow night, sir?'

'I thought dinner on the patio. I trust you can organise something special, James. For eight o'clock?'

'Any dislikes I should know of, sir?'

'Only seaweed soup.'

'Ah! Splendid to have so much leeway in preparing culinary masterpieces. Fussy eaters are very restricting.'

'Please feel free to be as creative as you like,' Hugo drawled, amused by his butler's enthusiasm.

A sigh of pleasure. 'At last! A lady who will appreciate my training with gourmet food.'

'Let's not lose perspective here, James. I have always appreciated your skill in the kitchen.'

'Thank you, sir. I didn't mean to imply…'

'Fine! I also want flowers sent to Miss Blessing's

office today. Let her know I'm thinking of her. What do you suggest? She likes pink.'

'Then it has to be carnations and roses, sir. And lots of baby's breath for contrast.'

'Baby's breath?' Hugo wasn't sure he liked the sound of that.

'Tiny white flowers, sir. Very feminine.'

James sounded so smugly satisfied with the idea, Hugo let it go, telling himself the exotic Singapore orchids had certainly served their purpose. 'Okay. Get it done. The note should read...*Until tomorrow.*'

'That's all, sir?'

'It's enough, James. Sorry if that blights your romantic soul.'

'As you say, sir, best not to go overboard. Less can sometimes be...'

'When I want your advice on how to deal with a woman, I'll ask for it,' Hugo cut in dryly. 'In the meantime, I have another task for you. Do you know about the Overton family?'

'Old establishment posh people, Wallace and Winifred Overton?' was instantly rattled out. 'Son, Paul, heading for a Blue Ribbon seat in the Liberal Party?'

'The same. I want you to find out what parties or social events they'll be attending in the next month or so. Very discreetly, James. I'd prefer not to have them know I'm interested in meeting them.'

'With a view to business, sir?' Clearly his curiosity was piqued by this uncharacteristic interest in *posh people*.

Hugo was not inclined to explain. This was personal. Deeply personal. 'Just report back to me as soon as you can. Anything to do with politics won't suit, but a fashionable ball or a premiere…'

'A social occasion that you might naturally attend,' James swiftly interpreted.

'Exactly.'

'And I should wangle you an invitation to it?'

'Two invitations. I shall be escorting Miss Blessing.'

'Does Miss Blessing have an interest in the Overton family, sir?'

Hugo grimaced at the linkage James had uncannily seized upon. 'No, she hasn't,' he said emphatically, though, in fact, Hugo felt a compelling need to have that proven. It wasn't just winning over Paul. He wanted to be certain there was no rebound effect running through Angie's attachment to himself. 'Nor do I want this mentioned to her,' he added. Surprise gave no room for pretence.

'Miss Blessing will simply be accompanying you,' James smoothly interpreted.

'I want her at my side…yes!' he answered curtly, finding himself somewhat discomfited by these questions.

Was he sure he wanted to do this?

Paul Overton wasn't part of his life anymore, hadn't been for twenty years. Though he had been a motivating force behind the desire to make big money, to build up so much wealth that winning or losing no longer depended on what could be given. It came down to the man.

Who was the better man for Angie Blessing?

Because it was Paul she'd been with for the past three years…Paul who had dumped her, not the other way around…Hugo wanted him to fight to get her back. Fight and lose.

Then he would know beyond any shadow of a doubt that Angie was his.

Not by default.

Her choice.

Regardless of what Paul offered her.

And he'd offer her all he could because it was Hugo who'd taken her over and that could not be tolerated by Paul Overton.

What it came down to was Hugo wanted closure on that old battleground. And he especially wanted closure because Angie Blessing was involved.

The confrontation had to take place.

CHAPTER TWELVE

DINNER on the patio was going brilliantly. The balmy summer evening made being outdoors particularly pleasant and James congratulated himself on perfect stage management.

Of course, the location itself—overlooking the very creatively landscaped swimming pool right above Middle Harbour, plus the clear starlit sky—had its natural beauty, but the addition of strategically placed candles with subtle floral scents added to the romance of it all, and his table setting with the centrepiece of miniature pink roses was pure artistry.

Miss Blessing had obligingly worn pink, as James had anticipated she would after yesterday's gift of flowers—subliminal choice—and his boss was wearing the white clothes which had been laid out for him. They looked a very handsome couple. A fitting couple.

James found himself humming the wedding march as he worked away in the kitchen, loading the silver tray with the sweets course. Highly premature, he told himself, but all his instincts *were* picking up promising signs.

The weekend in Tokyo had clearly inspired desires that were far from quenched. One could say they were burning at furnace heat out there on the patio. And never before had James received such meticulous and far from the usual instructions about the continuation of an affair.

Ballet!

And not just flowers to be sent. Exotic Asian flowers last Thursday. *Pink* flowers on Monday. When had his boss ever taken note of a woman's favourite colour?

Then there was the Overton family element that also had to be connected to this new relationship. What could his boss possibly want from self-styled upper class snobs? Normally he'd avoid them like the plague. Total contempt for their values. Surely the only reason he would go out of his way to meet them was for the sake of Miss Blessing.

Whose photo, apparently, should not have been on that billboard. This circumstance certainly added to the fascinating scenario. James had actually thought it was rather a dodgy self-marketing stratagem, coming from a lady who shone with natural class. Nice to know his judgement had not been astray. On the other hand, there was no doubt that Miss Blessing did have a flair for taking bold initiatives...giving his boss a Samurai sword.

That cut to the quick.

Clever woman.

Yes, it could very well be that his boss had met his match.

James carried the tray out to the patio, benevolently observing the glow of contentment his dinner had raised, not to mention the holding of hands across the table and two faces happily absorbed in drinking in the sight of each other.

'My pièce de résistance,' he announced. 'Orange almond gateau with drunken apricots swimming in Cointreau. King Island cream on the side.'

'Oh! How blissfully sinful!' cried the lady, her

lovely green eyes lit with delight at this special offering.

James barely stopped himself from preening over
his gourmet masterpiece. He did so enjoy having his
talent appreciated. 'A pleasure to serve you, Miss
Blessing,' he crooned.

'I've never had such a wonderful meal!'

'Thank you.' James swiftly passed on the credit to
get the flow of appreciation moving in the right direction. 'Mr. Fullbright did request something extra
special for you. Without seaweed.'

She laughed and squeezed the hand holding hers.
James felt an emanation of hungry urgency coming
from his boss that had nothing whatsoever to do with
food.

'You have quite outdone yourself, James,' he said,
smoothly adding, 'Just leave this with us now. I think
we'll forgo coffee in favour of finishing the wine.'

Rampant desire barely held in check.

Clearly aphrodisiacs were not needed. However, no
harm in having replenishment on hand. A dish of the
Belgian chocolate truffles he'd purchased to serve
with the coffee could be put on the bedside table.

'Very well, sir.' He clicked his heels and bowed
stiffly from the hips. 'May I wish you both a very
good night.'

He loved doing that stuff. It was so deliciously
camp under the guise of proper formality. Though he
was tempted to swagger a little as he made his exit,
as his acute sense of hearing picked up Miss
Blessing's whispered words.

'Your butler, chauffeur—whatever he is to you—
is worth his weight in gold, Hugo.'

'Mmh…that's just about what he costs, too,' came the dry reply.

Worthy of my hire, James thought, sailing out to his kitchen with all the majestic aplomb of the Queen Mary 2. He'd laid the scene. It was up to his boss now to capitalise on it. And there had better not be just sex on the menu, because Miss Blessing—bless her marriageable heart!—had the stars of love in her eyes. Anyone could see that.

As Angie savoured the glorious taste of the sweets course, she felt as intoxicated as the drunken apricots. Though not from alcohol. She couldn't help thinking this was the kind of courtship dreams were made of— being magnificently wined and dined in an exclusive romantic setting, everything arranged for her pleasure. Life with Hugo had felt so extraordinary during the weekend in Tokyo. She hadn't really expected that sense of awe to continue, but here she was feeling unbelievably privileged again.

She loved his beautiful home. She loved everything about the man sitting opposite her. She even loved his butler. Best of all was the mounting evidence that Hugo was certainly not viewing this relationship lightly.

When the masses of pink roses and carnations had been delivered to the office yesterday, even Francine had commented, 'What we have here are serious flowers, Angie. You've definitely got him hooked.'

Angie had shaken her head. *Hooked* was the wrong word. Hugo Fullbright would never let himself be caught. He was the hunter, the jungle cat, the wolf, the warrior. If he took a partner, it was for his pleasure. The big question was, would she be a lasting pleasure?

The hope she was nursing had certainly received a big boost tonight with Hugo's announcement that he had acquired tickets for them for the rest of the ballet season. This had to mean he planned on their being together for months, at the very least. And he cared enough about *her* pleasure to open his mind to sharing her interest.

It wasn't just lust on his part. It couldn't be. Besides, she had to concede those feelings were mutual. The sizzling desire in his eyes had her body buzzing with excitement, and there was no denying she loved his touch. Simply holding hands was enough to set her mind racing towards—wanting—more intimate contact.

Having consumed most of the delicious gateau, Angie set down her spoon, smiling ruefully at Hugo. 'I'm so full I can't eat any more. Will James be terribly offended if I don't finish it?'

'No.' The vivid blue eyes glinted wickedly. 'He'll probably think I raced you off to bed before you could.'

'Is that what you usually do?' tripped off her tongue, instantly raising a tension she didn't want between them.

Making comparisons to previous relationships was an odious intrusion when she should simply be revelling in being the sole focus of his attention. Yet once the challenge was out, she realised the answer was important to her.

Did Hugo have seduction down to a fine art?

Was the aim to dazzle her into compliance with whatever he wanted?

He'd sat back in his chair, the sexual magnetism suddenly switched off as he looked at her with the weighing stillness of every sense alert, sifting through what was coming at him. Angie's pulse skipped into a panicky beat. The warm harmony she had been revelling in was gone, supplanted by this tense stand-off. Had she spoiled their evening together?

'Yes, it is what I usually do,' he stunned her by saying, his eyes locking onto hers with searing intensity. 'I won't deny I have a strong sex drive and I've never been involved with women who don't want to go to bed with me. On an evening such as this, the natural follow-up would be to seek and enjoy more physical pleasures. Do you find that wrong, Angie?'

'No.' It was reasonable. Perfectly reasonable. And she felt stupid and flustered by his logic. 'I just…wondered…'

'How special you are to me?' he finished softly.

Heat flooded up her throat and scorched her cheeks, but she bit the bullet and stated the truth as she saw it. 'I still feel I'm on your magic carpet ride. All this…' Her hands moved in an agitated gesture to encompass the luxuries he could and did provide. 'You could overwhelm any woman if you set your mind to it. And I do feel overwhelmed by the way you're treating me, but I don't know what's in your heart, Hugo.'

'My heart…' An ironic little smile tilted his mouth, softening the hard look of a keenly watchful predator, weighing up the most effective way to pounce.

It gave Angie's own heart a jolt when he surged to his feet, swiftly stepping around the table to seize her hands and draw her up from her chair.

'Feel it,' he commanded, pressing her open palm to the vibrant heat of his chest.

Her whole body seemed to be drumming at his closeness—the forceful contact, the compelling intensity of his eyes blazing into hers. Was she feeling his response to her or hers to him? Angie didn't know, was helpless to discern anything beyond the physical chaos he stirred in her.

'You hold it,' he fiercely declared. 'You're pounding through my bloodstream. I ache for you. I can't take another second of separation.'

His mouth swooped on hers, passionately plundering, obliterating all Angie's concerns with the sheer excitement that instantly coursed through her. A melting relief soothed her jagged nerve-ends as Hugo swept her into a crushing embrace. She wanted this. Needed it. Loved the feverish possessiveness of his hands renewing his knowledge of her every curve, fingers winding through her hair, holding her in bondage to him.

Hungry kisses.

Greedy kisses.

And the desire for more and more of him erupted like the hot lava of a volcano, a force of nature that was unstoppable.

'Come with me.' Gruff urgency.

He broke away, grabbed her hand, pulled her along with him.

Angie's legs seemed to float in the wake of his stride, weak and wobbly yet caught up in the flow of energy driving him. She was too dazed to question where he was taking her. He tugged. She followed. Strong purposeful fingers encompassed hers, transmitting a ruthlessly determined togetherness, no separation, feet marching to a place of his choosing. Into the house. The luxurious living room facing onto the patio was a blur. Down a wide corridor.

A bedroom.

It had to be his.

And he'd raced her there.

Her dizzy mind registered a strikingly minimalist room, just the bed dominating a huge space—a king-size bed with many pillows—and lamp tables on either side, a soft glow of light from them. The top bed-sheet was turned down, ready…*ready*…and there was a silver dish of chocolates…*seductive* chocolates…

'Look!'

The command meant nothing to her. She *was* looking, feeling a terrible jumble of emotions, telling herself that the *readiness* didn't matter. Whatever had gone on in this bedroom in the past didn't matter. Only what she and Hugo felt together mattered. Yet if it was no more than elemental chemistry…

'Not there!' Terse impatience.

He spun her around to face the wall opposite the bed. A huge plasma television screen was mounted on it, and below that a long, low chest storing what seemed like massive amounts of home theatre equipment. Obviously he could lie in bed and…

'You see?'

His pointing finger forced her gaze upwards, above the mind-blowing size of the television screen.

The Samurai sword!

Angie's heart kicked with a burst of wild exultation.

Hugo had not set her gift aside as a meaningless souvenir. He had been so impressed—so pleased—by her choice, the sword was now hung in a prime place for his private pleasure, mounted on brass brackets that made it a fixture, not something that could easily be moved, on or off display as it suited him.

'It's the last thing I see at night and the first thing I see in the morning,' he said, stepping behind her and wrapping his arms around her waist, drawing her back against him. He lowered his head beside hers, purring into her ear. 'It's like having you speak to me, Angie. Does that tell you how special you are?'

'Yes.' The word spilled from a gush of a delight in the wonderful knowledge that she had touched him deeply. This was not a superficial attraction. Not for her. Not for him.

His hands slid up and cupped her breasts and the pleasure of his touch swelled through her on a blissful wave of happiness. She leaned back into the powerful cradle of his thighs, wanting to feel his arousal, wanting him to know it felt right for her.

He grazed soft kisses over the one bared shoulder of the silky top she wore—a warm, sensuous, tasting that made her quiver with anticipation. 'I want to make love to you, Angie,' he murmured. 'I want to sink myself so far into you that we're indivisible. I want…'

'Yes…yes…' she cried, not needing to hear any more, wanting what he wanted.

But he did not race into it.

'Don't move,' he growled. 'Let me show you how special you are. Look at the sword, Angie. Look at it…and feel how I feel about you.'

She looked at it, stared at it, remembering what she'd said about him being a warrior, determined on getting past anything that stood in his way…and he slowly removed her clothes, caressing them from her flesh, his hands sliding, stroking, palms gently rubbing her nipples into pleasure-tortured peaks, fingers finding the moist heat he'd excited, using it to drive her awareness of her own sexuality even higher. And his mouth trailed kisses everywhere, a hot suction that was incredibly erotic, a gentle licking that was intensely sensual.

The sword…an anchor engraved on its handle.

Was Hugo the man who would anchor her life?

Always be there for her?

She had the sense of being completely taken over by him, territory he was marking as his own, and she stood there, so enthralled by what he was doing to her that passively letting it happen didn't seem wrong. She didn't know if he was taking or giving. Somehow that was irrelevant. She felt…*loved*.

And when he finally moved her onto the bed, a mass of tremulous need crying out for him, the image of the sword was still swimming in her mind, and as the strong thrust of him slid deeply inside her, she saw herself as made to receive him, a perfect fit, like the black lacquered scabbard encasing the steel of the man, holding the heart of the warrior.

True or not…it was what Angie felt.

No memory of Paul Overton flitted through her consciousness.

And the women in Hugo's past…no substance to them. None at all.

The only reality was *their* union.

CHAPTER THIRTEEN

WOULD she spend the coming weekend with him?

Angie's mind was still dancing with *yes* to that question—*yes, yes, yes* to anything at all with Hugo—as she raced into her apartment to get ready for work the next morning. Francine accosted her before she reached her bedroom, taking in her bright eyes and flushed cheeks, not to mention the happy grin.

'So…Take Two went off with flying colours,' she concluded.

'And Take Three is already on the drawing board,' Angie literally sang.

'Well, I've had some luck, too,' Francine drawled smugly, stopping Angie in her tracks.

She looked expectantly at her friend, hoping that somehow *Hot Chocolate* had produced some magic for her.

'You'll never guess.' Francine laughed, shaking her head as though even she thought it was a miracle. 'I got an e-mail last night from the boy next door.'

'What boy next door?' There were no eligible guys in this block of apartments.

'From the old days. When we were kids in our home town before I moved to Sydney. Tim did an engineering course at Newcastle so our lives kind of diverged and we lost track of each other.'

'He saw your photo on the billboard?'

'Uh-huh. Then wrote to ask if it was me. Gave me his e-mail address in case it was. We've been chatting on the Net half the night, catching up and feeling out where we are now.'

'So where is he?'

Francine grinned. '*Not* married. And we're meeting for lunch today.'

'For the spark test?'

It had been Francine's prime requisite for starting a relationship, yet she wasn't dressed in her sexy *out there* best. She was wearing a yellow linen shift dress, more classy than sexy, though the colour did stand out enough to say *look at me,* stating a confidence in herself which Francine never lacked.

'You know, I haven't even thought about that,' she replied in a bemused tone. 'I like Tim. Always did. We were buddies in our teens though…' She grimaced. '…he never asked me out or anything. Never asked any girl out. He always had part-time jobs to help out with his family. Big family. Not much money.'

'Then you're just looking to renew a friendship?' That didn't exactly jell with this degree of pleasure.

She shrugged. 'Who knows? Tim was always a bit of an enigma. Most of the kids considered him a nerdy type but he wasn't really. He was just too smart for his own good. It's not popular, having stand-out brains, always questioning how things work. But you could have a really good conversation with him, not just slick boy-girl talk.' She heaved a happy sigh. 'I'm *so* looking forward to having that kind of company again.'

Without the strain of always trying to sell her attributes, Angie thought. Which answered the question of why Francine wasn't doing her power-play. However, she was in such a good mood, Angie hoped the meeting would work out well for her. With *a spark* happening, as well. Francine deserved a really good guy, one who truly appreciated the person she was. Though it was still a worry that the billboard photograph was the means of reforging this contact.

'This Tim...what's his full name?' Angie asked, a warning on the tip of her tongue.

'Tim Haley.' Francine rolled out the name as though it tasted like a sweet, heady wine.

Angie instantly checked herself from possibly striking a sour note. It had been a long time since their teens. *Hot Chocolate* might have provoked some sexual fantasy Tim Haley was now pursuing, taking the advantage of previous acquaintance. However, if this was so, Francine would find out soon enough.

Angie smiled. 'Reminds me of Halley's Comet. Zooming into your life out of the blue. I wish you all the best with him.'

Francine laughed. 'Thanks, Angie. At least I know he genuinely likes me.'

Genuine liking...

Yes, it was all important in a lasting relationship, and Angie thought about that on and off all morning as she worked beside Francine in their Glebe Road office. The materials they'd priced for the Pyrmont apartment block had to be ordered, contractors lined up to do the painting and tiling. It was difficult to focus her mind on the job when it kept returning to what she had with Hugo.

Strong sexual attraction was such a powerful distraction to really knowing how deeply the liking went. In that respect, an old-fashioned courtship was probably a much better proving ground. Would Hugo have pursued an involvement with her if she hadn't gone with him to Tokyo?

Impossible to ever know that now.

She had plunged headlong into this relationship and now she had to cope with having moved way out of her comfort zone.

So far there was nothing not to like about Hugo and she was fairly sure he thought the same of her. They enjoyed each other's company…just talking together. Though how much was he actually listening to her? Weren't his eyes always simmering with what he wanted to *do* with her?

Making love…

Angie had no doubt about the physical loving.

Apart from that, she did have the certainty that she'd touched something in Hugo's heart with the gift of the Samurai sword. He was also willing to take her to the ballet. Both of which proved he listened to what she said. Cared about what she said.

And their work sort of dovetailed, with Hugo being the driving force behind building new places and her colour co-ordination expertise making them even more attractive. This provided a common interest, making them compatible on more than one level.

It was probably foolish, worrying about sex being a dominant factor in their relationship. If the spark wasn't there, nothing would have happened between them. In fact, she'd be wallowing in depression from being so summarily dumped by Paul, hating him, hating herself for ever having thought she loved a man who could wipe her off for something she hadn't even done.

Three years…

How long did it take to really *know* a person?

Maybe never.

The thought slid into Angie's mind... *We colour them in how we want them to be.*

Yet instincts played a part, too, she quickly amended. Her instincts had been questioning Paul's *rightness* for her before last Thursday, and they were definitely signalling a great deal of *rightness* with Hugo.

All the same, after Francine left for her lunch date with Tim Haley, Angie found herself on tenterhooks, waiting to hear the outcome of their meeting, wanting to know if 'the spark' meant more than liking. The two didn't necessarily go hand in hand and her friend could be in for big disillusionment if Tim came onto her hard.

It was a very long lunch. When Francine finally returned to the office, she walked in as though floating on Cloud Nine, the dreamy smile on her face telegraphing that friendship had definitely turned into something else.

'Well?' Angie prompted impatiently.

The dreamy smile turned into a sparkling grin. 'I think I've found the man I'm going to marry. And what's more, I think he's got the same idea in mind.'

'From one meeting?' It seemed too incredible.

She laughed in a giddy fashion. 'Even I can hardly believe it.' She threw up her hands in a helplessly airy gesture. 'There I was, explaining about the bill-board, trying to find a marriageable guy because I just wasn't meeting anyone I fancied as a possible hus-band, and Tim asked straight out if I could I see him in the frame.'

'And could you?'

Francine nodded as she hitched herself onto

Angie's desk to confide all to her. 'I was hoping he might be interested if I toned myself down a bit. Not hit him full on. But it was he who knocked me out.'

'Big improvement on the past?'

'Just…a lot more impact. Grown up. Filled out. And the way he looked at me…'

'Wicked?' Angie quickly slid in, since *intelligence* was not in question.

Again Francine laughed, her own eyes twinkling with happy anticipation. 'Lurking behind warm and cosy, I think. Waiting for the green light.'

'Did you give it to him?'

'Not straight up green but certainly a very encouraging amber.'

'You're truly attracted to him?'

'I sure am!' came the delighted reply. 'It turns out that he patented an invention of his in the U.S. and made pots of money from it, and he's so confident now…'

'So he can well afford a wife and family,' Angie said, mentally ticking off Francine's requirements.

'No problem.'

'Then why amber? Why not green?' Angie queried, not understanding why Francine hadn't seized her chance.

'I didn't want Tim to think I was considering him for marriage out of sheer desperation. Like I'd grab him just because he was putting himself on the line. He's special. And I want to feel special to him.'

Yes.

Hugo had made her feel very special last night.

And he was special, too. Incredibly special.

'Besides…' A determined look settled on Francine's bright face. '…I still want my husband to win me. Show me I'm truly *the one* for him. Convince me of it.'

Angie nodded. 'Passion,' she murmured, her heart lightening with the certainty of Hugo's passion for her.

'Deep and abiding,' Francine said with considerable passion herself, making Angie realise how very serious her friend was about Tim Haley.

'He did give you reason to believe he might have serious intentions and wanted to pursue them with you?' she pressed worriedly.

'No question.' She lightened up, bubbling with excitement again. 'I tell you, Angie, I was so flabbergasted, I had to keep on testing if he was real or not. He said, like me, he's ready for marriage and wants to have a family. When he saw my photo on the billboard he started remembering what a good connection we'd had as kids, and our chatting last night, and again today, demonstrated a level of easy communication he'd never had the pleasure of with any other woman. Tim thought that was an extremely good basis for marriage.'

'Smart man,' Angie couldn't help commenting.

'I told you he was smart.' Francine grinned. 'And I do love smart.'

Hugo was smart, too, picking up on her needs, answering them, but had the thought of marriage even vaguely crossed his mind? Did she answer *his* needs?

'I've invited Tim to dinner with us tomorrow night.'

'Us?'

Francine slanted her a wise look. 'I can control what happens in our own home. You can be the chaperone, Angie. Make it proper and respectable. I want Tim to court me.'

Courting…not plunging into an intimacy that overwhelmed every other consideration. In fact, Angie realised she wasn't in control of anything with Hugo. He just kept sweeping her away…

'If he's truly serious, it won't put him off,' Francine ran on. 'Besides, I don't want him to think I'm after his money and what it can buy. If he comes to our place, it won't cost him anything, and the apartment will show him I've done well for myself, too.'

Angie frowned…shades of Tokyo with Hugo prepared to buy her the necklace. That had been bad. Bad, bad, bad.

'You're sure this marriage frame is not just a ploy to pull you in?' she asked, worrying if they were both giving their trust to men who were on different paths to the one she and Francine wanted them to take.

'Tim wouldn't do that to me.' With a very direct look that burned with conviction, Francine added, 'I know him, Angie. Long-time knowing. People don't change their character. I think his success in business has given him the confidence to go after what he wants and he figures the timing is now right for us.'

Long-time knowing.

Angie wished she had that with Hugo. Though it hadn't served her well with Paul, had it? Three years to find out what came first with him. Though that wasn't entirely true. She had known Paul always came first for Paul. She just hadn't wanted to see how little *she* meant to him.

It was different with Hugo. Completely different, she fiercely told herself.

Francine hugged herself exultantly as she waltzed

from Angie's desk over to her own, then flopped into her chair, arms opening out to encompass a whole new world. 'Just think! Last Thursday, life was the absolute pits! Six days later and our prospects are looking bright! You've got Hugo and I've got Tim. Happy days ahead!'

It sounded good.

It was good.

Angie vowed to give up negative thinking right now. Just because she hadn't known Hugo very long didn't mean she couldn't be blissfully happy with him. As she had been last night. And this morning. And was sure to be next weekend, too. They were on a journey together. There was no solid reason to think this journey wouldn't have a happy end.

CHAPTER FOURTEEN

THE State Governor's black tie dinner and charity auction…

Angie eyed her reflection in the full length mirror on the door of her clothes cupboard…hair up in an elegant style, make-up as good as she could do it, around her neck the gold pendant necklace on which hung a pseudo emerald—costume jewellery she'd bought to go with the black strapless evening dress, earrings to match—and the dress itself, so perfect for her it had been impossible to find anything better.

The only problem was she'd worn it before.

With Paul.

Which made it feel…somewhat tainted…with memories she didn't want.

And Paul was bound to be at *this* function. Angie had known it the moment Hugo had mentioned he'd bought a swag of tickets for it, saying it was a very worthy cause, raising money for a new children's hospital. At a thousand dollars a ticket, he'd put out a lot of money, booking a table for ten, inviting his closest business associates and their wives along, Francine and Tim included especially for Angie, making a party of it.

Hugo's obvious pleasure in his plan, and the expense already incurred, had made it impossible for her to say she didn't want to go. If she'd tried to explain it was because of Paul, it would have been like a negation of what she felt with Hugo. He might have thought she still cared about Paul Overton and she didn't.

The truth was, she just didn't want a night with Hugo spoiled by any show of Paul's contempt for her. The brutal call he'd made to dump her demonstrated an attitude he would undoubtedly carry through in public. Pride alone would demand it of him.

His parents, friends and associates would be there, as well, all of whom probably regarded her as something of a tart because of the billboard photo. And Paul wouldn't have told them the truth about that. Oh no! It would have messed up *his* story of what had happened.

Maybe she should tell Hugo…warn him there might be some unpleasantness. But if he then thought she still cared about Paul…

No!

Best that she try to shut the whole horrible business out of her mind. Concentrate on Hugo and how great their relationship still was, even more intimate after three months of being together in most of their free time from work. She would not let Paul's presence spoil anything, not even her pleasure in this dress. It looked great on her. In fact, this was as good as she could look…for Hugo.

'Anything wrong, sir?' James asked.

Hugo instantly smoothed out the frown James had observed in the rear-vision mirror. 'No. Where are we?' he asked, glancing out the side window of the Bentley.

'Almost at Miss Blessing's apartment. Five minutes away. We're on time.'

'Good!'

Angie was always ready on time, another thing he liked about her. He hated being kept waiting. Only at their very first meeting…and that was because of the shock of seeing her photo on the billboard instead of Francine's, probably worry about Paul Overton's re-action to it, too.

'The State Governor's dinner… I did get it right, sir? Meeting your requirements?' James asked a trifle anxiously.

'Perfectly,' Hugo assured him. 'Thank you, James.'

No way could he not go through with it now. He hadn't liked Angie's reaction to attending the special charity function…going all quiet, probably realising instantly it was the kind of event the Overtons would attend. She shouldn't have cared. With him at her side, she should have been happy with the opportunity to defy whatever they thought.

The hell of it was, he still felt uneasy about it.

He would win over any machinations Paul Overton came up with to take Angie away from him tonight.

Of course he would win.

That wasn't the point anymore. The problem was…Hugo suspected he'd made a bad move where Angie was concerned and he didn't know why it was bad. Tonight should be a triumph for her. Why wasn't she feeling that? Given everything they'd shared over the past three months, nothing the Overtons could do should touch her.

The Bentley came to a halt. Hugo picked up the jewellery box, determined on getting Angie to wear his gift. He hoped it would make her feel better about appearing at his side tonight, lift her spirits, give her joy.

'Good luck, sir,' James tossed at him as he alighted from the car.

Hugo didn't answer.

Luck had nothing to do with tonight.

If he was the right man for Angie, nothing should touch what they had together.

The doorbell rang.

Angie grabbed her evening bag, took a deep breath, told herself she had nothing to worry about, and went to open the door to the man she truly did love with all her heart. He looked breathtakingly handsome in his formal black dinner suit and his smile instantly sent a rush of warmth through her.

'Is Francine gone?' he asked.

'Yes. Tim picked her up half an hour ago. He wanted to take her somewhere else first.'

'May I come in for a minute?'

She nodded, slightly mystified by the request. Though his eyes sent their ever-exciting message of wanting to make love with her, a minute wasn't long enough and they were all dressed up and ready to go. Nevertheless, once inside with the door closed, he took her hand and drew her into her bedroom with such an air of purpose, her stomach started to quiver.

'Hugo…' she began to protest, then fell silent, mystified even further by the box he set on the bed.

'Face the mirror,' he commanded, moving her to do so and positioning himself behind her. His hands lifted to the catch of her necklace. 'This looks lovely on you, Angie,' he purred, 'but I want to see you wearing something else.'

He whipped the pendant away, opened the box, and Angie was stunned to see him lifting out the necklace she had admired in Tokyo. 'You bought it?' she gasped as he hung the exquisite collar of garnet flowers around her neck.

'Over the telephone when we got back to the hotel.' He flashed his wolf grin. 'While you were in the bathroom. I arranged for it to be delivered to the reception desk for me to collect before we left.'

'I told you not to.'

'You bought me the sword, Angie.'

'But…' She touched the fabulous piece of jewellery, loving it, yet feeling confused about Hugo's motives.

'No buts. I've kept it for you until now so you can't have any doubt about its being a true gift, without any strings attached. There's no reason for you not to accept it,' he stated unequivocally, making it a churlish act to even quibble about it.

Angie sighed, surrendering to his forcefulness, telling herself this was solid proof of how much Hugo cared about her, buying this gift and holding on to it until he felt the timing was right. 'Thank you. It's beautiful,' she whispered, choked up by a flood of mixed emotions. A ring on her finger was what she really wanted from him. To hide her inner turmoil she busied herself taking off the pseudo emerald earrings. 'I can't wear these with it.'

'Put these on.' He held out a matching set for the necklace, long tiers of the exquisite garnet flowers, almost like miniature chandeliers, probably costing as much as the necklace.

Her fingers fumbled over putting them on. At last they were fastened in her lobes and the effect with the accompanying elaborate collar was mesmerising…dramatic, exotic, an abundance of richness that dazzled the eye.

'You look magnificent,' Hugo declared, his eyes burning possessively at her reflection in the mirror.

Angie found her voice with difficulty, but the image facing her demanded she ask the question. 'Is this why you wanted to take me to a formal function? An occasion fit for the gift?'

Something savage flickered in his eyes. 'The gift is worthy of you,' he growled, then bent his head and kissed her bare shoulder, hotly, as though he wanted to brand her as his. But a necklace, however magnificent, didn't do that, Angie thought. Only a ring did. And the ring didn't have to be anywhere near as extravagant as this gift.

'Now we can go,' Hugo murmured, meeting her gaze in the mirror again with a look of searing satisfaction.

Angie nodded and smiled, though she wasn't smiling inside. She felt distressingly tense as Hugo tucked her arm around his to escort her out to the Bentley.

James was standing to attention by the open passenger door, waiting to see them seated. He flashed Angie an appreciative once-over. 'May I say you look splendid, Miss Blessing!' Warm approval and admiration were beamed at her.

'Thanks to Hugo,' tripped off her tongue, touching the necklace nervously as the thought slid through her mind that the fabulous showpiece jewellery had turned her into an ornament on his arm tonight.

It was not a happy thought.

Shades of being with Paul.

Angie fiercely told herself Hugo wasn't Paul. He was nothing like Paul. And she was not going to let her experience with Paul Overton twist up her feelings for Hugo.

The boss has made a big mistake with that lavish jewellery, James thought, covertly observing his passengers as he drove them towards Government House. The lady was not impressed with it. She kept touching it as though it was an uncomfortable cross to bear, not a glorious pleasure to wear.

She wasn't like the other women who'd traipsed through his boss's life. Couldn't he see that? He was going to stuff up this relationship if he didn't realise he had real gold in his hands. And James was nursing quite a few doubts about the purpose of this charity function that the Overton family would be attending.

A few subtle questions in the right places had elicited the information that Angie Blessing had been Paul Overton's partner for three years, the relationship breaking up just before the billboard incident. So what was the boss up to? Proving he was the better man? Loading the lady with flamboyant jewellery to show that she was his?

This was not a good scenario.

James had bad vibes about it.

Very bad.

As he drove into the grounds of the Governor's official residence, he hoped his boss was right on his toes tonight, because James figured some very fancy footwork would be needed to come out of this situation the winner.

Angie had been to Government House before. With Paul. Tonight it was to be drinks on the terrace first, then dinner and the charity auction in the function room. As James drove the Bentley into the grounds, she saw a string quartet playing on the terrace over-looking the gardens and a good smattering of people already there, enjoying the ambience of the evening. She wished there was a crowd. The jewellery she was wearing was so highly noticeable, she would have felt less on show in a crowd.

But, of course, they were arriving at the stated time on the tickets. Hugo had no patience with unpunc-tuality. He considered being fashionably late an af-fectation that was plain bad manners.

There would inevitably *be* a crowd, Angie assured herself. This was definitely a top A-list function. Everyone who was anyone would come, some to be seen, others to prove how wealthy they were, movers and shakers.

It was a relief to see Francine and Tim strolling up from the gardens. Angie needed her friend's support tonight. Not even the secure warmth of Hugo's hand holding hers could settle her nerves.

Francine spotted the Bentley and waved. The flam-boyant red car undoubtedly stood out like a beacon in the cavalcade of black limousines arriving. Red…garnets…did Hugo want her to stand out, too? Showing her off…*his* woman? She had to stop think-ing like this. It wasn't fair. It wasn't right.

There were ushers lined up to open car doors, sav-ing the time it would take a chauffeur to do it. The moment James brought the Bentley to a halt, the back door was opened and Hugo was out, helping Angie to emerge beside him, tucking her arm around his again. *Curtain up,* she thought, and hated herself for thinking it. There was nothing wrong with Hugo feel-ing proud of her. She should be glad he was.

Francine and Tim were waiting for them on the edge of the terrace. Angie noted her friend was glowing with happy excitement, almost jiggling with it beside Tim who wore the air of a man enjoying sweet success.

Francine's sparkling eyes rounded in astonishment at seeing the spectacular jewellery that had replaced Angie's far more modest choice. 'Wow!' she breathed, her gaze darting to Hugo and back to Angie with a raising of eyebrows.

Angie nodded, acutely conscious of the elaborate earrings swinging back and forth.

'That's some gift, Hugo,' Francine said in an awed tone.

'Angie carries it off beautifully,' he purred with pride.

'That she does,' Tim agreed, grinning away, his confidence in himself and Francine's attachment to him not the least bit dented by Hugo's extravagant giving.

He thrust out his hand in manly greeting and Hugo had to detach himself from Angie to take it. Francine skipped around Tim and thrust out her hand for Angie to see. 'Look! Look!' she cried, positively bubbling with excitement.

A diamond ring!

A beautiful big sparkling solitaire firmly planted on the third finger of her left hand!

An engagement ring—marriage proposed and agreed upon!

A stab of envy sliced through Angie so fast, shame drove her into babbling every congratulatory expression she could think of, hugging Francine, hugging Tim, forcing herself to be happy for them because she was. She truly was. Especially for Francine who had finally found the kind of husband she'd wanted. And the love shining from both of them left no doubt about how they viewed their future together. Absolute commitment.

For them this was a night to remember.

For Angie...her friend's happy situation underlined her darkest thoughts about tonight.

She wasn't Hugo's bride to be.

The jewellery he'd placed around her neck made her feel like a high-priced tart.

She wanted to feel good about it.

But she didn't.

Couldn't.

It felt the same as it had in Tokyo...the kind of thing Hugo habitually did for his women. It didn't mark her as anyone special to him. It said she was just another one in a queue who would eventually pass out of his life. Regardless of the three months they'd been together, nothing had really changed for him.

Though maybe she was wrong.

Angie fiercely hoped she was.

CHAPTER FIFTEEN

As soon as the Master of Ceremonies requested guests move into Government House, ready for dinner which would soon be served, Hugo wasted no time leading his party inside to the function room. They were ushered to their table and he designated the seating, ensuring for himself a clear view of the people streaming in for the business end of the charity evening. Angie, of course, was placed beside him.

He had not spotted the Overtons in the crowd outside and he had not tried searching for them. The mood of his own group of guests had been very convivial, celebrating the happy news of Francine's and Tim's engagement, and he'd wanted to keep it that way, especially since he'd sensed Angie's tension easing as bright repartee flowed back and forth, evoking merry laughter.

Besides, he felt no urge to hurry the confrontation he'd wanted. In fact, he was in two minds whether to push it or not. Mostly he wanted Angie to feel happy with him, happy to be at *his* side.

Waiters served champagne. Appreciative comments were made about the table settings, the floral decorations, the chairs being dressed in pastel blue and pink covers, a reminder that this function was to benefit children. Hugo kept a watchful eye on the people being ushered to their tables.

He saw Paul's parents come in with a relatively senior party, their haughty demeanour instantly striking old memories of them looking down on his parents as not worth knowing, and being vexed with him whenever he snatched some glory from their son. Though they had deigned to congratulate him. With thinned lips.

It occurred to Hugo that Paul had been born to live up to their expectations, bred to an arrogant belief that he should be the winner. But that didn't excuse some of the tactics he'd used to be the winner. The self-styled noble Overtons did not have nobility in their hearts. They simply had a mean view of others.

Angie didn't notice them. She was busily chatting to his guests, being a charming hostess, very good at drawing people out about themselves. Which was another thing he liked about her, not so full of herself that she always had to be the focus of attention. She even took an interest in James' life, not treating him as just a super servant on the sidelines. No meanness in her heart.

How the hell had she been fooled by Paul into staying with him for three years?

That really niggled at Hugo.

Especially since Paul had dumped her, not the other way around. As it should have been. How could she not have seen, during all that time, what an egomaniac he was?

At least she knew it now.

But something about Paul Overton still affected her and Hugo needed to know what it was.

Focusing all her attention on the company at the table and forcing herself to make bright conversation had served to lift Angie's spirits. She was determined on making this a fun night for Francine, setting her own inner angst aside. They were all here to enjoy themselves and she was not going to be a spoilsport.

The champagne helped.

Though she almost choked on it when Francine, who was sitting beside her, leaned over and whispered, 'Paul has just come in.'

Angie swallowed hard and flicked her friend a derisive look. 'I'm not interested.'

'Neither you should be,' Francine fervently agreed. 'But I've got to say the woman on his arm isn't a patch on you, Angie. Big come down.'

'His choice,' Angie answered flippantly.

'And Hugo leaves him for dead.'

In every way, Angie fervently confirmed to herself. It didn't matter that he hadn't yet offered her an engagement ring. The jewellery was a special gift, bought months ago to please her when the time was right. Hugo went out of his way to please her, which surely meant she was special to him. She just wished this gift had been presented to her on some other occasion.

She smiled at Francine, then directed a question at Tim, not wanting to even look at Paul. Though Francine's comment about his new woman piqued her curiosity enough to take a quick glance towards the entrance to the function room.

Recognition was instant—Stephanie Barton, daughter of one of the leading lights in the Liberal Party, one of the best political connections Paul could make. Well, the grass certainly wasn't growing under Paul's ambition, she thought cynically, and her set course of ignoring him was suddenly made much easier.

His view of her was totally irrelevant. In fact, he

could look at her with as much contempt as he liked. He was the one who deserved contempt, trading himself for political advantage.

Hugo watched Paul scan the room, budding politician in action. He was not paying any attention to the woman hanging on to his arm. Not a beautiful woman like Angie. Not even a pretty woman, although she had certainly worked hard on effecting a stylish appearance. Hugo decided she had to be a well-connected woman—silver spoon matching up to silver spoon.

As Paul's gaze roved around, picking out notable people, nodding and smiling when he received some acknowledgment, Hugo rather relished the shock that would hit him when he caught sight of his old rival. It had been a long time, but the animosity on Paul's side would undoubtedly still be there. On his own side? Only the problem with Angie's feelings weighed heavily. That had to be resolved.

The moment of recognition came.

A visible jolt and double take, his mouth thinning in displeasure as he visually locked horns with Hugo, silently challenging the effrontery of *his* presence in a place where he didn't belong. Except money was the only requisite here, and his contemptuous grimace revealed he knew Hugo was now loaded with it.

The contempt did it.

Irresistible impulse took over.

Hugo leaned back in his chair and stretched his own arm around the back of Angie's chair, deliberately drawing Paul's attention to her, ramming home how big a loser he was, despite the silver spoon cramping his mouth. Angie should have been treated as a queen, which was what she was—so far above other women she was right off the scale. And for Paul to have dumped her...well, let him at least acknowledge her worth now!

The moment he saw Angie, his whole face tightened up. He stared, then jerked his head forward, jaw clenched with determination not to look again. At either of them. Especially the two of them together.

His party was ushered to a nearby table and since all the tables were round, he could and did manoeuvre the placings so that he sat with his back turned to Hugo and Angie—an act of disdain, but Hugo wasn't fooled by it. Paul didn't want to face what he'd just seen. He had no weapons to fight it.

Unless Angie gave him an opening.

Hugo swiftly tuned in on what was happening at his table. Tim was explaining one of his inventions to the rest of the party and Angie was turned to him in listening mode. She seemed more relaxed now and Hugo relaxed himself, reasoning that if Angie had been disturbed at the thought of meeting Paul again, she would have kept a watchful eye out for his arrival herself, and clearly she hadn't.

Or was determined not to.

In which case, there was still a problem.

The dinner served was of the finest, most expensive foods, all beautifully presented and accompanied by a selection of wines chosen to complement each course. Francine raved about everything but Angie found it difficult to eat. She was still too conscious of the elaborate collar around her neck. It felt as though it was choking her.

A children's choir came in to entertain with traditional Australian songs, starting with *Waltzing Matilda* and finishing with a rousing rendition of *I Still Call Australia Home*. Angie turned around in her chair to face and applaud them. She caught sight of Paul's mother staring at her from the table closest to the stage. Or rather staring at the jewellery Angie was wearing. Then her gaze flicked up and she raised her nose in a sniff of dismissal before looking away.

Fine! Angie thought savagely. I didn't want you as a mother-in-law, anyway!

Yet she found her gaze skimming around the tables for Paul and found Stephanie Barton seated almost parallel with her on the other side of the room. The man next to her faced away from where Angie was but it was Paul all right. Had he seen her and deliberately chosen to keep his back turned to her?

That was fine, too, Angie decided.

Ignoring each other was the best way through this function.

But the garnet collar felt tighter than ever.

It was a relief when the sweets course was taken away and the auction started. Tim bid for and eventually won a walk-on part in a movie which was about to be shot in Sydney.

'I didn't know you wanted to be in movies,' Francine quizzed when he was triumphant.

'It's for you,' he answered, grinning from ear to ear. 'I couldn't afford to take you to the movies when we were kids. Now I'm going to have the pleasure of seeing you in one.'

They all laughed and Angie thought how nice Tim was, and how lucky Francine was to feel free and happy about accepting any expensive gift from him.

He wasn't buying her. He loved her. And the proof of that was on Francine's finger.

Coffee and petit fours were served as the auction continued at a wild pace, an amazing variety of goodies up for grabs. Huge interest was stirred amongst the men when Steve Waugh's autographed bat was offered. The recently retired cricket captain had been named 'Australian of The Year' and had reached the status of legendary hero amongst the sport's fans.

The bidding for the personal bat was fast and furious. Hugo joined in. Angie couldn't help noticing Paul did, too. Hugo's jump bid to ten thousand dollars seemed to be the clincher for him, but as the auctioneer wound up the sale, Paul suddenly called, 'Fifteen,' opening it up again.

'Twenty,' Hugo called, without so much as blinking an eyelid.

A hushed silence as everyone waited for a possible counter-bid. Paul didn't look around to see who had beaten him. He faced the auctioneer and raised his hand, drawing the attention of the whole room to himself as he called, 'Thirty,' in a terse, determined voice.

The auctioneer raised his eyebrows at Hugo, 'Do we have a contest, sir?' he asked, clearly wanting to whip one up. 'It's for a very good cause and this bat hit a century for Steve Waugh.'

'Then a century it is,' Hugo drawled. 'I bid one hundred thousand dollars.'

It evoked a huge burst of applause.

When it finally died down, the auctioneer gestured to Paul and whimsically asked, 'A double century, sir?'

Paul forced a laugh and waved the offer away, conceding defeat.

'That's very generous of you, Hugo,' Angie said warmly, impressed that he had contributed so much for a children's hospital.

He swung around to her, his eyes glittering with the savage satisfaction of a warrior who has swept all before him, his mouth curling with a deep primeval pleasure in his victory. 'To the children, the spoils of war,' he said.

'War?' Angie didn't understand.

'Cricket might be a sport but it's also a battle. A fight to the finish,' he explained.

'Well, you sure hit that other bidder right out of the playing field,' Tim said appreciatively.

'What you might call a deep six,' Hugo agreed with his wolf grin.

The other men at the table chimed in with good-humoured comments involving cricket terms which clearly amused them. Not ever having been a cricket fan, the repartee was completely lost on Angie. Francine, as well, who suggested they slip off to the ladies' powder room.

'Paul was livid at losing,' Francine whispered as soon as they were out of earshot of their party. 'I bet he was deliberately bidding against Hugo because of you.'

Angie glanced at Paul's table before she could stop herself. Stephanie Barton was staring venomously at her and even as their eyes caught, she said something to Paul, and from the nasty twist of her mouth Angie assumed it was some jealous snipe. Paul, however did not look around and Angie quickly turned her own gaze away.

'More likely he wanted to make a charitable

splash,' she muttered to Francine. 'He'd be angry at being frustrated, having decided what to bid on.'

'Well, I'm glad he's not having a happy night,' Francine shot back with smug satisfaction. 'Serves him right for being such a stupid snob as to dump you because...'

'That's water under the bridge,' Angie sliced in.

'True. And Hugo is much more giving.' She heaved a happy sigh. 'I do love generous men.'

Generous, yes, but what of the motive behind the generosity?

Angie didn't voice that thought. It touched too closely on the current ache in her heart—an ache that grew heavier as she refreshed her make-up in the powder room and the ornate jewellery from Japan mocked her dream of a forever love with Hugo.

Self-indulgence...that was what he'd called his impulse to buy it for her in the first place. He was still indulging himself with her. He'd wanted the pleasure of seeing her wear his gift and she'd let him have his way. He'd won her compliance. Won it all along. And maybe winning was what it was all about with him. Like with Steve Waugh's bat—decide on something—get it!

Interesting question...what was he going to do with the cricket bat, now that he had it? Angie resolved to ask him when she returned to their table. However, she and Francine were no sooner out of the powder room, than they were waylaid by a furiously determined Paul Overton.

'I want a word with you, Angie. A private word.' He grabbed her arm. 'Out on the terrace.'

'Let go of me,' she cried, angered at his arrogant presumption. 'I have nothing to say to you, Paul.'

'Well, I have a hell of a lot to say to you,' he seethed, the hand on her arm a steel clamp as he started pulling her away with him.

'If you don't let Angie go, I'll get her guy to come,' Francine threatened. 'You don't want a scene, Paul,' she added sarcastically.

'By all means get Fullbright,' Paul snarled at her, carelessly revealing knowledge of his name. 'While I tell Angie the truth about my old school buddy.'

'What?' Shock weakened Angie's resistance to Paul's dragging her outside with him. Her feet automatically moved to keep up with him.

'You're just a pawn in his game,' he shot at her, his eyes glittering with the need to shoot more than her down. He dropped a scathing look at the necklace as he jeered, 'Dressing you up like a queen to checkmate me.'

'You have nothing to do with us,' she protested, though a host of frightening doubts were clanging through her brain.

'I have *everything* to do with him parading you here tonight,' Paul grated out viciously.

Was that true?

They were outside, away from everyone else. The auction was still continuing in the function room— the auction that had provided a battle between Hugo and Paul, with Hugo bidding an enormous sum...to be charitable or to thwart a rival?

It had been a gorgeous Indian summer day but the night air was crisp now, bringing goose bumps to Angie's skin. Or was it the chill of a truth she didn't want to believe? She told herself Paul was an egomaniac and he was reading the situation wrongly, hating being publicly beaten, taking his anger out on her.

'This is absurd!' she insisted. 'Hugo was interested in me before he ever knew I'd had a relationship with you.'

'Sure about that?' Paul whipped back at her.

'Yes, I am,' she retorted heatedly.

'How soon did he learn about me?'

The quick insidious question stirred more emotional turbulence. She'd given Paul's name to Hugo at Narita Airport, at the end of their *dirty weekend.* But he'd bought the jewellery before that, on the Saturday, she reasoned feverishly, so he'd meant to continue their affair. Hugo's interest in her could not hinge on Paul.

'It doesn't matter,' she muttered, firmly shaking her head.

'You think it's not relevant?' Paul mocked. 'When you told him about me, did he mention we knew each other?'

No, he hadn't. Not a word. 'School was a long time ago, Paul,' she argued, not wanting to concede any substance to the point being made.

'Some things you don't forget.'

'Like what?' she demanded.

He told her.

About the intense rivalry between them.

About the chip on Hugo's shoulder because he hadn't been born to a life of privilege.

About the girl who'd dumped Hugo for Paul.

He fired bullets at her so fast, Angie was reeling from the impact of them. She could see the influence they might have had in forming Hugo's ambition, motivations...and they hammered home the point...*some things you don't forget.*

But there was one big flaw in Paul's scenario and she leapt on it. 'But *you* dumped *me*. Why would Hugo want your discard?' she flung at him.

'Good question.'

The drawled words startled them both into swinging around.

Hugo strolled forward to join them. He appeared completely relaxed, supremely confident, yet Angie sensed the powerhouse of energy coiled within, ready to be unleashed. It played havoc with her nerves which were already torn to shreds under Paul's very personal attack on her position in Hugo's life. She didn't want to be a bone of contention between them, yet all her instincts quivered with the sense that it was true. Terribly true.

It was a dangerous smile Hugo bestowed on Paul, and the airy gesture he made as he closed in on them had a mesmerising sleight-of-hand about it. 'The answer is...I want Angie because she is beautiful...inside and out. Nothing at all to do with you, Paul. Though I do wonder that you were such a fool as to let her go.'

Paul's jaw clenched. Sheer hatred burned in his eyes. 'Not such a fool that I didn't finally see she was no more than a cheap whore who'd sell herself to the highest bidder,' he bit out in icy contempt.

Angie gasped at the painful insult, her hand instantly lifting to her throat, wishing she could tear off the damning necklace.

'You're welcome to her, Fullbright,' Paul jeered.

'Always the sore loser,' Hugo mocked silkily. 'Do choose your weapons more carefully. You wouldn't want that vote-winning smile rearranged.'

Paul's shoulders stiffened, bristling with the aggression stirred. 'I didn't lose anything worth having,' he snapped.

'No? Then why drag Angie out here? Why do your venomous best to destroy her trust in my feelings for her?'

'Feelings?' He snorted derisively. 'I was doing Angie a favour, letting her know she'd been used by you.'

'How benevolent! Strange how I never noticed that trait in your character. Much more in keeping that you'd badmouth me so I'd lose, too.'

'You kept her in the dark, Fullbright. That speaks for itself.'

'Or does it say you were simply not a relevant factor?'

'Angie's not stupid. She can put it together.'

'I'm sure she can…from the way you treated her.'

'Still got your debating skills, I see.'

'Sharp as ever.'

'But not sharp enough to pass the real test, Fullbright.' A glint of triumph accompanied this challenge.

Angie had been sidelined as a spectator to the contest being waged, but suddenly she found herself the target of Paul's *test*. 'If you hadn't cheapened yourself on a public billboard, I would have married you, Angie,' he threw at her. 'If you think Fullbright's *feelings* for you will lead to marriage, think again. He'll never take you as his wife and you know why?'

She stared at him, feeling all the vicious vibes being aimed at both of them.

'Because I had you first,' he flung down, then

swung on his heel and strode off with the arrogant air of having finished with people who were beneath him.

Which left Angie and Hugo alone together—an undeniable statement hanging between them.

She had given herself to Paul first.

CHAPTER SIXTEEN

SOILED goods…

It was an old-fashioned phrase, out of step with life as it was lived now, yet it slid into Angie's mind and set up camp there, burning into her soul.

'Are you okay, Angie?' Hugo asked, his laser blue eyes probing hers for possible problems.

She looked blankly at him, feeling herself moving a long distance away from this whole situation, detaching herself from the entangled relationships with Hugo and Paul, standing alone. Chillingly alone.

'You can't believe I'd be influenced by what Paul is,' he said in a tone of disgust. 'But if you need to talk about it…'

'No!' The word exploded from her need to be done with the mess she had been drawn into. 'I want…' *to finish this right here and now.* Yet wouldn't Paul feel some filthy triumph if she left the scene before the night was over? Not only that, her disappearance would worry Francine, cast a shadow on her friend's happy night. She lifted her chin with a heightened sense of holding herself together and said very crisply, 'I want to return to our table. We've been missing too long already.'

'Fine! Let's go then.'

He clearly interpreted her reply as a positive decision towards him, smiling his relief and pleasure in it as he offered his arm. She took it, merely as a prop to present the right picture so Francine would be pleased that she had sent Hugo to the rescue. And Paul would not have the satisfaction of knowing how deeply she had been hurt.

Oddly enough, the physical link to Hugo had lost all its sexual power. There was ice in her veins, not one trickle of heat getting through from the contact with him. She hated being a trophy woman. Once this evening was over and they were in the privacy of the Bentley, she would stop being one, and never, never again fall into that horribly demeaning trap.

Hugo was delighted that Angie was dismissing the confrontation with Paul as not worth any further consideration. Sour grapes on Paul's part. Which, of course, it was. Clearly her mind was satisfied that her former lover did not impinge on their relationship in any way whatsoever and she was well rid of him.

Closure had definitely been effected.

Though as they reentered Government House, Hugo noted Angie's cheeks were flushed and she was holding her head so high it smacked of proud defiance, which told him she had been stung by Paul's personal insults to her. Perhaps badly stung. And his previous doubts about whether he was making the right moves came crashing back.

What had he achieved tonight?

Yes, it had felt good to outbid Paul in the auction, though that wasn't particularly important to him. He'd meant to bid for something anyway, giving to a charity that would benefit children.

And it had felt good, seeing Paul's reaction to finding Angie attached to him now.

Being the winner always felt good.

But at what cost if Angie was hurt by it?

Out there on the terrace, he had felt savagely satisfied that Paul's behaviour had stripped any wool from Angie's eyes where her ex-lover was concerned, but now he had the strong and highly disturbing sense that it had not righted the wrong he'd been feeling.

Far from it!

Paul's last childish shot of the night—*I had her first*—started some deep soul-searching which Hugo pursued relentlessly while he played out the charade of continuing a bright happy party at his table.

Had he been driven to arrange this encounter because he needed affirmation from Angie that she truly felt he was the better man? Right from the beginning he'd felt possessive of her. Finding out she'd been with Paul for three years...and it hadn't been *her* decision to break the relationship...had definitely struck him hard.

Not the sexual aspect of it. That didn't matter a damn. After their first night together in Tokyo, he'd had no doubt he and Angie were so sexually attuned to each other, the kind of physical intimacy they shared was something uniquely special to them. That had never been a problem.

It was the long attachment to Paul that had niggled.

Would she have married him if the billboard mistake hadn't happened?

Hugo's gut twisted at that thought.

But she knew better now, he told himself. Tonight Paul had surely obliterated any lingering sense of being robbed of a good future with him. She couldn't possibly regret losing him now. He'd demonstrated beyond any doubt what a mean-spirited bastard he was.

All the same, Hugo was acutely conscious that

Angie was not turning to him with a renewed flow of positive feeling. She was focusing almost exclusively on the others at the table, barely acknowledging his contributions to the conversation, not touching him and not welcoming any touch from him, actually detaching herself from contact with him. Not obviously. Under the guise of turning her attention to someone else or making a gesture that seemed perfectly natural.

It made Hugo increasingly tense. He craved action, a resolution to whatever was distancing Angie from him. As the auction drew to a close, he took out his mobile phone and sent a text message to James, ordering the car up, ready for a quick departure. He suffered through the wind-up speech by the M.C., applauded the end of it, then rose from his chair, thanking his guests for their company, wishing Francine and Tim well again, and taking his leave of them, ruefully announcing his work schedule demanded an early night.

Angie was quickly on her feet without any assistance from him, but she did submit to having her arm placed around his for the walk out of the function room. Again she held her head high and despite the many admiring and envious glances she drew as they made their exit, her gaze remained steadfastly forward, acknowledging nothing.

The Bentley was waiting.

James sprang to attention the moment he saw them, opening the passenger door with his usual flourish. 'Did you have a good evening, sir?' he asked as Angie stepped into the car and settled on the far side of the back seat.

Hugo handed him the cricket bat. 'Belonged to Steve Waugh. Take care of it, will you, James?'

'A prize, indeed, sir,' James enthused.

Not the one he most wanted, Hugo thought darkly as he moved in beside Angie who sat with her hands firmly in her lap, her gaze averted from him, not the slightest bend in her towards the intimacy they had so recently shared.

Hugo waited until the Bentley was on its way out of the Royal Botanic Gardens before he broke what he felt was highly negative silence. 'I'm sorry about what happened with Paul tonight,' he started gently, hoping she would unburden the hurt she felt so he could deal with it.

'Are you, Hugo?' she answered in a flat, disinterested tone.

He frowned, sensing one hell of a chasm had opened up between them.

Then she turned her head and looked directly at him, her green eyes as cold as a winter ocean. 'You planned it. Please don't insult my intelligence by denying it. You planned how this evening would play out.'

'No. Not how it did,' he quickly corrected her.

'You knew Paul would be there, just as I knew he'd be there,' she said with certainty.

'You could have said something if you didn't want to risk a social meeting with him,' he countered.

A mocking eyebrow was raised. 'Avoiding him would have given him an importance he no longer had to me.'

'Sure about that, Angie? I sensed you didn't want to see him and I readily confess I didn't like the feeling that…'

'It was bound to be unpleasant if we met,' she cut in crisply. 'That was my only concern. But you must have known that, Hugo. With your old history with Paul, you must have known he'd force a meeting…and you deliberately led me into it.'

The accusation sat very uncomfortably. Hugo didn't have a ready reply to it.

'But *I* didn't matter, did I?' she continued. 'It was between you and him. I was just the means to…'

'No!' he asserted vehemently. 'You do matter. Very much. And I'm deeply sorry Paul subjected you to…'

'The truth?'

'I doubt Paul Overton has spoken the truth in his whole damned life! As for *his* version of my history with him, I'm sure that was twisted to suit the purpose of undermining what we have together.'

His aggressive outburst didn't stir one ripple in her icy composure. She simply sat looking at him, apparently weighing the strength of what he'd claimed. Then very quietly she asked, 'What do we have, Hugo?'

'You know what we have,' he shot back at her. 'A great rapport. We enjoy each other's company. Every time we're together it's good.'

Her mouth twisted in bitter irony. 'Good enough to think of marrying me?'

Marriage!

Hugo shook his head in furious frustration at how poisonous Paul's barbs had been.

'Well, at least you're honest about that,' Angie commented wryly, misinterpreting his reaction.

'For God's sake, Angie!' he protested. 'I needed to get your hangover from Paul out of the way first.'

'*My* hangover!'

She didn't believe him. The scorn in her eyes

goaded him into saying, 'We've only been together three months. Let's be reasonable here. You were content to be with Paul for three years without getting a proposal from him.'

Big mistake.

Huge mistake!

Incredibly stupid to compare the two relationships!

Her face instantly closed up on him and she sat facing forward again. Her hands lifted and one by one, removed the earrings from her lobes, dropping them onto her lap.

'What are you doing?' he demanded in exasperation at her apparent choice not to argue with him.

No answer.

It was all too obvious what she was doing.

She removed the necklace, too, then gathered the jewellery together and placed it on the seat space between them. 'I don't want this, Hugo. I did tell you not to buy it,' she flatly stated.

'It suited you. It looked great on you,' he asserted, feeling a totally uncharacteristic welling of panic at this clear-cut indication she was cutting him off. 'There's no reason for you not to keep it,' he insisted heatedly.

She flicked him a derisive look. 'It makes me feel like a high-priced whore.'

Paul again!

'You know you're not one, Angie!' he threw at her furiously.

'Yes. I know,' she said dully, her head turning towards the side window, away from him.

'Then why are you letting Paul Overton colour my gift to you?'

'He didn't. I felt it when you put it on me tonight,

Hugo,' she answered, speaking to the night outside, the darkness seeping into her mind, shutting him out.

'You gave me the Samurai sword,' he fiercely argued. 'Why can't I give you a gift without you thinking...'

'The sword wasn't for public show,' she cut in wearily.

How could he make her understand? He had wanted her to wear his gift tonight to show how much *he* valued the woman Paul had rejected, to make her feel like a queen compared to other women. For her to know that this was how he thought, and feel it, especially when she saw Paul again.

'I would have broken up with Paul if he hadn't leapt in first,' she said, and slowly, slowly, turned her gaze back to his. 'You see, I finally realised I was a trophy woman to him, not someone he really loved for who I am...the person inside. I guess I was dazzled by other things about him but I did finally see...' Her mouth twisted. '...and I have no intention of spending the next three years being your trophy woman, Hugo.'

'That's not what you are to me,' he swiftly denied.

Rank disbelief in her eyes.

He threw out his hands in appeal. 'I swear to you, Angie...'

She recoiled away from him. 'Don't! The contest is over. You won whatever points you wanted to make. Just let me go now, Hugo.'

'No. I don't want to lose you.'

'You have already.'

He sought desperately for words to hold on to her. His mind seized on what she'd said about Paul not loving the person she was. He did. He very much did.

She *was* beautiful, inside and out. In a wildly emotional burst, he offered that truth.

'Angie, I love you.'

She flinched as though he'd hit her. 'Do you say that to all your women?' she flashed at him with acid scepticism.

'I've never said it to any other woman. You're the only one,' he declared with more passion than he'd ever felt before. 'The only one,' he repeated to hammer home how uniquely special she was to him.

He knew Angie had never been with him for the ride he could supply. His wealth truly was irrelevant to her. She was not out to get anything from him except his respect. And the love she deserved. He had to make her see she had both his respect and love.

Before he could find the words to convince her of it she tore her gaze from the blaze of need in his, jerking her head forward. Her throat moved in a convulsive swallow. She spoke with husky conviction. 'This is only about winning. It's all been about winning. A man who loves me would not have put me in that firing line tonight, knowing Paul as you did.'

'Knowing Paul as I did…' God damn the man and the baggage they both carried because of him! '…I hated the thought of you still feeling something for him, Angie. And yes, I wanted to win over him tonight,' he confessed, desperate to set things right. 'I wanted to be certain you're now mine.'

'I'm not a possession,' she flung at him, her cheeks burning scarlet. 'I chose to go with you. Be with you. I told you so before I ever went to bed with you, Hugo.'

But he'd seduced her into his bed. He'd done it very deliberately. Because he'd wanted her. And he'd used sex to tie her to him ever since. But sex wasn't going to work tonight. She'd hate him, despise him, if he tried it.

He told himself to calm down, reason through the important points he needed to make. He was fighting for his life here—*his life with Angie*—and suddenly he knew that was what he wanted more than anything else, and if he didn't make it happen, he'd face a terrible emptiness in all the years to come.

'I do love you, Angie,' he repeated quietly. 'I just didn't like how Paul had belittled you over the billboard photo and tonight I wanted to punch him out with how magnificent you truly are. I didn't plan for you to get hurt. I wanted you to feel proud that you were with me. The truth is…you're the woman I want to spend my life with, not a trophy for show. If you'll do me the honour of marrying me…'

'Don't!' Tears welled into her eyes, and once again she jerked her head away.

'I mean it, Angie,' he pressed, harnessing every bit of persuasive power he had to bring into play.

She shook her head. 'This is still…about winning,' she choked out.

'Yes, it is. Winning you as my wife.'

'It's the wrong time. The wrong time,' she repeated in a kind of frenzied denial.

'Then I'll wait for the right time.'

She looked at him with eyes swimming in pain. 'How can I believe you? Paul threw this challenge at you, Hugo. Paul…' She bit her lips and looked away again.

'Do you imagine I'd let him dictate how I spend the rest of my life, Angie?'

Her fingers plucked at the skirt of her dress, agitatedly folding the fabric. 'This is too much for me. Too much…' Her whole body suddenly jerked forward in alarm. 'James, this is my street,' she cried. 'You've just driven past my apartment block. Stop!'

'Missed the parking spot. Thought I'd just drive around the block, Miss Blessing,' James hastily explained.

'Please…back up!' she begged.

'Sir?'

'Stop and back up, James.'

While he appreciated James' ploy to give him more time, Hugo knew force would only alienate Angie further. Besides, she was right. It *was* the wrong time to make anything stick. He could only hope he'd made strong inroads on the barriers she was still holding on to.

The Bentley was reversed and brought to a halt. James alighted to open the passenger door. Angie rushed out an anxious little speech. 'I don't want you to accompany me to my door, Hugo. I need to be alone now.'

He nodded, not wanting her to be afraid of him, but his eyes locked onto hers with all the searing intensity of his need to convince her of his sincerity. 'Please think about what I've said, Angie. Think about us and how good it's been. And how much more we could have together. Promise me you'll do that.'

The passenger door was opened.

She didn't promise.

She bolted.

'James, see Miss Blessing safely to her door,' he quickly commanded.

'Yes, sir.'

He waited, the need to rein in all his aggressive instincts reducing him to a mass of seething tension. As soon as James had resettled himself in the driver's seat, Hugo asked, 'Did she say anything to you?'

'Miss Blessing thanked me for my many kindnesses, sir.'

'That doesn't sound good.'

'No, sir. Sounded like goodbye to me.'

'I have to win her back, James.'

'Yes, sir. Shall I drive you home now, sir?'

'Might as well. Breaking down her apartment door won't do it.'

'No, sir.'

The Bentley purred into moving on.

Hugo concentrated on coming up with a positive plan of action. 'Flowers tomorrow. Red roses for love. Masses of red roses delivered to her office, James.'

Throat clearing from the driver's seat. 'If I may be so bold, sir, I don't think flowers will do the trick this time. Not even red roses.'

'It's a start,' Hugo argued.

'Yes, sir. Shouldn't hurt,' came the heavily considered reply.

'But it's not enough to swing a change of opinion. I know that, James. You don't need to tell me.'

'No, sir.'

'I have to back them up with something else. Something big. Utterly convincing.' A sense of urgency gripped him. Failure to break this impasse with Angie in double quick time could mean losing her.

'Are you asking me for a suggestion, sir?' came the somewhat dubious question from the front seat.

'If you've got one, James, give it to me,' Hugo bit out.

More throat clearing. 'Please forgive me for…uh…
overhearing what was…uh…most certainly a private
conversation…'

'Oh, get on with it, James,' Hugo broke in impatiently. 'This is no time for sensibility or sensitivity.
I have a crisis on my hands.'

'Right, sir. Well, it seemed to me, Miss Blessing
felt you'd made a public show of her for…umh…
self-serving reasons, and you'll need to somehow
counterbalance that.'

'A show. A public show.'

Hugo seized on the thought, an idea blooming in
his mind so fast, it zapped into the mental zone of
perfect move. There'd been times in his life where he
knew intuitively that all the pieces pointed to taking
one single winning action—an exhilarating recognition of *rightness*. And when he'd followed through,
it had worked for him. Worked brilliantly.

'I've got it, James!' he declared.

'You have, sir?'

'And I'll see to this myself. Push it through. Bribe,
coerce…whatever it takes.'

'If I can be of any assistance, sir…'

'What I'm going to do is…'

And he outlined the plan.

Once again, James felt proud and privileged to be
in the employ of Hugo Fullbright. Not only did he
have the perspicacity to see Miss Blessing as the perfect wife for him, his plan to win her hand in marriage
had that marvellous touch of flamboyance that made
him such a pleasure to work for.

It was to be hoped—very sincerely hoped—that it
would produce the right result.

CHAPTER SEVENTEEN

ANGIE barely slept. The mental and emotional turmoil revolving around everything that had happened with Hugo and Paul gave her no peace. It was impossible to sort out what she should do—give Hugo another chance or end a relationship that felt hopelessly entangled with motives which made her shudder with wretched misery.

She dragged herself out of bed the next morning, red-eyed from bouts of weeping and so fatigued that the idea of facing a day at the office with a happy Francine, fresh from a night of loving with Tim, made her heart quail. But it had to be done. Best that she did occupy herself with work. She'd probably go mad if she fretted any more over whether Hugo truly loved her or not.

The marriage proposal after what Paul had said…it had felt so wrong, so terribly, terribly wrong…how could she believe anything that came out of Hugo's mouth now?

She pushed the whole mess to the back of her mind and determinedly kept it there, even when Francine sailed into the office one hour late and poured out all her excitement and pleasure in Tim's proposal once again, raving about how *perfect* he was for her, how well he understood her, how sweet and generous he was, etc etc etc.

Angie agreed with her, managing as many smiles as she could, feeling sick about not having understood anything about Hugo, except his drive to win. Fortunately, she had a meeting with a contractor after lunch, giving her a break from Francine's blissful contentment. *Unfortunately,* it was at the Pyrmont apartment complex where she was assailed by memories of her first meeting with Hugo.

He hadn't known about Paul then—impossible to doubt that his desire for her company had been genuine. During the whole Tokyo weekend it had definitely been genuine.

Could he be sincere about loving her? Nothing to do with ensuring he didn't lose before he wanted to? These past three months had been so good, everything feeling *right* between them. Even when he'd taken her to the new ballet performance, he'd enjoyed it with her, finding the dancing quite fascinating. And erotic, he'd told her wickedly. Definitely interested in sharing this pleasure with her.

What if he truly didn't want to lose her at all?

What if the marriage proposal was genuine, too?

But he shouldn't have done it last night!

It still felt hopelessly wrong.

At four o'clock Angie returned to the office and winced at seeing a huge arrangement of red roses sitting on her desk. 'You'll have to move Tim's roses somewhere else, Francine,' she tossed at her friend. 'I need the work space.'

'They're for you!' The announcement came with a delighted grin. 'I think Tim's plunge into a marriage proposal has fired up Hugo. Red roses for love, Angie.'

Her heart fluttered nervously, wanting to believe, fearful of believing. Her agitated mind reasoned it was nothing for Hugo to order up flowers. James had probably done it for him. But *red* roses was definitely a first from him.

'There's a note for you,' Angie brightly informed her.

Angie set her briefcase down beside her desk and settled in her chair, needing to feel calmer before reading the attached note. She opened it gingerly. The note was actually hand-written in Hugo's strong scrawl, not some anonymous printing from a florist.

> *I do love you.*
> *I want us to spend the rest of our lives together.*
> *Please don't turn your back on what we have together, Angie.*
> *I'll contact you tomorrow.*
>
> *Hugo*

Tomorrow… Angie drew a deep breath. She had another day to think about it. Not that she was getting anywhere much with her thinking.

'What does he say?' Francine asked eagerly.

Angie shrugged. 'Just that he'll call me tomorrow.'

'He adores you, Angie. Every time he looks at you, it's like he wants to eat you up.'

'That's sex, Francine, not love,' she said with some asperity.

'Oh, yeah? Well let me tell you, when I told him last night about Paul waylaying us and taking you off, he charged out like a bull to get you back with him. That's not sex. That's love.'

Or reclaiming his possession, Angie thought. Francine was rosy-eyed about everything right now. Nevertheless, Angie was reminded that the sense of intimacy she had known with Hugo had extended far beyond the bedroom. If it hadn't been for the too-extravagant gift of jewellery and the nasty encounter with Paul last night, would she be doubting a declaration of love by Hugo?

Wasn't it her own insecurity about the previous women in his life—all of them *temporary* attachments—that had made her see the gift as so much less than a ring of lifelong commitment?

And after all, their relationship *was* only of three months' standing. Three very intense months. But it was still a far cry from Francine's and Tim's situation, the two of them having known each other all through their childhood and teens. It was quite reasonable that Hugo hadn't seriously considered marriage...until she'd challenged him on it in the car last night.

She'd forced the issue.

He'd risen to it.

Why couldn't she accept that it was right for him?

Was she going to let Paul take from her what she most dearly wanted?

If only she could believe Hugo would have asked her to marry him, anyway.

She stared at the note.

He didn't mention marriage...just living together. But he did say...*for the rest of their lives.* And this note wasn't written in the heat of the moment. Hugo had had all night to think about what he wanted.

Tomorrow, Angie thought. *I'll see what happens tomorrow and take it from there.*

Thursday morning...

Angie felt more refreshed, having gone to bed early and slept like a log. Francine had also crashed out at home, and since neither of them had separate plans for today, they both travelled to work in Francine's car. They were in the usual tight stream of traffic crossing the Sydney Harbour Bridge when Francine remarked, 'Change of billboard today. Let's check out who's on it.'

'You don't need to check out anyone anymore,' Angie dryly reminded her.

'I have sympathy for the hopefuls.'

'Well, keep at least half an eye on the traffic as the billboard comes into view.'

She didn't.

She put her foot on the brake and stopped dead, causing mayhem and much honking of horns behind them. And Angie was too shocked to say a word. She didn't even hear the fracas around them. Her stunned gaze was fastened on the one mind-boggling, heart-squeezing photo of a man covering the entire billboard...

Hugo!

A much larger than life Hugo with a bunch of red roses resting in the crook of one arm, his other hand held palm out, offering a small opened box lined with white satin, and nestling in the middle of it, a blindingly gorgeous ring—an emerald with diamonds all around it.

Text was flashing with a kind of spectacular urgency.

Angie—will you marry me?

'Now that...is some proposal!' Francine muttered breathlessly.

Someone rapped on her window and an angry face yelled. 'Have you got trouble, lady? You're holding everyone up.'

Francine rolled down the window and yelled back, 'Have you got no romance in your soul?'

'What?'

'Look at the billboard!' She pointed. 'That's my friend's fiancé up there. Or he soon will be. Right, Angie?'

'Right,' Angie replied faintly.

'You can't get a more public commitment than that,' Francine told her stunned critic.

No, you can't, Angie thought dazedly, and wasn't the slightest bit aware of the rest of the journey to their Glebe office.

Where the red Bentley stood parked at the kerb.

'Stop!' she cried to Francine, totally unprepared for facing Hugo here and now.

Francine brought her car to a screeching halt, causing more mayhem to the traffic behind them on Glebe Road. 'Better get out, Angie,' she advised. 'Guess you won't be working today.'

'I don't know. I don't know,' Angie babbled nervously.

'Out you go and say yes. That's all you have to do. I have no doubt Hugo will take it from there. He's one hell of a go-getter,' Francine said admiringly. 'And all the best to both of you!'

'Thanks, Francine,' Angie mumbled and made herself move, alighting from the car to a blast of honking horns.

Francine stepped on the accelerator, shot forward, braked again as her car came level with the Bentley, honked her horn to draw the notice of the chauffeur, then carried on to drive around to the parking area in the back lane behind the office building.

Angie's suddenly tremulous legs managed to carry

her from the street to the sidewalk. Her heart was galloping as she saw James alight from the driver's side of the Bentley, resplendent in his chauffeur's uniform. He raised a hand to her in a salute of acknowledgment, rounded the gleaming red car, and opened the passenger door on the sidewalk side. He stood at attention beside it, his usual stately dignity slightly sabotaged by the hint of a smile lurking on his lips.

Angie paused to take a deep calming breath and unscramble the assault of wild thoughts in her mind. Was Hugo in the car? Or had James been ordered to take her somewhere to meet him? In which case, should she go or stay? It was a bit presumptuous of Hugo to send his man to collect her when she hadn't even said *yes*.

'*Please* step in, Miss Blessing,' James urged, a slight frown replacing the slight smile. His dignity even cracked so far as to beckon her forward.

Well, it wasn't fair to upset James, Angie reasoned. Besides, it was absurd to play hard to get at this point, when Hugo had well and truly put himself on the line for her. 'I'm coming,' she announced to James, giving him a grin as assurance that all was well.

He actually grinned back!

Which lightened Angie's heart immeasurably as she hurried to oblige him. James definitely approved of her marrying his boss, which should make for a happy household. She dived into the Bentley and straight into another heart-fluttering situation.

Hugo *was* in the car, sitting on the far side of the back seat. 'I've been waiting for you, Angie,' he purred at her as she flopped down beside him, his bedroom blue eyes sizzling with wicked intent. 'Waiting all my life for you to join me.'

'Oh!' was the only sound that came out of her mouth. Her dizzy mind registered that Hugo had just voiced exactly what she'd wished to hear from him. *Exactly!*

James closed the door, locking her in with the man who was fast proving to be the man of her dreams.

'Will you marry me?' he asked, wasting no time in pressing the critical question.

Angie looked askance at him but her heart was dancing, performing cartwheels. 'I'd have to love you first, Hugo.'

His mouth quirked into a very sensual smile. 'I think I love you enough for both of us. Why not give it a chance?'

She laughed. She couldn't help it. A cocktail of happiness was bubbling through her. 'Well, since I love you to distraction, I might just do that.'

'Then you will marry me.'

'Yes. Yes, I will.'

'I need your left hand.'

She gave it to him.

He immediately produced the ring that had glittered so enticingly on the billboard and slid it onto her third finger. 'Perfect fit!' he declared smugly.

'How did you guess?'

'Angie, there is nothing about your body that I don't know intimately. There's nothing about your heart that I don't know intimately. If you'll just let me fully into your mind…'

'I think if you kissed me…'

He did.

And the magic of knowing Hugo really, truly loved

her, and meant to love her all his life, made it the most special kiss of all, making them both sigh with satisfaction when it ended.

Some heavy throat-clearing from the driver's seat signalled that James was ensconced there, ready to drive off. 'To the airport now, sir?'

'Yes. Straight to the airport.' The furred edge of Hugo's voice was very sexy.

'May I be the first to congratulate both of you on your forthcoming nuptials, sir?' James said somewhat pompously, returning to form now that everything was satisfactorily settled.

'You may. Thank you, James.'

'Thank you, James,' Angie warmly chimed in, then turned quizzically to Hugo, 'Why the airport?'

'It's time for meetings with parents. We'll fly to Port Macquarie for mine to drool over you, then on to Byron Bay for yours to look me over. Or we can do it the other way around if you prefer.'

'All in one day?'

'I thought today and tomorrow with one set of parents and the weekend with the other. Enough time for everyone to get to know each other.'

It was a wonderful idea, but...I can't wear the same clothes for four days, Hugo. Can we go home first...?'

'No time. The flight is scheduled.' He gave her his wolf grin. 'You can give me the pleasure of buying whatever you need. That has to be allowable for my future wife!'

Staking out his territory, Angie thought, and laughed, moving to cuddle up to him, blissfully content for Hugo to indulge any pleasure he liked as long as it was with her. 'My warrior!' she murmured happily.

'At your service,' he said just as happily.

Angie sighed. 'Fighting for me from a billboard in full view of everyone crossing the Sydney Harbour Bridge is a story I'm going to relish telling our children.'

'And grandchildren,' he said with equal relish. 'Worth the price,' he added. 'Worth any price to have you, Angie. I just feel the luckiest man on earth to have found you.'

Amen to that, James thought.

The boss sure had a prize in Angie Blessing. And the pitter-patter of tiny feet was clearly on the drawing board. James felt he could now look forward to a fascinating new phase in his life.

LET'S TALK
Romance

For exclusive extracts, competitions
and special offers, find us online:

f facebook.com/millsandboon

⊙ @millsandboonuk

y @millsandboon

Or get in touch on 0844 844 1351*

For all the latest titles coming soon, visit
millsandboon.co.uk/nextmonth